ON THE TIP OF HER TONGUE

His mouth closed on hers. All coherent thought washed away like a sand castle at high tide. His lips were firm and warm.

The room spun a bit, but his hands were there to catch her. He wrapped his arms around her, drew her against the hard length of his body. She felt a moan rise in her throat and had enough sense to clamp down on it.

He really knew how to kiss.

She thought of power and heat. Then she thought of nothing. Her mind zapped white for a brief instant; then her body zapped red hot.

His kiss was a long, lazy perusal of her lips. He tasted of caramel-covered popcorn. She lost all sanity. Giving no thought to who watched, she raised her hands and gripped his head. She drew him closer and bit his lower lip. With a jerk of his head, he responded; his lips moved against hers, his arms tightened. . . .

Other *Love Spell* books by Ann Lawrence:
LORD OF THE KEEP
VIRTUAL HEAVEN

RAVE REVIEWS FOR ANN LAWRENCE'S *VIRTUAL DESIRE*!

"SPLENDID!! 4 ½ Bells!!"

—*Bell, Book & Candle*

"*Virtual Desire* is a romantic and sensual tour de force. I give it my highest recommendation."

—*Word Museum*

"*Virtual Desire* tells a wonderful tale of love, friendship, faith, honor and courage. . . . It's pure enjoyment from the first page to the last!"

—*Old Book Barn Gazette*

"P.E.A.R.L. award-winner Ann Lawrence is a natural storyteller. Slow and sweet, hot, spicy, and unpredictable, [her book] is a testament to the power of love."

—*Paranormalromance Reviews*

"An adventurous tale that will sweep the reader into its fantasy world. Ann Lawrence demonstrates a definite flair for creating characters and stories that leave the reader begging for more!"

—*Bookaholics.com*

"Sinfully delicious . . . A must-read by star-quality author Ann Lawrence!"

—*The Belles and Beaux of Romance*

"*Virtual Desire* is the perfect read for anyone who loves the mix of fantasy and romance elements. Packed with intrigue, adventure, mystery and magic."

—*Writers Club Romance Group (WCRG) on AOL*

"*Virtual Desire* is a book guaranteed to please."

—*BookNook Romance Reviews*

"In *Virtual Desire*, Ann Lawrence has written another powerful and moving story with the perfect blend of humor, intrigue, fantasy and sensual romance. *Virtual Desire* grabs you from the first line and doesn't let go until the end. . . . Bravo, Ms. Lawrence!"

—*RBL Romantica*

MORE PRAISE FOR ANN LAWRENCE!

LORD OF THE KEEP

"Ms. Lawrence brings a maturity to *Lord of the Keep.* The portrait of awareness drawn between the hero and heroine is clear. Their emotions seep into the readers, rendering it impossible to put the book down. Disappointment does not follow any reader of this tale."

—Writers Club Romance on AOL, Reviewer Board

"Lawrence weaves a dazzling, sizzling page-turner. *Lord of the Keep* will capture your heart and quench your thirst for a satisfying romance. 4 ½ stars!"

—*Word Museum*

"Ann Lawrence has penned a thrilling and unusual novel in *Lord of the Keep.* This well-detailed plot paired with the excellent historical details and characterizations makes *Lord of the Keep* a definite keeper in my opinion."

—Lisa Hamilton, *CompuServe Romance Reviews*

VIRTUAL HEAVEN

"A *Romantic Times* Top Pick! Brilliantly done, *Virtual Heaven* is a must for fans of fantasy and recommended for anyone else seeking something new and exciting. 4 ½ stars!"

—*Romantic Times*

"*Virtual Heaven* is an incomparable debut novel that shatters the soul and touches the heart with passion and high adventure. Brava!"

—Deb Stover, bestselling author of *Another Dawn*

Virtual Heaven is "one stunning story. Ms. Lawrence is without a doubt one writer on the way to the top. Splendid! 4 ½ bells!"

—*Bell, Book and Candle*

"Ann Lawrence's clever and imaginative debut novel establishes her as an exciting new talent. With a modern-day heroine and a hero perfect for any reality, *Virtual Heaven* is a nonstop romantic fantasy."

—Kathleen Nance, bestselling author of *Wishes Come True*

Virtual Desire

Ann Lawrence

LOVE SPELL BOOKS NEW YORK CITY

A LOVE SPELL BOOK®

August 2000

Published by

Dorchester Publishing Co., Inc.
276 Fifth Avenue
New York, NY 10001

ISBN 0-505-52393-0

Printed in the United States of America.

For My Parents . . .

This book is for my father in thanks for the delightful treasure maps he drew my children through the years. Those maps and the accompanying stories inspired this tale. He is also responsible for telling me about POTS and U R A BUS. This book is also for my mother in thanks for her support, encouragement, and the best of Thanksgiving dinners!

Thanks, Dad and Mom!

Virtual Desire

True love's the gift which God has given
To man alone beneath the heaven:
It is not fantasy's hot fire,
Whose wishes soon as granted fly;
It liveth not in fierce desire,
With dead desire it doth not die;
It is the secret sympathy,
The silver link, the silken tie,
Which heart to heart and mind to mind
In body and in soul can bind.

—*The Lay of the Last Minstrel*
Sir Walter Scott (1805)

Chapter One

She appeared in a glittering column of snow. Her long white skirts floated about her as she came toward him in the indigo night. She was a creature of the vast ice fields.

Beautiful. Sensuous. Alluring.

He stood frozen in place and watched her, his body numb in the icy wind despite the heavy furs he wore. His mind refused to believe what his eyes saw and his body craved. Golden hair, like a close-fitting cap, hugged her head. Sinuous movements of her arms beckoned him near. Ribbons of silvery fabric streamed behind her as she lifted her arms to him.

With a quick turn of his head he scanned the horizon. Where were her retainers? Her protectors? The ice fields stretched unbroken in the moonglow save for a few treacherous red rocks that pierced the snow and tripped the unwary foot. He rubbed his gloved hands over his face.

Reluctantly, he turned east again to the beguiling ice

woman. A new fear, fear that he had lost his mind, joined with an older fear that he might not survive this formidable land. He drew a deep, steadying breath and caught a hint of summer flowers along with the scent of ageless ice.

She waited in silence, many yards away, and raised her hand to him again. He obeyed her summons without thought, mesmerized by her, unable to resist.

The thick snow crust crunched beneath his boots. The wind rose in a mournful ululation as it lifted her sheer gown and twisted it against her body. The fabric traced her lush shape, her full, womanly curves.

A man might warm himself in her embrace.

He pictured her lying naked on his furs, arms open in invitation as they were now, welcoming him. The enticing vision tumbled about in his head. He tried to grasp the warm thoughts, but his mind stumbled along with his feet.

A shriek of wind jerked him back to his path and his goal. The woman blurred a moment before his eyes, then became sharp-edged. Touches of her femininity appeared and disappeared in the eddies of her swirling gown. A sweat flushed his skin beneath the layers of his clothing.

For moments he staggered forward, drawing no closer to her. Touching her became imperative, necessary, as necessary as drawing the chill air into his lungs. He imagined her kiss. Her lips would be full and ripe and gleaming with moisture, as if she had just licked them. He imagined that her taste would heat his blood. He craved the warmth of her body, the intoxication of her scent, the comfort of her long white arms.

He stepped into her embrace and clasped . . . nothing.

He howled at the pain of it, clenched his fists, and fell to his knees. Around him lay nothing but vast empty space. A blast of raw wind cut his cheeks and harrowed his spirit. With little will to go forward, he knelt, his head hanging down, and cursed the gods.

How smooth and slick and beautiful the world had looked when he'd begun his journey. He had lost count of the sunrisings. Three? Four? Seven? His body yearned for sleep. Clumsy with the cold and fatigue, he fell to his side. A sudden stab of pain tore at his cheek and burned like fire up his face to his eye. The flames of pain defied and mocked the cold.

A wounded-animal sound echoed in the empty expanse of wasteland. Had the sound come from him? Struggling on limbs that repeatedly refused to obey, he staggered upright, ashamed of his lapse.

There at his feet gleamed a bright red gem. It glittered against the icy white moonglow. As he watched, more gems appeared. They bounced and rolled away, scattering in the snow. With shaking hands he tore off his gloves and reached for one that lay alone, perfectly round and gleaming. The numb tips of his fingers were clumsy as he tried to lift the fine jewel. It burst and became blood, running between his fingers.

His blood.

Another bright red drop fell to the ice, congealed, and was magically transformed into another gleaming gem. He dashed the drop away with an angry sweep of his hand. More appeared, but he understood now and would not be tricked again.

Relentlessly, he trudged along, too tired to take his direction from the moons overhead.

Why was he crossing this merciless field of ice?

For love. For the love of a friend more brother than any man of blood family could be. For a bond more precious than that with a lover.

As his strength waned, he found himself standing and staring at the four blue-green orbs slowly aligning overhead.

He was lying—if only to himself. The love of a friend

might have sent him on his mission, but the salvage of his honor, his good name, kept him moving forward through ice fields no other warrior had dared to cross.

For without his friend, honor was all he had. He had no family, no illustrious ancestors, no lifemate waiting dutifully for his return.

Time passed. He knew this from the growing indigo shadows cast by the moonglow that defined the sharp red rocks tripping his feet. He knew this from the nearly perfect alignment of the moons.

If he did not survive his quest, his name would be forever inscribed on the roll of cowards and traitors, there for all future generations to see and vilify. Surely a just end for a man with no lineage.

Where was he?

Confused, he turned first in one direction, then another.

He stared down at the fur cloak in which he had wrapped himself. Blood matted the front. Where had the blood come from? Was he wounded?

Idly, he wiped at the frozen red stains. Where were his gloves? Lethargy prevented him from searching for them. His gold ring looked copper in the night. He wasted long moments staring at it, turning his hand this way and that.

Finally, he conceded the ice to be the victor, the cold a merciless conqueror, impervious to a warrior's sword or knife. With regret, he fell to his knees and scrabbled in his furs for the stone he carried close to his heart. The stone, captured in delicate strands of silver, reflected the color of the orbs overhead. The talisman slipped from his clumsy fingers and fell to the ground. He dug about near his knees, searched the ground in all directions, but the stone had disappeared, lost in the soft snow.

He tried in vain to rise, but his legs no longer obeyed.

"What more do you demand?" he asked the heavens,

fists clenched. Try as he might, his strength was gone. As was the stone.

And lost with it was his desire to go on.

He would not fulfill his quest.

Dignity demanded he not collapse cravenly but meet his fate with his face to the heavens. The four small moons beckoned overhead. He liked to think they were watching over him and would ease his passage from this life to the next. The moons drew closer, like friends rushing to meet in a stellar embrace.

"I failed," he whispered. His eyes drifted closed. Thunder rumbled in the distance. Lightning streaked across the barren horizon.

Gwen Marlowe twirled across the ballroom floor, spinning and laughing. She came to a halt before a young man who had entered the Ocean City Music Pier's ballroom in a blast of rain and salt-laden wind. "Neil, my *Tolemac Wars* ball is going to be a real winner."

Thunder echoed across the cavernous room.

"Only if this storm doesn't close the bridges and keep everyone at home," he said, and handed her a foam coffee cup.

"Pessimist." She took a swallow, then threw out her hand toward the long row of floor-to-ceiling windows. "The weatherman said the brunt of the storm is going to miss us."

"If you say so." He dug her sneakers from under a chair and held them out.

Gwen ignored them and gulped her coffee. She peered from one of the tall windows. The two-mile-long Ocean City boardwalk had only a few piers extending out into the ocean. The Music Pier was one of them. Glowering clouds and intermittent bursts of rain obscured the view. The radio had predicted that the storm would move east and miss their small coastal island, which lay midway between the bright lights of Atlantic City and the Victorian charm of Cape May. She hoped the meteorologists were right. "Don't you feel like we're on a ship right out in the ocean?"

"Maybe the *Titanic*? Only the iceberg's in here."

"Don't say things like that!" She bit her lip. Maybe the weather *would* ruin the ball and all her work.

He touched her on the shoulder. "Don't worry; this old place has taken hammerings since 1928. I don't think one small nor'easter is going to knock it down. And the tickets are sold. It'll be standing room only in here tonight—storm or no storm." He moved about the ballroom, gathering assorted litter from her decorating efforts and stuffing it into a trash bag.

"Come on, Neil. I need your honest opinion. Does this look like the ice fields from *Tolemac Wars Two* or not?"

She held her breath. Neil Scott examined the ballroom, hands on hips. Water dripped off his ancient black leather jacket and beaded in his short dark hair. Gwen noticed circles etched beneath his eyes.

"I feel like I'm in the middle of a blizzard, not a rainstorm—a Tolemac blizzard. Relax. You've recreated the game." He grinned. The sudden smile wiped away the biker-from-hell look and hinted at the handsome man he might be if he got enough sleep. "You should do stage design," he said. "It looks great. Even if the Tolemac warrior himself showed up, he'd be impressed."

"Really?" She skidded along the polished floor in her socks and adjusted one of the drapes that gave the impression of a mountain of snow on red rock. "I spent a fortune on all this. And wait till you see my gown."

"I draw the line at fashion commentary." He bent and retrieved the remnants of silver streamers and tossed them into the trash bag.

"But I could use a guy opinion. I made it myself, you know. I hand-painted each layer of white silk with seven shades of white and silver. I hand-stitched the silver sleeve ribbons—"

"Enough. This is really more information than I need."

Gwen scooped up a handful of artificial snow and threw it at him. It clung to his shoulders and hair. "What's wrong? Up too late with your coven?" He took off his jacket and shook off the snowflakes. A snake tattoo slithered around his upper arm, just showing at the sleeve edge of his T-shirt.

Perhaps prompted by the angry gray sky outside, Neil was garbed all in black. Daggers and skulls hung from one pierced ear. Gwen never minded Neil's many personas. He was just as likely to appear at the video game shop they owned together in a white shirt and a tie. He worked hard, was always on time, and did grunt work without complaint. He was the perfect business partner.

On the front of his black T-shirt, a hideous skeleton wielded a lacrosse stick. Neil had once been a star attack player for Johns Hopkins. These days he attacked nothing more challenging than cardboard boxes that needed to be broken down for the recycling bin, his weapon a utility knife.

"Are you finished in here?" He pulled his jacket back on.

She nodded and took a last look around the room. "All that needs to be done is putting out the food. If I do say so myself, the room looks like a winter snow scene straight out of *Tolemac Wars Two*." *Tolemac Wars II* was the latest and hottest virtual-reality game. Thanks to her friendship with the game's creator, she had a monopoly on the game. If you wanted to play *Tolemac Wars II* in South Jersey, you had to patronize her boardwalk game store, Virtual Heaven. "Let's take these trash bags back to the shop."

They ran the two blocks on wet, slippery wooden boards. Her store stood in the nearly unbroken row of shops that graced the northern end of the two miles of Ocean City's boardwalk. Wind gusted from all directions. Rain fell in sheets. The Atlantic Ocean hammered the boards with savage pleasure. On the horizon, lightning flickered.

"Should there be lightning in November?" she said in a gasp, out of breath. "What if there's a power failure?"

She cast a longing glance up to the apartment she rented over her shop. She'd left a light on. It splashed a yellow glow over the small balcony fronting the apartment. She resisted the urge to go back to her warm, snug bed. Fatigue was creeping in. She'd started her decorating at dawn, and now, even though it was still early in the morning, she wanted to crawl into her bed and sleep the rest of the day away.

"If the power fails, you're cooked." He ducked under the awning over their shop door.

Gwen saw his half-hidden grin and turned the key with a jerk. "I get it. I'm obsessing. You're the pessimist and I'm the optimist. Okay. The ball will be a huge success, written up in game magazines nationwide, the extra ten pounds I gained this summer will be adequately hidden under my flowing . . ." Neil dragged a finger across his throat. "Never mind," she finished.

Once inside, she punched in the code to turn off the security alarm. Neil flipped several switches, and light flooded the shop. She tossed her raincoat behind the service counter.

Neil scooped up a white envelope that lay on the rubber mat by the front door and placed it on the counter. He slipped a CD into the boom box sitting next to the cash register. She winced as Mozart's "Jupiter Symphony" filled the shop. "Jeez," she called to him. "Do we have to listen to that stuff so early in the morning?"

Neil didn't answer. Perhaps he hadn't heard her over the music. She smiled. More likely he was ignoring her.

She guessed she'd pushed him over the edge with her Tolemac ball worries. He shrugged out of his jacket and began to open cardboard cartons.

Gwen set up the cash register for the day. Usually she opened her shop only on weekends in November, but this was the week of the war-game convention in nearby Atlantic City, and she'd been open every day for the conventioneers, especially women, who'd flocked in to play *Tolemac Wars II.* She'd started her plans for the ball the minute the game con had booked into Atlantic City.

She picked up the envelope Neil had found, examined it a moment, then flipped it into the trash unopened.

"Why'd you do that?"

Gwen started as Neil spoke. "It's just a letter from my mother."

Neil salvaged the note. "Why don't you open it?"

Gwen rounded the counter, took it from his hand, and threw it back into the waste can. She sniffed the air and wrinkled her nose. "Did you sleep in those clothes?"

Neil retrieved the note and again slapped it on the counter. "I showered," he said. "It's not me. I thought it was you, no offense."

When Neil turned his back to crank up the CD player's volume, Gwen surreptitiously sniffed her underarms. "Not me." She tapped the letter with a finger for a moment, then slit the envelope flap open with her thumb.

She scanned the short note as she picked up Neil's jacket. It smelled innocently of old leather.

"What's it say?" Neil plucked his jacket from her hand and folded it onto a shelf behind the counter. He also picked up her raincoat, shook it out, and hung it on a hook.

Gwen shoved the letter into the back pocket of her jeans. "It's just the usual invitation to Thanksgiving dinner. You know. Everyone will be there, why not good old Gwen?" She lifted the wastebasket and sniffed. "This place smells like wet wool." She glanced overhead. "Could there be a leak somewhere?"

A sharp rap on the window glass made Gwen whip around. "Oh, dear." She waved Neil off and went to the door. She opened it a scant inch. "I'm sorry, Mrs. Hill. We're not open yet. Not until ten o'clock." She pointed to her watch, which said nine. "The game needs to warm up. I haven't even turned it on; I'm sorry." She needed all her strength to pull her shop door firmly shut on the woman swathed in a raincoat, who flapped a twenty in her face. With a sigh and a decisive turn of her key, Gwen locked the door.

She turned to Neil. "These women have no life. Don't you think it's worse now that we have *Tolemac Wars Two*? The women are even more gaga over this warrior than the first one."

Neil nodded, then touched her arm. "How come you're not going to your folks' for Thanksgiving?"

"You've never tasted my mother's cooking. If you had, you wouldn't ask." Gwen shook her head. She was not about to tell Neil her family troubles. Neil had enough trouble of his own. He'd just dropped out of graduate school to look after his alcoholic mother.

"I'll take out the trash. Maybe that will take care of the smell." Neil propped the back door open and gathered up several plastic bags.

Gwen grabbed the vacuum cleaner and dragged it across the shop to the virtual-reality booth that daily stuffed her cash register with tens and twenties—or her and Neil's cash register. The boom in virtual-reality game popularity had necessitated a partnership—she just didn't have the ability to run the shop alone anymore.

She gave the Tolemac warrior an affectionate pat on his chest as she passed his poster. Women flocked to the shop to play his game. They made no effort to hide their addiction to the eerie experience of donning a headset and entering the handsome warrior's world.

"Hope you're ready for business, buddy," she informed the warrior. "Mrs. Hill's getting anxious."

Neil ran back into the shop, accompanied by a blast of salty wind. "Are you talking to me?"

Gwen shook her head. "No, I'm talking to this guy up here." She jerked her thumb at the poster.

"If he ever starts talking back, I'll know you're working too hard." Neil hefted an armload of recyclables.

Gwen frowned as she plugged in the vacuum. Her fingers traced a jagged tear across the bottom of the *Tolemac Wars* poster. "Oh, no, Neil, look at this."

Neil came to her side. "I guess someone tried to steal the poster again. What is this? The fourth one this month? Must be those nutty women from the game convention."

"More like Mrs. Hill. These posters are so hard to come by," Gwen complained, but Neil didn't answer. The door banged shut behind him.

Gwen swore aloud. She looked up at the warrior, who glowered at her as if blaming her for the desecration of his poster. His silver-blond hair blew back from his magnificent face. His black leather breeches and elaborately embroidered white tunic molded his body. Gwen always imagined he stood foursquare to the wind so that his fans could admire the honed contours of his body and the straight, noble lines of his profile. "Vanity, thy name is not woman. Or at least not in Tolemac," she muttered.

Abandoning her vacuum, Gwen leaned over the service counter and dug up a roll of tape. As she plastered the poster back on the wall, she spoke to the warrior. "Don't blame me if every Tanya, Dawn, and Helen tries to steal you off the wall. If you weren't so damned perfect and beautiful, they'd leave you alone. Maybe a few scars and scuffs would wipe that haughty sneer off your face." She laughed and patted the warrior on a well-muscled thigh, tossed the tape onto the counter, and returned to her vacuum. "Of course, Mr. Tolemac Warrior Snob, if you weren't so beautiful, you'd be just another game—and I'd be poor." She sniffed. "Whew. Whatever it is, it reminds me of a wet sheepdog—or maybe just the wet sheep."

She stepped into the entrance of the freestanding chamber that housed the *Tolemac Wars* game. It was formed of four matte black walls with an inner chamber, also with walls of unrelieved black.

The classical music rose to a crescendo behind her, masking something else, something close and furtive. A rustle. A soft, mousy sound that tickled her spine with apprehension and froze her fingers on the light switch.

Gwen stood poised, her ears straining. The sound was not repeated. She ran to the counter and hit the eject button on the CD player.

Silence pounded in her head as she listened. Had she imagined the sound? Had a trick of wind playing over the roof carried in the sound of a distant foghorn? Trembling, Gwen tiptoed farther into the virtual-reality chamber and flicked the switch. Light filled the game chamber.

A polar bear was her first thought. A huge, dirty polar bear lay sprawled in her game chamber, filling the space with its body and wet-animal scent.

With a scream in her throat, Gwen turned, tripped over the vacuum, and ran. She skidded on the smooth carpet and lunged out the back door.

Rain pounded the wooden boards of the back steps. Wind lashed cold drops against her face. Salt air and low-tide smells choked her as she gasped for breath and fought the panic that welled within her.

Lightning pierced the sky. Neil stood next to the trash Dumpsters, black against black, and frowned at her.

Gwen felt suddenly foolish. Shame that she'd panicked and run made her press her hand to her pounding chest and take a deep, steadying breath.

The back parking lot held only her car, the trash containers, and Neil. "What is it?" he called. Water lapped over the sidewalks and gushed in gutters.

"I-I-I heard something." She rubbed her cold hands on her arms. Her fleece top and jeans were getting soaked.

Neil bounded up the steps two at a time. "What?"

"In the game booth." She omitted what she'd seen. Something made her hold her tongue. *Let Neil see for himself.* Together they went back into the shop. As they entered, she caught a whiff of sweat. It underlaid the wet-animal scent as well as the salt and sand smells that were such a part of a shore community that they went unremarked.

Gwen held up a hand to Neil for silence. Not far from her front door, the Atlantic Ocean snarled. Wind rose and fell with a whine. Nothing else stirred. She tiptoed to her counter and pulled out a long metal bar that was supposed to be locked onto her car's steering wheel. She just couldn't remember to use it. As she brandished it like a sword, she slipped cautiously into the game booth, Neil right at her elbow.

The game booth was really a small room inside another. The inner room held a raised platform and a wide screen for spectators to view the game while it was being played. The players had no use for the screen. They wore a headset that covered their eyes and ears; they experienced the game as if living it.

Gwen took a deep breath, poked the bar around the curved wall, and followed slowly after.

Neil shoved past her and stood with his hands on his hips. "These gamers!" he said in disgust. With his work boot, Neil prodded the mountain of fur that lay half on and half off the control platform.

Gwen relaxed at Neil's apparent unconcern.

After all, she thought, polar bears did not wear leather boots.

Neil gave the lump a harder kick. "Yo, bud. Up and outta here." The small mountain didn't move. "Should I call the cops?"

Gwen frowned. *And say what? "A polar bear in boots is snoozing in our shop."* Now that Neil had demonstrated the thing's harmlessness, she grew brave and made a few fencing moves at the mountain. She prodded and poked and circled.

"Or maybe we should call the exterminator." Neil bent over, hands on knees. "Come on, bud. This isn't the Seaview Motel."

The offending gamer shifted. Gwen squeaked and danced away. The disgusted look Neil aimed at her made her straighten up and justify herself. "Well, it moved." She feigned nonchalance, but she did not lower her "sword."

While Neil cajoled, Gwen took in the small details. Dirty fur, like a matted bath rug, swathed the figure from head to foot. Boldly, Gwen poked the pile again.

Nothing happened. She prodded the flat, scuffed sole of one boot. The furry mountain abruptly shuddered. Gwen jerked away, her back coming up against the wall. The pile shifted and rolled off the platform onto its back on the floor.

It flopped back like a beached whale and snored—a decidedly loud snore.

"Sound asleep," she whispered in disgust.

"Maybe drunk," Neil whispered back.

"At this time of morning?" Gwen held the metal bar in both hands, ready to whack the man if he stood up.

"He probably sneaked over from Atlantic City." Neil reached down and dragged the furs open in the center of the long form. "How the hell'd he get in here, anyway?"

Gwen dropped her bar. She hated it when Neil was right. Under the furs, the man was garbed exactly like the warrior in *Tolemac Wars II.* Costumes were *de ri-*

gueur at the game convention as well as at the ball scheduled for that night. A dirty, blond beard covered the lower half of the man's face, yet his features were hauntingly familiar. "Boy, lose the beard and he'd win the prize in any Tolemac warrior look-alike contest, wouldn't he?" she asked.

Neil grunted. "Not unless he takes a bath before the final judging." Then he frowned. "Did you forget to check the back door last night?" His implied "again" didn't need to be said.

She winced and busied herself examining the man. He opened his eyes and licked his tongue over dry lips. "Come . . . warm . . . me."

Gwen found herself staring. His eyes were as blue as a northern fjord, his voice low and seductive. His eyes fluttered closed. A smile curved his mouth.

"Oh, great. A rude Tolemac impersonator," Gwen muttered. "What should we do with him?"

Neil scratched his chin. "I don't know. If you call the cops he might get thrown in jail."

"Gamers are not criminals," she said.

"You're right. They also spend tons of money in shops like ours."

The man rolled his head and snorted like a large boar. It was then that Gwen noticed a long gash that extended from his right eye nearly to his chin. Dried blood matted the front of his furs. "Oh, Neil, he's hurt." She dropped to her knees at the man's side. He was a long, tall mountain of fur. "And he's really dirty. It's his fur coat we're smelling. He must've swiped it from a bear. A wet, muddy bear." She wrinkled her nose in disgust.

Yet despite the coat's condition, where Neil had separated the furs, she could see an elaborately embroidered shirt. She'd seen that pattern of black and gold on white so many times, she could not fail to recognize it now. "His coat might be dirty, but his costume is beautiful." She reached out cautiously and touched the man's shirt.

Heat zinged up her arm. She snatched her hand back.

As if his body had become aware of his surroundings, the man began to shiver. He tucked his hands into his armpits and curled onto his side. The small chamber once again filled with his harsh, growling snores.

"We could at least clean his cut," she said. Neil frowned. "He's shaking; he must be cold. Shouldn't we at least get him upstairs? I could clean his cut."

"Yeah, I guess we don't need him lying here when we open up."

"Kered?" the man whispered. His eyes remained closed, but his hand groped toward her.

Involuntarily, she took it. He shivered. His hand was hot—feverishly hot. While she held it, the heat seemed to flow up her arm. The hair on her nape stirred. With difficulty, she extracted her hand from his hard grip.

She stripped the furs open all the way down the man's body. The garment revealed itself to be a long fur parka with a deep hood. The man's dirty, matted hair lay plastered against his skull—it could be any color from dark blond to white. His beautifully embroidered tunic, once soaked in sweat, now lay stiff against his skin. Yet he was the image of the man from the poster. "This might be the guy the agency hired for my ball, Neil."

The man's breath whistled through his nose.

"Looking like this?" Neil shook his head. "Let's call the police instead."

In her mind's eye, Gwen saw herself locking the back door and checking it. "I know I didn't leave the door open. I just know it."

"Then he sneaked in while we were busy with customers yesterday and hid in the bathroom. No, that's ludicrous. How could a guy this big sneak past us?"

"Regardless of how he got into the shop, we can't leave him lying on the cold floor. And if he's from the agency, I can't exactly turn him over to the police either.

The agency would never supply another event for me." No matter how imprudent it might be, she decided to help the stranger. She rose to her feet. "Let's get him upstairs to my apartment."

"Are you sure?" Neil asked. "He could be dangerous. He was reckless enough to break in here."

Gwen took one more look at the man. "You know, Neil, I think he just needed somewhere to sleep. Maybe he was broke and couldn't afford a hotel room." She put her hand on his forehead. It was cool. She grabbed his arm. The same zing of heat pulsed through her hands, but this time she ignored it.

Neil jammed his hands on his hips. "Are you sure?"

She tugged and pulled. The man did not budge. "I'm sure. After all, the ball's tonight. What's a few hours? Come on. Help me."

As Neil continued to catalog his protests they hefted the man to a sitting position. "Yikes," Gwen said with a gasp, "he's a deadweight."

"Smells dead, too," Neil quipped.

The man's eyes rolled in his head, then seemed to focus on them. "I was . . . not . . . quitting. I was just . . . resting," he said through perfect white teeth.

"Anything you say." Gwen grabbed one arm, while Neil grabbed the other. After several false starts, they succeeded in hauling the man to his feet and propping him against the railing of the game platform.

She was five-foot-seven. The man was almost a foot taller.

"I'll unlock the back door to your apartment." Neil dashed from the chamber, leaving Gwen in sole possession of a very large male.

Her hands planted in the center of his chest, Gwen took a deep breath and staggered as the man's weight sagged forward. "Hurry, Neil, he's heavy," she shouted, looking up at the man who now towered over her. He began to list to the side. “And huge!” She wrapped her arms around his waist.

The man opened his eyes and stared down at her. Gwen could not have looked away if ordered. His beguiling blue gaze swept over her face and hair.

“I dreamed of you.” His hands stroked up the column of her spine. His long fingers slid along her neck.

Hurry, Neil, she thought as the slow caress of his fingers wandered to the hair at her nape. The zing had settled to a warmth that flooded her system.

“You . . . disappeared.” He closed his eyes and began to slide. She accepted the inevitable and tried to ease his collapse to the floor. He fell to his knees, his arms loosely clasped about her waist.

He nuzzled his face against the soft fleece of her top and sighed. In moments he was snoring again.

Gwen buried her hands in his matted hair and pulled his head back. His eyes fluttered open. She swallowed hard. She had never seen a man so dirty—or so handsome.

“I dreamed of you. Your . . . taste. Your scent.” His hands moved over her hips. Heat pooled where his hands journeyed. A memory of long-buried sensations coursed through Gwen’s body as the warmth of his hands penetrated her jeans.

Drunk gamer or warrior wanna-be, he was providing an unwanted reminder of how a man’s hands felt on a woman’s body. His hands stroked down her legs.

He gasped.

His fingers gripped her tightly just above the knees and shoved. She squealed at the pain and landed on her bottom.

He lurched to his feet, stumbled backward, and gripped the game platform. He swayed and stared down at her.

An expression of confusion crossed his face. The cut

on his cheek oozed bright red blood. Then his features settled into the haughty lines she recognized from the *Tolemac Wars* poster.

Disbelief filled his voice. "You are a boy!"

Chapter Two

"I'm not a boy!" Gwen stifled a laugh. Then heat swept up her face. Maybe it wasn't so funny to be mistaken for a boy. She scrambled to her feet. "Who the heck are you? How'd you get into my shop?"

"Shop?" The man's body tensed. He swept a trembling hand across his brow.

A wave of sympathy made her soften her voice. "Yes," Gwen said, "my shop. How'd you get in here? Who are you?"

"I crossed the ice fields?" It was a question.

Gwen sighed. He was going to act out the part for which he'd dressed. He was definitely into *Tolemac Wars*. She'd met all kinds. From the small—she perused the war gamer from his black leather boots to his matted hair—to the tall. "Yes. Yes," she said, playing along. "You've crossed the ice fields. You're in Ocean City, now."

"Ocean . . . ? The place of legend with sea creatures three times the size of dragons?"

She pressed her lips together to remain as serious as he was. "Yes, that's the one. Now, who are you?"

He straightened to his full height and stared down his perfect nose at her. "Vad."

Of course. If she looked so much like the Tolemac warrior, she'd call herself Vad, too. "Okay, Vad. How'd you get in here?"

A look of real consternation settled on his face. "I do not remember." He staggered. His hand shot out to the game platform.

"No. Don't touch that!" Gwen lunged for his hand. She grabbed his arm and jerked him away. He'd come dangerously close to leaning on the game controls. "I don't need any accidents. Do you understand?"

"Uh, Gwen?" Neil spoke from the entrance to the game booth. "Your back door's unlocked, but Mrs. Hill and some friends are lined up out front."

"Gwen?" The man said her name very distinctly. In fact, he sounded as though he belonged on the public television station, maybe in one of those British mysteries she watched on Thursday nights.

"Come on." She tugged at the man's arm. "Let's get you out of here. If the women outside see you, they'll strip you naked in a minute."

A look of sheer terror crossed the man's face. Gwen grinned. "Yep. Less than a minute. Maybe in ten seconds." He scooped up his fur parka. She wrinkled her nose. "You'd better get your coat to the cleaners, pronto."

He swayed. His hand settled heavily on her shoulder. Slowly he removed it and forced himself upright. "Forgive me. Perhaps you might take me to your master."

Gwen opened her mouth to make a sarcastic remark, then realized he was just staying in character. "Sure. Right after I rescue you from Mrs. Hill."

He jerked his arm from her hand. "I do not need a pathetically small female to rescue me."

Gwen settled her hands on her hips. "Look, Vad. You're on thin ice here. You broke into my shop. Play all the games you like, but keep your insults to yourself."

She did not wait for him to follow her. She hurried from the game booth. If he wanted to be attacked by Tolemac fans, that was up to him.

Behind her, Vad slowly straightened.

He felt as weak as a spring lamb. He took a cautious step. Then another. At the chamber doorway he staggered. Lights and sounds and smells assaulted him. Drums pulsed and beat in his head. Pain shot from one side of his skull to the other. Bright colors burned his eyes. He bumped into a table. A slither and clatter of glittering objects made him jump. A man grabbed him. He pulled away.

The man, garbed in all black, had no arm rings or visible weapons, but this was the land beyond the ice fields. Vad did not know what laws applied here, nor what enemies he might encounter. Legends told of strange people, strange customs, and stranger weapons to be found if one could but cross the ice fields.

He went on guard. His burning eyes swept the long chamber he'd entered. Colors warred with light bouncing off glossy surfaces. Nothing looked familiar. Glass windows, impossibly large and clear, ran with rain. In sharp contrast to the room, the world outside looked strangely washed of color. He stifled a moan as the pain in his head rose with the crashing sounds that pulsed through the chamber: drums and cymbals. They came from nowhere and everywhere at once.

Vad forced himself to concentrate on where the immediate danger lay: the dark-haired man. He gripped the hilt of his knife. The double-edged blade was sharp enough to sever a man's arm from his body—even snake-protected arms. The man might be a slave without arm rings, but he wore a symbol of evil and temptation about his upper arm. What significance the symbol carried here, in the lands beyond the ice fields, he did not know. But in Tolemac, the snake was feared. It struck swiftly, its poison deadly. His blurry vision settled on the symbol on the dark one's shirt. A death's-head, wielding a strange weapon.

The little female jerked him from his thoughts. "Vad, meet Neil. Neil, meet Vad. Vad's a little under the weather." The woman touched the snake man on the shoulder. "Do you mind getting the shop ready while I take him upstairs?"

Unbelievably, the snake man nodded and silently went to stand behind a long table. The woman gave orders to the man? Vad watched warily, but the man made no threatening moves.

"Yo, bud. Are you going with Mrs. Marlowe or not?" The snake on the young man's arm writhed as he leaned surprisingly strong-looking hands on the table. "The shop will be opening in a few minutes."

"Sh-shop? Msssmrlow?" He glanced around, bewildered by the man's words.

"Make up your mind."

Make up his mind. Vad felt as if his mind had slipped into madness. He found nothing familiar on which to anchor his senses.

He closed his eyes and groaned. A sharp blade of pain twisted through his skull. He could not let it gain control of him. He opened his eyes and sought the only familiar thing in his sight—the woman.

She stood in a rear doorway, held out her hand, and beckoned him to the strange gray world outside—a world with the comforting scent of the sea.

She had beckoned before, called him to her. His bone-deep fatigue warred with the hot pulse of desire that surged through him. The ice woman had invaded his dreams—and his reality. The image of her seemed burned into his mind. The woman before him could not be her. He raked the boyish female with his gaze from gold-capped head to blue-clad legs.

The wind pressed her men's garments against her body. How could he have ever doubted she was a woman? In his mind, her garments dissolved into white gossamer robes draping lush female curves.

Vad concentrated on the pain behind his eyes and followed her. He had no time to study his surroundings. The woman held open another door but a step from her shop. He had no strength to do more than follow her up a narrow set of stairs.

It took most of his remaining concentration to ignore the woman's buttocks in the tight breeches as she climbed the stairs before him. His thigh muscles ached with fatigue from the endless time of trekking across the ice.

At the top of the stairs she opened another door and stood back so he could enter. Her master must be poor, he thought, to live in such a place. The chamber was long and narrow. A thin rug covered the center of a wooden floor. The only furniture was a tall wooden cupboard, a padded bench with a high back, and several straight-backed chairs about a round table. All looked old. Dishes and bright fabrics were piled on every surface. Didn't her master require her to keep his chambers clean?

"Where is your master?" he asked her, edging slowly from the doorway, one ear cocked for male footsteps.

"Sit down. Relax."

He ignored her invitation and paced the long room. The ceiling was low. It would be hard to fight in such a space. Two other doors led from the chamber. One, amazingly made of glass, faced a small balcony and the gray world outside. He rubbed his eyes. Even the roiling waves were gray. They should be dark purple in a storm such as this one. Staring at the dazzling white of the ice fields must have damaged his eyes. Slowly he moved close to the glass door. It looked pathetically weak, the glass fragile and thin. He could be through it in an instant and gone, should danger threaten.

"Where do those doors lead?" He pointed to the far end of the chamber.

"My bedroom and the bathroom." She flitted about, grabbing the scattered colorful rags from the padded bench and the dishes from the chest, then swept a curtain aside and disappeared. Ah, he thought, a hidden chamber. He peeked inside. The room was very small and cramped, naught but an alcove, too small in which to even swing a sword. It was filled with cupboards and a white basin into which she dumped the dishes.

"Out of here." She pushed him—pushed him!—one hand flat on his chest.

Outrage surged through his body. He gripped her wrist. "A female should not touch a man without invitation." He emphasized the final word so she would know he held her in contempt. Only women of pleasure were so bold. He held little esteem for women of pleasure.

Her face flushed. She wrenched her wrist from his grip. He stared as pink colored her cheeks. The urge to touch her face made him whirl away. Many a warrior had used a woman to lure his enemy. Alone, a woman offered little threat. Women might lure a warrior to destruction, but a man would deliver the death blow.

The memory of how seductively she had called to him from the ice made him redouble his efforts to steel himself against temptation now. How he had conjured her into his dreams he did not know, but until he met her master and took his measure, he could not let down his guard.

In a careful inspection he studied everything in the room. His mind flooded with questions. But a warrior did not reveal his weaknesses to a possible enemy. With every footstep, pain throbbed in his head. His cheek had begun to burn.

The woman came near. Her flowery scent came with her. He shook his head.

"Why don't you sit down and explain to me how you got into my shop? Are you here for the war conference?"

Vad stiffened. Her words confused him. "War? Conference?" A conference meant a discussion. A war conference meant planning and strategy—and other warriors. "What conference?"

"The one in Atlantic City."

The wan light from the glass door gleamed off her short cap of hair. "Why are you disguised as a boy?"

"Why are you disguised as the Tolemac warrior?"

He sneered. "I *am* a Tolemac warrior. No man may claim to be *the* Tolemac warrior."

"You stink, you know?" She wagged a finger at him.

He felt chastised and ashamed. Never in his life had he been accused of uncleanliness. Never had his skin crawled so with the urge to scratch. "There are no bathhouses on the ice fields," he spit back.

She giggled. The sound, lighthearted and sweet, sent a shiver down his spine. Her amusement annoyed him.

"Suit yourself." She sank onto one of the wooden chairs.

Suddenly his stomach felt none too steady. Would he shame himself before her? He forced himself to breathe slowly and carefully, to remember every lesson he'd learned about control from his awareness master.

His mind became acutely aware of the many discomforts of his body and the strange world around him. The stormy sea churned so close by, and yet it was all but silent. He heard the continuing sounds of drums and strange instruments beneath them in her shop of many colors.

The woman's soft scent of summer flowers filled his

head. "Why are you garbed as a man? Where is your master?"

She bent her head—to hide a smile, he suspected. Indignation overshadowed his pain. When she looked up, the smile she gave him was kind, not mocking.

"Look, Vad. Here, beyond the ice fields, we have no masters or slaves. I can dress any way I like, and I feel very comfortable in men's garb." Boldly she met his eyes. "Could I fix that cut on your cheek?"

"No," he snapped.

"Have it your way." She shrugged and bit her lip.

He regretted his abruptness, but something warned him to maintain a distance from this unusual female. His stomach shamed him by growling loudly in the silence that followed his words.

She shot to her feet. "You're hungry. Why don't you tell me how you got into my shop after I make you some soup? Sit down."

He remained standing. She disappeared behind the curtain. As soon as she was gone, he grasped the knob of the glass door. It wouldn't turn. He shook it. As frail as the door had looked, it held fast beneath his hand. The sea—and escape—lay beyond a wide wooden road that stretched as far as his eyes could see along the shore. Wind and rain lashed the wooden boards. He caught a glimpse of a man, or possibly a woman, hurrying along, wrapped in bright yellow. He did not relish going into the storm in his weakened state.

If he stayed with the woman, he would be fed.

He must prepare a satisfactory answer to her question. If only he knew what was satisfactory in this place. Turning, he dumped his fur cloak onto the long, padded bench and circled the room until he came to one of the closed doors. Did she pleasure her master in her bedchamber? The woman was humming behind the curtain. He gripped the hilt of his knife and eased one door open—a bedchamber.

The space was gloomy, the curtains drawn. A raised bed stood against one wall. Decadent amounts of lace pillows and covers lay in disarray on it—a bed of pleasure. Garments were strewn on every surface. He grazed his fingers on the dust on a standing chest. He'd sell a slave who kept such a slovenly place.

Delicate slippers littered the floor. He shoved them aside with his boot as his eyes fell on a flowing white garment draped across the disheveled bed. Giving in to temptation, he lifted it and pressed it to his face.

Sweet summer flowers—her scent. The garment had pieces he could see right through and trailing ribbons of silver. He crushed the gossamer fabric in his fist. The gown would tempt the most stalwart warrior.

A bell chimed in the other room. He cast the garment to the bed and strode quickly and quietly back into the front chamber.

Just in time.

The woman came through the curtain carrying a tray with a bowl on it. "Sit," she ordered him.

The rich scent of meat wafted from the bowl—it was a simple broth with chopped vegetables and meat, but not much of either. Without thought, he sank onto one of the chairs at the table. His mouth watered. For a moment, hunger overpowered his aching head and his wariness.

Without ceremony she plunked the bowl before him and handed him a silver spoon. He turned it about in his hand. When his hand trembled, he dropped the spoon. He could not show weakness to this female. Her chambers might appear poor, but the gold-rimmed bowl and the silver spoon bespoke some former time of greater prosperity. Or perhaps they were from her master—gifts for her services.

The woman settled across from him. She had a sweetly heart-shaped face with a stubborn little chin. Her nose was small, her mouth full with soft lips. Her teeth were good and her eyes the color of new ale. Except that she'd shorn her hair like a boy child's, she was perfect for a pleasure slave. A man liked a wide mouth and large breasts. He also much enjoyed well-cushioned buttocks.

She interrupted his thoughts with more prattle. "Now, how'd you get into my shop?"

Lifting the bowl, he gulped the broth and promptly scalded his mouth. He thought of at least three ways to improve the broth, the first of which was to add more meat.

Slowly, to avoid her unanswerable question, he finished the broth, then searched for something with which to wipe his mouth.

She flapped a square of cloth at him. "Is this what you're looking for? I'm glad to see you have some manners."

He snatched the cloth and wiped his hands and mouth. "Manners? Where are yours? You sit next to a warrior as he eats?"

The crack of her hand on the table pulsed through his head. He moaned.

"I'm sorry!" she cried. In an instant she was standing, reaching for him, touching his forehead with her small, smooth hands. Her chest was dangerously close to his face.

It took all his awareness training not to lean in and rest his head on those lush breasts. He shook her off and rose.

"I will leave now." He retrieved his cloak.

"And where are you going?" She stood before him, fists on hips, a small, insignificant barrier to the outside.

"You said there is a gathering of warriors."

"You are not leaving until you give me some answers."

Her chin went up and her eyes snapped fire.

A man also liked a little heat in a woman.

He briefly touched his three arm rings, concealed by his shirt. "I am a warrior. I command an army of Tolemac warriors, the least of whom would strip you naked and flay your back for your impertinence."

Gwen did not move. While she'd microwaved the soup, she'd thought about this man's uncanny resemblance to the warrior in the poster. She had to have him at her ball. If *Video Game* magazine sent a reporter and photographer, her ball was sure to make the cover with him—if she could get him cleaned up.

She blew a strand of hair out of her eyes and blocked his exit. She could not let him get away, but he stood there stubbornly, silently daring her to move away from the door.

"Look. You can't meet other warriors looking like that. No offense, but you're a mess."

He touched his cheek. A crust of blood lay on his beard.

"No one will believe you're the—a—Tolemac warrior if you don't clean yourself up. Neil can take your clothes to the cleaner. You could bathe, maybe shave. You'd look more like Vad if you lost the beard."

His chin jutted out. His hand went to his knife—a very authentic-looking prop. "I am Vad."

"Sure you are," she said, humoring him. It was really difficult to think a guy this gorgeous could be dangerous. Nutty, maybe, but not dangerous. His gaze kept darting from door to door. "There isn't anyone here. No one will disturb you."

"The man in black?"

"That's Neil. And no. He wouldn't think of coming up here without permission. He might look like a hell-raiser, but he's really a gentleman. Anyway, he has to watch the shop."

She decided to take matters into her own hands. She left him looming and glowering in the center of the living room, and flipped on the bathroom light. Hastily she swept several damp towels and a pair of panties into the hamper. A sound behind her made her yelp.

The man paid her no attention as he shoved past her, his gaze riveted to the full-length mirror on the wall. She watched as he reached out and touched its surface. "By the sword, 'tis magic. I must truly be beyond the ice fields."

The wonder on his face and in his voice made her frown. He must have hit his head. He no longer seemed to be playing a role.

The bathroom felt small and crowded with him at its center. The bathroom was the only thing she liked about her apartment, other than its convenience to the store downstairs. Once a spare bedroom, the bathroom was tiled white. A whirlpool tub sat in the corner on a raised, tiled platform. The toilet sat behind a privacy screen she'd fashioned from a tall bookshelf crammed with plants. Her late husband had been shamelessly immodest and laughed at her need for privacy. He might not have minded sharing the facilities, but she had.

The man stared up at the rain drumming on the skylight overhead. His posture drew attention to the long lines of his throat and the perfection of his profile. Her own throat dried.

A thought entered her mind and spilled out of her mouth. "Why don't I fill the tub for you? You could soak and even shave, if you like."

He impaled her with a suspicious look.

"Okay." She held her hands palms outward. "Stay that way. So what if you smell like a dead goat? So what if—"

"Enough, woman. Draw the water." He turned and left the bathroom. She watched him pace and stride from one end of her apartment to the other. The black leather of his trousers hugged every inch of his well-muscled thighs. She knew he was in pain. His hand sought his forehead far too often. A muscle beneath his eye twitched.

Gwen turned on the faucets. The water thundered into the tub as hard as the rain drummed on the skylight. The sound drew him to the doorway, where he stood and stared at the tub as if it might bite.

Impulsively, Gwen lit a candle. The soothing scent of lavender filled the bathroom. She arranged several thick white towels on the tiled ledge at the head of the tub. Anything else he might need stood at hand: bottles of shampoo, shower gel, washcloths, pink plastic razor. She giggled. She was sure a Tolemac warrior would be heartily insulted to use such a feminine-looking device.

She turned off the taps and dug out two aspirin, glanced at his size, and decided to offer him the whole bottle.

"These are for your headache," she said, tugging at his arm. When he made no move to take the pills, she sighed and put the pills and a cup on the edge of the tub. "Give that cut a really good scrub. I'll give you some ointment for it later." Whatever she had expected him to say, it was not his next few words.

"Are you planning to help me bathe?"

Gwen nearly swallowed her tongue. "No. Not likely. Wouldn't think of it."

Vad grinned as the woman flew out the door, slamming it behind her. He had evaded her questions and rid himself of her presence with little effort.

In a moment he had stripped naked. He sighed with relief at finally being free of his malodorous garments, yet shame filled him anew. A warrior should take as good care of himself as he did his weapons. He tossed his filthy clothing from the room to the floor outside the bathing chamber. He unsheathed his knife and slipped it under the edge of his cloak, which he laid nearby on the floor with his boots.

He looked around, studying the slick, shiny walls that reminded him most painfully of the ice fields. The walls were smooth and cold to his touch.

Although the tub looked inviting, with steam rising over the water, it was the shining glass that drew him. He pressed his palm to it. His breath misted the surface. Even reflected in a still pool, he'd never seen himself with such clarity. The whites of his eyes were threaded with red. The deep cut on his cheek looked as nasty as it was painful. Dried blood crusted his beard. His hair lay matted against his brow. Dirt streaked his skin. In fact, there was a line of grime about his neck that he eyed with fastidious displeasure.

But a wide grin split his mouth, opening a crack in his chapped lips. A low rumble of laughter came from deep in his chest. He slapped his hands against the reflective glass and leaned his forehead against its cold surface. He swallowed his glee lest the female be drawn near. He met his own eyes. *Nay.* She would not be tempted by this damaged face, this human wreckage.

An elation born of a lifetime of being mistaken for one of the angels of the gods bubbled and churned in him. No one would make that mistake now. He appeared as what he was: a mortal man, a warrior. He had no healing powders to prevent scarring. He grinned with satisfaction.

His muscles trembling, he fairly collapsed into the hot tub. The water nearly burned his buttocks. With an oath, he fell back with a splash and groaned. The heat embraced his hips, reaching only to his waist. He had to fold his long legs to fit in the hard white tub. The bathhouses in Tolemac had water taps that brought water from rain butts on the roof, but none with such force as this one had, none that poured hot water. He was much more used to it bubbling up from the earthen bottom of a bathing pool.

A moan of pleasure escaped him. He swallowed it

whole as he heard the woman's footsteps outside the door. She called to him through the door: "Are you all right?"

"Aye," he bellowed back. *I am more than all right,* he thought. *I am scarred and marked as if from battle.* He propped his legs on the platform surrounding the tub and slid down until his head rested on the edge. In an instant, he was sound asleep.

Gwen heard the snores. She smiled and tossed the man's clothes into a garbage bag. Slinging it over her shoulder like Santa's pack, she ran down the stairs and dashed into the shop. "I'll take over for a few minutes, Neil. Would you run these over to the dry cleaners? Tell Harry one hour."

"I don't think you should leave that guy alone upstairs. How'd he get in here? He's probably stealing your jewelry right now."

Gwen glanced down at her wedding band, as simple and unadorned as the gold hoops in her ears. She remembered the day her husband had slipped the ring on her finger. Forever, he'd said. Who could have guessed forever would last for only one year? The thought never failed to raise a huge lump in her throat. "I'm wearing my jewelry, Neil. Now get a move on with this stuff. I don't think he's a thief. I think he's just a wacky war gamer, like you said—and harmless. And I want him at my ball. Just think of all the publicity. But"—her eyes glazed over—"he needs his clothes; he's buck naked right now."

"There's no way Harry can get that stuff back in an hour if his leather stuff is in there."

She dug into the bag and drew out the leather trousers. The black leather was incredibly soft and supple in her hands. For a moment she mused on how the leather had clung to the man's legs. "Bribe him." She folded the trousers carefully and tucked them back into the bag.

Neil took the laundry. "Stop thinking about his ass and cover your own. He's a nut."

Gwen felt the heat rush into her face. Had she been that transparent? The instant Neil was out the door, she lifted the phone and punched in a familiar number. When an answering machine stated its neutral message, she swore under her breath.

"Maggie? If you're fooling around, stop it and pick up the phone." No one obliged her. "Okay, listen, I have this guy here at my place. He's the spitting image of Vad. In fact, he claims to *be* Vad." She mentally cleaned him up and shaved him. "He's beyond gorgeous. Tell your husband the poster doesn't begin to do him justice. Think Nordic god. Sure wish you could meet him."

Maggie was Gwen's best friend and was married to the creator of *Tolemac Wars*. They were staying at a farmhouse Gwen owned in the New Jersey pine barrens, left to her by her maternal grandmother. Gwen was grateful her friends could use the house. She personally found it lonely. The six bedrooms were meant for a large family. She had no family—or no family she wished to acknowledge. Her little apartment suited her needs much better, and was handy to her business; and whatever remained of Bob was here, too. Bob. He'd always said she'd end up on the farm, tending a garden and cooking up huge meals in the vast kitchen. How wrong he'd been.

For the next half hour Gwen absentmindedly handled the crowd in her store. A turmoil of questions about the man upstairs prevented her from really attending to the customers. When Neil returned, she gave him a grateful smile. He popped out her Garth Brooks CD and slid in another.

Gwen made a face as she ran a credit card through for approval. "Oh, no, not that pathetic Tchaikovsky symphony again."

Neil shook his head and took over for her. "That's 'Pathétique,' you infidel."

"Whatever you say." She patted him on the shoulder. "On that note, I'm going to see how Mr. Sleeping Beauty is doing."

Neil gave the customer the charge slip to sign. He grabbed Gwen's arm. "Look, I know it's none of my business, but are you sure you should be alone with that guy?"

Gwen edged around a customer who had settled a stack of computer games on the counter. "I'm sure. I think he's as much a gentleman as you, in fact."

In a few moments she stood outside the bathroom door, listening to snores as loud as the crash of the cymbals in any of Neil's symphonies. She rapped sharply on the door. The snores ended in a snort and a grunt. "You okay in there? Can I get you anything?"

Vad swore and fumbled the bottles he'd knocked into the tub back onto the edge. "I am bathing, woman." His voice sounded like a hoarse croak to him. He swallowed. "If I wished assistance, I would call for it."

"Suit yourself," she hollered back to him, a touch of sour wine in her voice. Her footsteps receded.

There were no pots of soap for washing in sight. Although the bathing tub was more the size of those found in a children's bathhouse, the edge of the tub had deep recesses decorated with bulky silver ornaments. On closer examination, he realized they moved. He gave one an experimental turn. A soothing bubble tickled his thigh.

He sighed and thought of calling the woman to bring him soap. His eyes settled on a green bottle. The green liquid looked suspiciously like some witch's potion, but the words on it said, *For Cleaner, Silkier Hair. Normal to Dry.* He ran a hand over his hair. Definitely dry, like straw, and filthy. Thank the gods he could read the language of this strange place. He read the bottle. *Ammonium Lauryl Sulfate.* On second thought, there were many words here he did not know.

He struggled with the bottle for a moment, trying to pull out the smooth white cork. Instead it popped open. He peered into the tiny hole at the top. The wonderful scent of green grass in spring teased his nose. He tipped the bottle and poured a generous amount into his palm. The many experiences he'd had in bathhouses told him this was some potion meant to please and tantalize.

He slid down until his head was underwater, his knees sticking into the air. In a rush, he surfaced and shook. He rubbed the liquid into his hair. The joy of finally bathing made him groan aloud. He dunked. Pouring the green liquid over his head, he twice more lathered his hair until it really was cleaner and silkier.

He sniffed the other bottles. One said *Jasmine Body Gel.* Only the middle word did he know. The thick liquid's scent was even more alluring than the one for his hair. Not a manly scent, he must admit, but potent—spicy and intoxicating. As he rubbed the gooey pink liquid across his chest and belly he bumped his elbow on one of the silver decorations.

A whooshing sound filled the room. A gush of water surged between his thighs. He yelped. His knees disappeared in a froth of water pulsing from the sides of the tub. The empty bottle he'd discarded in the water bounced and jumped about. Suds foamed and rose, spilling over the sides and across the floor. He stared in fascination and poured more liquid into the tub.

Gwen heard the jets come on in the bathroom. "I guess warriors like a whirlpool, too." she muttered. She lifted her late husband's worn green velour robe from the hook on the back of the bedroom door. It was one of the few articles of his clothing she hadn't donated to charity. As she approached the bathroom door she heard an ominous bellow and a huge splash.

She flung open the door. The man lay submerged in suds.

He floundered indignantly to his feet. Bubbles covered him from shoulder to thigh. Her mouth hung open. Then she realized what he'd done.

She shrieked and pointed to the controls. "Off. Turn it off. You'll gum up the works. Turn it off!" Frantically, the man twisted the controls. The jets fell silent.

"No," she mouthed as he turned one final knob. In a blast of water, the shower overhead washed him clean.

She cleared her throat. The robe dropped from her hand. "Well, *you're* definitely not a boy."

Chapter Three

"Unless you are offering your services to clean the floor, woman, I suggest you leave." Vad stepped over the side of the tub. His foot slipped in the slick mess of water and suds. He skidded across the room, his arms flailing.

Gwen thought of a hockey goalie stretching for a save. She'd never again be able to attend a Flyers game without picturing the players naked. There was something quite magnificent about a well-honed man in motion. Any motion.

He righted himself and reached for his furs. Around his beautifully sculpted right biceps were three silver arm rings. Then light glinted off the long blade in his hand.

"Oh, my God," she said with a gasp. Her throat dried.

Then the man lifted one of the towels and wiped the blade. "Water plays havoc with fine steel," he said. She remembered to breathe when he turned away and inspected the knife's leather sheath. Tension flooded through her again as he swung back to poke the sodden mass of fur at his feet.

"Put the sword down." She hated the tremor in her voice.

Puddles of soap and water slowly crept in her direction. They would soon soak the robe she'd brought for him, but she couldn't make herself move.

His sword pointed toward the floor, he came to her. "I wish you no harm."

How she wished she believed him. He was too big and too near—and way too naked. His steady blue gaze held her frozen in place. The touch of his fingers to her cheek was gentle, but she could not stop herself from flinching.

"A warrior must think of his weapons first, and 'tis naught but a small knife. Nothing to be afraid of, woman." Her head bobbed in assent, but she took a step away from him, then another. He bent and lifted the robe. It was heavy and soft. A floral scent clung to the fabric. His body responded.

With as much disdain as possible, he donned the robe. Still, she stood in the door as if ready to flee. Her ale-dark eyes were huge in her face. Her fear insulted him. He had never harmed a female in his life. Well . . . there had been that time he had dropped his shield on a slave's foot. But surely that did not count—it was an accident. She had recovered quite nicely once the healer had stitched her up. Perhaps this one, too, might regain her humor, given the opportunity. It was not often his weapons gained more attention than his manhood.

Shaking out a white cloth, he once again lifted his blade. He began to stroke the cloth up and down its length. "Unless you wish to polish my other sword, woman, be gone."

She flitted away. A cold breeze replaced her. He sheathed his knife and, although it was the work of slaves, he tossed cloths upon the floor to sop up the mess he'd made. There were piles of cloths, cloths enough to dry many bathers. In a cupboard he found more. They joined the others on the soapy floor.

He donned the robe to conceal the knife sheath and sighed over the dampness of the leather. Unbidden, his fingers stroked the green fabric. It was like none he had ever felt before. It had a nap like fur, yet inside it was woven, proving it to be cloth of some kind. He shrugged and scooped up his sodden cloak.

A commotion brought him from the bathing chamber, dripping a trail of water from his furs. So . . . she had feared him enough to fetch the snake man. The woman half hid behind her champion and prattled something about his knife.

"By the gods, woman! Are you so spineless you quail at a small blade?" Keeping one eye on the snake man, he heaved his cloak onto her table.

Her shriek burned his ears.

"How dare you! That was my mother's table. She loved that table. I learned to write at that table." Before he could stop her, she dragged his cloak off the battered wood and, after twisting and turning the silver knob on the glass door, heaved the furs out like so much refuse to be discarded.

He shoved the snake man aside. The man went down like a sack of feathers. Vad leaped to the deck and snatched up his furs. He clasped them to his chest. Anger warred with compassion. The woman was scrubbing the water from her scarred table. He knew well the value of ancestors. As an orphan, he had no mother's table to preserve.

The snake man picked himself up off the floor. "Get downstairs, Gwen. Call the cops." He spread his arms to protect the woman.

Wind whipped at Vad's robe and tore at his hair. It thrummed like the wings of a thousand ravens about his ears. Vad considered how best to handle her protector without hurting him or offending her further.

Gwen giggled. Her Vad look-alike pushed through the deck door, struggling a moment as six and a half feet of man and a mountain of fur were caught between the uprights. He looked ridiculous. The robe came only to mid-calf on him. The ocean winds flapped it about his legs and threatened to once again reveal a tantalizing length of muscled thigh—and other important stuff.

Somehow she could not be afraid of a man who nursed a dirty cloak like a beloved child. Any fear she had dissolved. "Let him alone, Neil. I'm sorry I called you."

Neil ignored her. He took matters into his own hands. He strode to the kitchen, lifted the phone, and punched 911.

Gwen sighed. "Prepare yourself, Vad. You're about to answer a zillion questions."

"From whom?" He hovered at the deck door, arms clutching his cloak.

"The police." When he tipped his head and looked confused, she smiled. "Here, beyond the ice fields, we don't have an army in charge. We have what we call the police. In fact, if you listen, you should hear them any moment now."

He dropped his furs. With fluid grace, he drew his knife. He looked as if he were preparing to confront an army. "What is a zillion?"

"A lot. Take it from me." Gwen sighed heavily at the distant wail of sirens on the sea air. It made her heart beat faster. She didn't want him arrested. She wanted him at her ball. "Now put the knife away."

"Yo, bud. Take it easy." Neil encircled Gwen in his arms and put her behind him again.

As much as she appreciated the gallantry, it blocked her view. Robe open, blade in hand, the man looked so much like the Tolemac warrior—from his straight, noble nose to his honed, muscular body—she almost fainted. Beard or not, there was no mistaking that arrogant sneer.

She whispered in Neil's ear, "He must have posed for those posters. Look at him. Really look at him." Her heart slammed in her chest—and not from fear.

The police hammered on her door. Neil jerked it open.

"Oh, no," she said with a groan. The man who stepped into her apartment was the last man on earth she wished to see. Her former fiancé—now her older sister's husband. Talk about grand larceny. What the heck was the traitorous detective doing answering a routine call?

"Gwen? Are you okay?" R. Walter Gordon stepped into her apartment. Two other officers stepped in behind him. There were no guns drawn, but Gwen knew that if Vad made a move, there would be.

"I'm fine. We really don't need you," she said, hands up, palms out. Her voice sounded shrill and peevish to her. This was her warrior. Nut case or not, she'd invited him into her apartment. If someone hurt him, she'd never forgive herself. "Just go away. Please."

"The guy's got a knife," Neil said.

The officers ignored her as they faced Vad. If they'd missed the knife, they must be blind. Relief came from an unexpected quarter. Vad turned his blade hilt out and offered it to Gwen; then he belted his robe and yawned. He scratched his ear. He looked like a harmless, sleepy guy who'd just climbed out of bed.

Oh, no. What would Walter think? And what story would he spread—like a bad flu virus—to her sister and her mother? She hugged Vad's knife to her chest as he had his furs. She acted without thought. She slid an arm around Vad's waist and hugged him close as well. "There's nothing wrong here, Walter."

Neil gasped. Vad stiffened, but did not move from her embrace. It was like hugging a petrified tree.

With little of the air of a bed companion, Vad said,

"This impertinent woman tried to take my cloak. The snake man overreacted. 'Tis ofttimes seen in poorly trained warriors."

She wanted to kick him in his perfect shins.

Walter froze. *Oh, no,* Gwen silently groaned. The British accent had done it. Walter was a hopeless Anglophile. He'd bored her to tears reading droll Inspector Morse lines from his favorite British mysteries—until he'd run off with her sister, that was.

"What's going on here?" the detective asked.

"Neil? Who's watching the shop?" Gwen used her sweetest voice. "Could the customers be stealing us blind? Should we take the shortages out of your share of the profits?"

He took the hint and left the apartment.

Walter, his eyes on Vad, took the knife from Gwen. He stroked his hand over the decorations that graced the silver crossguard of the long blade. "Is this Celtic?" He gave a low whistle as he examined the handle. The handle looked as though it was made of solid turquoise wrapped with a band of gold. "It's beautifully done."

Vad graciously accepted the compliment. " 'Tis an ancient design."

Gwen sighed. Once Walter got going on Celtic folklore, they'd be here all night. He'd minored in mythology at school. It was how they'd met each other—paired on a mythology project and then later paired in other ways.

One uniformed officer, behind Walter, moved forward and bent over the knife. But Gwen was very aware of the other man, one hand resting casually on his gun, still standing by the door. Vad, Walter, and the one policeman discussed double-edged versus single-edged blades. She wanted to bang their collective heads together.

She sank onto the sofa and rolled her eyes. She patted the place next to her and Vad joined her. He leaned back and crossed his arms on his chest.

Now he looked as if he'd spent a few hours in her bed—and shower. Wouldn't that fry Walter's scrapple?

Vad's long, wet hair hugged his head. His robe gaped over a smoothly muscled chest. She averted her eyes but leaned against him and clasped his hand. She sensed tension sweeping through his body, but he entwined his fingers with hers. A slow warmth built in the pads of her fingers and spread throughout her palm. He wore a wide gold ring on his left hand. Its design echoed the Celtic knotwork on his blade. She hadn't noticed it before.

Was he married? The feeling of his strong fingers wrapped about hers reminded her most poignantly of how lonely her life had become. She dropped his hand. Married men should not hold hands with lonely widows.

Judging from the questions Walter directed at Vad, there was little chance he'd arrest anybody. Instead, Vad received a severe lecture on waving weapons around. Gwen came into her share of censure, too. After a hiatus of seven years, Walter was on a roll. She tuned him out as she had when they'd dated, nodding now and then, her mind uncomfortably occupied with the warmth of the man whose long thigh and hip pressed against hers.

One of the uniformed officers frequented her store. He eyed Vad with something akin to the look she saw on rabid fans just as they donned the headset for a virtual-reality experience. When her ex-fiancé ground to a halt, she introduced her guest to the officer.

"This is Vad, the Tolemac warrior. He's my boyfriend." She enunciated every word in case Walter had missed the more subtle hints.

"*A* Tolemac warrior," Vad corrected.

"You're coming to the ball tonight, aren't you? You're sure to win a prize," the officer gushed.

"Prize?" Vad and Walter spoke simultaneously.

Gwen shot to her feet. Vad followed suit. "Sure, best costume. Finest weapon," she said as she tucked Vad's robe more securely about his waist. The man had no modesty. "That's why Vad was showing me his sword."

"Knife," the three men said in unison.

She took the blade and put it on top of her entertainment cabinet.

The officer thrust his notebook into Vad's hands. "How about an autograph?"

"Go on, give him your autograph," Gwen urged. Then they might leave. The sooner the better. Preferably before Vad said something to make Walter escort him to the funny farm.

They stood around in silence while Vad turned the notebook over and over in his large hands.

"Aut-o-graph?" Vad stared at what he held in his palms. He drew his fingers carefully over the paper. It was fine, far finer than any he'd ever seen. The writing instrument was curious. He sniffed it. Wood. He touched it to the fine paper and it left a mark.

"Sign your name. Big. Across the page." The woman patted his arm. He felt as stupid as a small child.

Boldly, he slashed his name across the page, the way he would if putting his name to an important peace treaty.

The blue-garbed man snatched it up. "Wait until Marlene sees this. She'll shit. Whoops. Beg pardon, ma'am, Lieutenant." Vad watched, fascinated, as brown speckles on the man's face glowed against a flush of dark red. He'd seen this changing skin once before, in a woman who had claimed to be from beyond the ice fields.

The man called Lieutenant drew out his own writing implement and ignored the other man's lapse. Vad would have ordered a flogging for such familiar behavior.

"Let's run through your story again so we can all get home to our families for lunch," the lieutenant said.

For some reason, the woman's expression became

stiff and sour. He sensed an unease that had naught to do with what had summoned these men.

Thunder crashed, shaking the house. The woman winced, her eyes going to the storm outside. She twisted a ring about. He walked behind her and dropped his hands onto her shoulders and squeezed.

"One last time, Walter," she said on his behalf. Her voice trembled just a bit. "Vad is here for the war-games convention. He didn't sleep very well last night, so I guess he's kinda grumpy. His costume stinks a bit. You know how fur smells when it gets wet—so I threw it out on the deck to air. He wasn't too happy. My fault. I should have asked his permission. Neil came in just when Vad was checking his knife. Neil overreacted. End of story."

Vad bit his lip. The woman had lied to the man—with a remarkably agile tongue and straightforward gaze.

The lieutenant tapped his writing tool against his teeth. Vad decided the man looked a bit like an amiable rabbit. He had hair cropped quite close to his scalp. What hair he had was tinted an unfortunate reddish hue, and yet Vad sensed a quality about the man that would be alluring to women. There was no softness about his belly. Vad stood up straighter and sucked in his stomach. He squared his shoulders.

The lieutenant scowled. "Why does this remind me of the stories you spun in college, Gwen? When you were playing that stupid *Tolemac Wars* game? When it was still just a pencil-and-paper amusement. You know, the one like Dungeons and Dragons? The game nonathletes played."

"Yes, R. Walter. The stupid game I loved and you hated."

The man had insulted the woman. Vad clamped his hands on her shoulders and held her in place. Her small fists were clenched. The Rwalter man rose from his seat at the mother's battered table.

All the names confused him. Later, when he had gained this woman's confidence, he would delve into why this unlikely man had angered his little friend.

Nay, not friend.

Possibly an ally.

He shrugged. As it stood now, she was his only ally. But she was an ally who glibly lied to men in authority. And with but a word, the snake man did her bidding.

At the door, the Rwalter man turned. "Hey, Vad. Mind if I bring my son over to meet you?"

Vad dropped his hands from the woman's shoulders and bowed formally from the waist. If the same rules applied here as in Tolemac, the man would recognize an obeisance of equal to equal. As superior as Vad felt to this man who came only to his shoulder, he understood the tactics of flattery. The man did not return the bow. Was the man ignorant or deliberately insulting him?

Once they were alone, Gwen slumped onto the sofa. "I think I just aged ten years."

"Why did you lie for me?" Vad stood before her, tall, angry, and magnificent. He spread his legs and crossed his arms on his chest.

Oh, brother. How was she supposed to think with a Tolemac warrior looming over her? "I lied to save your butt, you ungrateful idiot. If I'd known you wanted to spend the night in a cell, I wouldn't have bothered."

A muscle twitched in his jaw. His eyes narrowed.

"Would you sit down? I have a headache." That was no lie. Her head pounded. What were the chances that Walter would come to her apartment after seven years of silence? And just when she was making a complete fool of herself. She'd given him one good dig—he hated being called R. Walter. She glanced at her warrior. At least Walter and her family would know she didn't need them, had someone in her life.

The thought depressed her. There was no one in her life. With a conscious shake she chastised herself for her soppy mood. This was how she wanted her life to be—well-ordered, with no messy entanglements. No lovers to desert her or her husbands to die on her. Besides, she couldn't get burned if she avoided the fire.

The warrior inspected his cloak. He crouched down and spread the furs out, ran his hands over them. She cocked her head and enjoyed the play of muscle beneath the soft velour of the robe. She sighed. Her hand went to the tight waistband of her jeans. She should have lost those extra ten pounds during the summer.

Contemplation of her weight always made her cranky. "There's no way I'm putting up with that smell. Give it to me." She leaped up from the sofa and grabbed his cloak.

He trotted after her as she hustled back to the bathroom. "Just great," she muttered, and stared at the floor. Every towel and sheet she owned lay in a sodden mess. "Now I remember why I didn't want a man in my life." She glared at the warrior. And the last thing I need, she mused silently, is to be attracted to a man who thinks I'm a slave.

She flung open the folding doors that concealed her washer and dryer. Stepping gingerly over the piles of linens at her feet, she tossed the furs into the dryer. She added a scented dryer sheet. He made a strangled sound in his throat. "Don't worry, big guy." She patted his rock-hard chest. "This will make you sweet-smelling again." On second thought, she added two more dryer sheets. "Oh, what the heck." She added the whole box.

He bent over and peered at the control panel as she punched the button for air fluff first, then one hour.

With a sigh, she scooped up the soapy sheets and towels, wrung them out in the tub, then dumped what she could into the washer and squashed the rest into a laundry basket.

Vad opened the dryer door. The light popped on and he nearly put his whole head into the dryer looking about. He closed the door. She pushed the on button. Two seconds later, he jerked the door open again.

She patted his arm. "Relax. Nothing's going to happen to your precious coat. I'm just airing it out."

Like a soldier called to battle, Gwen pulled out a mop and tackled the floor. She consoled herself with the idea that the job was overdue.

Behind her, Vad's stomach growled. "I suppose that means you're still hungry. Why don't I get us a pizza?" she said, shoving the mop behind the washer.

A curious expression crossed his face. "Pepperoni," he said softly. He said the word as if it were too big for his mouth.

"Sure. Pepperoni. I'll just run down the boardwalk and pick one up." She contemplated her large guest. "Maybe I'll get two . . . or three. If the dryer buzzes, your coat's done."

He watched her pick up a black leather pouch. With a wave and a smile, she left him.

Wandering about her small home, he rolled the odd word about on his tongue. *Pepperoni.* The word had popped unbidden into his mind. His headache returned with a vengeance. He massaged the ache in his temples and groaned. What did the word mean? Where had it come from? The woman certainly understood its meaning.

The sound of the door opening drew him to the front room.

"Your clothes," the snake man announced, standing at the door with a bundle in his arms. "Where's Gwen?"

Vad tried the unfamiliar word on the snake man. "Pepperoni."

"Oh." The man nodded, then stepped in and closed

the door behind him. He tossed his bundle on the table. "Look, bud. Gwen's a nice lady. Don't screw around. Get it?"

Vad searched the man's face. Although the warrior lacked a few inches, he did not lack bravery. He had no weapons save his audacity. Vad understood the import of the man's words, if not their actual meaning. "I will not harm her."

The snake man paced to the glass door. He opened it and stepped into the rain. After standing there a moment, hands on hips, the man came back inside. Challenge radiated from him in tangible waves. He pointed to the bundle of clothing. "Get dressed. When Gwen returns I'll take you to Atlantic City. She doesn't need any hassles, and you look like a king-size hassle to me."

"What is in this Atlantic City to interest me?"

"A thousand people just like you."

A thousand!

The snake man tore a thin, clear wrap that looked like spun glass from the garments. An unpleasant smell wafted from the package, yet his clothing was clean. The leather gleamed. His shirt was completely free of wrinkles. Garbed thus, he would once more feel himself. And surely, if his friend had crossed the ice fields, he would be at this Atlantic City. Someone there must know him. "I will do as you ask."

"Great. Gwen should be back in about ten minutes. After you eat, I'll run you up."

Vad frowned. He did not relish running with this pain pounding through his head. Nor did he relish being lured to an enclave of a thousand warriors, all of whom might be snake men. He would seek his friend—and entrance to the war talks—in his own way.

When the man left, Vad carefully folded the robe and dressed. The familiar feel of his clothing canceled much of the confusion from his mind.

In a whirlwind, he searched the place, looking for

other weapons he might use. His mind reeled at the strange and inexplicable objects he found. He saw tiny portraits of people in strange garb who looked almost alive, the artist who had painted them so talented Vad could discern no brush marks. And then there were the silken articles of clothing hidden in a chest that seemed to have no purpose. And the chest had odd boxes in it that slid. It was marvelous, and he wasted time shoving the little boxes in and out.

Perhaps he could pay the woman for her services and see the gossamer garments on her lush flesh. His head throbbed with an intensity that made him groan. He stuffed the garments away and closed the door on temptation.

He had taken a personal oath against spending his seed with cheerful abandon—once a rather bad habit of his, but one he thought he had learned to control.

Cooler of mind, he rummaged in jumbled boxes in the alcove where the woman had prepared his broth. He found only a paltry collection of small knives. One, with an oddly curved blade, he shoved into his boot. Finally he fetched his cloak from the bathing chamber.

The scent it gave off was intoxicating. Her scent. It clung to all her silky garments. As he shook out his furs, small white squares of fabric fluttered to the floor. He lifted one to his nose and took a deep breath. She would not miss one. He tucked it into his shirt; it would serve as a remembrance of her.

Using the tip of his knife, he made a tiny slit in the lining of his furs. A polished blue-green stone dropped into his palm. He placed it in the center of her scarred table.

Footsteps pounded on the staircase. Soundlessly he moved to the glass door, and with barely a fumble at the catch, he was through it. He swung a leg over the railing.

An arm snaked around his neck and jerked him off his feet.

The colorless world tilted, spun. A vision of a dark place rose in his mind as the scent of dirt and dust filled his nostrils. Black mist swirled through the air and blinded him.

A distant voice called his name. He felt the clasp of a hand on his. He coughed, then tried to grasp the hand, but it slid away. He thrust his out, groping in the darkness, but felt nothing. With a mournful howl, he gave himself to the ebony mist.

Chapter Four

"Vad!" a voice said by his ear.

The arm about his neck slid away along with the encroaching darkness. He took in a deep breath and steadied himself.

Where was he? *Ah, yes. Ocean City.*

A metallic taste filled his mouth. He shook his head and focused on the man who had called his name. The snake man stood over him, his features blurred and foggy.

"Are you all right? You nearly went over the railing," the snake man said, taking his arm again.

"I was deliberately going over the railing," Vad said, jerking his arm from the snake man's grasp and stumbling back into the chamber. The room spun around him, changed for a moment, filled with blues and greens. The furniture shifted, stretched, the shapes elongating or shrinking from one moment to the next.

He gripped the back of a chair and took a long, deep breath. He'd dreamed the black mist, the strong grip of the hand, and the grief of its loss before—but never while awake. He had also dreamed the blue and green room.

This time when the snake man took his arm, he did not shake him off.

"I don't think Gwen would be too happy about—" the snake man began.

"What wouldn't I be too happy about?" Gwen asked from the doorway, her arms full of white boxes decorated with royal purple. Her gaze swept over him, lingering on his cloak, and a look of distress crossed her face, then quickly disappeared behind a bright smile. Her helmet of golden hair was wind-tossed. It gave her the look of a small child. "Oh, I see," she said. "You were leaving." With no ceremony she plunked the boxes on the table. She shrugged. "So why don't you go? I certainly can't keep you here. Go if you want."

Her words might appear to be uncaring, but a tiny hint of something else colored them. Finding his friend was all important; he should not concern himself with one woman's disappointment.

Vad sighed. He'd never been very good at ignoring a disappointed woman.

"You brought food?" he asked, stalling for time until the room settled down and the colors shifted back.

The snake man lifted the lid from one of the shallow boxes and revealed a tray of flat bread. "Why don't you have some pizza? As usual, she bought too much. This is enough for an army."

"An army?" he repeated, eyes on the woman. "I thought you said there was no army in charge here."

"Oh, we have armies for keeping peace in other places," she said with a negligent wave of her hand. "Neil's just being sarcastic, aren't you?" She disappeared into the curtained alcove and then returned with gold-rimmed plates.

Vad hated the confusion he felt, the words he did not

understand, the lack of familiar objects and places to rest his eyes. He rubbed his temples. His head pounded, as it had when he'd first awakened in this strange, colorless place.

"Vad." Gwen touched his shoulder and held out a plate. "Why don't you eat something? Then you can go if you want. We won't stop you."

The plate she offered him held the unappetizing flat bread cut into a triangle. Its scent was pungent and familiar. For a moment he was a child again, sitting on a bright blue chair, eating . . . then the image slipped away. He accepted the plate and turned it around and around in his hands.

"I suppose there's no pizza in Tolemac."

He shook his head and regretted the action; pain jolted behind his eyes.

"Go like this," she said with a whisper of a laugh. The sound ran up and down his spine like warm fingers. The image did nothing for his resolve to ignore her. She bit the point from a piece of bread. He stared at her mouth. It was a mouth made for pleasure.

He followed her lead, biting carefully into the bread. His mouth flooded with flavor: strong, spicy—cheese, bread, tastes he didn't recognize. The childhood image returned, sharper, bolder this time. He could smell a sharp, metallic odor and the tang of the circles of strange meat on his bread.

"It would be nice if you could come to my ball," Gwen said.

Her words ended his musings as effectively as an ax chopping off a tree limb.

"What is a ball?" His plate was empty. Somehow the bread had disappeared, though he couldn't remember eating all of it.

"Oh . . . hmmm . . . a ball's a festival of sorts, similar to what you'd have after the harvest in Tolemac." She smiled warmly, but he was not going to be distracted by frivolous activities.

"I have more need to go to the war conference in Atlantic City."

She trilled a laugh. The snake man shook his head and scooped up a piece of the bread, eating it from his hand.

"Well, Vad," she said, "you might as well wait right here. I think everyone who was at the conference will be at my ball tonight."

Waiting was not something he did well, but could he risk missing an opportunity to complete his quest? "I will attend your festivities."

Gwen thrust another piece of bread onto his plate. "Great! Now eat up, and then you can shave."

The smile she gave him could melt the ice through which he had traveled. Such an alluring manner, calculated to distract a man from his goals, must be useful in a slave.

"I will not shave," he said around a piece of the tantalizing bread.

"If you don't get that cut cleaned up, it'll scar," said the snake man. "It looks bad."

Vad did not want to give up even one whisker of his disheveled beard. Women would surely recoil from a man who looked as he did now. "No. I will not shave." He placed his plate on the table, crossed his arms, and spread his legs.

"Neil's right, though; your cut needs tending. You can't do much with it unless you shave around it. You don't want it to become infected, do you?"

"Infected?" Another word he did not know.

"Sure." Gwen nodded. "You know, rot, grow disgusting and putrid. Like worms eating your flesh."

Vad glanced from Gwen to the snake man, who rolled his eyes. She knew of the flesh-eating worms. He had battled them only once, an experience he did not wish to repeat. "I will perhaps shave around the cut."

"I'll help you," she said with a look that boded ill for his composure.

"Gwen—" the snake man started.

"Neil? Could you go over to the Music Pier and see if the food's arrived?"

The man went to the door, a huge grin on his face. "I can tell when I'm not wanted."

Vad did not understand the man's amusement, nor the small woman's ability to command his swift obedience.

When the door had closed behind the snake man, she went to the bathing chamber door. "Be careful where you put that coat this time," she called to him.

A repeat of her stormy emotions over the table would drain the last of his energy, so he draped his cloak carefully on the back of a chair. He scooped up the stone he'd left on the table and took it to her in the bathing chamber.

"This is for you, for your trouble." He held it out. The stone—its color—was sacred. If the stones meant little here beyond the ice fields, he truly had nothing but his wits on which to depend.

She took the stone with the tips of her fingers, as if reluctant to touch him. "It's beautiful. The color is gorgeous." Her warm brown eyes looked up at him. How small she seemed.

"I had such a stone, decorated with silver, as a talisman, but in my journey here, I seem to have lost it." The loss of the stone boded ill for his mission. It had served as a reminder that the person he sought was real. But with its loss went some of his conviction that he would succeed. He was not used to feeling unsure.

"It's almost the color of your eyes. Not quite as . . . lush a color, but almost."

Her skin flushed red, and he knew she regretted making the personal remark. All of the inhabitants of this strange place must have changeable skin, perhaps to compensate for the lack of color in their world. The woman who had given him the pendant—the woman who had journeyed beyond the ice fields and beguiled his friend into leaving Tolemac and all he'd held most sacred—had had such skin. *This* warrior would not be so easily beguiled.

He shrugged. "It will perhaps pay for any damage I have done to your bathing chamber."

With a slow, sensuous motion, she rubbed her thumb back and forth over the stone. "Thank you. I'll treasure it."

Her words pleased him. She understood its value.

"The philosophers say the stone's color will intensify through time from contact with the skin." Her color deepened to a darker rose. "It is also said that one may know the health of the stone's holder by how rich the color is."

"I guess you must be very healthy, then."

"Why do you say so?"

"Your dagger handle is so beautiful. I assumed it was just from being handled for many years."

He touched the knife's hilt self-consciously, but tipped his head in acknowledgment of the compliment.

She put the stone into an opening in her men's breeches. They were tight. His body heated as he watched her hand slide down her hip and tuck the stone away.

"Come on." She led the way to a small white seat. It was hard and uncomfortably low for his long legs. He put his hand into his boot. "I borrowed this small knife."

"What were you expecting? Killer grapefruit?" She took the knife and hefted it in her palm. "Why don't you keep it? It's not worth what the stone is by any means."

"What has this knife to do with grapes?"

Unexpectedly, she placed her fingers under his chin. A soothing warmth spread from the contact. With a gentle pressure, she urged his chin up. He could not avoid her intense gaze. Her smile continued to hold a hint of amusement.

"The knife is for a special fruit. It has tiny sections and the knife's curved tip helps to cut each . . . Now, look, I don't think I really need to explain it to you."

If she was going to refuse to explain, then he must accept it. A warrior did not need the condescension of a mere woman.

He slid the knife back into his boot. When he looked up, her chest was dangerously close to his face. So was a small pink object she held. "Now, let's deal with your cut." Her tone brooked no disobedience.

Gwen sat abruptly down on the edge of the bathtub. What had she done? What had she unleashed on the unsuspecting female world? She licked her lips. He'd dozed off for only a moment when the devilish thought had burst into her head, and before she'd been able to stop herself, she'd acted on it. Now Vad was glaring at himself in the mirror, looking ready to strangle someone—her.

He swung around, fists on hips. She clutched the edge of the tub. Oh, Lord, he was even more devastating in person than on his poster. The artist had not captured something . . . intangible, slightly dangerous about him.

"Stop staring at me," he said between tightly clenched teeth.

"Huh?" she said. The room was suddenly way too small and way too hot.

"Not you, too."

Gwen's back stiffened at his haughty tone. It matched the haughty face she saw every morning on the poster in the shop. "I beg your pardon? What does that mean? Not me, too?"

"I do not need—nor wish—your attention."

"Well!" She shot off her seat and ducked under his arm, escaping to the clearer air of the living room. All her pictures rocked askew as he thumped after her. "If that isn't the most conceited comment I've ever heard. I-I-I was just checking out your hair. It's terrible."

His hand went to his head. His haughty look vaporized to one of confusion. "My hair? What has my hair to do with the fact that my beard is gone?" His anger rumbled through the small apartment. "And I liked my beard!"

"It was a pretty scruffy beard, believe me. Here." She pulled out a chair. "Sit down and let me fix your hair. If I didn't know better, I'd say you really were crossing the ice fields—without a hat."

She whipped a comb out of her purse and separated the dry, broken strands of hair at his brow from the rest of the shoulder-length mass. She tried to ignore the fact that he was frowning at the center of her chest again. Of course, the last time he'd stared at her chest, he'd fallen asleep—not much of a compliment.

"So what did you want in Atlantic City?" she asked to distract him, but when he looked up, her hands fumbled at her chore. His deep blue eyes were fringed with dark lashes—not gold, not brown, but a pewter color.

"I am seeking my friend Kered," he said, interrupting her thoughts on eyelashes. He was silent for many moments, and she thought he was wrestling with some decision. Perhaps he was going to tell her he was from the modeling agency.

"Your friend Kered? Sure. I guess all you warriors are friends." She swallowed a smile. "I know his wife—lifemate—Maggie. Did you know she's going to have a baby?"

His smooth brow wrinkled in a frown. "Nay. I did not know." The expression on his face was troubled. His blue eyes locked on hers. "He possesses a dagger I must retrieve and return to the council. I would not tell you this, except that I fear that without someone's assistance, I would become lost searching for Kered."

She was lost, almost unable to tear her eyes from his. They were the blue of a stormy sea right now.

"Uh, what? A dagger? What kind?" She forced her mind to focus on what he'd said. His hair was very thick and heavy in her hands, like skeins of rough silk.

"A jeweled dagger. About this long." He spread his hands about a foot apart. " 'Tis just a trifling piece."

His broad shoulders rippled as he shrugged and she almost sighed aloud. She knew just the knife he wanted. Maggie had given it to her with a cryptic message that one day she, Gwen, would believe Tolemac really existed. "If the dagger's not worth much, then why do you want it?"

"That is not something I can tell you, a woman." His eyes dropped to her chest again; his frown deepened. Despite the cold words, she did not sense that he was insulting her. Warriors rarely gave women any credit, she imagined.

Whoa. He is not *from Tolemac. He is not really looking for a dagger. He is . . . What is he?*

A confused cover model sent from the agency? A wacky war gamer too into his role? Or . . . An idea burst over her. Maybe he was payback.

Payback for inviting a gang of *Tolemac Wars* fans to her friend Maggie's wedding. Maybe she and her husband were playing a practical joke on her—bent on making her think this guy was really from Tolemac and then—zing—he'd whip out a cell phone and call them to tell them she'd been well and truly suckered.

The idea made more and more sense. Her friends had sworn vengeance. After all, the fans had been a tad disruptive at the wedding. So she'd forgotten to tell the group not to bring their swords . . . So a fight had broken out . . . Well, there was no way she was giving Vad the dagger and playing right into his practical-joking hands—not that they weren't really nice hands.

However, it might be fun to go along with the joke

and somehow turn it back on Maggie and her husband.

"This knife you're seeking, is it sacred?" she asked, smoothing his hair through her fingers, checking his body for a lump that might indicate a concealed cell phone. No. She'd seen him buck naked and taken his clothing away with her own hands. No, any lumps or bumps ruining the smooth leather expanse of this guy's leather pants belonged to him. The room was suddenly hot again. Sweat broke out on her palms.

"No, the dagger has no holy meaning."

He wasn't picking up on his cues. Most relics in the *Tolemac Wars* games were holy. Their value was to priests or wisemen. Warriors killed for them, or devoted their life to finding them.

"Okay. Don't tell me why the knife's important."

"Okay." He mouthed the word as if he were taking part in a language experiment. "What are you doing to my hair?" His eyes crossed as he peered up at her hands.

"I'm braiding it. I once saw this painting of a Native American who had these skinny braids down one side . . . Never mind. I'm fixing the dry, broken ends so they don't show."

"I do not care if my hair is damaged." He began to rise, pulling her hard work apart with a jolt.

"Sit still." She shoved down on his shoulders. It was like pressing on a steel girder. "There's no way I'm taking someone as messy as you to my ball."

Color heated her cheeks from her misplaced indignation. His head could be shaved and he'd be spectacular. In fact, he could stripe it blue and purple and he'd still be the best-looking man on her little barrier island—or in the state of New Jersey . . . or east of the Mississippi, for that matter.

Vad's hair slid silky soft through her fingers as she redid the braids. Good old-fashioned common lust raced right through her. She bit her lip to concentrate. He was not going to be right. Women might fall all over him, but she was not going to be one of them. *Ever.*

She made a decision: practical joker, agency model, or nut case, she would go along with his contention he was Vad until the ball was over. Eventually he'd step out of his role, and then she'd tell him she'd known what he was up to all along.

In the meantime, if she could get him to the Music Pier, her ball would go down in history as the best Tolemac ball ever.

Finally she dug through the jumble of thread and needles in her sewing box until she found exactly what she wanted—a steel gray embroidery thread to match his eyelashes. She wove it into the narrow braids she'd constructed from his damaged hair.

When she stepped back and examined her handiwork, she knew she was a liar. She was no different from any other woman.

He was no longer more beautiful than a Nordic god. He was way past that. He was all the really great-looking gods rolled up in one.

"Well, Vad. There's not much more I can do for you," she said, slamming her sewing box closed. "I can't work miracles, you know."

Chapter Five

Getting to the Music Pier with Vad was like walking a giant two-year-old. He jerked to a halt for the fifth time, nearly pulling her arm from its socket.

"What is it this time?" A seagull he had to examine? A trash can he had to peer into, sniff, circle? A woman she had to peel off his arm?

She followed the direction of his intent gaze. A police cruiser was coming toward them on the boardwalk.

"Nilrem's Seat of Wishes," he said, his eyes wide. "I have dreamed of the seat many times. . . ." He frowned. "No. The seat in my dreams is black, without . . ." He waved a hand at the bubble lights as the car drew even with them. "If you know Kered, do you know Nilrem? Do you know the legends of Nilrem's treasures?"

"No, I'm sorry, never heard of them." She lifted her hand in greeting to one of the officers who'd come to her apartment earlier that afternoon. The cruiser stopped; the window lowered. The headlights illuminated the fine mist swirling about in the high winds like smoke curling from a chimney.

Vad's arm tensed beneath her hand. He did not move, but she knew instantly that he was upset about something.

"You'll get a great crowd at your ball tonight," the officer said. "Wish I wasn't on duty."

"I'm sorry you can't be there, too. See you." She urged Vad the last few steps to the Music Pier. "What's wrong?"

He shook his head and took a last look at the police car.

"Nothing is wrong, but I do not understand what the Seat of Wishes, surely Nilrem's most famous treasure, is doing here—beyond the ice fields."

He was really good. Just the right touch of confusion. A soupçon of distress. The treasure idea was cute. "Well, why can't the seat be here?" she asked. She could also tell he wasn't budging until he'd said what he had to say.

" 'Tis said in legend that Nilrem buried eight treasures, with a challenge that any man who found them might know great wisdom. To my knowledge, no warrior has yet located the treasures, and yet there is one of them." He turned around another time to stare after the police cruiser.

Gwen smiled. Any moment now, someone was going to jump out and yell, "Gotcha!" She just knew it. Were her friends hiding in the Music Pier rest room? Or across the way, tucked beneath the boardwalk?

This was a practical joke of the highest caliber. And her friends would be really disappointed if she didn't at least appear to believe that this guy was from Tolemac.

Vad wiped a hand over his brow. Cracking under the pressure, she thought. It must be really difficult to stay in character so long.

" 'Tis magic," he said.

"No. There's no such thing as magic."

"But can you not use the Seat of Wishes to go wherever your heart desires?"

She swallowed a laugh. He looked so adorably earnest. "Yes, the Seat of Wishes will take you wherever your heart desires, as long as you are pure of heart. Now move it. I'll melt if we don't get out of this rain."

"Melt?"

His voice dropped, and he examined her in a way that made her feel hot but at the same time naked and exposed.

"Come on." She grabbed his arm and hauled him into the Music Pier. She took his cloak and tossed it behind the blue-and-gold stage curtain with her own coat and Neil's leather jacket.

Moisture beaded Vad's hair like a dusting of tiny diamonds. With Vad facing as he was now, to the rear of the Music Pier, staring at the huge, roiling waves, she could not see his damaged cheek, and for a moment he looked just like who he said he was . . . the warrior from *Tolemac Wars II.* He must be the model for the character. But she imagined when he'd signed on for this practical joke, he hadn't expected it to go on so long. It probably paid really well, though. Her friends were richer than a Tolemac councilor.

A fleeting thought, that he would not need to camp in her game booth overnight if he was paid well, was quickly replaced by another thought when he turned her way.

Maybe he was mentally ill. Maybe he really thought he was the warrior. A strong protective instinct overcame her. There was something vulnerable about him.

An hour later, Gwen rocked back and forth on her heels as she surveyed her ball. It was more than successful; it was a megahit. Despite the downpour outside, the ballroom was wall-to-wall people, or creatures and Tolemac free folk, if you went by costumes alone.

"He's great, isn't he?" Gwen asked Neil. "I thought he'd be completely overwhelmed by the women. But he's just taken it all in stride. He's so charming. No matter how many of them want his autograph or want a photograph, he obliges."

Neil nodded. "Yeah, I guess they have photo shoots in Tolemac all the time. But if he takes another step back, he'll be cornered. And he keeps touching and turning the programs like he's never seen paper before."

Neil crossed his arms and leaned on the edge of the stage. His costume consisted of the clothes he'd worn that day to work—black jeans and a T-shirt. There was no getting Neil into warrior garb—or out onto the dance floor. Her gaze went to Vad again. She swayed and hummed to the music—a Celtic piece, mournful and somehow alluring. "Vad hasn't danced yet, has he?"

Neil shook his head. "Somehow he doesn't look like the dancing kind." He took her glass of punch and sniffed it. "How many cups of this have you had?"

"It's great, isn't it? Who made it? There's this spicy hint of—"

"It's spiked. Or it was," he said. "I took care of it, but some wicked warrior added a little extra ingredient."

"Oops. I hope we don't get arrested." A giggle bubbled in her throat. "Imagine R. Walter storming in here and arresting us for spiked mead or ale or whatever we're pretending it is."

"Yeah, well, Ocean City is dry—and R. Walter will never believe you didn't know the punch was spiked. Now, how many cups have you had? You're grinning like a fool."

"I only had maybe four . . . maybe eight cups."

"You'll feel great in the morning!" He shook his head and stalked off with her cup.

Mrs. Hill took his place. Her long blond wig and two silver arm rings proclaimed her a Tolemac free woman of rank. "Vad is such a doll, isn't he?" she chirped.

"Yep." Gwen smiled. Mrs. Hill's cheeks were flushed a hectic red.

"I don't think he's used to giving autographs, though."

"No."

"He gave me the most wonderful recipe for hart stew."

Gwen coughed. "He gave you a recipe? That's a new one."

"Oh, yes, although he was a bit sheepish about it. Cooking is women's work in Tolemac, you know. Of course, he told me quite sternly that one should never take the meat of the white hart." Mrs. Hill's voice was a grave imitation of Vad's.

"Oh, of course not, not the white hart."

"Strange, he's never heard of turmeric. I used to make quite a venison stew myself when Kurt, my husband, hunted, and I always used a touch of turmeric. By the way, your costume is gorgeous! You're the ice woman, aren't you?"

"Yes, do you really like it?" Gwen felt inordinately pleased. She'd spent hours on the costume. For once, she felt almost beautiful in the billowy layers of silk.

Mrs. Hill nodded approval. "I love it. I never quite understood the ice woman's role in the game. She's just a suggestion, a swirl of snow and ice. Somehow you've made her into a living, breathing entity." She adjusted one of the many jagged layers of Gwen's gown. "And how's Neil doing? Is his mother still recovering from her accident?"

"Yes," Gwen said. She was not going to discuss Neil's mother with Mrs. Hill. Everyone in Ocean City knew Mrs. Scott had driven into a bridge abutment of the Garden State Parkway and had had a blood alcohol level way over the legal limit. Unfortunately it wasn't her first DWI.

"I know she's had skin grafts and God knows what done, poor woman."

His mother's history of problems had made Neil quit graduate school and return to Ocean City in the first place—this latest tragedy merely meant he was home indefinitely. Neil always turned the conversation when it veered toward his widowed mother and her accident. What a pair they made—both unable to deal with their family problems.

"And remind me to introduce you to that Gulap over there," Mrs. Hill said sotto voce. "He's single and making a very good living."

Gwen groaned. The man Mrs. Hill indicated, dressed as a leopardlike Tolemac creature, was three times Gwen's size—around the middle.

"It's time you married again, you know. Time for some babies!"

Tears filled Gwen's eyes. What chance had she of having her own children? She needed a husband for that. She needed to fall in love before she could have a husband, and she never wanted to take a chance on love again.

She'd loved twice. R. Walter had defected with her sister, and Bob . . . She didn't want to think about Bob.

It's just the punch making me maudlin, she decided, and surreptitiously wiped her eyes. "Thanks for the offer, Mrs. Hill. But I'm really not in the market for a husband. I'm quite happy by myself."

"Nonsense. Look at your sister. Two boys and a third on the way."

A third on the way. She hadn't known Pam was expecting. "I've got to go, Mrs. Hill." For a moment the room spun, and she felt the full effects of her cups of spiked punch.

"Oh, stand still," a woman of almost six feet cried. She aimed a camera at Gwen and fired off a few shots. The chief photographer for *Video Game* magazine, Liz

Williams, bore down on Gwen like a Tolemac army besieging a fortress. Liz was instrumental in obtaining coverage for Gwen's ball each year.

"Hi, Liz." Gwen welcomed the interruption. Mrs. Hill walked away. "I'm so glad you could make it."

"I wouldn't miss it! I get to dress up like a medieval princess and take pictures of devastatingly gorgeous men. I've got at least two rolls of him!" The photographer jerked her thumb in Vad's direction. Behind her stood a small man who was scribbling on a notepad. As diminutive as he was, he would be the one to translate the event into words. Gwen gave him a warm smile.

Liz spoke in exclamations all the time and at the top of her lungs. Her yellow costume clashed badly with a purple totebag bulging with lenses and film.

"Do you have everything you need?" Gwen asked. *Video Game*'s feature on her ball last year had meant thousands of dollars in mail-order business for Virtual Heaven.

Liz leaned near, her breath a blast of spiked punch. "No!" she shouted in Gwen's ear. "I want that warrior! And maybe that evil-looking dark guy standing next to him. He'd make a tasty appetizer!"

Gwen followed the direction Liz pointed and saw Neil talking to Vad. The contrast in the men's hair color and garb was striking. They did look inviting together—edible, even.

Neil caught her eye and winked.

Whoa. I must be drunk, Gwen thought. *Neil never winks. Never.*

"What a pair of great asses!" Liz gushed. "Do you think a man's penis is in direct proportion to his height?" Liz's reporter flushed red across his balding forehead.

"Liz! Lower your voice." Luckily the classical music, surely something Neil had picked, soared into a crescendo and drowned her words. Gwen fanned herself with a program.

To distract Liz, Gwen guided her around the perimeter of the room, past the refreshment tables, the only non-Tolemac spot in the room. Modern buffet servers were filled with hot and cold foods and mountains of saltwater taffy and bowls of caramel-covered popcorn.

"Do you think that guy who builds the hardware for the *Tolemac Wars* game—what's his name . . . ?"

"Gary Morfran, the hardware genius?"

"Yeah, that's him. Do you think he'll be making any changes to the virtual-reality gear this year? I'd really like to interview him," Liz said.

"I don't know. I'd personally like him to make the headset lighter. Mrs. Hill's always complaining."

"And where'd you learn to make such fabulous costumes?" Liz asked as she peeled a lemon taffy and crammed it into her mouth. Her next remarks were lost in garbled-candy exclamations. Something about icicles and ribbons.

"I majored in textile arts in college, and I've been painting fabric ever since. Usually I make quilted bags or vests, but this time I went all out and did a whole dress. It's silk. Seven shades of white and silver painted on—"

"Stand in front of that fake snowdrift," Liz interrupted her. "The lights overhead make you sparkle." She fluttered her hands through the silver ribbons on Gwen's sleeves. "In fact, let's open a door, blow some wind through here."

"No! Liz, no." But it was too late. In a burst of salty, watery wind, Liz tore open a door. All Gwen's snowdrifts lifted, swirled, and gusted into the air.

"Shit."

"Now that was far from ladylike," Neil said, and helped Gwen haul the door closed. A crack of lightning flashed over the water, painting the black water silver, spotlighting a small boat near the horizon.

"Shut up, Neil. I could cry. Look at my decorations."

She stared miserably about. Her red rocks were barren; her drifts were all on the south side of the ballroom.

He put an arm around her shoulders. "No one cares. They're either three sheets to the wind or just happy to be here." He gave her a gentle squeeze.

"You're right." She sighed, and dropped her head on his shoulder. "No harm done, I guess."

Vad did not enjoy the uncomfortable pang of jealousy that he felt when the snake man—Neil—embraced Gwen.

"May I have your autograph?" a tiny woman with hair a strange color, like melting metal, said. In her hand was a bound set of papers of magnificent colors. Each time he touched the beautiful papers, he thought of the hours it must have taken to write each word and paint each design. With reverence, he wrote his name.

The woman seemed to value the documents more once he had written on them.

The snake man came to his side. "Gwen told me to see if I could help fend off some of these fans."

"Help me?" Vad frowned. "Everyone is very polite. I enjoy their conversation. They see to my comfort."

"Really? How many cups of punch have they brought you?"

"Punch?" In truth, he understood only one in every five words they said. But he was learning their language. *Caramel corn, turmeric, quickie.* Each woman added to his vocabulary. "What is your status here, Neil? What is the meaning of the snake in this place?" *What harm could come from asking?*

"I'm part-owner of Gwen's shop. When my father died, he left me a little money, and I used it to invest in Gwen's business. She wasn't doing so well after her husband—lifemate to you—died. She needed a partner. I used to work at Virtual Heaven when I was in high school, so I knew the business.

"And the tattoo means I was drunk one night and not thinking clearly—typical college state, I'm afraid. Other than that, don't read too much into it."

Vad took a deep breath, but kept himself from asking for a better explanation. Involuntarily, he looked about the room for Gwen. So she had lost a lifemate. It explained the contrasts of wealth and poverty in her home.

These festivities did little but delay his mission. He kicked a boot at the polished floor. Snow lay over everything—or had until the loud one had opened the door. Sparkles radiated from glowing colored glass in the ceiling. It was all false. Like the spectacles after the harvests.

His head ached. When he lifted his hand to his brow, it trembled. Quickly he tucked it into his knife belt.

"You'd be perfect!" Liz yelled over the loud hum of conversation. "Come on."

"Where?" Gwen asked as Liz hauled her through the crowd.

"Over there!" She pointed vaguely toward the ceiling. "I need an ordinary woman to kiss that hunk in the corner. What a shot that will be—front-cover material."

"Whoa." Gwen skidded to a halt. "No way. I'm not kissing anyone."

Liz leaned down from her nearly six-foot height. "What's the matter with you? Think of the PR for Virtual Heaven. Not to mention an opportunity to lock lips with—"

Liz's words were lost as she hustled Gwen at a quick trot through a wall of people. "There he is!" Liz cried as she halted in front of a mob of women waving programs for Vad to sign. Miniexplosions of camera flashes reflected on the wall of windows behind him. So Liz was not the only woman intent on a photo op.

"We'll need to stand on a chair to see over this crowd," she said to Liz.

"Watch this. . . ." Liz's iron grip on Gwen's arm tightened as Liz used her elbows to hurl Gwen through the mass of women and into Vad's chest.

Vad grunted and closed his arms about her.

"Liz, I don't think—" Gwen began.

"Quick. Kiss each other; I don't have all night."

"Oh, sure, I guess—"

His mouth closed on hers. All coherent thought washed away like a sand castle at high tide. His lips were firm and warm.

The room spun a bit, but his hands were there to catch her. He wrapped his arms around her, drew her against the hard length of his body. She felt a moan rise in her throat and had enough sense to clamp down on it.

He really knew how to kiss.

She thought of power and heat. Then she thought of nothing. Her mind zapped white for a brief instant; then her body zapped red-hot.

His kiss was a long, lazy perusal of her lips. He tasted of caramel-covered popcorn. She lost all sanity. Giving no thought to who watched, she raised her hands and gripped his head. She drew him closer and bit his lower lip. With a jerk of his head, he responded; his hips moved against hers, and his arms tightened.

His mouth no longer explored; it pressed hard, crushed, possessed.

Gwen moaned softly, dug her fingers into his hair, and opened her mouth. He opened his, and she plundered his mouth with her tongue.

With a groan he lifted her high into his arms. Her arms slipped about his neck. She felt naked against him, every bone, every muscle defined.

A white-hot blade skewered his vitals. It twisted and dug so deep he gasped. The woman in his arms led him places he had only imagined. He followed. The path led to short breath, a rapid heartbeat, sweat on his brow.

Now. End it now. Now . . .

He spread his hands over the delicate bones of her back and held her even closer. *End it. End it.* The words ran over and over in his mind.

He ended it. He put her away from him, safely at arm's length. His mouth ached. His loins throbbed.

She stared up at him, her lips half-open. Then she snapped them closed. "You're about as comfortable to kiss as a stone wall."

So she was going to pretend she'd felt nothing? He unlaced his tunic and opened it.

An audible moan rose from the women surrounding him.

"Geez, keep your shirt on. These women are rabid," Gwen said. Her hands drew the edges of his tunic together.

"You will protect me, I think," he said, and flicked her hands away. He drew out various colored lumps wrapped in smooth paper. "You flattened my sweets."

She burst into laughter. "You have saltwater taffy in your shirt?" Her smile reminded him too much of the heat of her kiss.

"Aye," he said. "The women offered it. It would be unkind not to accept it." He felt as if he had some of the sticky goodness stuck in his throat.

"We crushed it, didn't we?"

In truth, the sweets were soft and warm from his body and hers. "You were overly fierce in your attentions."

"Me?" She smacked his arm. "You're the one who crushed me."

"I did nothing. You kissed me—"

"Now, children! Enough bickering!" Liz angled her camera between them. "Maybe you could open your shirt just a wee bit more. . . ." Deftly, the loud woman spread his tunic open, revealing his chest. "Boy, you must work out twenty-four-seven!"

His precious square of scented cloth slipped to the floor from where he'd tucked it in his tunic.

Gwen was glaring in the strange woman's direction. He bent and retrieved the scented cloth.

"Or maybe you'll catch cold," the tall, yellow woman said, jerking his tunic closed. She stepped away from Gwen's glare.

The crowd enfolded the loud woman. Gwen turned back to Vad. "Let me help you," she said, even though he was sure she knew he was perfectly capable of lacing a garment on his own. "Why do you have a dryer sheet?" She drew the fine cording together at his throat.

He shrugged and changed the subject. "So I am like embracing a stone wall, am I?" he asked.

"Yes. Too bad you're not comfy like that Gulap over there."

He frowned. *Not comfy.* The word he did not know, but the meaning was clear. "When is this festivity over?"

"Oh, we can go back to my place in about an hour."

Go back to her place? Perhaps she could show him what *comfy* was.

"And you can explain your dryer-sheet fetish." She made a low, musical sound of laughter in her throat.

It did not please him to amuse her. "What is a fetish?"

"A passion for something," she said, and walked away.

As he watched the sway of her skirts, he imagined she could define all the words he did not know if given the proper persuasion.

A sudden hush fell over the crowd. Only the pulsing beat of the music continued. Gwen looked toward the door, in the direction of everyone's gaze. A blond man of about twenty stood in the doorway, his hair and Tolemac warrior costume drenched with rain. With a collective sigh, the crowd turned away.

"Uh-oh. I think the model from the agency is here," Gwen said to Neil. That made it more certain than ever that her other warrior was a practical joke waiting to happen. She hurried to the dripping young man, who stood not much taller than she did. "I'm Gwen Marlowe." She held out her hand, but he ignored it as he tossed his dripping blond hair off his face.

"I'm Vad, and your directions stink," he said. "I got off the wrong exit of the Atlantic City Expressway and I've been driving . . ."

Gwen tuned him out. He was a fairly attractive young man, but she was sure Tolemac warriors didn't whine. "Look. Have a cup of punch." She snagged one from a passing warrior and offered it to the model. Maybe a few cups later, he'd be bearable—unless Neil had weeded out all the spiked stuff. While he sniffed the cup, she slunk away.

An hour later, the crowd fell silent again, eyes on the door. She ignored them. All the Vads were in the house.

"Holy mackerel!" Mrs. Hill cried, and ran past her.

"Gee, what'd you do to get him here? Sell your soul to the devil?" Neil asked. Gwen turned around.

Another warrior was making an entrance.

This man, who easily stood an inch or two taller than Vad, scanned the crowd with a frown. His hair was a sun-streaked brown, pulled back and secured at his nape. His black-and-white costume was a twin of Vad's. A sword hung at his side. There was nothing of the prop about it, however.

The three heartbeats of silence ended. In a squealing rush, women hurtled in the newcomer's direction.

"It's Kered!" Liz cried, and hugged Gwen in an embrace that would bruise. "Who'd have believed it? Does this mean *Tolemac Wars One* will be available again? Just think . . . two Tolemac warriors in one room."

Gwen glanced at the short, wet version of Vad busily gorging himself at the buffet. "Don't you mean three?" Gwen muttered, and disentangled herself from Liz's viselike grip. "I guess the practical joke is just about to crank up a notch. Now, where's Kered hiding my dear friend Maggie?"

"Why didn't you do some promo on this meeting of the two Tolemac warriors?" Liz asked, quickly loading new film.

But Gwen didn't need to worry about her answer. Liz was flying across the room, camera over her head, flash working overtime.

Gwen turned to Neil. "He hates publicity. I didn't really think he'd come. And where's Maggie?"

"Don't bother about that right now. Look." Neil held her arm.

Warrior God Number One was stealing away with Warrior God Number Two. "Damn, they can't leave," she said.

But Neil held her still. "Let them go."

A wall of fans followed the two men to one of the rank of double glass doors, but Kered turned at the door and held up his hands. As if by magic, the crowd halted. He closed the doors in their faces.

Her warriors had deserted her.

"They're still outside. Stop checking on them." With a groan, Neil swept a pile of fake snow into a dustpan. "We'll never get this cleaned up. And were you into the punch again? You can't stand still."

"I'm not drunk. And you disposed of the punch, remember? I'm just worried about Vad out there in the rain. He felt kinda feverish this afternoon."

"Did he?"

Neil's grin annoyed her. "I was just helping him shave, and he felt hot."

"I'll bet."

"Oh, shut up," she muttered. Neil was right. She couldn't stop pacing. Her ball had completely collapsed when the two Tolemac warriors had gone outside. And she'd never even awarded the prize for best costume or best Vad look-alike, as the soggy Vad had informed her before departing in a huff.

She knew *her* Vad and Kered were only a few feet away outside, standing at a railing, their faces to the icy wind, because they were illuminated on a regular basis by the flashes of jagged lightning.

Uncannily, not one guest had trespassed on their intense conversation, but the ball had died with their exit nonetheless.

"I am sorry, my friend," Kered said. "I will not be returning to Tolemac."

Vad gripped the iron railing and felt waves of grief as huge as those splashing below wash over him. He had crossed the ice fields in vain and had known it since Gwen had mentioned that Maggie was with child. Kered would never leave her now. So be it. He would survive this as he had survived so much else—being orphaned, fighting for his place at Kered's side, the curse of his face.

No one must ever know how he felt. No one. With a deep breath, he turned to his friend. "You have not been here even one conjunction and already your speech is deteriorating—"

"Vad. You must listen. This is where you belong, too."

"No, do not try to convince me again to remain here with you. My honor lies in Tolemac. If *you* choose not to return, then it is left to me to prove us innocent of the council's charges or our names will be forever inscribed in the rolls of traitors." *My* sword displayed there for all to see."

"It doesn't matter. This matters! Here. Now. This place." Kered clamped a hand over his on the slick railing.

"What is here for me? If it is as you say, and I came

from here at some time, long ago in my childhood, then where is my family?"

Kered's hand on his reminded him too poignantly of years of friendship, years of serving beneath this man, trusting him, obeying his commands, looking up to him not just as a leader, but as a brother. Now his life felt blasted in a furnace of betrayal.

"I'm sorry, my friend. I tracked them down and they're dead, but I could show you their graves."

"Graves? What use have I of graves?" Vad's jaw ached from clenching his teeth. Long moments of silence reigned between them. "So I have only you, as was true for so many conjunctions. My adoptive brother . . . my commander, fellow traitor."

"You're not a traitor! Neither am I. This is where I belong. It is not dishonorable to follow what you know in your heart is right. One day you will understand. No matter your ties there, you will find a need to be here—"

"You are tied to a woman, not a place!"

Kered nodded. "And the need I have for my new family. The place doesn't matter, as long as I'm with Maggie, and I know she's safe." He shook his head. "I can't explain it."

"Then give me the jeweled dagger, and I will leave you to your chosen life." Every muscle in Vad's neck ached. He wanted to lash out, to howl with the pain of finding his friend, but losing him at the same time.

Kered frowned. "So be it. I'll search for the dagger. I'm sure Maggie must have it. I just sent her home this morning because her grandmother has broken her hip, and Maggie wanted to help care for her. I know she would want me to take you out there to see her."

But Vad shook his head. He looked out at the sea. How far could he go and not be lost completely?

"Vad, I'll find the dagger; I promise. But you must make a promise, too."

"What promise do you desire of me?" Vad asked. How many promises had been made and broken in the name of friendship?

"If you won't come with me, stay here until I find the dagger. That's all."

Vad nodded. How long would he have to wait? Long enough to be seduced by the women, the strange food, the hypnotizing music, to want to remain? "Do what you must to find the blade. It is all I have to prove my innocence."

Gwen pressed her face to the window. Both men were as rigid as soldiers at attention.

"I'm going out there." She jerked the door open and was nearly blown off her feet. Vad was at her side in an instant, shoving the door closed for her. "You're soaking wet—both of you. Vad's been ill. He shouldn't be out here." She had to shout over the wind and a low rumble of thunder.

"I am not returning to the festivities," Vad said. Something in his tone told her he meant it.

"Okay," she said. "We'll all go back to my place, then." She pointed to the gleam of light that was her apartment, a couple of blocks away.

Kered shook his head. "I can't stay. I have to tell Maggie Vad's here and have her look for something . . . at home."

"Really? Maggie's not here?" Gwen braced herself for Maggie to leap out of the shadows and yell "Surprise!"

"That's right. Vad can fill you in. Now I have to go and secure something Vad needs for his quest."

With a sudden turnabout, she smiled and clapped. "You guys are really good. Superb. Do you do amateur theater back home?"

"We're not acting," Kered said.

"Oh, sure. And he's really Vad." She swallowed a laugh.

"Yes. He is Vad," Kered said. "But he's Nicholas Sandav, too."

Chapter Six

Gwen tossed and turned and knotted herself in her sheets. The fact that the most beautiful man on the East Coast was sleeping on her sofa bed shouldn't be keeping her awake, but it was. Her mind kept returning to that moment when the shower had washed him clean.

"Oh, brother, whoever spiked that punch should be ashamed of himself. I'm really going to feel it tomorrow." She threw off the covers, got out of bed, and turned on a small desk lamp so she could look for a book to read that would put Sleeping Beauty out of her mind. Far out of her mind. How she wished Maggie had not gone home. Maggie could be persuaded to tell the truth.

When would Vad admit he was just a guy playing a role and not a man tragically pulled into the *Tolemac Wars* game when he was a child, as Kered so adamantly claimed? A child thought lost forever. A child named Nicholas Sandav, whose parents died before learning the truth that their son had survived—in another world. What incredible imaginations!

Vad's name also disturbed her sleep. Not as much as his body, but almost as much. Where had she heard that name before? *Nicholas Sandav . . .*

To be honest, she could not imagine calling him Nick. Vad he looked like, and Vad he was.

Her fingers danced along a row of books and settled on one R. Walter had given her the first—and only—Christmas they'd spent together. After that, he'd spent them all with her sister Pam. *Jingle all the way.*

The notation inside brought a lump to her throat. *For Gwen, as legendary as any heroine.* Oh, sure, she thought. Until he met Pam, anyway, and broke her heart—a heart that had not healed until she'd met Bob. She looked at her bare finger. Each night she took off her wedding ring and placed it in her jewelry box. Each morning she put it back on. Bob would have laughed at her sentimentality. He was one man who did not believe in dwelling on the past.

She settled at the desk and thumbed through the book, flipping here and there at random. The book was beautifully illustrated with examples of Celtic art. She lost herself in the familiar legends that had colored her world, inspired her fabric designs, and added so much romantic mystery to her college years. With delight she pulled the light close, examining the intricate lines and forms that decorated shields and caldrons, much like the designs engraved on Vad's knife. And his ring.

Then she gasped and jumped to her feet, dropping the book.

Sandav.

She sat down hard on the chair. Why hadn't she realized immediately where the name had come from? Hadn't her love of Arthurian legend led her to take that fateful class where she'd met R. Walter? Hadn't a love of legend brought them together?

Bending over, she reached for the book. It lay open to the pages on King Arthur's final—and mortal—battle. *Sandav.* The knight had survived, one of the few to do so, because he was so beautiful men would not fight him, just in case he was a messenger of God, an angel from heaven.

Vad fit that description. He was beautiful in a masculine, hard-edged way. His bones were those of a man whose genes had been bred to perfection. His cheekbones were meant to be carved in marble or on a wooden figurehead at the prow of a ship. Or was that always a woman? Her mind was muzzy.

She shot from her bedroom and stood over him before she could stop herself, the book clutched to her chest. The light from her bedroom painted a single golden stripe across his bare shoulder. For a moment she just stared in sheer appreciation.

Outside, thunder rumbled, and for a brief moment the room flashed white as lightning split the sky and broke the spell.

"Vad." She touched his shoulder.

He came awake in an instant. The long knife appeared in his hand.

"It's me," she whispered, sitting at his side. "You can stop pretending now." She pushed the knife away. "I know who you're not."

Wow, she thought as he shook his hair from his eyes; he gave new meaning to the term *pillow head.*

Vad slipped the knife back in its sheath. Then his hand clamped about her wrist. "Woman, you had only to ask if you wished to share my bed."

"Huh," she said, distracted by the way the sheet pooled across his hips.

"Now hear me. Clearly," he said, his voice low and rough from sleep. "You are quite small and, I doubt not, would take up little space to disturb my rest, but I do not want you in my bed."

The furnace heat of his body chilled to ice cold as he rose from the bed. The light from her bedroom gleamed on his naked flanks as he pulled on his leather breeches, jerking the lacing closed over a flat stomach furred with golden hair.

When he straightened, his hair loose about his shoulders, his ring-adorned arms folded on his chest, she almost swallowed her tongue. The cheekbones she'd just been musing on were hard slashes of anger.

"If I want a woman, I ask her. I did not ask you."

"How dare you!" she screeched, leaping to her feet on the sofa bed. She flapped the book at him, rocking on the thin mattress. "I was not trying to jump your bones. I found your name, stupid. You can stop pretending."

"My name? Stupid? Pretending?" He raked his hair back, dragging the braids behind his ear. His face was harsh, every line intensified by the deep shadows. "I am not pretending."

"Sure." She turned the book and thumped her finger on the decorated page. "It's all here. Your name—Sandav—that was really a stupid pick. Sandav is famous. It took me a minute to remember because of . . . well . . . the spiked punch, I guess, but I remember now. It's all right here." She tapped the page again. "So now you can tell me who you really are. Come on. Is it really Nick? Or Nicky? Nicky what? Come on. Confess."

Nausea crawled through his belly. *Nicky. Nicky.* The name twisted in his mind. He heard a voice, a faraway voice—a woman's. The dark mist spun from the corners of the room, rose behind Gwen like the waves behind her Music Pier. He swallowed to contain the sickness burning up his throat.

"Vad, what's wrong?" She jumped off the bed and extended her hand.

He avoided it and hurried to the bathing chamber.

There he stood at the tub, confused, looking for the water spigot. Impatiently he jerked on the silvery handles. Water thundered into the tub. He splashed it on his face and gulped great handfuls of the icy water.

When she placed her hand on his back, it was like an iron brand laid on his skin to sear and scar. "Nilrem's throat," he swore, twisting from her touch. "Have you some evil power that you can burn with your fingertips?"

"It's you. You're burning up." She placed a palm on his cheek. "Are you sick?"

Incongruously, her hand, which a moment ago had scalded, felt cool and soothing on his skin.

"I don't get it," she said. "I could have sworn . . ."

"What is it you could have sworn? That I was a liar?" How could a woman be so sweet-faced, so alluring one moment, so infuriating the next?

"Look. I just read through my legends, and Sandav is there. Vad is part of Sandav—backward. What did your family—"

"My name is Vad. I have no family."

Her touch was light, a dance on his forearm. "I know. Kered said they were dead, years ago. I'm sorry. When I lost Bob, I thought I'd never get over it. Now where are you really from?"

"I am from Tolemac. I crossed the ice fields."

Anger and amusement warred on her face. "Sure. Stick to that story. I almost believed you guys. You were so sincere—the way you greeted each other, your intensity. But I'm not in a ball gown, under the influence of too much Tolemac punch. You can drop the act. It's stupid and childish."

Her words were small hammers smiting his honor. "I am stupid and childish?"

"Never mind." She ruffled her hair with her hands, causing it to stand up like a cock's comb. "I didn't mean it. Wait here."

She dashed away in a twirl of her white gown. He heard the door bang shut.

As unsteady as he felt, he went into the room to the strange bed she'd pulled from the padded bench. He'd wasted several long moments under it, examining the way it worked. Now he just wanted to sink onto its lumpy surface and sleep this nightmare away.

The mist no longer swirled through the room. He was dressed and sheathing his blades when she burst through the door again, her hand extended before her.

He froze. The blood in his veins felt as cold as the ice fields. In her hand was the jeweled dagger. "Where did you find it?" He could barely say the words. Men were willing to ruin a warrior's life for this blade.

"Here. Take it. Isn't this what you were on a quest to find? Well, here it is." She shoved it into his hands.

"Where did you find it?" he repeated. The blade was smaller than he remembered. The gold handle was studded with gems of poor quality. He turned it over and over in his hands.

"I didn't find it. My friend Maggie gave it to me, and I've been using it to open letters down in my office."

"And why did you not tell me you had it when I told you I sought it?" I have been betrayed, he thought bleakly, betrayed by my friend's woman. Maggie had given the blade to Gwen—given away the key to his future.

"To be honest, I thought you were a bit wacky."

"What is wacky?" He grasped the knife's handle and pulled. Nothing happened.

"Oh, not wrapped too tight. Mad. And why am I explaining myself to you? You're the one who's playing games."

"I do not play games—or not here. You are like so many other women I have known—unworthy of trust."

"I am not. This isn't about trust."

He silenced her with a look. "It is to me." Finally the

handle shifted, then turned a mere hairsbreadth. "This blade means everything to me. It holds my future."

The handle suddenly turned, slid, pulled from the blade. Whatever the future might hold, he would know it now. He went to where a lamp gleamed in her bedchamber.

He avoided the strange lamp on her table and stood at the foot of her lush bed to shake the blade handle. A small, rolled piece of paper dropped onto her blanket.

He was gratified that his hands did not shake as he unrolled the paper. His vision blurred. It was not a map of a route through the ice fields.

"Oh, it's beautiful. It's a map, isn't it?"

Gwen stood so close to examine the map, he could feel her breath on his hands. To distract himself, he studied the map. His gaze scanned the territory from the Sleeping Mountain known as Gog to the Ford of Ravens. Places far from the ice fields.

A crash of thunder outside made her jump. He felt as if the thunder outside was loose in his chest.

"Aye," he said. " 'Tis a map—showing the way to Nilrem's eight treasures."

Gwen could not change his mind about returning to Tolemac. Not that he could get there from here . . . He must still be taking his role seriously—or the practical joke wasn't over. And at this exact moment, she was darned tired of it.

After turning the game on, she trotted at his heels as he walked determinedly to the game booth. "Look," she said, still playing along. "I know you think this map means the council tricked you, but maybe they were just wrong about what was in the knife."

"I will explain this one more time," he said. With great deliberation, he folded his cloak on the floor by the control platform in the game booth. "I was brought before the council and accused with Kered, who had been my commander, of traitorous acts against Tolemac. Kered was believed to have left Tolemac with his slave woman and the knife. 'Twas claimed that Kered knew the knife's handle contained a map of the way through the ice fields."

"And why would they want to get past the ice fields?" She propped her elbow on the platform railing. Her head pounded from too little sleep and too much punch.

"For what men have always craved—weapons. The best weapons. And the legends describe weapons of destruction beyond our imaginations—here, beyond the ice fields." He lifted the game gun. "This is such a weapon. I have seen its like—once. And know of what it is capable."

With a look of contempt, he put the gun back on the control panel.

"The last thing Tolemac or the Selaw need is a weapon of such potency. But my honor demanded I regain the dagger with the map. It was Samoht's charge to me. The reward? My name restored to honor."

"Samoht's the high councilor of Tolemac, isn't he?" She rearranged the gun, next to the headset.

Vad nodded. "He has a streak of evil . . . but he is not what matters here."

"So if you did what this Samoht asked and found your way here, why do they need a map?"

"Many have set out on the journey to cross the ice fields; none have returned. A map would allow a legion to make the trek. And if the dagger had contained the route through the ice fields, then all they accused us of would have been true. They said Kered's adoptive father, Leoh, was once enamored of a Selaw woman. It was through her Leoh obtained the map. He kept it hidden through the years in the knife's handle. The council, and Samoht, claimed Leoh died before he could make use of the map. And Kered was said to know of its existence. Now I know it was all lies, lies to conceal the council's real goal—the treasures. A lie to conceal simple greed."

"I have a headache." With a yawn, she plopped down on his fur coat. Playing this game was getting tedious. Tomorrow Mr. Warrior God was out on his tight buns if he didn't own up to who he really was. "So go on. The council's greedy. What difference does it make which map you found?"

A very convincing hauteur entered his voice. "Warriors do not seek treasure. The very idea is dishonorable. I was sent to bring back Kered and the dagger and prove our loyalty. It seems I was really sent to obtain a treasure map. If I had died doing so, they had lost only a man with a traitor's name." His voice dropped; his hand turned the dagger over and over. "They knew what it was they sought—something far more valuable than mere weapons. They lied to me."

"Maybe they didn't know what was in the dagger either." She might as well go along with him for a few more hours. It was almost dawn. Another yawn overcame her.

He stepped off the platform and went down on one knee before her. "Gwen, I have allowed my anger to spill over on you a number of times. For that I am truly sorry. It is not my nature to be ill-mannered."

When he closed his fingers around hers, his heavy gold ring heated, and a tingle went down her spine. She pulled her hand away.

"You said I arrived here by magic. How does this magic work?" He gestured to the platform and the keyboard.

The ring on his outstretched hand was deeply incised with Celtic knotwork. She remembered seeing the pattern on one of the caldrons in her book of myths. The pattern had a name, but it eluded her. "The game should have warmed up by now. Hit the green button and then put on the headset. It's automatic," she murmured, trying to dredge the name from her memory.

He tucked the headset under one arm and rested his long fingers on the keyboard. The familiar hum of the game filled the room.

His expression was impassive, his voice filled with emotion. "You called me stupid. You were right."

"Vad, I didn't mean it that way." When was he going to give up this charade? "It's just an expression."

"But still, 'twas stupidity to think the council trusted me. Or that Kered would return." A crooked smile twisted his mouth, pulling his wound, painting his face with pain.

He put out his hand.

Automatically she took it. His fingers tightened on hers; his ring bit into her hand. Heat whipped up her arm, across her shoulder, and down into her breast.

A whisper of thunder rumbled outside.

Flames of pain hammered her hand, her arm, her chest.

"Vad," she said in a gasp as he disappeared in a blinding white light.

Chapter Seven

The dream was wonderful. A fresh breeze kissed her cheeks, and the scent of damp earth filled her nostrils. A few wispy clouds scudded across the lavender sky.

Lavender?

Gwen groaned and sat up. She felt the full punishment of the spiked punch. Vad stood ten feet away, hands on hips, contemplating the landscape.

Or lack of it.

As far as Gwen could see, the world dropped off at his feet—a purple world. She rose to her knees and scrabbled backward. Her stomach lurched.

Vad whipped around. "Ah, you are awake." He strode to where she knelt, hooked a hand beneath her elbow, and hauled her upright.

"No," she cried and jerked back. The world did drop off. They stood on a cliff.

"Be still," Vad ordered.

"No, I am not going to be still," she said slowly and distinctly. "I am getting as far from here as possible."

She went nowhere. Vad's grip could hold a tractor in place.

"And where would you go?"

The question confused her for a moment. She looked about. Behind her rose a steep mountain meadow, carpeted in emerald green and capped with fir trees. It could be any mountain in Pennsylvania or New York, but in front of her lay a vista as foreign as the moon. She knew it well, saw it every day when she or a customer played *Tolemac Wars II.*

The rocky red ground before her was the same color as the huge red sun overhead. The barren landscape stretched for miles, and seemed miles below them. In the distance, their tops obscured by low white clouds, rose craggy mountains as forbidding as the highest Rockies.

Yes, she recognized it all from the game; only when playing the game, she didn't really have to cope with it.

"How did this happen?" she asked, changing her mind about running away. She tucked herself against Vad's warm side instead. He smelled like home—caramel popcorn and dryer sheets. "I won't believe we're where we are. I won't. I'm dreaming. I'll wake up soon. I drank too much punch—"

"Enough." The word was a command, but it was kindly spoken. He hugged her against his side and swept a hand out to the land before them. "We are home."

Gwen squeezed her eyes closed. "I'm not. I'm in a dream. My sky is blue. My cliffs are out west. Ocean City is flat. I like flat. I'll wake up and be lying in my bed, hoping Liz did a huge layout on my ball for her magazine."

"We must go."

"It's a cliff. I'm not going anywhere." The sky darkened from lavender to nearly black; an angry buzz filled her ears. Her knees buckled.

* * *

Vad scooped her into his arms. He hurried from the precipice's edge to a patch of mountain meadow. Carefully he laid her on the long grass. Her face was as white as her gown, as white as the tiny star-shaped flowers that clustered about her like errant flakes of snow.

He swallowed and shook off the temptation to kiss her awake. Kisses led to more problems, not fewer. He had kissed many a woman, but unlike those many kisses, the kiss Gwen had given him at the ball still remained on his lips. The sensations that had coursed through his body surged back if he let himself dwell too long on the feel of her in his arms. He would not think about how he'd stood like one of the beams holding up the Music Pier while she had taken control of his every sense.

No woman should control a man. He never lost control to a woman. They were easily acquired and easily forgotten. At least until this little one.

He went down on one knee and picked up her hand instead of kissing her. "Gwen. Wake up." He chafed her wrist.

In the next moment, she rolled over and emptied her stomach into the grass.

"You are not very feminine," he said. He withdrew to allow her privacy for her suffering. Perhaps if he could make her angry, she would forget her discomfort. Anger chased other emotions away, according to his awareness master.

He had but a small ache behind his eyes from the strange journey, and whatever else he felt, the overwhelming feeling was exhilaration. He was home, in a place where all was familiar, where all made sense. Here—and nowhere else—he could reclaim his honor, his reason for being.

Before him stretched the Scorched Plain, and his life would be as the land was, parched, useless, deadly, were he no longer a warrior. If he returned with the dagger and map, he would at least prove to the council and

Samoht that he had obeyed their commands. Should they reward him with the return of his sword, his good name, all he had suffered would be as nothing.

"I need a drink of water," she called out to him.

He turned around. She was sitting cross-legged, her gown tucked about her knees. Her face was almost its usual color. Wind riffled the short golden strands of hair on her forehead. She looked childlike and yet womanly at the same time.

"Come." He offered her his hand. She stared at it warily, then took it. He helped her rise, then steered her away from the cliff and up the mountain. "The wise man will have water, and perhaps a potion for your belly."

She trembled as she wiped her mouth with the back of her hand. "I'm feeling better, but my mouth tastes like I ate your fur coat."

He smiled. Her humor was returning. She would survive. Then he thought of his coat and the fortune stitched inside, lost because he had forgotten it—forgotten it because he wanted one last contact with her and, in truth, did not believe standing in the black room would send him anywhere.

All the legends would need rewriting.

She stumbled. He tightened his hold on her and looked down. Her tiny feet were bare.

He lifted her into his arms.

"What are you doing? I can walk. The grass is nice and soft."

"You may be able to walk, but your pace will slow me down."

"And here I thought you liked me," she said.

When she wrapped her arms about his neck, he grinned. How well she fit in his arms. Then he lost his smile. It was liking her that complicated everything . . . liking the taste of her mouth. . . .

"I like all women." Her arms loosened their grip. "Your presence is a complication I can do without. Nilrem will see to your care and perhaps figure out a way to send you home."

Her body tensed in his arms. "You're going to leave me here? What's the point in that?"

"I did not ask you to come."

She arched and twisted in his arms, breaking his hold. He almost dropped her. She shrieked and pushed. He let her go.

"Are you mad, woman?" He rubbed his neck where her sculpted nails had scratched him.

"Yes. I am mad. How dare you blame me for this? I didn't want to come with you. You held my hand. It's your fault I'm here."

Vad stared at her for a moment. He expelled a long breath. Like it or not, he was responsible for her safety.

"We will not argue who is at fault. You should have stayed in your chamber; I should have pushed you away. Now let us proceed." He held out his arms.

"I'll walk." With her little nose pointed into the air, she stalked off through the meadow. "And I'm not staying with anyone named Nilrem," she said over her shoulder. "Nilrem!" She halted. "Oh, no." She turned in a whirl of skirts that displayed an enticing amount of leg. "Vad, hurry up; catch up."

How like the ice woman she appeared in her flowing white gown, which fluttered in the rising wind. Was his vision of her on the ice fields a prophecy of this moment? And just as she had that time on the ice, she lifted her hand and beckoned to him.

Unable to resist, he went to her. "What is wrong? Are you going to be ill again?"

"No." She trotted along at his side when he reached her. "Don't you see? Your name, Vad, comes from Sandav. Nilrem is Merlin backward. He was a famous magical person of legend."

Vad heard the echo of his laugh across the hillside. "Magical? Nilrem may be wise, he may even be a bit backward, but he has no pretensions to magic."

"Okay," she bit out, and it amused him to see the becoming flush tint her skin. "Forget I suggested it, but treasures like the Seat of Wishes sound pretty magical to me."

"As you wish; the magic insult is forgotten."

"Grrrr." She stalked away, her arms straight and swinging. The funny little noise she made in her throat told him her anger was at a fever pitch. At least she would forget her discomfort.

Within moments they had cleared the mountain meadow and entered the trees. Vad imagined her feet suffered for her pride, but he did not offer again to carry her.

The trees opened into a small clearing. Before them stood Nilrem's hut, but the sight made him frown—no smoke curled from the smoke hole.

"It doesn't look like he's home," she said. "Should we knock?"

"Why? Do you think there is some magical knock we can use to conjure him up?" Her frown became a scowl, and he grinned at her as he pushed open the door to the wise man's home. He inspected the hut and finally returned to where Gwen stood on the threshold.

"The hearth is cold and the ashes swept away. There is no food on the shelf. He is gone, possibly for a long time, as his stick is gone as well."

"Stick? Is he really old? And maybe he just went out for more food."

"No one knows how old Nilrem is—ancient, some would say—but not magically so," he hastened to add before she could interrupt him. "As for food, Nilrem wants for nothing. Many bring him offerings in payment for his help and his prophecies. I fear that if there is no food, it must be generally known he will be gone for a long time."

"What does that mean for us?"

"For me, it means I will have no ancient wisdom to read the signs and portents before I make my decisions. For you . . ."

"Oh, no, you're not leaving me here. Not by myself. How would I eat? What if someone came?" She backed a few steps to the door.

Vad forced himself to remain impassive. The last thing he had expected was Nilrem's wandering off. "There is another place I can look for him. He often goes to a sacred cave for silent contemplation."

"You meant we, didn't you? *We* can go look for him. I'm not staying here alone."

Vad opened his mouth and then closed it. "You are ill equipped to sustain yourself. Even the smallest child of Tolemac can snare food, choose the proper herbs, catch—"

She held up her hand. "Enough. I get it. I'm incompetent to survive in the wilderness. So take me with you."

"We must deal with your feet before you can make even the shortest of journeys." He retreated into the hut and went to a pile of blankets on a low frame. He rummaged beneath it.

Gwen came closer and sidestepped the flurry of objects he tossed her way.

"Ohhh." She picked up a silvery trinket. It was a chain of large links that was too long to be necklace and might instead be a woman's belt. Every other link contained what appeared to be a cabochon ruby. "This looks like it belongs in a museum—in the ancient-stuff collection. It's beautiful."

Vad looked over his shoulder and shrugged. "Many are grateful to Nilrem for the wisdom he offers."

She stirred the growing pile of tributes with her toe. "Some payment. What's he do? Cure disease?"

"Only the gods can cure disease." Dusting his hands on his thighs, he rose. "Try some."

An assortment of shoes and boots lay tangled in jewelry, leather belts, daggers, and cooking utensils. The items ranged from humble wooden bowls to objects as magnificent as the silver belt.

A few moments later, he fitted her on the sword side with a silvery painted-leather slipper that might have been made specially for the long gown in which she'd appeared the night before, and for her shield side, a low boot that was down-at-the-heel.

"Nothing matches," she said, but he was glad she did not concern herself with the trifles of fashion. "Where do you think the other shoes are?"

"Who can guess at the needs of a wise man?" Vad touched her shoulder. "How does your belly feel? I am sorry there is no water or food to offer you."

"What are we going to do? Aren't you hungry? How am I going to get back to Ocean City? All I wanted to do was apologize. I felt really bad about calling you stupid. I was unkind. And now . . ." She paused and licked her full lips. "I see that all you said was true. This place does exist. I'm so, so sorry, and—"

"Enough. I do not need your apologies." She looked pathetically small and out of place. She was out of place, he reminded himself, as out of place as he had felt in Ocean City.

He shoved the remaining shoes and objects back under Nilrem's bed. "I am leaving."

Without a backward glance, he turned and went through the door.

"Wait for me," she called, stumbling in the mismatched shoes as she followed him. "Where are we going?"

"First, to find you water. Second, we will seek Nilrem's cave."

"I'm not very fond of caves."

Vad shrugged. "I, too, do not care much for caves. They are dark, wet, and ofttimes inhabited by creatures."

She glanced about her and limped along. He imagined she could feel every pebble and twig on the sloping terrain. They walked quickly down the mountainside and into a row of trees.

"When you say creatures, just what do you mean?"

"Within the cave or without?"

"Oh, let's start on the outside." She had to hurry to keep pace with him, as his stride was almost twice hers. Low brush caught at her hem, hampering her movement, but he did not pause to accommodate her. She must toughen herself or she would suffer all the more.

"The white hart and hind graze Nilrem's Hart Fell," he began, to distract her from her feet. "They are sacred and never hunted, except by the Gulap."

"Gulap? I forgot all about them. Gulap means claw, doesn't it?"

Vad wanted to laugh at the way she glanced about her and hugged her arms around her waist, but stifled the temptation. *Temptation. Aye.* She represented many temptations. "The Gulap range these mountains, feline, fierce, and black as Samoht's heart."

"Remind me not to run into either of them." She glanced over her shoulder, anxiety written on her small features.

He placed a hand on her shoulder. "A Gulap wants only the sweetest morsels—you are safe. And also we have snakes, much like the one about your snake man's arm."

"That's Neil, please." A cold wind swirled about them. Gwen gathered her nightgown closer to her legs. "Geez, it's cold here. I might as well be naked."

Naked. He did not want to think of her naked, either. "Other creatures you must fear are men. Outcasts range the foothills."

"You do know how to use that knife, don't you?"

Vad made an impatient gesture with his hand. "You

would do better to be wary of men rather than the woodland creatures."

"Slow down. I feel dizzy. Anyone with . . . any . . . sense . . ."

She stopped as if rooted to the hillside. Without a sound, she fell to her knees. Her eyes rolled up into her skull. Her lips moved, but no sound came out.

"Gwen?" Vad caught her as she slipped into unconsciousness. He touched her forehead. It was damp and cold, as were her hands. Gently he lifted her into his arms.

The rest of the trek down the mountainside took twice as long as Vad would have liked, and it had nothing to do with the womanly burden in his arms. Once he needed to backtrack and take another ancient path. Few feet trod the way to Nilrem's cave, and the markers were often obscured by lush vines. The cave was considered sacred. Unless invited, only Nilrem would venture there.

They were not among the invited. Legend said that only evil would come to those who intruded. That was why the path was faint and ill-marked. But he did not believe in legend—not those of Tolemac or those of Gwen's place.

Legends were for ignorant slaves, and he was a warrior. He dealt in life and death, honor and truth. What he wanted from Nilrem was his wisdom, his common sense, his understanding of the intrigues of the Tolemac councilors.

He came to a tumble of rocks in the hillside. The rocks were reddish in color now, not black and gray, as they had been higher on the mountain. A spray of water erupted from them and became a small stream flowing down the mountainside. In ancient times such springs, the source of the rivers, were sacred. When he placed Gwen on the ground, he thought that if such ancient tales held truth, it was good he had brought her here for revival.

Using the hem of his tunic, he soaked it and touched it to her cheeks. As he drew the cool cloth over her lips, she moaned and stirred.

"Vad?" she whispered. "Are you trying to get in my bed again?"

"No, woman. And it was you who tried to get into my bed."

Gwen sat up and pressed her hands to her temples. "Oh, my head." She looked about and up at the brilliant amethyst sky.

He watched tears well in her eyes and down her cheeks.

"I thought it was a dream."

Vad crouched on his haunches. "We have no time for your tears."

She wiped at her cheeks. "Well, I do! I'm thirsty. My head hurts. I'm in my nightgown in a stupid, purple place."

"Stupid? Did you not just offer your apology for speaking thusly to me?" He cupped his hands in the icy water and offered it to her. " 'Tis typical of a woman. I should have known your words meant nothing. You withheld the dagger. And now . . ."

Gwen ignored his outstretched hands and crawled to the low stream bank. She scooped up the cool water, splashed it on her face, and gulped it down.

"Sorry. I feel like a petulant child, but I can't help it. I was calling this place stupid, not you," she said. "I can't believe you're still miffed about the dagger. I did apologize. I told you, I thought you were playing a hoax on me. How was I to know you really were Vad and needed that knife? Can't you put that behind you?"

He looked over his shoulder. "What? Put what behind me? You speak in riddles."

"It's an expression that means accept my apology."

Somehow her words did nothing to assuage the bubbling irritation he felt. "Your words come too late. Now move." He took her arm.

She stumbled along with him. They followed the stream downhill for at least a mile longer. As they hurried along, Gwen paused repeatedly to exclaim over the delicate ferns and tiny, bright red flowers nestled by the water's edge. She asked their names.

"We have no time for lessons," he said with a grunt as the forest grew denser, the vines more thickly twisted about trunks and branches. The terrain sloped more steeply downward.

Finally he halted. Gwen rubbed her arm where he'd held her, and he thought that although there were many times she'd wanted to free herself from his grip, there were also many other times she'd welcomed his hold as he boosted her over roots and jerked her out of the way of low branches.

"Are you recovered yet?" he asked as she wayed and stumbled for the tenth time.

"Things are a little blurry still, and my head pulses with every step, but don't let that hold you up."

The stream disappeared into a hillside covered with thick vines. Vad drew his long blade and hacked at the foliage. A maw of darkness appeared. It grew as he chopped and slashed. The stream did not end, but looked like it flowed into the hill.

She planted her feet in the soft, muddy bank. "That's a slit, not a cave. I'm not going in there."

He sighed. "You will find it opens up almost immediately, once inside . . . or so they say."

"Who's 'they'? Elves?"

His eyes narrowed. "Elves? What are elves?"

"Little magical people."

"We have small people, but they have no special powers."

He reached out and skimmed his thumb over her cheek, rubbing at a red spot high on her cheekbone. She sighed, the sound stirring a memory of the small sigh she'd given in response to his kiss. "I am sorry you are cold. I will give you my tunic."

Her small hands wrapped around his, preventing him from unbuckling his knife sheath. "No, absolutely not. You can't give me your shirt. You'll freeze."

The heat of her hands held his immobile. A mad desire to clasp her hands tightly against his belly swept through him, but then she jerked them away and pressed her fingertips to her temples.

"Your head still troubles you, does it not? That is why you are so—"

"Peevish? Irritable? Cranky?" She smiled up at him. It cost her greatly, he saw. "Yes, my head still aches, but now my feet hurt, too. I'll try not to be so cranky."

"Cranky. I like the word. It is hard-edged, just like you." Then he turned to the cave, using his blade to hack away the remaining vines and ferns and put the touch of her hands from his mind. "I fear all this growth indicates that Nilrem has not visited his cave in many conjunctions."

Gwen stood on a flat rock and peered into the shadows over his shoulder. "Look, isn't that light in there?"

Vad sheathed his knife. Before Gwen could protest, he hoisted her into his arms and stepped cautiously into the shallow, running water. It swirled in chilly rapids nearly to his knees, seeped into his boots, crept with icy talons into his composure. He turned sideways and eased his way past the cut vines. Gwen bit off a small scream as the cave claimed them.

For several moments he stared forward into the gloom, putting aside his hatred of dark, dank places, seeking a glimmer of light. As his eyes adjusted, he saw it—an exit from the cave, curving off to the right on the far side of a huge cavern.

"Loosen your hold, woman," Vad said, his mouth to her ear lest his words echo about the chamber and alert whatever creatures, human or otherwise, inhabited the place. Her stranglehold eased.

The rush of water filled the small space. Rock surrounded them, inches from his shoulders and head.

The light in the distance grew and swelled, and they emerged in a large, cavernous room lit by the opening on the opposite side through which the stream exited. Long, jagged dripstones hung from the ceiling. Lines of blue traced the walls like veins in an arm. "No wonder Nilrem treasures this spot for contemplation. 'Tis filled with the sacred stone and must offer him its power."

"I thought you didn't believe in magic?"

"The power of a stone is not magic," he said with a shrug. "Its possession, just for the mere pleasure of rubbing its smoothness between one's fingers, can ease tension. And the stone does take on different hues depending on the wearer's health—that surely is not magic."

"Point taken." She rested her head on his shoulder, an intimacy he did not want. He dropped her to her feet with no warning, but she made no protest, merely rubbed her arms and crouched down by his side as he stirred the ashes of a fire long gone cold.

He shook his head. "Nilrem has not been here in a very long time. There is no other entrance from his side of the mountain, either."

"Where does that opening go?" She pointed to where the stream flowed toward a bright, coppery light.

He shrugged. "Out."

She frowned at him. "Of course. But where is out?"

Gwen had difficulty keeping her temper. A few moments ago he was offering her the shirt off his back; now he was stiff and formal. His few smiles were quickly swallowed. This was not the man who'd kissed her with such passion at the ball. This was more like the man who had so cuttingly told her he did not wish her in his bed. Why did that thought raise a lump in her throat when she didn't want him in hers, either?

She much preferred the man at the ball. He would care that she was out of place and underdressed. She shivered. Dampness seeped into her mismatched shoes.

They walked toward the light. As the cavern widened, a small beach of stones revealed itself, allowing them to walk on dry ground. There was a cathedral quality to the space. Even the stream seemed to have quieted as it flowed along. The high ceiling disappeared in black shadows overhead. How high it was, Gwen could not say. She tried to imagine an elderly wise man contemplating philosophy in such a place and succeeded. It was as filled with reverence as a church. The veins of turquoise and the gentle light held her mesmerized.

Vad raised a hand, cautioning her to silence, and drew his knife.

"What's wrong?" she whispered.

"I think I heard a man's voice—not Nilrem's." With a quick nod in the direction of the cave's exit, he crept toward the gleam of light—and whatever lay outside. She followed him, holding her nightgown high to prevent the hem from dragging in the watery puddles scattered about the cavern's floor.

They moved quietly along the curving rocky wall. Ahead loomed a huge opening, decorated with hanging foliage. Light from the red sun bore down from above and dazzled the eyes. The stream widened and flowed from the cave's mouth in an amethyst glitter, touched with sparkles of red. Gwen shielded her eyes.

The far bank was a tangle of trees, festooned with deep green vines.

Out of the verdant shadows stepped a woman.

"Selaw," Vad said, and pushed Gwen behind him.

Chapter Eight

Garbed in a long, green cloak, edged with purple and gold embroidery, the woman glided forward to stand at the stream's edge. Her face was but a suggestion in the shadow of her hood.

Gwen could feel the tension emanating from Vad's body.

"Stay back and be silent."

Gwen was about to bite off a retort about men who gave orders when she saw that the woman was not alone. Three men, garbed in green like the woman, emerged from the shadows behind her. They flanked her. She lifted a hand and they remained where they stood.

The men were dressed in cross-gartered trousers, long tunics, and cloaks all in shades of green—and each held a long bow, with arrows nocked for flight. They blended well with the surrounding foliage. Gwen swallowed. There was something rather deadly about an arrow when it was pointed right at you, she thought.

The woman swept off her hood. "Do you also seek

the wise man?" the woman asked. Her voice was low and melodic. Her words carried well across the wide stream. The sun painted a reddish gleam on the dark blond hair that tumbled about her shoulders.

"What I seek is my business. What do you want here?" Vad held his knife loosely by his hip.

"He has no sword," one of the men in green said to the woman. "We can—"

The woman lifted her hand, and the man fell silent. With another quick gesture from her, the men lowered their bows.

"You appear to be a warrior," the woman said. "You wear the Tolemac colors, but do not bear a sword. Why?"

"What need have the Selaw of Nilrem?" asked, ignoring her question.

"Even the Selaw have matters of concern that are outside the province of our healers and priests."

"That's no answer," Gwen said in a hiss at Vad's shoulder.

His shoulder twitched. "The Selaw are not welcome here."

The men moved closer to the woman. They stood in deep, sylvan shadow, their intent hidden, their protection obvious.

The woman made a small gesture with her hand, and the men stepped back. Her cloak skimmed the grass as she moved gracefully forward to stand on the edge of the opposite bank, still protected by her guardian archers. "Nilrem has always made me welcome." She lifted her arm. Gwen tensed for some signal to fire, but instead the woman opened the throat of her cloak and pulled out a long silver chain that ended in a lump of turquoise. "A gift from the wise man."

Vad nodded. "Come forward to the cave—alone."

The woman tipped her head and stared at Vad for a moment, then nodded. She turned to her companions and spoke softly, then walked along the stream bank to a spot where erosion had cut a path to the stony beach of the stream, lifted her skirts, and stepped delicately down the incline. Her path took her to the water's edge. There she untied her low green boots, set them on a stone, lifted her skirts to midcalf, and stepped into the water.

Gwen thought of a water nymph, or a green swan come to life. In a few moments the woman had reached Gwen's side of the stream, where she dropped her hem.

She and Vad joined the woman, but not before Vad assured himself her men were still standing on the far bank.

As though reading Vad's mind, the Selaw woman spoke. "They would not think to disobey me."

"Why does a woman of the Selaw seek a Tolemac wise man?"

"First," she said, "who are you?"

"Who are you?" Vad countered.

"I am called Ardra."

"What need has a Selaw woman with a Tolemac wise man?" he asked again.

The woman paced back and forth at the cavern entrance. The coppery light shone on her long tresses, which cascaded from her shoulders nearly to her waist. Her stride was so graceful, she seemed to float. Her face was a pale oval, her brows delicately arched, her cheekbones high and patrician, her lips full and sensuous. She reminded Gwen of someone advertising ski holidays in the Alps, except for one stunning feature that set her apart from most other women—her amber eyes.

Gwen wondered if it was her eyes that had immediately told Vad the woman was Selaw and not Tolemac.

She came to a halt in front of Vad. "The help I need cannot be found in Selaw. There is peace between your people and mine now. I had hoped we might extend that peace to helping one another." She tucked her hands up into her sleeves and began to pace again. "I have come far and have little time. If Nilrem has gone on a wander, I am in grave trouble."

"Can you help her?" Gwen asked Vad, who impaled her with a dark glare. "Well, you could try to help her, couldn't you?"

"I am grateful for your offer," the Selaw woman said with a breathiness to her voice that bespoke her agitation.

Vad shook his head. "My companion speaks too quickly. I have my own duties of which I must think, and my own time is short."

The woman bowed her head. A look of sorrow crossed her face, then was quickly masked. "I see." She turned and went to the stream. Again she lifted her hem to wade across.

"Wait," Gwen cried. "At least tell us what your problem is."

"Gwen!" Vad hooked her arm and dragged her into the shadows. "I must get to the capital and confront the councilors. I have no time for women in distress. I must . . . Oh, by the sword . . ." He stomped in a circle, then called to the woman, "Come back."

She quickly waded back into the cave entrance and out of her men's line of sight. "You wear the colors of the Tolemac army, and the gold on your uniform is a symbol of leadership. Surely you can help me."

Gwen eyed Vad as he nodded. She hadn't thought of his embroidery as anything beyond decoration. She'd have to have a word with the man who'd written the *Tolemac Wars II* manual. It was sadly lacking in detail.

Vad crossed his arms over his chest. "First, who are your ancestors?"

"I am called Ardra. My father is Ruonail of the Fortress of Ravens."

"Ruonail? I know of him. Your father holds vast lands in Selaw. Some say to the detriment of his people."

Ardra nodded her head. "In the past he was thoughtless on occasion, but now he is . . . cruel. It is for him I have come . . . and for my people."

"What changed him?" Gwen felt left out when they ignored her questions. There was nowhere dry to sit in the cave. Her legs quivered with sudden fatigue.

"But how could I, a Tolemac warrior, help a Selaw chief?" Vad asked.

"My father is a powerful chief, controlling the mining of the ice. He has great influence in Selaw, but it is the influences on him I fear."

Gwen felt a prickle of apprehension as Ardra continued. Beneath Ardra's serene appearance Gwen sensed a turmoil of emotions.

Ardra continued. "A man first appeared more than four conjunctions ago. He comes and goes, sometimes staying for several sunrisings, other times from feast day to feast day. It is his influence over my father that I fear. Until this man, Narfrom by name, arrived, my father was for the peace between our people and yours."

"And now?" Vad prompted.

Her pacing grew more agitated. "Now Narfrom controls my father's every thought. He has convinced my father that our people will be richer and more powerful without the Tolemac peace. Narfrom claims we made a mistake exchanging the ice for food."

"Ice?" Gwen said.

"Yes." Ardra looked Gwen up and down, as if she were seeing her clearly for the first time. Her gaze lingered on her hair. "We Selaw stand between Tolemac and the ice fields."

Gwen knew the basics of the politics from the game. Tolemac wanted the ice. It allowed them to enjoy foods out of season, but she assumed it was also wanted simply because the Selaw had it and Tolemac didn't.

Vad added to her thoughts. "The ice fields stand between the Selaw and the lands beyond. If the legends of those lands are true, then the Selaw have access to those lands, and Tolemac does not. It behooves us to negotiate that access."

Ardra nodded. "I know the peace with Tolemac is good. For the first time, our people can plan their lives without the constant fear of invasion. Stop at any settlement now and you will no longer see the seasonal starvation that prompted so many years of war."

"Have you talked to your father about your concerns?" Gwen asked. She linked her arm about Vad's and leaned on him for support.

The woman looked from Gwen to Vad. "Who is this woman, and what has happened to her hair?"

"Forgive us," Vad said. "We have not returned the courtesy of an introduction. I am called Vad—"

"And I'm Gwen."

Vad did not even glance in Gwen's direction or acknowledge her touch. "She is my business. As to her hair . . . she was too vain and I decided to cut it off to tame her spirit."

Tame me? Gwen thought.

Ardra shrugged and dismissed Gwen. "Is she trustworthy? Should we be speaking before her?"

"If there are spies about, they are of Selaw origin." Vad put a staying hand on Gwen's.

The woman weighed Vad's words. Then her shoulders slumped. "I must trust your word. I have no one else to turn to."

"To question a Tolemac warrior's word is—" Vad began.

"—natural. After all, you don't even know us," Gwen quickly interjected.

"It is as you say. I know you not." Ardra began to wring her hands. Some of her stateliness crumbled. "I must trust someone! Why not you?"

"What of your men outside?" Vad asked. He impaled Gwen with a glare to silence her.

"They are my father's men. They brought me here at

his behest to secure a sleeping potion. My father is unable to sleep, you see. He wanders the fortress ramparts hour upon hour. He is aging before my eyes. But it is not just for a sleeping potion that I have come to Nilrem. I had also intended to query the wise man on how to break this chain of influence Narfrom has forged about my father. My men escort me with my father's blessing, but if questioned will tell him—and Narfrom—anything they think he needs to know. I cannot allow them to know my true mission."

Vad nodded. "My time is limited, as is yours. State your wishes."

Ardra glanced about, looked Vad up and down, then just as carefully inspected Gwen. Finally she took a deep breath. "Narfrom has taken hostages—the maiden daughters of seven Tolemac councilors—and is holding them in the fortress."

"By Nilrem's beard! And your father does not know?"

"Oh, my father actually took the hostages, but it is Narfrom who thought of the idea and made the plans. If not for him, my father would never have thought of such treachery!"

"What madness!"

"Aye. Surely 'tis a madness to want such power. You men are all sick with it. You cannot be content to have your small part of the world. You must have it all."

Vad bristled.

Ardra swept in agitated circles, her skirts forming a perfect bell about her legs. "And yet, he is my father—my only family since my mother died. I love him. Or love the man he was." She wrung her hands. "I would not have believed him capable of such treachery a few conjunctions ago. I thought the wise man might know of some spell Narfrom has cast that has made my father unable to think clearly, unable to see the folly of his actions. I came in hopes that Nilrem could break the spell."

Vad's voice was gentle. "Nilrem is a man of wisdom. He is not a witch to cast or uncast spells."

"You may be right, but it matters not, since he is not here. I have visited all his places, including climbing to the top of Hart Fell, and he is gone."

"Aye. He is gone." Vad nodded.

Gwen felt an immediate need to pat the woman on the shoulder and tell her Vad would take care of her.

Wherever had that thought come from?

Vad went to the curve of the stream, where he could see Ardra's men. He crouched down on his haunches and watched them, but spoke softly so only the women could hear him. "Has Tolemac launched an attack on Selaw to regain the maidens?"

"No. The councilors would never let anyone know my father has their daughters. It would prove the fathers unable to protect their own." Her eyes glistened with unshed tears. She took a step toward him and sank to her knees by his side as if begging.

"Vad?" Gwen caught Ardra before she could fall. Vad did not move.

Gwen gripped Ardra's shaking shoulders. "Aren't they concerned about their daughters' safety?"

"Narfrom has promised the maidens' deaths should the councilors tell anyone of their abduction."

With a nod, Vad rose. He propped his shoulder against the cave wall and shrugged. "It is an age-old means of ensuring compliance. Take a hostage and it will be easy enough to dictate behavior and decisions. The hostage is rarely harmed."

Ardra stayed on her knees, her hands raised in supplication. Gwen tried in vain to get her to rise.

"You must help me. Narfrom threatened to put a rope about the maidens' necks and toss them off the ramparts to hang there for all to see if the councilors do not obey him. 'Tis no idle threat. It was done to a serving boy who dared to defy an order of Narfrom's. It is why I have hastened here."

"And your father's response to the hanging?" Vad asked. "Such executions for petty disobedience were banned in Tolemac and, I thought, Selaw, ages ago."

"I swear to you my father knew nothing of the order. He is haunted by the image of the boy—a fetching lad he liked well—and imagines the maidens' fate. He will not admit he has lost control of Narfrom. 'Tis why he cannot rest. Only some spell of madness could make him behave in such a manner as to support Narfrom. Please help us. I have little with which to reward you—"

"An honorable warrior does not seek reward." He shook his head.

For a moment Gwen thought he might refuse the woman's plea.

"Think of the maidens," Ardra begged. "They are but pawns in the games of men."

Gwen held her breath. She knew it was not her place to convince Vad to help the woman.

"My time is limited. I have until the next lunar festival to return to the capital. It is my charge from the Tolemac council. If I am late, dire consequences will befall me."

"More dire than the end of peace and the death of the maidens? One has lived only eight conjunctions!"

Vad met Gwen's eyes. She tried to keep her expression neutral. He had to make his own decision. It was his life and his honor.

"Well, my little one?" he asked her. "Where shall we go? To Selaw to rescue maidens or to the capital to see Samoht and complete my mission?"

He did not ask idly, she realized, though he still leaned indolently on the cave wall. The day of fighting for an honorable cause, no matter the personal cost, was gone in her world.

She held her hands out like a balance and moved them up and down. "Rescuing kidnapped maidens or facing evil Samoht? Hmmm. Either works for me. I'm still trying to cope with the purple sky."

Vad touched his hand to the hilt of the jeweled dagger tucked in his belt. "Mistress Ardra, it will be an honor to rescue your maidens."

The boat in which Ardra had come was a sorry excuse for a sailboat. Gwen eyed it with disdain. The sail was square-rigged and clumsy. She imagined the oars were used more often than not. In the bow was a rolled set of blankets and a painted wooden chest the size of a picnic basket.

Small as the stream had been that flowed from Nilrem's cave, it had taken but one sharp bend to join a wide and swiftly running river. The river had no name, according to Vad. It was unlucky to name rivers, he'd said.

The sail was not raised, but instead of being carefully folded on the boom, it was dragging on the deck. Deck? The boards were rough and splintery, and Gwen couldn't imagine why they weren't leaking like a sieve.

Vad sat in the bow by the painted box, his warm hip against hers, and kept an eye on the three Selaw archers in the stern. They took turns at the tiller, refusing Vad's offer to spell one of them. He did not, however, look at Ardra, who sat on an embroidered cushion in the center of the boat.

At the moment, handling the boat seemed fairly effortless to Gwen. The current was with them, and the only tricky part was negotiating gentle rapids.

Her headache returned with a vengeance. The scenery was alien and yet . . . not. If one ignored the sinking red sun and the lavender sky, it could have been a trip along any river in New York or Pennsylvania, or for that matter the Cotswolds of England.

She'd honeymooned in the Cotswolds—in a tiny cottage with rough stone walls and hanging baskets thick with flowers. The wound of her husband's death usually seemed well healed until suddenly, the sight of a flower, a scent, and it would all come flooding back. She had learned to live with his passing, but not the loneliness of their parting.

She thought of the Tolemac maidens and the anguish of their fathers, forced to make decisions in fear for a child's life.

"Gwen." Vad touched her shoulder. "What do you think of these men?" He spoke softly by her ear. His breath was warm and woke nerve endings long dormant. She swatted at her ear as if a mosquito buzzed there.

She inspected the men. The one at the tiller had a sullen mouth and a blind eye, its iris milky white.

The second was tall and slim, his eyes an uncanny amber, tawny and quite beautiful. He had the hard expression of a man who had seen much and looked as if he'd steal a person's purse—or her virtue—given the chance.

The last was fair-haired like Ardra and the other men, but his greasy hair was less carefully tended than the others'.

Gwen propped her chin in her hand and barely spoke between her lips. "I think the men are not happy escorting Ruonail's daughter. They think they've better things to do than row her around the countryside."

Vad wrapped her into his embrace, drawing her close to his body, his mouth at her ear. Wonderful warmth flooded her.

"I think they intend to kill us."

Gwen jerked in his arms. "Kill us?" She said in a squeak against his throat, all warmth gone in an instant.

Vad pulled her closer and more tightly against him. He brought his mouth very close to hers. She felt the heat of his breath, imagined it scented with caramel popcorn. "Aye. They exchange looks when Ardra is not facing them. They have noted my lack of sword. The one at the tiller has nodded twice to the one on our right."

"Maybe they're just afraid of you."

He tipped her chin back and whispered against her lips. "How able are you? If they come for me, can you defend yourself?"

A quiver ran through her body. Vad's hand moved like a lover's against her hip, caressing, moving up to her waist and then to her stomach. Something cold and hard pressed against her. She covered his hand, as if to stop its progress toward her breast. Her fist closed over the jeweled dagger.

She swallowed hard. "I can't," she whispered against his lips. "I can't."

Chapter Nine

Every muscle screaming with tension, Gwen sat silently at Vad's side. He remained as still as if carved from marble—very warm marble, his long thigh hard against hers.

Gwen clutched the jeweled knife in her skirts for several miles, her nerves taut, her hands cramped into fists. With every foot they traveled, they drew farther away from what was familiar—or familiar to her from the game. The terrain grew rockier, although the greenery remained thick, the trees still mostly conifers. The air cooled despite the bright red disk overhead.

Abruptly, Ardra rose. "Put to shore. I need a moment of privacy," she said, staggering as the boat rocked violently. Vad shot from his seat to steady her, putting an arm about her waist. He held her hand and eased her onto her cushion.

With a lack of skill that made Gwen grit her teeth, Greasy Hair beached the boat with a jarring scrape of the bottom on marl. He leaped out and wrapped a frayed rope about a jagged boulder.

Then he attacked.

He whipped in a circle, snatched up a handful of muddy pebbles, and cast them in Vad's face.

But Vad was gone—over the side in a long, flat dive.

In moments, a flurry of arrows hit the water where Vad had disappeared.

Gwen screamed. Blind Eye yanked her over the side and onto the muddy ground. Her feet tangled in her nightgown hem, bringing her to her knees. She almost lost her grip on the jeweled dagger. With a vicious jerk, the man dragged her forward. Her feet sank into the stony mud; her skirt slapped heavily against her legs. He threw her to the ground.

"Stop!" Ardra shouted at her men. "What are you doing?"

The remaining two men sent another hail of arrows into the water. "Be still," Beautiful Eyes growled. "He is an outcast."

"My father will hear of this treachery," Ardra cried as she scrambled over the side of the leaning boat and grabbed Blind Eye by the cloak. "Let her be!"

With a quick thrust of his arm, Blind Eye pushed Ardra away.

"There," Greasy Hair shouted, and another barrage of arrows entered the water.

Blind Eye turned away. Gwen wrenched herself from his grip, the dagger caught in the folds of her skirt as she raised it.

"Do it and die."

Beautiful Eyes stood in the boat's stern facing her—not the river. He raised his bow. "Give me the knife."

"What are you doing?" Ardra gasped. Water sloshed about her skirts as she ran to where he stood.

"She has a knife!" the man said. "Take it from her!"

"Enec, you do not understand. You shall rue the day

you attacked him," Ardra sputtered, and wrung her hands. "The warrior said she has healing powers. She is needed to help my father. *He* was needed!"

Blind Eye burst into laughter and turned from his deadly task. "Then we shall keep her alive until we get to the fortress. Just a mite worn around the edges." He wiped his arm across his brow and asked over his shoulder of the other two bowmen, "Any sign of him?"

Enec turned his beautiful eyes on Gwen. They touched her with a tangible stroke of malice. "He is surely dead. A man cannot stay beneath the water for so long. But he is unimportant. We have this one."

Gwen's body quivered with fear. She glanced behind him for Vad—or blood. The other two bowmen peppered the water and nearby reeds with arrows.

"Have you no idea, Mistress Ardra," Enec asked, "what it means when a warrior has no sword?"

Ardra locked eyes with Gwen and shook her head. Gwen fought to keep her expression neutral. She had never questioned why Vad had no sword. No one had swords in Ocean City.

"It means he is a traitor. Tolemac strips traitors of their swords. They inscribe their names in the rolls of infamy and display their weapons for all to see. For him to be so close to our border, with no weapon, means he is an outcast. Fair game. Perhaps even with a weighty reward on his head. Listen!"

They all stood in silence. Gwen's every muscle quivered. The river sounds, the rustling of small creatures in the ferns and vines, the soughing of boughs in the wind was all Gwen could hear. But it was obvious the men sensed something. They stood alert, eyes wide, heads swinging to and fro from riverbank to forest growth, bows aimed at the water—except Enec. He kept his bow and his beautiful eyes trained on Gwen's chest.

Ardra moved closer to Gwen. "This one is naught but an innocent pawn in men's games."

"Hand over the knife. Now." This time Enec did not wait for an answer. He fired. The arrow hissed through the air, penetrated Gwen's hem, and buried itself deeply in the ground.

"Next time I aim for your breast. Now, Mistress Ardra, take the knife and bring it here." He stepped slowly from the boat and stood, his legs braced in the knee-deep water.

With wide, frightened eyes, Ardra thrust out a trembling hand.

Gwen shook her head and put the dagger behind her.

Vad erupted from the water like an ancient water god, spraying a silver cascade in a huge wave behind him.

Blind Eye threw aside his bow. A knife appeared in his hand. Its curved blade flashed red in the sunlight as if dripping blood as he raised it overhead. Vad moved in a blur. Blind Eye screamed. He fell forward, hands clutching his middle. Vad tipped the boat. It rocked, but Greasy Hair managed to raise his bow.

Vad jerked his long blade from Blind Eye's belly and swung his arm in a short arc. Greasy Hair turned in surprise. He looked down at his chest, then collapsed over his friend.

Enec charged Gwen, knocked her flat, stepped on her wrist, and plucked the jeweled dagger from her fingers.

He turned and lunged for Vad.

Vad fought with savage grace. He was taller than Enec, his reach longer, his blade heavier and more deadly. Enec parried, thrusted, then incongruously backed off again and again in a confusing cycle of fight and flight.

Vad mirrored each move in an ancient deadly dance Gwen knew he'd done before. He was who he said he was: a warrior, bred to fight—nothing more.

Men feared to fight him lest they harm an angel of God. The ancient legend came back to her. She saw the words on the page, and the stylized illustration of an angel fighting at King Arthur's side. Vad was Sandav, or a descendent of that ancient knight. The evidence of what he represented was before her eyes.

Each twist that turned his scarred side toward Enec's beautiful eyes brought a vicious, slashing attack. Each turn that presented his unblemished cheek sent Enec stumbling back, half-crouched in indecision.

Ardra shrieked and cried out for them to halt.

Gwen inched to where a bow lay in the mud. She lifted it.

"Stop," Ardra cried, clutching Gwen's sleeve. It ripped at the shoulder. "You will harm someone."

"Vad needs help." She dodged the men, skirted the bodies, and drew an arrow from a quiver on the boat deck.

She nocked the arrow. The bow seemed to weigh a ton and trembled in her hands as she lifted it and aimed.

The string resisted her efforts to draw it. Her arms shook.

Vad turned. He saw her. With a low laugh, he leaped into the boat and out again on the other side, callously stepping on one body in the process, and snatched the armed bow from her hands.

The arrow flew.

"Enec!" Everyone froze. Ardra's scream echoed down the river. Gwen stared at her, shocked by the unexpected anguish in Ardra's voice and etched on her face. Was Enec more than just a servant to the Selaw woman?

The two warriors stood still, gazes locked on one another. The jeweled dagger fell from Enec's hand. He fell with a soft splash into the water.

Ardra ran to the riverbank. "Enec!" she cried, but he had drifted, facedown, out into the current. In moments he disappeared. "No. Oh, no." Her distress touched Gwen. How must she feel knowing her father's men had betrayed her, especially if Enec was more than just an escort?

"What will we do?" Gwen whispered.

"Remain with Ardra. I will go along the bank and see if he survived." He lifted the quiver of arrows from the boat. "Are you injured?"

She shook her head. "I-I-I'm all right."

Ardra half rose from her knees, her eyes on Vad's bow. "You plan to kill him."

"Nay. I will pull him ashore if he yet lives," Vad said. "Then you may decide his fate." Vad disappeared into the trees.

Gwen's body began to violently shake in reaction to all that had happened. Ardra stood tensely by the boat, her gaze fixed on the spot where Enec had fallen. Abruptly she reached into the water, withdrawing the jeweled knife Enec had dropped.

Gwen did not know how Ardra could stand so close to the dead men. What if they weren't actually dead? One glance told her they were—very dead.

Her head ached from the strain of listening for Vad. All she heard were river sounds and the wind in the trees.

Biting her lip, not sure what to do, she knelt on a dry patch of grass and peered into the verdant shadows. A rustling sound drew her to her feet. Vad appeared.

"There is no sign of him," Vad said gently to Ardra. "Just be grateful he did not harm you or Gwen."

"I do not understand what happened. They would have killed you all. Enec has always been . . . loyal to me," Ardra said, her eyes still watching the swiftly flowing water.

Vad lifted Ardra's chin with his fingertips. "You placed some value on the man?"

Ardra whipped away from his grasp. "Should we bury these treacherous knaves?" Unlike Gwen, Ardra showed no reluctance to look at the dead men.

"I think we will give them a water burial. We have not the time nor implements for digging. Say whatever words you want over them now and be done with it." He began to pile up stones by the boat. Gwen helped him, keeping her eyes averted from the bodies.

Ardra closed her eyes and touched her breast, then opened them and touched the men on their foreheads. "May you be forgiven for your sins against my house." But Gwen sensed she was thinking more of the man with the glittering amber eyes than of those lying so silently before her.

Together Ardra and Vad stuffed stones into the men's clothing. With some coiled rope from the boat, they wrapped the men securely like bundles of wood. Gwen stood by and tried not to watch.

When the bodies were prepared, Vad assisted Gwen and Ardra into the boat, then shoved it into the water. The current caught it, pulled it into the center of the river. He carefully rolled each body overboard. They sank quickly, only tiny streams of bubbles marking their passage.

Gwen swallowed and blinked. I will not be sick, she thought.

The boat turned, the stern swinging violently toward the bank. Gwen swore.

"Sit down!" she shouted at Vad and Ardra, who moved about as if on dry land. She hauled the crude sail up and, with motions learned in childhood, secured the line. Stumbling over Vad's long legs, she jerked her nightgown away from a splinter of wood and grabbed the tiller bar. The boat drifted ever nearer to the shore, and with one eye on the sail, Gwen watched it, willed it to catch the slight breeze.

Slowly, slowly, the boat responded to her touch. The sail filled. The bow turned. With a nod of satisfaction, she steered the boat into the current.

Ardra sank to her cushion, her hand wound tightly about Vad's arm. Blood stained his sleeve. "Are you hurt?" She ran her hand over his arm and up to his shoulder.

"The blood is that of your men," Vad said briefly, and touched her hand. "But your concern should be for yourself. You are wet, and Enec could have killed you."

Ardra shook her head. "But he did not. Perhaps he will survive to repent of his sins." She stroked Vad's arm rings.

Gwen contemplated a tacking maneuver that would probably dump Ardra overboard, but decided she was being childish. So what if she was wetter than Ardra and in nothing but thin cotton, while Ardra had a cloak as well as a heavy gown?

Tears burned in her eyes a moment. She wiped them on her sleeve. She was just tired. That was all it was. She was just tired and cold.

Ardra did not take Vad's word for his lack of injury and insisted on rolling up his sleeve. She ran a hand from Vad's wrist to his shoulder, her fingers lingering and exploring the three engraved arm rings he wore.

"At least there is now a use for Gwen," Ardra said when her inspection of his arm was over. She rolled Vad's sleeve down. "You will want this back." She handed Vad the jeweled dagger.

"Aye. 'Tis a valuable piece. Thank you for saving it." He made his way to the bow and sat down. He thrust the dagger into his big boot.

A flash of cold ran through Gwen. It overpowered the chill of her wet nightgown against her legs and hips. It overpowered the uncomfortable longing she'd felt when Ardra had touched Vad.

Ardra's words made her feel as if she'd been invisible, useless. Vad's lack of response hurt more deeply. She wasn't useless. Why didn't he come to her defense?

He tugged off his high boots and emptied them of water. As he pulled them back on, he frowned. "We must assess our supplies. There are only these few blankets to keep us warm. Where did you pass each night on your way here?"

"There are several settlements along the river. While waiting for Nilrem on the mountain, we suffered the elements. It was proper to do so."

He nodded. "Gwen is not garbed to suffer the elements. She needs heavier clothing. Will we reach one of the settlements before the moon-rising?"

"No, and we must avoid the one that offered us shelter on our outward journey. Surely they will question why my men are . . . missing. We must make another choice—farther along the river. If Gwen manages the boat properly, we shall be there ere the light fails tomorrow."

He nodded. "Then we must find our own shelter this night and seek a settlement on the morrow." With an intent stare, he asked. "Why did your men attack me?"

"They said it was because you have no sword." Ardra kept a wary eye on the boom and crept to where Vad sat in the bow. She positioned her cushion near him and bent her head to his.

The low sound of their voices barely reached Gwen. The rising wind cut through her nightgown. Her wet feet were numb.

Gwen realized she might not be useless, but she was invisible.

The terrain grew more forbidding with each hour on the water. High, sharp rocks lined the bank. The foliage thinned; the trees became bent and gnarled. When Vad directed her to put to shore, Gwen could no longer feel her hands on the tiller or the line controlling the sail.

The landing was clumsily done, bumping them hard on the riverbank. Vad soaked his boots again when he jumped over and hauled the boat onto the bank. He might have been lazing in the sun all day for the effortless manner in which he swept Ardra into his arms and carried her to the bank.

He returned for her. Gwen looked at Vad's outstretched hands. She didn't think she could rise. She shook her head.

With a shrug, Vad left her and set about starting the fire. It took Gwen many long moments to straighten and feel able to climb over the side. The thought of putting her feet into the muddy water again made her regret giving Vad the brush-off, but she couldn't allow him to see how weak she felt.

Her whole body trembled as she put a leg over the side.

Vad was there in an instant. He plucked her off the boat and carried her to the fire. "Sit as close to the heat as you can." He lifted her hem and spread her skirts wide. Without a word, he pulled off her mismatched shoes and rubbed her feet between his large hands. They were warm and gentle.

Gwen stared wide-eyed at him. "Why are you being nice?"

"Nice?" His hands stilled. "Ardra and I cannot sail the boat. What use will you be if you sicken?"

How could she have thought his solicitude meant anything more? Ardra's men had thought she was a slave. Ardra thought she was a slave. In fact, she had so little worth, Enec had seemed to want the jeweled dagger more than her. So she might as well face the fact that without arm rings, she was a slave to the people of Tolemac and Selaw. How many arm rings Ardra had under her gown and cloak, Gwen didn't know, but one was enough to relegate Gwen to lowest in the pecking order.

"I'll try not to get sick. I wouldn't want to be a burden." She pulled her foot out of his hand. Rising, and staggering slightly, she moved to the other side of the fire.

"What do you mean, you cannot cook?" Vad tried to keep his temper. He felt it surging up from where he kept it hidden and controlled.

"I really haven't ever cooked over a fire," Gwen said. She poked a stick at the row of birds he had snared and laid out at their feet. "I've never plucked a bird, either."

Vad turned to Ardra. She was also looking at the birds with a puzzled frown on her face. "And you? Do you know the proper manner to roast a bird?"

"I have a number of women who tend to such things. . . ."

"By the sword!" Vad dropped to one knee and gutted and plucked the birds.

The two women were useless. Or almost. Gwen, at least, could sail a boat. He was very impressed. He had never been called upon to learn. Swords he knew. Horses he knew. Not sailing vessels. The skill with which she had handled the boat told him she had learned many conjunctions ago.

He hoped she had properly dried her gown. Her refusal of help was foolhardy. "We must secure warmer clothing and shoes for Gwen." He'd seen harsh red blisters on her toes and heels before her fit of pique had taken her to the opposite side of the fire.

Responsibility for her weighed as heavily as an iron weight about his neck. In truth, he had not just held her hand a moment too long, he had gripped it, locked her fingers so tightly in his, he wondered how he'd not crushed the bones.

Gwen was frowning at him. What had he done to earn her anger? Other than drag her into a situation fraught with danger and the possibility of death?

"Shouldn't we try to find something else to eat?" Gwen asked him.

"I have some bread!" Ardra said. She stepped daintily to the bank. "But I will surely wet my feet obtaining it."

Vad swallowed an oath. He jerked off his boots and stepped into the mud again. How he hated the feel of slime between his toes. They should have spared one of

Ardra's men to fetch and carry for them. In the stern, he found a sturdy painted box.

When Ardra opened it, she pursed her mouth like someone tasting a disagreeable potion. "The bread is gone! Those greedy men!"

Of food, there was naught but crumbs and bare bones in the box. However, they would dine in luxury, he saw, as Ardra set out four painted bowls. She unrolled a length of dark red cloth to reveal four each of silver spoons and eating daggers.

His stomach growled. "Do either of you know the plants that are safe to . . ."

They both stared at him wide-eyed.

"How do you feed yourselves?" he asked, disgusted.

"Microwave meals," Gwen said.

Ardra gave her a puzzled look. "I do not need to feed myself. My father strove and toiled that I and my children should never need to."

"Not too happy, is he?" Gwen said with a nod in Vad's direction.

Ardra nodded. "He expects quite a lot from a woman, does he not?"

He ignored their remarks. He expected little from women. They had a very distinct place—beneath a man.

A quick forage among the plants at the river's edge produced several tubers of a plant he knew well. He washed the green tops, chopped them, and stuffed them beneath the skin of the birds. The thick tubers he wrapped in damp leaves and set among the rocks to bake. His mouth watered as he skewered the birds and began the roasting.

It was most fortunate that his ban on women servants when his company was on the march had forced this simple learning on him years ago. The alternative had been dining on dried and poorly preserved provisions, or the toleration of serving women constantly pestering him. It had just seemed easier to learn the skill himself.

"When we have reached a settlement, we will barter the bowls and cutlery for warmer clothing and more arrows," Vad said. "Then we must be on our way. Neither your maidens—nor my quest—can wait much longer."

Ardra stepped into the dark shadows, leaving him alone with Gwen. Her next words were not about the food he prepared. "Maybe we should make a copy of the map. We almost lost it today."

"I have it committed to memory. I have no need to reproduce it."

"You think I want it for myself, don't you?" There was a small quaver of anger in her tone.

"Nay. But the council wants the original, so a copy is useless anyway."

"Hmmm. Am I allowed to know about the treasures? Or is that betraying some trust, too?"

"The legends of the treasures are common knowledge: a sacrificial blade, a whetstone to ready it for the kill, a cloak to warm the body, a caldron to feed the belly."

"That's only four."

He poked one of the birds with his blade tip to see if it was ready. "The Seat of Wishes, a game board that predicts the victor in a battle, and the Vial of Seduction. I can only guess that it is the game board the council covets most. Imagine knowing who is going to win a battle before it begins."

"Wow. Think of the wasted lives you could save. The council gets the board, and before any battle, they watch it. If they're the losers, they just don't fight, right?"

"Nay. It would merely mean regrouping, reassessing terrain, and so forth to turn the odds, then the playing of another game to see if the outcome had changed."

"Oh," she said softly.

His words brought the conversation to a halt, each of them lost in contemplation of the flames, of lives lost and battles fought.

Ardra returned and sat by his side, her eyes on the

river. "Do you think Enec survived?" she asked.

He shook his head. There was little point in raising false hopes. Ardra lifted her hood and concealed her face in its shadows.

An uncomfortable silence followed, which he refused to break. Enec had betrayed his mistress's trust, and yet here she sat, her grief plain on her face. He supposed she had been lured by Enec's pleasing features. When would women begin to look beyond a set of beautiful eyes or well bred bones to what was inside a man?

"What are those plants?" Gwen asked when finally he shoved a bowl at her.

"I do not know their name, but they are nourishing. Eat." He demonstrated how to cut the tuber to reveal its rich yellow center. "How can you train your cooks if you have no knowledge or skill yourself?"

Gwen ignored him. Ardra just stared up at him. Her eyes were deep amber in the flickering firelight. All around them, night creatures began to stir.

Ardra lifted a spoonful of the tuber to her mouth.

Gwen was still peering at the roasted birds. "Are you sure this is safe to eat? I usually draw the line at meat that's blue," she said.

He felt his anger bubbling. Blue creatures were a delicacy in Tolemac. To insult the meal when one had not the skill to prepare it oneself . . . "How do you train your cooks?" he asked again.

"My mother trained our cooks, before she died," Ardra said between delicate bites. She nibbled around the edges like a bird herself.

"Oh, all our cooks were trained at Cordon Bleu," Gwen said. She ate with less daintiness and more purpose. Her hands shook.

"Come, you are cold." He pulled her closer to the fire. Her gown still felt damp, and she quivered as he wrapped his arms about her. She still smelled of her exotic scent. It came to him from her hair. "You are not yet dry," he said near her ear. "Eat and I will warm you."

"How? It's freezing here." She was rigid against him.

He grinned and briskly rubbed her arms. He was quite adept at warming a woman. In fact, he knew more ways to start a fire than most men.

Chapter Ten

A shadow fell across Gwen's lap. She looked up. Ardra stood there, her hands extended.

"Please take my cloak. It is quite dry now and very warm," Ardra said.

"That is most kind of you," Vad said. He put the cloak about Gwen's shoulders, drawing it tightly closed. "Now you will be warm."

His arms felt perfect around her. But in the next moment he withdrew to the fire. He scraped the remnants of their meal into the flames and offered the bowls to Ardra. She stared at him and he sighed.

"Bob and I had a strict rule: whoever cooked did not wash up." Gwen rose and held out her hands for their bowls.

"Bob? Who is Bob and what kind of name is that?" Ardra tipped her head and wrinkled her nose. How Gwen hated a woman who should have looked as if she'd been dragged through a bush and instead looked picture perfect.

"Bob was Gwen's lifemate," Vad said. He unceremoniously dumped the dishes and cutlery into Gwen's outstretched arms. "He is dead."

Dead. In another world and another time.

"I did not know slaves may lifemate," Ardra said. Her hair glistened like spun gold. Her curious amber eyes were filled with firelight.

"Look, Ardra, I'm not a slave. I'm from beyond the ice fields. Vad here is just taking me home. So forget the slave nonsense." Her hands shook along with her voice.

"Nonsense?" Ardra's voice was a whisper.

Vad stepped between them. His face was inscrutable in the shadows cast by the fire behind him. "Gwen wishes you to put aside the idea that she is a slave. She is to be afforded the same dignity as a Selaw worthy."

Vad blurred before Gwen's eyes. She whirled away, clutched the bowls to her chest, and ran to the riverbank. Her eyes stung as she knelt on a rock and washed the bowls. His kindness only made it worse.

"I will not cry!" she said. The water was ice cold on her hands as she dunked the dishes. She'd cried her last at Bob's funeral. Before that, only R. Walter had made her cry. She'd cried buckets over them both. She had vowed never to cry over a man again.

She scrubbed the bowls to exorcise her tears.

The bowls were made of some substance like marble. The cutlery was silver. The handles were a bit tarnished, and she wasted time working on the intricate carvings. Overhead, the moons had risen along with the wind. The breeze whipped the cloak and rattled the reeds at the river's edge. She looked over her shoulder. Vad was sitting beside Ardra, deep in conversation.

How could she sleep? Her whole body shook with cold and fatigue. Ardra might have been unselfish to give up her cloak, but Gwen knew she could not keep it. On closer inspection, the pale green gown Ardra wore looked like a soft woolen weave, the kind she saw scarves made of rather than dresses. It clung and swayed as she moved. It hugged a reed-thin figure. Vad could have spanned Ardra's waist with his hands. She certainly had no fat layer to keep her warm.

Gwen closed her eyes. The feel of Vad's hands was easily conjured. Her eyes burned again.

"Stop it!" she chastised herself. Gathering the bowls, she stomped to the couple at the fire. "Here, all done." Her back to them, she packed the box and took her time securing it with the small peg-and-loop closure.

The wind ripped through the small clearing and showered sparks across the black shadows. With a shiver, she took off the thick cloak.

"It was very kind of you to lend me your cloak. I'm nice and warm now. Here." She held it out. Ardra rose and took it.

Vad shot to his feet and jerked it from Ardra's hand. "You cannot be warm. I can see straight through your gown."

"Can you? I hope the view's to your satisfaction." Gwen sank to the ground. She tucked her nightgown tightly around her feet.

In the next moment, she was enveloped in his embrace. He lifted her like a small child, strode to a tree, and sat down where he had placed the blankets. He tucked her against his side and arranged a blanket about her shoulders. For one luxurious moment, Gwen reveled in the hard feel of his arm about her. Heat surged from where they touched. It danced along her nerve endings, zipped across synapses.

"Come, Ardra. Sit close to us. We will offer each other the warmth of our bodies. Tomorrow we will find a settlement and secure proper garments." His words were worse than a cold shower.

Ardra moved into the circle of Vad's other arm.

"You both shall rest and I will keep watch," he said.

His arm tightened about her, drawing her even closer. The scent of him mingled with that of Ardra's perfume.

How wonderful. She was in the arms of a man as handsome as a god and she had to share.

She'd never been very good at sharing. Ask her sister.

Vad leaned his head against the tree trunk. A spot in the center of his back itched. He had difficulty ignoring it—a sign his body was tiring. Fatigue was an enemy.

His mind drifted. He remembered well his first time lying with a woman—two women, in fact. His awareness master had purchased their favors upon his attaining the fifth level of awareness along with his warrior status. It was forbidden to indulge oneself with women before that moment. It tainted the training.

The two women had been but a few conjunctions younger than he, but moons beyond him in other ways. They'd sated him within but a few hours. Never again had he wished for two women. He'd felt fed upon, devoured, without control.

Now here he was in the darkest hour of night, his senses on fire, his body oddly hot on Gwen's side. Her legs were snuggled tightly against his hip. At first he'd thought the intense heat a fever. And surely after such a soaking, and in such harsh wind, she could easily have sickened. But her skin was cool when he stroked a hand along her cheek.

Within his other arm, Ardra lay sleeping as a child might. Her hand cradled her face where it rested on his chest. Her other hand had slipped into his lap. But her hand felt weightless and insubstantial. It was the other woman who heated his blood.

He imagined he could have them both. Ardra would be delicate, full of gentleness. Gwen would be fierce and probably give him directions. He grinned at the thought. *Aye.* She would tell him exactly what she liked and then demand it.

Having two women as a responsibility reminded him far too much of having the two women in his bed. He must spend every moment thinking of them, where they were, what they were doing, in order that he did not disappoint or neglect them. More a burden than a pleasure.

Ardra must be satisfied as well as Gwen with his performance, else he would be a failure. The responsibility of it weighed heavily. He wanted to slip into the forest and make his way to the capital. There he would present the dagger, and prove that despite the council's dishonesty, he had behaved with honor.

He would again feel the weight of his sword in his hand. Until then, until it was placed there by the high councilor, Samoht, he would never pick up another.

As he stared into the dwindling coals of the fire, he thought of the attack by Ardra's men. It had not come until Ardra had stood in the boat, until he had moved forward to steady her, until he had turned his face, scarred side to the men.

In the past, few had wished to engage his blade. Few wished the consequences of angering the gods. It was foolish, superstitious nonsense, in his opinion, and yet, time and again, he had found that he must attack first to force the issue. But this time, as soon as he'd turned his cheek, the men had attacked.

Only when fighting Enec hand to hand had he seen the true ambivalence his face engendered. With his scarred side to his opponent the fighting was fierce. With the unblemished cheek to the fore, he faced naught but defensive moves, retreating, dancing about.

Vad's shoulder ached to move, but Gwen had snuggled even closer, her nose buried in his tunic, and he was loath to shift her and risk waking her. He knew how she must feel. Had he not faced disorientation and pain upon waking in Ocean City? Then there was the curious familiarity with surroundings he had surely never seen before. The feeling was one of his world tipping. Would not a night of quiet sleep have eased his way there?

A final question disturbed him only a bit less than the ache in his shoulder: why had Enec not dropped the jeweled knife and drawn his longer, more useful blade? Why had he taken the dagger from Gwen in the first place? Its value was trifling. Surely he had not feared so small a weapon in the hands of so small a woman?

Chapter Eleven

At dawn, which came in a burst of red streaks in the purple sky, they took to the river again. Vad and Ardra glanced at Gwen occasionally as they moved down the river. A frown knitted both their brows. While a scowl merely rendered Vad more handsome, Ardra looked like a disapproving older sister, and the last thing Gwen needed was a surrogate sibling.

With a sharp shake of her head, she tried to ignore them. Sisters and men did not mix. Sisters, men, and lust didn't either. Lust? Why had she thought of lust? She didn't need lust. Lust rotted your brain, scrambled the circuits, made you do ridiculous things like follow gorgeous warriors into games—deadly, cold, frozen, windy games.

Vad's frown deepened. Her thoughts scattered as internal cold was replaced by a fizzy, hot feeling between her eyes. She rubbed the spot. Vad's eyes tracked the movement of her hand. His frown became a hard glower.

The look did interesting things to the shadows the dawn light cast over his features.

The slash on his cheek did nothing to detract from his devastating looks, either. It added a bit of danger to his appearance. His beard was growing back. The memory of shaving his face while he dozed did nothing for her composure.

He shoved his hair behind his ear and stepped across the boat in one long stride. Ardra took a more cautious path, clinging to the gunwales.

"Gee, did you want a sailing lesson?" Gwen asked him as he crouched on his haunches before her. Ardra dropped to her knees at his side. They looked like a matched pair. Fair. Great-looking. Perfect—for each other.

He slapped his palm to her forehead. "She is cool."

"Still," Ardra said to him, "she looks ill."

The spot where his hand touched pulsed a moment and began to grow warm.

"I'm not sick. What makes you think that?" Gwen felt like a mood ring from the 1970s. If Vad touched her, she was suddenly hot. When he retreated, cold swept in to replace the warmth.

"You are sick," Vad said. "The skin about your eyes is turning black. You are puffing up along the jaw. Perhaps you are rotting."

Gwen touched her chin. "One of Ardra's men hit me with his elbow. It's called a bruise. I suppose you perfect folks don't bruise. I have noticed your skin is darn near perfect—scars excepted. I'll probably look even worse tomorrow, but it's nothing to fret over." Then she picked up the hem of her nightgown and wiped it beneath her eyes. She contemplated the dark stain and burst into laughter. "And this is just mascara and eyeliner. It's smeared makeup."

"Makeup?" Ardra said softly, and turned to Vad. "What language is she speaking? Where is she from?"

"Ocean City—" she began.

"Ocean City!" Ardra cried. "Is this the city on the great ocean that holds the mighty serpents? The huge fish the size of three horses?"

Gwen stifled a giggle and adjusted the sail. "Sure. That's the place."

Vad glowered at her mirth. "Ocean City is beyond the ice fields. It's flat and colorless." Turning his attention to Gwen, he took the scrap of cloth in his fingers and did as she had, only more gently, wiping it along the skin beneath her eyes. "This is very curious. This color is some kind of enhancement? Like the paint you spread on the cloth of your gown? Why would you put color on your eyes?"

"Oh, I could never explain it. It has to do with vanity—"

"Vanity!" Ardra pursed her lips. "A vain woman is despised by men. Selaw women sometimes rub berry juice upon their lips to stain them a darker red. *Those* women are accounted of little value, save to a certain portion of the male populace who have few funds to—"

"Well, it's easy for you to criticize." Gwen felt herself bristle. "You have cooks; you're beautiful—"

"I am?" Ardra smiled. Gwen decided Vad should not see that smile. It was a thousand-watt menace. She jerked the boat to throw them off balance and distract him. He was probably like most men when faced with a beautiful smile—easily attracted, easily landed—like a giant fish.

"Well," Gwen qualified, "maybe if you took a bath."

Ardra frowned. *Good.* She looked less wonderful with a frown. When Gwen turned back to Vad, he was grinning. She felt as if he'd read her mind.

"Here, Vad, hold the tiller. I could use some help. Did I tell you I used to take part in sailing races when I was a kid?"

An hour later, Vad ordered her to put the boat in to shore.

"Smoke," he said, although Gwen could smell nothing except her nightgown, which had the strong scent of river water. "There will be a settlement with food and clothing," he continued. "We can barter the bowls and spoons for what we need."

Familiar now with the little boat's idiosyncrasies, she beached it on a sandy spit of land with a small flourish and waited for Vad to carry Ardra to shore before she surrendered herself to the same treatment. She did really well ignoring the strength of his arms, the nearness of his wonderful warmth, but less well controlling the sudden heat that surged through her as she watched the muscles of his back and arms work to pull the boat farther up the beach for safety. With no anchor, or handy trees or boulders to tie up the boat, Vad had quite a bit of work to do. Gwen fanned herself. Yes, there was definitely something about a well-honed man in motion.

"We should see if we can get an anchor," she said when he was satisfied the boat was safe. "Will these folks be friendly?" she asked them.

Ardra nodded. "They will be Selaw, and thus subject to my wishes."

"There has been strife between the Selaw and Tolemac for generations. We must be careful not to offer offense," Vad answered more cautiously.

Somehow the idea of going in to territory she did not know from the game frightened Gwen. The game took a player only to the border, where all the skirmishes occurred. She rubbed her hands on her arms and scanned the landscape. The water was tinted red, and the beach was more orange than brown now. If this was home, she'd guess there was a high iron content in the soil, but here, she didn't want to hazard any guesses. The only thing keeping her from freezing into an ice cube was the exertion of sailing and Vad's uncanny effect on her, which heated more than her blood.

"When did we leave Tolemac?" she asked Vad.

"About the time Ardra's men were meeting their fate."

"Then we're deep in Selaw country." She shivered and stepped closer to Vad.

"Do not fear," Ardra said, laying a reassuring hand on her shoulder. "We will gain what we need."

Gwen trusted Vad's caution far more than she trusted Ardra's confidence. She was close on Vad's heels as he strode swiftly through the scrubby brush that edged the river. Taller trees formed a grove at the foot of a hill tinted with lavender shadows as clouds raced across the sky. Despite the pastoral surroundings, she thought Vad was too tall, too much a target. And the hand he held on his knife hilt looked far from casual. Even the bows and arrows he'd slung across his back did not reassure her. After all, they had only a few arrows. There might be hundreds of hostile Selaw hiding in the woods.

Instead of hostile natives, though, children burst from the woods when they reached the foot of the hill. Their faces were dirty, but their clothing was clean and sturdy. They stood and jabbered at Vad, jumping up and down before him with little fear. Several men and women melted from the shadowy trees and approached more warily.

" 'Tis his uniform, the Tolemac colors, that they fear. But they know well my father's name. I will speak for us," Ardra said, stepping forward.

Gwen plucked at the back of Vad's tunic, but he ignored her. His posture remained guarded, even militant, his expression impassive as he stood behind Ardra.

A man, garbed much as Ardra's men had been, in crossgarters and a long cloak the color of their surroundings, stepped forward. He gestured for them to follow him into the trees.

Gwen's heart picked up as they moved silently behind the man; the children and women brought up the rear. A hum of soft chatter followed them. The urge to look over her shoulder, to see if the looks on the Selaw faces were benign, was almost overwhelming.

They came to a clearing filled with scattered clusters of cottages. At the man's terse command, the children and other folk hurried away toward the cottages. Carefully tended vines climbed about the doors and windows. Here and there, lavender and white flowers bloomed on the vines.

Ardra bowed deeply at the waist to the man. He returned her bow, but did not take his eyes from Vad. Vad gave no greeting.

"Our boat capsized," Ardra fibbed, "and we lost much of our provisions. We have only these with which to trade." She set the wooden box on the ground before the man and stepped away to where Gwen and Vad waited.

The man knelt and pulled the peg. He inspected the contents between quick glances at Vad. "What do you need? These are very fine, indeed." His hands turned the bowls over and over.

Gwen noticed that his fingers were long and his hands well tended. He was not a man who toiled in the fields.

Ardra took a step forward. "We need warm clothing, blankets, shoes—"

"Thirty arrows," Vad said quietly.

"Thirty arrows," Ardra repeated.

The man stroked the silver cutlery. "May we have the box as well?"

"For ten more arrows you may have the box," Vad said.

The man sat on his haunches. Gwen could see him visibly relax. Ardra knelt before him and sat back on her heels. They bartered a few more moments. Vad stood as still as a statue throughout it all. A tangible wave of tension seemed to shimmer about him.

Finally Ardra rose, a dazzling smile on her features. “We have done well, as have they. Come. We will see to the clothing first.” She retained the box and bowls. The man took the cutlery. “When we are satisfactorily garbed and armed, we will complete the trade.”

They followed the man to a nearby cottage where he left them, gesturing Ardra to continue on with him in another direction. Its door was too low for Vad, who had to duck to enter. As their eyes grew accustomed to the dim interior, a woman shooed two children through the door before returning to the hearth.

Gwen examined the cottage. It was simply furnished. It had a stone hearth, shuttered windows, and an intricately decorated plaster chimneypiece, painted with delicate birds and flowers.

Unearthly birds, unearthly flowers.

A wave of homesickness swept through Gwen.

The village man arrived with armloads of clothing and blankets for their inspection. He dropped them at the foot of a high bed covered in many furs. He never acknowledged Vad’s presence at the hearth, but physically skirted the area each time he entered. Some of the tension that pervaded the room disappeared when the man left them.

The woman, less splendidly garbed than Ardra, but in much the same style gown, remained behind and proved as susceptible as every other woman where Vad was concerned. She stared at him, stumbling over her hem, bumping her elbows on chairs. Gwen resisted an urge to slap her silly when she almost upset a kettle as she pulled it from a hook over the fire. Her efforts to fill a washbasin resulted in half the hot water slopping over and steaming on the hearthstones.

Vad stepped forward and relieved the woman of the heavy kettle. The woman thanked him so many times, Gwen had to bite her lip to remain silent.

Finally, with many bows and smiles, the woman placed a small fabric-wrapped bundle by the water along with a length of linen and silently departed, her eyes riveted to Vad. She tripped over the doorjamb and practically catapulted backward from the cottage.

Once the woman had departed, Gwen looked about, unsure what was expected of her now that she and Vad were alone.

"You will bathe first and I will stand watch," Vad said. He drew his long blade and held it casually in his right hand. The flames reflected along the blade.

"Do you think you're going to need that?"

He shrugged. "One should always be prepared."

She glanced about and realized that she and Vad were alone in the cottage.

"Where do you think they took Ardra?" She sank to the edge of a chair. Beside her, on the well-scrubbed table, the basin of water steamed. A wonderful, spicy scent came from the small bundle. She lifted it and held it to her nose. She breathed deeply of the soothing scent.

"She will be given a more honored place to wash and better garments from which to choose."

Gwen nodded. "So rank has its privileges here, too."

She unwrapped the cloth to reveal a waxy bar of brown soap. She stroked her fingers along the surface and brought it again to her nose to inhale the fragrance.

"I seek nothing better," Vad said. "I do not need serving women pawing me either. Now disrobe. Bathe while I keep watch."

He nudged some clothing on the fur-covered bed with his dagger point. "These clothes will do well enough for you. They are warm, and with your butchered hair, you will excite less curiosity garbed as a man. Make many layers, especially for your feet. It will surely be bitter cold at the Fortress of Ravens."

"Okay." Gwen waited until Vad moved to the hearth and stood there, his broad back to her. The sharp edge of his blade glinted in the firelight as he warmed his hands.

Gwen shook out the clothing he'd indicated. He'd picked well. The long trousers and heavy woolen tunic were made for a man not much taller than she. The linen undergarments, like long boxer shorts, and a shirt with a huge tail looked so soft, she wanted to just put them on and curl up somewhere and snooze the night away.

With a sigh, she tugged off her boot and shoe, sorry she'd tramped mud through the woman's cottage. She pulled her grimy nightgown over her head, dropped it, and stood on it to protect her bare feet from the icy wooden floor. The nightgown was beyond saving.

Carefully she dipped her hands into the basin. The hot water felt wonderful. The cake of crude soap lathered well. The thought of being clean banished even her shivers. As she scrubbed her arms, her goose bumps disappeared and warmth took their place.

She worked slowly, savoring the rich lather, the spicy scent, the hot water. She saved the dirtiest part, her feet, for last. Finally she bent from the waist and began to stroke away the splashes of mud on her calves.

Behind her, Vad gasped.

She whipped around, hands spread to conceal her breasts. Water and soap trickled down her front.

"Gwen." In two quick strides he crossed the small cottage to where she stood.

How naked she felt. How suddenly hot. How suddenly vulnerable. Her vision blurred and her mouth dried. He seemed to have grown taller, stronger. Smoke from the hearth filled the room with a dull haze behind him, outlining his shoulders, his silvery hair.

He reached out and placed a hand on her arm, a caressing hand. He turned her about. Slowly, with great gentleness, he ran his fingertips along her shoulder, down her back, over the curve of her hip. "You are hurt." His voice was low, rough.

A shudder ran down her spine in the wake of his caress. Flames licked where his fingers touched. She began to tremble. No words formed on her thick, slow tongue.

He stepped even closer and dropped his weapon on the bed. He took the soapy cloth from her hand and began to wash her back slowly, in gentle, circular motions. She arched to the sensation, soothed herself in his ministrations.

"Why did you not tell me you were hurt?"

She could feel the whisper of his breath on the back of her neck. The room filled with a foggy mist.

"They're just . . . more . . . bruises," she finally managed. "They don't . . . really . . . hurt."

An errant thought—that he cared about her even if he didn't trust her—flickered through her mind. Then he wrung out the cloth and placed it in the bowl. Her whole body went ice cold when he returned to the fire. It flared to nearly burning when he took the kettle and renewed the water in the basin. He dipped his hands into the water and lathered the cloth again.

She could not move, her eyes glued to the motions of his strong hands. Her feet were somehow attached to the floor, her body frozen to immobility by an outside force. When he again stroked the warm cloth along her shoulders, across her back, a long, deep sigh of pleasure escaped her, and she didn't care if he heard it.

Vad felt anger crawl through his control.

He had caused these hurts by bringing her into his world.

Her sleek back muscles quivered as he bathed her bruises. He'd never seen such injuries. The dark marks spread in ugly patches on her delicate skin. Uncannily, he knew what she must feel. A throbbing, a dull, heavy ache, would underlie each mark. He felt the throb, knew the ache in his own flesh.

He'd also never seen a woman with such golden hair on her head and such dark hair . . . He forced his thoughts from the small swath of hair covering her femininity.

With the lightest touch he could muster, he stroked the cloth down the back of her damaged legs, wiping away mud, exposing more of the bruises and an angry red scrape.

He placed the basin of water on the floor and went down on one knee behind her. She stood as still as a statue, her head bowed, her hands clasped over her breasts.

How beautiful was the smooth column of her back, the ivory curve of her hip. A shimmer of heat ran along his fingers as he bathed her, and the tantalizing scent of the soap filled the room. Heady, spicy, it teased a memory, but then she turned, and all thoughts of the soap slipped away from him. Her flesh was soft and rounded, just the way he liked his women.

She sighed and swayed toward him. Her eyes fell closed.

Heat suffused him. Desire replaced succor. His body grew heavy with need. He leaned forward and pressed his mouth to a livid bruise on her thigh.

An arrow of want darted through him.

He rose before he touched his lips to the soft flesh of her belly. "I am sorry for your hurt," he said, taking her clasped hands and spreading them open. He placed the cloth in her palms. It should have been cold now, but was instead almost too hot to touch.

Her eyes fluttered open. Unfocused, vague, her huge,

dark eyes gazed up at him. A pulse beat frantically in her throat.

She licked her lips.

Slowly, lest he awaken her from the trancelike state in which she seemed to be frozen, he leaned forward and kissed her shoulder.

Not her moist lips.

He could not kiss her lips. He would be lost. Driven to forget his goals.

Goals of honor.

She tasted sweet. Her skin was soap scented, silk textured, inviting. He skimmed his fingers after his kisses, stroked the hollow of her throat with his tongue. How hot and fevered felt her flesh.

She moaned.

He forgot why he should not kiss her. Slowly he brought his lips to hers.

Her kiss was as he remembered—tasting of foreign lands and forbidden wants. Sweet, hot, forceful, possessive—beguiling.

With a jerk, Vad pulled away. She swayed to music only she could hear.

Beguiled, he thought. *I beguiled her.*

Or had she beguiled him?

He no longer cared. He swept her hot, damp body into his arms and laid her out on the furs.

With little effort, he urged her hands to his shoulders. Very slowly she stroked her fingers down his chest, then pulled up his tunic. Heat spiked low in his belly—hotter than any need he could ever remember with any woman. Her palms kneaded his chest muscles, aroused him, invited him to touch.

Her breasts were firm and fit perfectly in his hands.

"I want you," he said.

"Yes," she whispered, arching against his caress. Quickly, his hands shaking, he shed his clothes. When he was naked, he walked to the table; it seemed very far away. He washed his face, his body, sluicing the hot water down his skin.

When he turned back and gazed at her, he stumbled against the table's edge.

She lay stretched out on the furs, one knee bent, her legs spread open, her lips gleaming. Then she lifted her arms to him.

Her invitation was just as he'd dreamed it on his journey across the ice fields.

Would she disappear when he clasped her to him?

No. This time she wrapped her arms about him and urged him close.

His body flashed hot. Chest heaving, he surrendered to her seductive pull.

Her mouth was greedy. So was his. He wanted to devour her. Together they feasted on each other's mouths, tangling tongues, nipping lips.

He pressed her arms wide and climbed over her, resting on his hands and knees, caging her with his body.

The taste of her throat, her breasts, her belly was sweeter than the best wine. He drank in the scent of her, nuzzled the tiny triangle of hair, learned the smooth texture of her inner thigh, as he dragged his tongue back and forth on her from knee to hip.

"Now. Now," she said in a moan, twisting her hands in his hair, and thrusting her hips beneath his kiss. She embraced him with her thighs, urged him down with her strong arms.

He joined himself to her with a hard thrust. She was hot and ready—experienced—meeting him, moving in perfect rhythm with him.

They rocked together, sweat springing up between their bodies. She smothered her cries against his neck. Her nails scraped across his back in painful counterpoint to the silken heat in which he moved. He wanted more than just a joining. He wanted to inhabit her.

Suddenly her body arched frantically against him,

once, then twice. Her head lolled back, her arms opened. His knife clattered to the floor.

"By the sword," he said in a moan.

All around them blurred. The bed spun, tipped.

"Hypnoflora," he said with a gasp.

Chapter Twelve

He could not stop. Her body possessed him. Tides of desire swamped him.

"Vad!" called a muffled voice from outside the cottage. "Vad!"

With a near roar of pain, he tore his body from hers. His chest heaved as he stood over her, his heart pounding wildly, every muscle screaming for him to finish what had only just begun for him.

"Let me in!"

Ardra. She had come at the perfect moment to save him from foolishness. His ardor died a swift death.

Vad shook his head and took a long, shuddering breath. He turned to the door, then realized Ardra's voice was accompanied by a soft rapping on the window shutter.

Gwen lay in the deep shadows of the bed, her eyes closed, her mouth slack. "Sweet Gwen," he murmured. "This did not happen."

He touched his lips to her shoulder, then snatched up

his blade. With a groan and an unsteady hand, he dragged furs over her body.

The shutter resisted his efforts to open it.

Ardra's voice persisted in a whisper from behind it. "Vad. Open now! Hurry! Hurry!"

Finally he worked the catch and swung the solid wooden shutters wide. The midday light dazzled him. An icy blast of air swept into the cottage, and for a moment his head cleared and his mind recognized what he had done.

"Pull me in," Ardra said, lifting her arms to him, calling him to his duty.

He boosted her over the windowsill and set her on the floor.

"We must go. Now. Out this window. There are men watching this place from the clearing." Then she clapped her hands over her eyes and turned her back. "You are naked!"

"I was . . . bathing," he said, glancing at the bed.

"Hush. Lower your voice and garb yourself. Quickly," she persisted.

He could not make his feet move. "I think the soap was tainted with—"

"Aye." Her head bobbed agreement. "With hypnoflora."

Vad pulled on a pair of thick breeches, too short for one of his stature. He jammed his feet into his boots.

A swirling mist still hovered in the room. It inched in Ardra's direction across the floor.

"Throw the soap out the window," he said. Ardra reached for the small cake. "Nay! Do not touch it with your hands!" He must fight the heavy languor that was stealing over him again.

Taken in by hypnoflora—the mistake of a man half his age. He pictured the tiny flowers, fields of them, stretching as far as the eye could see—like snow—men picking them, women crushing them.

The images tumbled about so that he thought he was in the cottage one moment and the fields with the pickers the next. He leaned on the table. His head pounded. The heavy scent of the room was one of passions aroused but, thank the gods, not released. "Why have they done this? What purpose was served?"

Ardra pitched the soap from the window. "I overheard two men arguing. It was planned the instant we made our appearance." Ardra drew the shutters and helped him cross-garter his legs. "The women want to keep you."

"Keep me?" He shook his head.

She held out several long tunics. "Aye. The women were very taken with you. They wish to keep you for . . . for . . . I am not sure for what purpose." She looked about. "Where is Gwen?"

Vad indicated the bed and drew on a green cloak to conceal his knives. It also gave him an opportunity to ignore Ardra's scowl of censure.

She swung about and hurried to where Gwen lay buried. "We must wake her, clothe her. If the women can convince the men their plan has worth, they will come straight here for you. They have a pit in which to put you."

"A pit . . ." Vad looked away. *A dark place.* He trudged to the bed and tossed off the furs. He tried to jam Gwen's arm into a sleeve, but she was as limp as a dead eel. "This is hopeless."

With little ceremony, he rolled Gwen up in the furs and pulled her into his arms. "You can dress her later," he said. Ardra snatched up clothing and made a bundle of it.

Gwen burst into life. She locked her bare arms about his neck. The look on her face warned Vad before she began to kiss him. "No," he said, evading her questing lips. "No. You must stop."

"Why?" She leaned forward and nuzzled his neck. Ardra made a sound of disgust behind him.

He imagined that all that had passed between himself and Gwen was now apparent to Ardra. "It seems the village women wish to keep me."

Gwen burst into laughter, and he lost his grip on her. She unrolled in a boneless slither onto the floor.

How far away she looked—how naked—how splendid.

"They want to keep you?" She clutched her belly and rolled about. "Sure, who wouldn't?" she said between gales of laughter. "I mean, you can really cook—"

" 'Tis not his cooking they require," Ardra snapped. "She is acting the idiot, Vad, and her laughter will attract the men. She must be very susceptible to the hypnoflora's essence."

And so was he. "It would appear so." With gentleness—after all, he'd just known her intimately—he shook Gwen's shoulder.

Ardra shoved past him and took matters into her own hands. She slapped Gwen hard across the face. Gwen's laughter changed to gulping hiccups.

"We have no time for this," Ardra said close to Gwen's ear. "The women are adamant in their mission. If the men agree, they will put Vad in a pit, and where will they put us? I imagine wherever they plant their dead!"

The imprint of Ardra's hand stood out starkly on Gwen's smooth skin. Amazed, Vad watched as Gwen's head rolled about on her neck. When she jerked upright, a grin lit her features. "I want a dress as nice as yours."

Ardra threw up her hands at him. "Help me."

"Gather the bows, some furs, whatever you can carry—do not forget my other clothes."

Unaccountably, Gwen wriggled and laughed each time he touched her—especially on her sides. Finally she was garbed in a haphazard collection of men's clothing—enough to make her appear to be a well-fed Selaw merchant.

Ardra bundled clothing and then lashed the pile with several furs and outergarments to the two bows. Vad set Gwen on her feet. "Take her to the boat, Ardra. I will remain here and hold them off until you are safe." He thrust the bundle into Gwen's arms.

"You will come with us now." Ardra fisted her hands on her hips. "I know what will happen if you resist them. They will cut off your feet."

"I will not run away like a coward."

Gwen began to hiccup again. "Silly. You can't run without feet. Of course, you can still cook . . ."

Vad ignored her. She did not know what she was saying.

"Close your eyes and stand on one foot," Ardra ordered him.

He could not do it. The room spun and twisted.

"You are not fit to fight anyone! When the hypnoflora has worn off, you can return and burn the village to the ground if you wish!" Ardra shook out the white wool cloak in which she was garbed. She softened her tone. "Come with us, I beg of you. I need you. The maidens my father took need you."

"Ah, the maidens," Gwen said, and sagged onto a stool. "The maidens will probably want to keep you, too."

"How dare you make light of—" Ardra began.

"She is not responsible for what she says." *No,* he thought. *I am at fault here. I brought her here, I did not recognize the soap's danger, I took advantage of her. . . .*"

"Vad. Vad!" Ardra shook his arm.

Vad took a deep breath. In truth, his head was spinning, and his limbs took far too long to respond. What chance had he against dozens of determined men and women? He strode to the window. "Gwen, get on your feet. Ardra, throw her out the window if you must."

He climbed from the rear window and reached up.

Gwen tumbled out into his arms. She leaned drunkenly on the wall, gasping the fresh air, her face a pale oval. Ardra flung herself over the sill into his arms.

"Stay low. Now run," he whispered.

Ardra led the way, skirts raised to her knees.

He stumbled after her, still clumsy, but his head grew clearer with each step.

Behind him, he heard a raised voice. He grabbed Gwen's arm and urged her to a faster pace.

When they reached the beach, he shoved the boat into the water with both women on board.

"Look," Ardra said in a gasp as he jumped aboard. Between the trees, men and women could be seen running. Their voices echoed against the foothills.

Vad pulled the sail aloft and secured it as he had watched Gwen do a number of times. He folded her hand about the tiller. "Ignore it," he ordered as an arrow tore through the sail and Gwen gasped. "You are in Ocean City, sailing the sea breezes, racing the wind."

"Ocean City . . . racing?" she whispered. He felt her hand lock on the tiller beneath his.

"Aye. Ride the wind." Slowly he pulled his hand from hers. Arrows whizzed across the bow, but Gwen's eyes were locked to the fluttering strips she'd tied to the top of the mast.

"Vad, watch out," Ardra cried, but it was too late. An arrow embedded itself in his forearm. She shrieked and flung herself flat.

He jerked the arrow out. Blood welled from the wound. Another arrow thunked into the wood by his hand.

His bows lay at his feet, but there was no point in firing on the Selaw. He had no idea what the hypnoflora had done to his aim, and they still had precious few arrows to waste. He would not do as Ardra had either. Gwen must remain upright, sailing the boat. He must shield her as best he could. To that end, he lifted the bow and its burden of furs. Each time an arrow came too close, he used it as a shield.

Suddenly the boat heeled sharply, nearly spilling them all into the river. Ardra screamed. Gwen laughed and flung her body practically overboard as she hauled the sail close and shoved the tiller over.

In moments they were truly riding the wind, skimming the water, the Selaw arrows falling harmlessly behind them.

Gwen looked magnificent, her hair tousled, her face to the wind. He knew she was somewhere else, still under the hypnoflora's influence, probably on the gray waters of Ocean City.

And where had she been when he'd joined himself to her? Had she been in his arms? Or had she been in her lifemate's embrace again? Reliving her former life?

A burn, not unlike that in his arm where the arrow had entered, filled his throat.

Finally they drew far enough from shore to no longer fear the archers. Three arrows were buried halfway up the shaft in his makeshift shield. "Gather the Selaw arrows," he said to Ardra, who finally sat up. "Perhaps we can reuse them."

Ardra crawled about the boat, pulling arrows from the soft wood, her eyes round and frightened in her pale face.

Gwen shook her head. An odd exhilaration swept through her as she sailed along the water, looking neither left nor right, only to the clouds and the wind-filled sail.

Then she glanced about. She looked down at her own legs. When had she changed into this awful green costume?

"I see you are with us again," Ardra said.

"Huh?" Gwen licked her lips. They were dry. Her throat was scratchy.

She looked closely at Vad. He was dressed very

oddly—like the Selaw men who'd accompanied Ardra. Gone were his thigh-hugging leather breeches. A long red line of blood ran down his arm where he'd rolled back a sleeve. The blood dripped from his fingers as he played with some arrows and inspected their points.

"Vad! You're hurt," she cried, but he merely shrugged. He untied a strip of bloody cloth, dipped it in the river water, then tried to rebind the wound.

"I will see to it," Ardra said, and edged to where Vad sat.

Before Gwen could ask how he'd hurt himself, the wind kicked up and whitecaps danced across the water's surface, requiring her immediate attention.

The scent of wet earth and rain filled the air. She shivered. How had she gotten here? How had Vad been injured? Even the terrain looked different from what she remembered. Gone were the red, rocky shores, the stained water, the stunted green conifers. Ahead the river curved between two high cliffs of dark, striated stone. An apprehensive feeling of being watched filled her. What if someone awaited them up there?

A small rapid threatened to capsize the boat. She fought the tiller bar, hauled on the sail with all her strength. She wrapped a cloth about her hand to protect it from the rough rope.

When she next could look back to where Ardra tended Vad in the stern, she saw that the other woman was inspecting a deep gash across his forearm.

"Doesn't that need stitches?" she called over the rising rush of the wind.

Ardra nodded. "I have no healing skills. What shall we do?"

Gwen thought a moment. "Maybe we could put in to shore. We can boil some cloth and wrap it up."

"We will not be stopping," Vad snapped. "Just bind it and let it be."

This time it was Gwen's turn to shrug. Ardra bit her

lip and looked anxiously from her to Vad.

Her hooded cloak, lined with white fur and embroidered with gold, accentuated her ivory skin and amber eyes. As she leaned toward Vad, the cloak parted to reveal a matching fur-trimmed gown and shiny leather boots.

Well, Gwen thought, rank certainly does have its privileges. She groped beneath her rough wool cloak and pulled a long strip of cloth from around her middle.

"Here," she called. "Tear this up. At least it looks clean."

In the end, it was Vad who took the cloth and did the bandaging. Ardra patted his arm and made small, ineffectual fluttering motions over his work.

The effort of holding the sail against the strengthening winds made Gwen's arm tremble. No sooner had she felt the tremor run along her arm than Vad was there, sitting beside her, relieving her of the burden of holding the sheet.

"What happened? Where are we?" she asked him when the boat had settled into as smooth a glide as could be expected on the choppy water.

Vad kept his eyes on the sail, and Gwen sensed he was not going to be completely honest with her. "The Selaw attacked us. They were going to cheat us over the bowls, so we decided to move on. The soap we were given was tainted with hypnoflora. It muddled your mind."

Gwen frowned. "I feel so . . . strange. And . . . I had the weirdest dream . . ." Her body flashed hot. Sweat broke out on her skin. Her hand jerked on the tiller.

He placed a hand over hers, and together they brought the boat back on an even keel. "What did you dream?" he asked when he released her hand.

"Oh . . . nothing . . . I mean . . . I can't remember." The lie would have to satisfy him. There was no way she was going to tell him about her dream. She could

suddenly feel its effects. Her whole body felt bruised. In fact, she was vaguely sore in all the wrong places. Her mouth hurt, too.

"Gwen?" He studied her face. It was almost as if he was trying to see inside her mind. What could he read in her gaze or in the deep blush of color on her cheeks?

She lowered her eyes. "It's stupid—just a dream. I can't even remember it. Just . . . I feel a little dizzy." That at least was not a lie.

The scenery changed from one moment to the next as they rounded another bend. High black cliffs rose on either side. Jagged lichen-covered rocks hung over their small boat. The clouds darkened overhead to match the changing terrain. Deep purple shadows filled the crevices.

There would be no lights to guide them when the darkness fell. No Tolemac moons glowed overhead. She hoped they'd get to the fortress before dark. Her arms, back, and legs ached from sailing the boat.

Ardra pointed to a narrow offshoot of the river. "I think we should stop a moment to plan how we will gain entrance to the fortress and to eat," she said.

Gwen gratefully guided the boat into the sheltering cove.

"We are but a short way from the fortress," Ardra informed them. "There are two ways into it. One is used only by my father and his chosen ones—a waterway into an underground grotto. The other is the public way—over the drawbridge—a way you cannot use. You might be recognized as from Tolemac with your blue eyes. No man from Tolemac has ever entered the fortress."

Vad nodded. "Who guards each entrance?" he asked. He leaped onto a flat outcropping of rock and wrapped a rope around a jagged spur.

"The drawbridge is rarely raised now that we have peace. The people of the area come and go as they please. Sentries man the ramparts. Able archers all."

"At the grotto entrance?"

"Four of my father's men in watches of two on and two off. Little more is needed. The cliffs hem in the boat; there is no way out once you enter the canal leading to the fortress. How we will get past the guards, I do not know, but if we succeed we can disappear in the many underground caverns. If we choose the public way, many will see us, and my servants will immediately come to see to my care."

Vad made no comment, and Ardra continued her description of the grotto. "Warm springs rise from the earth in the caverns. Once, they were worshiping places of the ancients. The ways of the labyrinth were passed from father to son. With no son to inherit, my father entrusted me with the way."

"What's to stop Ruonail from telling Narfrom how to get around down there?" Gwen asked.

"It is not so simple that a single telling would suffice. It took several years for me to learn. One must trace the paths, walk them often, know the key to the markings. It is not something one learns quickly. Trust me, only my father and I know the true nature of the labyrinth beneath the fortress."

Gwen scrambled out when Vad pulled them close enough to disembark. "And if we can't get into the fortress?" she asked him.

He met her gaze squarely.

"The maidens will die."

Chapter Thirteen

Gwen tucked her hands into her underarms. "I've seen enough violence today to last me two lifetimes. Why can't we go now and get it over with?"

"I agree," Vad said. "Do what you need to. I will prepare food, and then let us be gone."

A little glimmer of an idea as to how they might enter the fortress had come to Gwen, but she wanted to think it through before telling them.

She jumped across a small gap between rocks and stood at the mouth of a large outcropping. Vad lifted Ardra across the gap and set her down.

After shaking out her snow white cloak, Ardra frowned up at the sky. Gwen looked up, too. The sky, now filled with angry, grayish purple clouds, looked low and threatening. Would it rain purple? High cliffs penned them in. The terrain was cold, alien.

"What is wrong?" Vad asked Ardra, but it was at Gwen he looked. She felt a strange discomfort from his intent inspection.

"I do not understand what is happening," Ardra said. "The weather is always fair after the harvesttime. This gathering of clouds is an ill omen."

"Just looks like rain to me," Gwen said, rubbing her sore rear. She caught Vad watching and stopped. A vision came to her of Vad kneeling over her. Naked. Every detail of his body was edged in a golden shimmer, as if a fire flickered behind him.

Gwen found herself staring at the long line of his well-muscled thigh, the way his woolen tunic pulled taut across his shoulders.

She jerked from her reverie. *Stop it. He's just flesh and blood. Whatever dreams you've had, you're awake now.* Still, warmth curled through her insides.

She hopped from rock to rock until she was out of their sight, then sat down, arms about her knees, and stared at the water. They needed to get past the guards so they could rescue the maidens.

Just saying the words—rescue the maidens—sounded absurd. The biggest thing she'd ever rescued was a seagull from a kite string. The whole concept of what Vad proposed to do was insane. Believing she was in a game was insane. And what possible help could she be to him? She couldn't even draw a bow, she was so weak.

Her reflection looked back at her in the waning light. "My hair's wrecked and I look like a giant lima bean." As she brought her cupped hands to her mouth to take a drink, she caught the scent of the soap from the cottage.

The purple-stained sky spun. The water slid sideways. "Uhhhh . . ."

"You were desirous of a swim?" Vad said as he snatched the back of her cloak and hauled her away from the water's edge.

"No. I-I-I feel so dizzy." Vad settled her a few feet from the rocky lip. "The soap . . ." She held her hands close to his face.

Treating her with little gentleness, he scrubbed her hands and used the point of the jeweled dagger to clean beneath her nails. She forced herself to look away from his strong hands and long fingers.

What was wrong with her? Why couldn't she watch him do the simplest thing without some erotic image taking over? She'd played *Tolemac Wars II* countless times, turned him off without regret, laughed when Mrs. Hill and other women went on and on about how spectacular he was.

Now she was worse than any rabid fan. She couldn't look at him without . . . An incredibly vivid image—his head bent to kiss her inner thigh—made her jerk away from his hands. She could feel the rasp of his unshaven cheek against her soft skin.

"Gwen? Something is wrong." Vad cocked his head to the side. He examined her with an intent scrutiny that made her insides churn.

"You'll think I'm crazy—mad—if I tell you," she whispered back. She edged away from him.

"Perhaps I will; perhaps I will not." His voice was low, seductively so. The scar coursed his cheek like a dark ribbon of blood.

"I had this dream that we . . ." He hissed in his breath. The look on his face stopped her. "Did we?" she whispered. He was silent. "Did we?" Her lips trembled, and she clamped her fingers over them.

"It was not a dream," he said equally softly. "Hypnoflora is very . . . powerful."

She bowed her head. *Not a dream. Reality. Each moment. Every caress.* Tears burned against her eyes. What had she done? She had slept with a man who had told her quite bluntly he did not trust her. She had slept with a man she did not love—who would never love her.

He touched her bent head. "I did not complete the act. You need have no fear of a child resulting."

Great. He did not complete the act. How cold he

sounded, despite the way he smoothed her hair with his warm hand.

"What stopped you?" He was a blur through her tears.

"Ardra. We were most fortunate she called me back to my duty. Why are you crying? You will not bear a child."

"Oh, I'm not worried about being pregnant." What could she tell him? "I'm just having a delayed reaction to that hypno stuff. My eyes are bothering me. You probably don't have problems like that here. Eat too much of something, drink the wrong stuff in Ocean City, and your eyes water, your nose gets all puffy and red—"

"I see," he said, but his voice said he did not believe her.

"Anyway . . . I can't get . . . have a child."

He rubbed away her tears with his thumb. "You are barren?"

"In a way." His hands were so comforting, but his voice had a hard edge that made her pull away from his seductive warmth. She extended her arm and tapped the inside of her upper arm. "I have an implant."

"Implant?" He took her arm. He skimmed his thumb along the inner flesh. Even through the heavy layers of clothing, he had the power to arouse her.

"Yes. In Ocean City we've figured out ways to prevent . . . birth. When Bob and I first lifemated, we wanted to wait a few years until we"—her throat tightened—"we had children. I had this thing put in my arm. It keeps you barren for years—I mean conjunctions—until you have it removed."

His fingers tightened on her arm. "Then you are free to lie where your whim leads you."

A heavy silence fell. The air between them crackled with something she didn't want to explore—was afraid to explore. She had to push him away.

"What's that supposed to mean? You probably lie about all the time," she said.

He frowned. "You are my first in three conjunctions."

Now why would he lie about such a thing? "Sure. And pigs fly." She jerked her arm from his grip.

"Perhaps pigs fly in Ocean City, but here they merely trot. And I have not had a woman in three conjunctions."

Gwen inspected his face. The dark shadows hid much of his thoughts. His awareness training would probably hide the rest even if she could see him clearly.

He raked his hand through his hair, snagged his fingertip in a braid, and jerked it free. The loose hair tumbled across his brow. "It is difficult to forgo pleasure."

Yes. She hadn't realized just how difficult. How she wanted that pleasure again, wanted to experience the full measure of a man's desire. She wanted to wrap herself in his strong arms and lose herself in that dream again, to feel his body moving over hers, to feel again the turmoil of emotions she'd not realized she so desperately missed.

But he would feel none of those things. "Why did you make love to me?"

"Hypnoflora."

Her head ached. "It was nothing more?"

"What do you mean?"

"Just . . . that you cared for me."

"I have always cared for my partner's pleasure." His voice was low, soft, sending a shiver down her spine.

"Of course. If they didn't find pleasure, that would reflect on your skill as a lover, wouldn't it? That would be a real kick in the pants. It wouldn't do for anyone to say the Tolemac warrior is a lousy lover."

She felt rather than saw him shrug.

Bitterness swept through her. He could make love to any woman he wanted—a different one each hour, if he was capable. She pictured women lining up to take a number. And lousy or not, he'd probably remain in each woman's dreams for years to come. Why should he care about their feelings?

He rose and offered her his hand. She ignored it. She felt small and insignificant. A rising wind tugged at her cloak and his, snapping them in the air, punctuating her agitation. Ardra was forgotten.

"I see my answer did not satisfy you. What is it you desire?"

"I don't know," she whispered, and didn't.

Desire. It filled the air about them, touched them like wings beating against the imprisonment of a cage.

He lowered his head, encircled her waist. His kiss was not the urgent, heated one of her dreams. No, this kiss was gentle, a whisper of a touch across her lips, like walking into a cobweb.

"I know what you desire," he said between kisses. His fingers were warm as they stroked up under her cloak to caress her. Ripples of sensation ran through her, making her shiver.

He skimmed a kiss over her eyelids. Instantly her body trembled in a liquid rush. With a moan, she jerked away. "Don't." What had she done? She felt like a teenager caught in the backseat of a car.

"Why do you stop? You want me, too."

"I can't."

"You are protected. Your body wants me." He pulled her hard against him. "My body wants you."

"But my heart doesn't want you."

He reacted immediately. He stepped back as if burned. "Your heart?"

"It's just occurred to me that when I next make love, I want it to be with someone who wants only me. Someone who hasn't had a thousand women."

Her words hit him like small daggers thrown from close quarters. *A thousand women.* "Is that what you think of me?"

"I have only to look at you to know every woman in Tolemac has probably been panting after you since you were old enough to have a wet dream. And I'm sure you didn't turn too many of them away."

"And how many men have you had with your protected arm?"

"Two, if it's any of your business. R. Walter and Bob. I loved them both—with all my soul." *And I lost them both.* She closed her cloak and knotted her hands in the rough wool. "What do *you* desire, Vad? Just a quick tumble here, with Ardra only a few feet away? Well, that's not the way I want it."

Without a backward glance at her, he spun away. The icy wind might scour his skin raw, but her words harrowed his spirit.

What had possessed him to embrace her? To even consider making love to her?

And how could he tell her how empty it was to lie with a woman who could not see beyond his face and form? Who cared nothing for the man inside, did not care if his heart was good or evil—was quite willing to excuse anything for what he might offer.

How many women had he lain with in his short life? Too many to feel comfortable admitting the number. Too few who cared for him beyond the few moments he granted them the right to touch him, slide their hands over his body, draw from him that blissful spasm of ecstasy. The emptiness had driven him to make a vow that he would not lie with a woman unless she was to be his lifemate.

In the space of one day, he had cast aside his vow as if it had no meaning. The hypnoflora was no excuse. He had wanted Gwen from the moment he had seen her on the ice fields.

What was it she desired? A mating with a man who offered his heart.

And what was it *he* desired?

Why had he withheld himself from so many women for so long and then taken the first opportunity to lie with her? A woman who held him in contempt? A woman who demanded he work for her every kind word?

The wind whipped the water to a whitecapped froth. The purple cloud-covered sky illuminated nothing—including his inner turmoil. "I must see my awareness master," he said to the wind. He touched the jeweled dagger at his hip.

The map.

The map inside would free him from suspicion, reinstate his respect.

He knew now how to answer her. He desired one thing and one thing only. It was not a woman. It was not that hot, quick twist of the guts one received with the pleasure of lovemaking. No. He desired one thing only—the return of his honor.

He would present the map, face the perfidy of the council, and show himself above it. Ancestors or not, he would make his own name, than lifemate with a woman whose lineage was a prized jewel. He could think of several. And as Gwen had said, what woman wouldn't want him?

His face assured his success with whichever woman he chose. Other skills would see she spent her moments in his bed well contented, full with child at each conjunction.

When Gwen could finally face him, and no longer resist the scent of the meat he was cooking, she returned. That they were waiting for her was obvious. They had eaten and were sitting idly by the boat. She ate quickly, licked her fingers, and sighed. "What was that?"

"Eel," Ardra said.

"Uh . . . never mind." In Gwen's estimation, an eel was a leech grown to mutant size. "Next time can you tell me what the meal is before I eat it?" she asked Vad.

He shrugged but didn't respond.

"We must be on our way," Ardra said as she settled herself like a queen in the bow.

Gwen took her place again and Vad cast off. Her insides churned with uncertainty at his silence. When he helped her hoist the sail, she took the opportunity to speak.

"Vad? I'm so sorry. I didn't mean to insult you. I don't know why I said those things. I guess I didn't want to admit I was just like—"

"All the other women I have had?" he said, acid dripping from his words.

She secured the sail. "No woman likes to think she's just another conquest."

"Then keep your distance . . . or you will be."

Chapter Fourteen

"I know how we can get past the guards," Gwen said as they moved into the center of the river. Vad and Ardra ignored her. "Okay. I'll just shut up and sail the boat."

A few miles later, she tried again. "I have an idea." When they ignored her, she fell into a state of irritation. She started humming.

Vad swung abruptly around. He'd been honing his knives for the past few miles. "What are you singing?"

"A song from a Disney movie."

A fleeting look of consternation crossed his face. " 'When you wish upon a star . . .' "

"That's it. You remember."

"What is it you remember?" Ardra asked, her own head tipped in question.

"Nothing," Vad snapped.

"Vad. If you remember something, you can't just ignore—"

"It is impossible to ignore you. You are like this festering wound on my arm. You are the drip of water from a spigot: you are—"

"I get it." She took a deep breath, then softened her tone. Maybe his arm really did hurt. "Do you think your wound's festering?"

"Aye," Ardra piped up. "I must get a potion from the healer once we are in the fortress." She pointed.

Gwen followed the direction Ardra indicated. She swallowed. Her stomach danced. A huge edifice seemed to hang from the black cliffs. It loomed over the horizon like a dark castle harboring bloodsucking vampires. Behind it loomed even larger jagged mountains. But it was the sight of Vad's arm as Ardra checked his wound that filled Gwen with alarm.

There were no telltale red streaks running up his arm, but the wound looked terrible. "Hold the tiller, Ardra," she said. As Ardra took her place, she admonished her firmly, "Don't change anything. Just hold her steady."

"This looks bad, Vad." Gwen pressed the puffy area around his wound. "No wonder you're so grumpy. Does it hurt much?"

"A warrior is trained to ignore bodily discomfort."

She probed around the wound. Then her eyes fell on the knife strapped to his hip. Alarm turned to stomach-churning dread. The handle was dull, with a grayish tinge.

She dipped his binding in the water and wiped some of the noxious ooze away. "You're probably at the sixth level of awareness, aren't you?" she said absently.

"Seventh." Despite his assurance that he was trained to ignore discomfort, she felt the tensing of his muscles beneath her hands.

"Hold still," she said, and touched his forehead with the back of her hand. He was cool. The heat that zinged through her each time they made contact was gone. "You don't feel feverish, but we should do something about your arm. Soon."

" 'Tis unimportant." He jerked from her touch. "We have more urgent matters to attend to. Such as entering the fortress."

"I think I can get us past the guards," Gwen said. "If we don't get there soon, this arm will be useless; you'll be useless to the maidens."

He grunted. "Ardra's healer will have a potion for the wound, but as you say, we will not be able to obtain it if we do not get past the guards. What is your plan?"

"Oh, it's pretty simple, really. I used to sneak out at night to walk on the beach. My mother and father never knew a thing. I used to stuff my bed to look like someone was sleeping there. If they peeked into my room, it looked like I was snuggled down in the covers—safe and sound.

"I thought we could use the same ruse. We can masquerade as Ardra's men. There are two of us, right? Besides Ardra, I mean. Well, she left with three men. We have plenty of extra clothes, and if we stuff them with furs and arrange them like a sleeping man, we could pretend it's one of her men—say he's wounded, sick, or just say nothing unless the guards ask."

" 'Tis a most wonderful idea," Ardra said.

"Vad can grease up his hair with some of the stuff he saved from his less than marvelous eel meal, and I can pretend to be Blind Eye. Don't you think I could pass for him if I'm sitting at the tiller, Ardra? Vad's the only oversize one here, and he can . . . I don't know, kneel in the bow, scrunch down and tuck his legs under the dummy."

The grin that lit Vad's face almost knocked her backward. He hoarded his smiles. The one he directed at her now was as powerful as the sun, as potent as straight Scotch to an alcoholic. Womankind had no chance near Vad with a smile on his face.

"What do you think, Vad?" Ardra asked.

"I think the idea as marvelous as my eels."

The boat drifted a bit as Gwen maneuvered it into the narrow cut that rushed to the deep labyrinth beneath the fortress. The river wound away from them and off to the front of the fortress. The rock base on which the fortress crouched was black, thick with lichens, encrusted at the water's edge with tiny gray barnaclelike animals, and it all looked even more forbidding up close than at a distance.

Arrow slits seemed to provide the only openings in the sheer rock walls of the fortress.

The Fortress of Ravens.

It looked deserted, brooding, aptly named.

A cloud of blackbirds lifted from the high walls as their boat skimmed along with the tide. The flock circled, screaming, then soared off toward a distant expanse of white.

"Great," Gwen muttered. "Birds of ill omen. What's that?" She pointed to a glaring white plain that lay snuggled in the vee between two high mountains dwarfing the fortress.

"The ice fields," Vad said.

It looked like ants were crawling along the sheer face of the ice wall. "Are those people climbing it?"

"Aye, they are cutting the ice. If you could see the base, you would see the wagons that will transport the ice to Tolemac. You would also see the necessary military escort."

"You were in charge of those escorts, weren't you?" Gwen asked.

He nodded and rolled his tunic down over his wounded arm. "It was an honor to be trusted with such a mission. I commanded men from each chiefdom and was entrusted to bring the ice back without incident. Under my care, no man lost his life, and no chip of ice arrived melted."

"Then you must know the fortress if you guarded the ice shipments." Gwen said. Ardra stuffed clothing with the furs, tugging and pulling the garments into a credible humanlike shape.

Vad shook his head. "Never did we have contact with the Selaw, save to direct them in the filling of the wagons. It was forbidden."

"Why?" As she asked, rain started. It came without warning, pelting them with stinging drops. Ardra and Vad pulled a fur over their heads. She remained face to the elements, the boat demanding all her attention.

"This rain is a blessing," Vad called above the hiss of rain on the river's surface. "It will not look suspicious that we hide beneath the furs."

"Be careful of your hair, else this will wash off." Ardra pursed her lips and wrinkled her nose as she dipped her fingers into the eel grease Vad had saved and wiped it through his hair.

Gwen thought that with dirty hair, Vad looked almost evil, if you saw him from his scarred side. She shivered—and not from the rain dripping down the back of her neck. She also realized he hadn't answered her question concerning the Selaw.

The sky went night dark with the driving rain. A swirl of purple-edged clouds scudded along with the harsh sweep of wind. Ardra seemed to shrink into the fur lining of her hood. Her confident manner had disappeared.

Gwen wanted to offer some encouragement, but knew her words would be whipped away. She held her breath and concentrated on her sailing. The rocky channel narrowed so that little more than an oar's distance stood between them and the walls on each side. The sail flapped as the wind died.

"They should call it the Fortress of Maidens," she muttered. "They haven't a chance—and neither have we."

Vad's hair was clumped in greasy hanks. She could smell him from her place in the stern. "You've never looked better," she quipped to keep her own spirits up.

He grinned and winked, then pulled a fur forward. His face disappeared in shadow.

She scrambled about, lowering the sail, securing it, letting the tide take them forward, using only an occasional push of an oar to steer them.

They bumped on the rocky wall, scraped along for a few feet, and rounded a sharp curve. A hewed rock entrance to the cliff base faced them. A creneallated ledge ran across it. In the openings stood two men, bows drawn, arrows pointed right at them.

"It is Ardra," Ardra called. She stood in the bow, lowered her hood, and shook out her hair. She made a quick gesture with her hand to where Gwen plied an oar to keep them from splintering against the rocks, and to Vad, who hunched by the fake Selaw man.

"You were expected days ago," called one man. Neither lowered their bows.

"Aye. We lost our way in a side stream and needed to backtrack. 'Tis lucky we found our way at all." There was a slight tremor in Ardra's voice. Gwen crossed her fingers.

One archer gestured them closer. Water sheeted down from the lip of rock over his head. Despite the rain, his arrow was clearly aimed at the center of Ardra's chest. "You will need to light your way." He lowered his bow. Setting it aside, he tossed down a rush torch and a small pouch. "I am sorry; it is very wet."

"You would do well to take better care next time."

Gwen stiffened at Ardra's complaint, then realized that for the woman in charge, making such a complaint would not be unusual.

The man bowed and took up his weapon.

Gwen felt as if the archer's eyes were burning holes into her back as she shoved the boat along with the oar. They entered a huge maw of blackness—and rapids.

Like an amusement-park ride, the boat rushed through the opening. Gwen swallowed a scream as the boat smashed against the rock wall, bounced off, and was swept inside.

Blackness enveloped them. A hand touched hers—Vad's. She clutched it—hard. They were being pulled along with the tide, with no steering, no ability to stop. A loud roar of water sounded ahead. A waterfall? Gwen's insides churned. She pictured them going over the falls, smashing in a pile of splintered wood and bone. Only Vad's hand reassured her.

Without warning, the boat stopped short. They were thrown forward into a heap of arms and legs in the bottom of the boat. Vad's hair whipped across her mouth.

"Yuk." She spat out the eel grease caught on her tongue.

"Stay where you are. That was a most terrible docking," Ardra said. Gwen stifled a retort about warnings. She could not identify the sounds coming from the bow, but when a smoky light gleamed out from where Ardra stood, she realized it was the sound of flint striking stone.

The cavern was so dark, the scant light of Ardra's torch made her feel as if they were in a tiny oasis and all about them was a desert of blackness.

"There," Ardra said, raising the torch and pointing at the set of slimy-looking steps cut into the rocky wall and leading to a long, flat landing.

Vad tied up the boat to a gleaming brass ring—a sign that the docking site was well tended despite the slippery steps—then he climbed out, turned, and assisted first Ardra and then Gwen from the boat. Gwen wanted to leap back into it and somehow leave this dark, moldy cavern.

"I know many rooms in the grotto that are not known to anyone save my father. He is far too occupied, too ill at heart, to be searching about down here."

"Don't you think you should make an appearance first? What if the guards mention you've arrived, but your father hasn't seen you yet?"

Vad agreed.

"I will at least take you to a safe spot to await my return. A warm place where you may bathe in one of the old springs." Ardra held the smoky torch aloft and marched forward. With the greasy smoke and dripping walls, Gwen felt almost smothered.

Within moments, Vad felt lost. They had turned and twisted through the underground caves until he did not know if he was facing in the direction of the sunrising or not.

Each step away from the boat reminded him quite sharply that he hated dark places. Something wet dripped on his neck. He almost cried out, but stifled the sound in time.

Finally, when he wanted to turn and run back, Ardra halted. She lifted the torch. A sheer wall faced them. Water ran down it in small rivulets.

"A dead end. Are we lost?" Gwen asked.

Lost. He could not be lost in this torturous place.

Chapter Fifteen

"No, we are not lost." Ardra gave a soft laugh. "I wish I could bring Narfrom here, though, and lose him."

Gwen looked from Ardra to Vad. He shifted the bows and settled his long knife lower on his hip. Her gaze followed the movement. "Vad, Ardra. Look." Gwen grabbed Vad's forearm, and he groaned at the contact with his wound. "Oh, I'm so sorry. I didn't mean to hurt you, but look."

She gestured Ardra near with the torch. The hilt of Vad's knife was almost gray. "The knife handle, it's losing its color. You're ill. Your arm must be much worse than it looks. You can't do this. Let someone else rescue the maidens."

Ardra touched the tip of her finger to the knife handle. "It is the light, or your imagination, Gwen."

"No, I'm right. I saw the knife in Ocean City, long before you did. It's losing its color. Come on, Vad, tell her I'm right. You're the one who said you can tell the wearer's health by the stone's color, didn't you? Well, it's changed! Why deny it?"

"And if it is changing? I feel quite capable."

"Really? How's your sword arm?"

"I have no sword!" There was a tightness about his eyes, a pain she knew ran deep.

"Can you draw a bow?"

"Well enough."

A burst of fear churned in Gwen's stomach. "Vad, I'm afraid. Can't we think of some alternative to direct confrontation?"

Vad shook his head. "We must do whatever is necessary."

Ardra drew near. The reeking smoke from her torch filled the air with its pungent odor. "You are truly a man of honor, Vad, not to abandon us. A man of great kindness." She dropped into a deep curtsy.

Gwen said. "What if you went to the council and reported what Narfrom has done, revealed the kidnapping plot. Won't the councilors look more favorably on you if you not only give them the dagger and map, but also Narfrom's plot?"

Vad and Ardra exchanged glances.

"Okay." Gwen bit out the word. Her head was beginning to pound. "What's going on? What did I miss?"

"You may say you know Tolemac," Vad said, "but you are sadly lacking in an understanding of the rites of punishment and retribution. First, if we report the kidnapping, each councilor whose daughter was taken becomes suspect from that moment on. They might lose their positions, forfeit two, possibly three of their arm rings—"

Gwen interrupted him. "Are you saying that a little arm jewelry is more important than the safety of a daughter?"

Ardra gasped. "Arm rings are not jewelry," she cried. "They mark one's place, separate the outcasts from those who are permitted to walk among good society."

"It is as Ardra says. In addition, if I do as you ask, Gwen, Ruonail will be hunted down along with Narfrom, and when caught, as he surely will be, his head will be severed from his body and piked on the fortress wall for all to see and revile."

Within the shadows of her white hood, Ardra's face looked ivory pale. Her lips trembled.

"I'm so sorry," Gwen said. Her stomach churned a bit at the grisly image Vad painted.

"We will do as we planned." Vad swept an arm out for Ardra to continue leading them forward.

"What did 'we' plan?" Gwen looked from Vad's face to Ardra's. Neither spoke. Whatever their plans, she was not privy to them. "Let me guess. You two have decided to solve this little maiden problem quietly so no one knows of anyone's treachery. Vad returns the maidens safely, and the councilors won't say a word because it would cause them shame and the loss of their arm rings. Ruonail isn't going to complain or his crime is revealed. The only wild card is Narfrom."

Gwen watched Vad and Ardra communicate with another silent glance. She felt like the proverbial third wheel. She also felt a chill deep within her that had nothing to do with ancient stone or vast fields of ice. "You have to listen to me." She grabbed Vad's belt and hauled him around until he was facing her. "I have this terrible feeling, deep inside here." She touched her chest. "I just know the changing color of your knife means something awful is going to happen. We have to leave—now."

Ardra wrung her hands. "I beg of you, Vad. Do not pay her any heed. I . . . the maidens need you."

His expression softened at Ardra's words, and he clasped her hands to still their distraught motions. "Be at peace. I have pledged to do my best to save the maidens."

Ardra turned to Gwen. "Will you help us free the maidens and prove that Narfrom has enchanted my father? If we can prove such a thing, then—"

"Wait," Gwen said. "First we were just going to rescue these girls. Now we're proving that Narfrom enchanted your father? That wasn't in the bargain." Vad shifted his bows from his injured arm to the uninjured one. "I see. So you two didn't feel you had to consult me?"

"A slave?" Ardra said.

Gwen felt the heat rush into her face. *Useless one moment, unconsulted the next.* "I am not a slave!"

Vad hoisted the two bows higher on his shoulder. "There is no slavery beyond the ice fields, Ardra." But Vad's rebuke was mildly spoken, said almost in an unthinking, automatic manner.

"So let me understand this." Gwen could not let it go. "You two were making decisions that involved life-and-death situations and didn't feel you needed to include me." She spoke to both of them, but looked only at Vad.

He didn't speak. His gaze met hers squarely.

"It's a trust issue, isn't it? You don't trust me."

"You withheld the dagger."

She wanted to howl at the unfairness of it. "I didn't know you were being serious. How could I have known Tolemac really existed? It was just a game to me."

He dropped his bundles and clamped his hands on her shoulders. "This is not Ocean City. Peace or not, there is little love lost between Tolemac and the Selaw. Here, without arm rings, you are a slave. If Ardra's men had killed me and taken you, they'd have used you until they were sated." Ardra made a mew of protest. "Say nothing, Ardra; she must understand her place here." He returned his attention to Gwen. His intent blue gaze held her frozen in place. "You know I speak the truth. Wherever those men were bound, if you had slowed them down, they would have killed you, but more likely they would have seen what is apparent for all to see—a lush woman worth a hefty purse of gold at the slave sales. If you protested your fate too loudly, they'd have cut out your tongue. To mark you as sold they would have carved an *X* on your breast. A man can tell how many exchanges a slave has had by those scars. The purity of your skin would have made your value immense."

She trembled against his hands.

"Tis not a game you are playing."

Tears burned in her eyes. A huge lump that felt like undigested taffy filled her throat. The picture he painted was as cold as the ice outside. Yet it was not the prospect of some man's mistreatment of her that hurt. It was his lack of trust.

Abruptly Vad released her and shouldered his bows once again. "It is time to move forward. Go with us, or not. Choose."

"Come," Ardra said, raising her torch and hastily lifting the latch on an arched wooden door strapped in iron.

In silence, they passed through, Gwen last. Behind her, Ardra closed the door with a solid clunk of metal that seemed like a death knell to Gwen.

Vad did not trust her, had not consulted her on his plans, and worse, she had slept with him. Tears ran down her cheeks, and she impatiently swiped them away with the back of her sleeve. *Think only about those seven girls,* she chastised herself. *You don't want a man's . . . what? Trust? Respect? Love?*

Angry as she was, she found herself checking the handle of his knife where it rested against his side. Was it her imagination that the color had dulled? Was she just looking for excuses to avoid this confrontation with Ruonail?

She didn't know what it was she wanted—or thought—anymore. But she did know what she didn't want—her heart broken. "Funny," she whispered to herself, "this feels oddly like heartache."

* * *

Vad felt sweat trickle down the center of his back. The massive stone fortress above them seemed to press down on him. For a few yards there was nothing save walls of solid rock—close, solid rock. Then another arched wooden door, built for men much shorter than he, was before them. Although smaller than the first door, it had huge straps with iron bolts and a bar. Ardra lifted it and pulled open the door. Another corridor stretched before them, lit with torches in iron brackets, obviously not a secret place. An eddy of cold, musty air twisted about his legs.

He could hear the whisper of Gwen's soft leather boots behind him. Regret at her misery could not color his decisions. He certainly regretted telling her of the stone's ability to predict one's health. The stone was changed. Each time he honed the edge of the knife, he saw how the tones were subtly altering. Perhaps Ardra's healer would have what he needed to treat his wound, but if not, he must push past the pain as he must push past Gwen's objections. Once committed to Ardra's aid, he could not allow womanly feelings or emotions to influence him.

From the moment of his being found abandoned on Nilrem's Hart Fell as a child, he'd been taught one thing only—to be a warrior. A man devoted, heart and soul, to honor.

Now, faced with his own disgrace, he knew redemption could come only if he proved himself worthy again. But that proof must wait until the maidens were rescued. Truly women were a constant trial—from those of only eight conjunctions to those who had lifemated.

Ardra turned and addressed them in a hesitant manner. He must reassure her that he intended to help her in any way he could. Gwen's words had undermined Ardra's stately confidence.

"Here," Ardra said, "we begin to make our journey in

secret. There are many doors in the caves. Some are known, such as this one, and will lead you straight into the upper reaches of the fortress. Follow me." She led the way along the stone corridor, pointing left and right to doors as she passed them. "Some open to a wall of rock, some to twisting corridors that go to blank walls, other caverns, or beautiful grottoes."

"Why aren't there any guards?" Gwen asked.

"Guards are unnecessary," Ardra patiently explained. "If you climb any steps, enter any room in the fortress, there are guards aplenty. Why have them stand in a cold place, bored and alone?"

"Because someone might kidnap you and coerce you to take them into the fortress? Say two people disguised as Blind Eye and Greasy Hair?" Gwen suggested.

Ardra smiled. "I gave the men a signal. You need not know it. It is a secret sign, and if I had not given it, you would be dead."

"I see," Gwen said, but Vad doubted she did. Still, he thought it better she ask questions when in doubt than make a blunder later.

After several moments of heavy silence, Ardra continued. "Once, in ancient times, men and women worshiped at the hot springs that flow from the earth beneath the fortress. It was a privilege to bathe in the healing waters. Now no one believes in the ancient gods or the water's power, so only my father and I know the ways of the labyrinth."

"Are the waters still here?" Gwen asked. At Ardra's nod, she continued. "Maybe Vad could bathe his arm." She spoke without her usual confidence, almost hesitantly, he thought. Perhaps she feared being spurned again.

"If it will offer you some measure of comfort, I will do so," he said. Then he became aware of a low, continuous rumble in the distance. It penetrated the rough stone walls. He thought of a herd of dragons, thundering to annihilate them. He liked a nest of dragons as little as he liked a dark place.

"What's that noise?" Gwen gave voice to his thoughts.

"The Eternal Falls," Ardra said. "They spring from the very rock and disappear into a bottomless pit."

"Great. A bottomless pit. Is that where you cast your worthless slaves?"

Vad gave a quick shake of the head when Ardra would have issued a reprimand. He thought it best to ignore Gwen's mutterings. He recognized the sharp words as her way of dealing with fear or disappointment.

From then on, the thunder of the falls grew louder as they paced wordlessly along corridors and through doors, twisting and turning in a dizzying maze.

The cavern in which Ardra finally stopped was as different from the fortress entrance as night was from day. It contained four identical doors. "Pick a door," Ardra said, a touch of amusement in her voice.

Gwen pointed to the second door. Ardra swung it open to reveal a blank stone wall. Again and again, Gwen pointed. Each time the door revealed the same stark stone.

"What's the trick?" he asked. "We are tired and do not need a puzzle to solve."

"Gee, your awareness training must be wearing off. You're getting testy," Gwen said.

"Forgive me. I did not mean to trifle with you. Gwen chose well the first time." Ardra opened the second door very slowly this time. As she did so, the stone wall behind it angled toward them. He ran his hand over it. It was simply an inner door with a thin layer of stone attached to it. He thought the ruse might not bear close scrutiny, but was effective for a quick look.

Ardra interrupted his thoughts. "Each door has the same inner door faced with stone, but the others lead to blank walls." She lifted her torch after securing the door, and they trudged after her into another twisting corridor, this one sloping downward.

"Does this journey have an end?" he asked, then gasped. The corridor opened into a large, circular cavern. In the light of Ardra's waning torch, he saw a many-colored room of ice. No, not ice. Sheer, almost transparent stone. Quickly Ardra moved about the cavern, touching her torch to others in brackets on the wall.

The rocky walls were striated in the tones of the Tolemac sky, sacred stones, and ice. Dripstones in the same colors stood about a large pool of steaming lavender water like sentries guarding a treasure. A vague scent of moss and age came to him. A memory teased at the periphery of his consciousness—another pool, sand between his toes—but Ardra's words sent it slipping away.

"You will find steps cut into the side of the pool, just here." Ardra indicated a spot where centuries of feet had worn a path to the edge of the water. "It is not very deep, but the bottom is smooth and sandy, so avail yourselves of it without fear. 'Tis said that in ancient times spirits abided here. The stones—the blue-green, the lavender—are sacred and impart their properties to the waters. Perhaps if you bathe your arm, it will be cured."

The pool enticed him. The skin of his face and neck crawled with the noxious eel grease.

"I will find clean clothes for us all, and see my father, so take this time to bathe."

Vad dropped his load of arrows and furs to the ground. Gwen knelt at the pool's edge and ran a hand back and forth in the steaming water. The sight of her well-cushioned bottom clad in the tight men's breeches made him feel as if a fever had gained control of him again, but it had nothing to do with suppurating sores.

With a conscious effort, he looked away and sat on a large boulder. "Concentrate on locating the maidens," he said. "Discover where they are being held. Ascertain the manner in which they are guarded and by whom. Who has access to them? How are they fed? If you can secure clothing for Gwen, she might be able to pass as a serving boy and help you in some way."

"Serving boy? Am I trustworthy enough for such a position?" Gwen jerked around to look at him.

"If you feel a desire to join Narfrom and Ruonail in their endeavors, then do so. But count the cost first."

She walked right up to him, her nose inches from his. "Do you think, for even a moment, that I might join them? Didn't I try to help you fight Enec? Wasn't I proving my loyalty then?"

"Any woman would oppose such men. They would have abused you—"

"Nay." Ardra rushed forward. "Enec would never do such a thing. He must have believed me in danger."

Vad could not contend with their roiling emotions. His energy was drained as dry as a leaking cask.

"You have to choose, Vad," Gwen said. Her earnest little face looked up at him and he thought of how he'd held her hand and brought her here—into danger. "Either you trust me," she said, "or you don't. I'm not going to rescue maidens for a man who doesn't trust me."

Ardra gasped. "You are impertinent."

Vad silenced her with a sharp slash of his hand. "Gwen has a right to an answer. I can offer provisional trust."

"Provisional? What's that supposed to mean?" Gwen asked.

"It means I have only one act of dishonor on which to base your character. Just as I have but one act of valor to weigh in the balance. What you do from this moment on will tip the scales—one way or the other."

"Great. And if I make a mistake and something goes wrong? I don't know your world, your customs. What if—"

He placed a weary hand on her shoulder. "There are no answers to 'what if' questions. Do your best."

To end the confrontation, he turned his back to them both and spread the furs on the cavern floor. He laid out the arrows, inspecting their tips. "I will sleep here tonight, you and Ardra above. Can it be done?"

"I shall send her to the kitchen," Ardra said. "She will not raise any curiosity there; it is filled with misfits. One more will not be noticed. If she binds her breasts, she can work alongside the men and listen to the gossip!" Ardra clapped her hands excitedly. "The worst of the gossips is in the kitchen."

"Vad?" Gwen said.

"What Ardra suggests makes great sense. And, Ardra, when you place her there, gather these few herbs for me. Perhaps I can cook up something particularly noxious. A potion to call everyone to chamber pots—at the same time." He grinned and took a piece of charcoal from a disused fire circle. Using the smooth side of a fur, he scratched some words. "Think of something everyone might eat or drink. Warriors fighting over chamber pots are not much of a threat." He offered her the fur. "This is what I need—no substitutes."

She read the list and then bit her lip. "What excuse have I to gather herbs in the kitchen?"

"Deep regret that you have shirked your duties until this day." His sharp words silenced any further protest Ardra might have had for visiting her own kitchen.

When Ardra had committed his list to memory, she bowed to Vad and turned away. To his relief, Gwen followed.

Reluctantly Gwen trailed Ardra into the belly of the fortress, her mind in turmoil. There would be a thousand opportunities to slip up. Vad's lack of trust was like a raw wound, chafed by his every word.

"What if I need to find my way back?" Gwen asked. Two turns and she felt lost, disoriented.

Ardra halted and turned to face Gwen. She lifted the torch. "You will never find your way to him. He must wait for us, and you must wait for me to guide you to him."

Gwen sighed.

"You are enamored of him, are you not?"

"What?" Gwen felt her face heat. "Enamored? Of someone who distrusts me?"

"You had congress with him, did you not? And do not deny it. I am not stupid."

"It—it was the hypnoflora. It . . . we were foolish."

With a nod, Ardra turned and continued along the stone path. It rose in a gentle incline. "Aye. 'Tis foolishness to lie with someone who is not your own kind. You were angry with me when I said you were a slave, and as I think on it, a slave would not need the nature of such things explained."

"Then explain it. I'm listening."

"He cannot mate with you, nor you with him. Such congress leads to naught but heartbreak." Ardra halted again before a wooden door, no different from any of the others. "You are not from here. I do not know these lands beyond the ice fields, but I do know there are a few rare folk who bear Tolemac blue eyes and Selaw bones. Their life is hard—very. They fit nowhere." She tapped her upper arm, and Gwen knew she was indicating her arm rings. "A misfit has no hope of status. Should you bear Vad a child, that child would suffer greatly."

A child. What a different set of emotions she'd be experiencing if she had such a worry. "If that's all that concerns you, then rest easy. I'm barren." It seemed the easiest explanation.

Ardra's face softened. "I am sorry for you, but still, I must offer you a warning: Guard your heart. A man of such perfection, such beauty, will never remain with one woman long—barren or not. Why should he, when he may have whomever he desires?"

Whomever he desires. Ardra was right. Why would Vad want her except when under some influence like hypnoflora? After all, he didn't even trust her.

Gwen slept poorly in an alcove off the kitchen, with Vad somewhere unreachable in the caverns below, and Ardra equally inaccessible, somewhere above. But upon waking she found she fit in with the kitchen workers very well. She was just another misfit—smaller than most, weaker than several, uglier than just about everyone, as the loud gossip made sure she understood; still, she was a pair of hands and a willing worker.

Status among the kitchen folk was based on that willingness. Men, Gwen now among them, carried wood to keep the fires beneath great boiling caldrons of water burning and hauled buckets of fresh water to the cooks.

It was backbreaking, mindless, hot work. Her hair was plastered to her head; her back and hands ached. At least she'd been given a pair of gauntlets to wear when handling hot pots and rough wood. But, to give Ardra credit, the place was a hotbed of gossip and innuendo—or it was once everyone got over Ardra's presence in their world. Their mistress puttered about the hanging herbs, asking questions, taking samples. Gwen thought she took more than Vad had requested to conceal what he wanted.

Once Ardra left, no one cared who spoke or what they spoke about—including her. Names whizzed about her, and Gwen soaked up information like her linen shirt soaked up sweat.

There was a general feeling of unease about the workers. It was based on the ominous clouds forming overhead. They bemoaned the lighting of torches in the daylight hours and repeated legends of dark times from the past.

Several women, those with less taxing duties than Gwen's, wore a single arm ring. Most of the men did as well. One woman, who did not, bent forward to feed small sticks beneath a caldron, and her gown fell forward. Gwen saw two white scars on her breast—each clearly an *X*.

At that moment, Gwen wanted to scream. The room was too hot, the air too thick, the future too frightening. This was not a game. This was not the role she always played, that of the ice woman, a whirling, swirling tempest that saved lives, plucked the hero from danger, and froze enemies where they stood. No, this was a stark and frightening reality of wounded warriors, kidnapped daughters, and evil villains.

Then she heard a tidbit that chilled her bones. Two men were wagering that a certain hostage maiden would not be a virgin by the next sunrising. Narfrom, whom they all spoke of with suspicion, was enamored of the girl.

The heavy, rich odors of roasting meat, baking bread, and simmering wine suddenly sickened her. Her stomach flipped. She glanced around and saw a basket. Filling it with bread and cheese, she asked a small boy how to find Mistress Ardra. He merely stared at her, his bright amber cat's eyes gleaming, his light brown hair falling over his brow. She forced herself to repeat her request slowly, with the best British accent she could fake, and left out the contractions. He nodded once and dashed away.

Gwen tucked her small basket under one arm, then shifted it in front of her, as the men carried things, and followed the boy.

As they climbed worn stone steps the air grew cooler, the scent of food less heavy.

The boy led her to the family rooms. Here it was not

apparent that one was in a hulking, Dracula-style fortress. The family chambers had polished wooden floors, whitewashed walls, and decorated chimneypieces. Somewhere, far below in the bowels of the earth, Vad waited for them.

Ardra stood before a narrow slit of a window, the only sign that her home was not just her living quarters, but also a stronghold. "Place the basket there." She pointed, and Gwen did as bid.

"Wait," Ardra commanded as the boy gestured Gwen out. "I wish a word with this slave."

The boy scampered off. "At least he is one person who seems unaffected by ill omens," Gwen noted.

"Aye. He is a happy child, the son of one of my seamstresses, born of a Selaw warrior who fell in battle."

Another warning? A thick silence fell between them as Ardra added various items to the basket. Outside, men shouted as they worked. A wagon rumbled by on cobblestones, sounding a little like the thundering water below in the grotto.

"Your gown is lovely," Gwen said to break the silence.

Ardra hurried forward, flapping her hands in a gesture of silence. "A male slave would not remark on a woman's gown."

Her golden-yellow wool gown was the color of her eyes. A long silver chain, dotted with turquoise and amber, wrapped several times around her slim waist before falling nearly to the hem. Her hair was loose and rippled to her waist. She no longer wore the silver and turquoise necklace from Nilrem. She wore a large silver disk with a center stone of polished amber about her neck.

While Gwen told her the gossip she'd heard, Ardra rubbed the disk thoughtfully.

Finally she turned with a swish of skirts. "We must get to Vad. We must plan quickly. It is all worse than I had imagined. If Narfrom forces her, it means that, rescued or not, she will no longer be a maiden."

"No kidding."

"She will be cast out."

"What?" Gwen's sweaty garments felt chilly against her suddenly cold skin.

"Aye. A tainted maiden is worthless."

Chapter Sixteen

Gwen hurried after Ardra through the dark maze of stone corridors and wooden doors. Some of the paths they took felt vaguely familiar; others did not. She thought she recognized a few of the corridors, with their twisting veins of turquoise occasionally illuminated by Ardra's torch. They reminded her of the tunnels of an abandoned mine.

"We're going a different way," she said to Ardra as the scent of the cavern and its heated pool came to her.

"Aye, 'tis a shorter way. There are several paths to each destination." She opened a door on the cavern.

Vad looked as if he had not slept the night before or at all during the day. Nor had he used the steaming waters; his hair was still thick with eel grease. Although he looked exhausted, when they entered, his blades were instantly in his hands, glinting, ready. Gwen swallowed, remembering the death of Ardra's men.

"Your voices arrived first," he said, and sheathed his blades. "What brings you back so urgently?"

"You tell him," Gwen said. She peeled off the wool tunic she'd worn all day and flapped her sweaty linen shirt away from her body. There was a steamy atmosphere in the cavern, but occasional breezes and errant drafts kept it pleasant, unlike the kitchen, where the heat and steam probably never dissipated.

"It is grave news I bring you. Narfrom is enamored of one of the maidens. The eldest, daughter of Ranoc."

Gwen saw that Vad did not need further explanation. "Then we need to act without delay."

"It's not so easy," Gwen said.

"If 'twas easy, Ardra would rescue the damned maidens herself." He scowled at Gwen, as if she had some control over their situation.

"I'll forget you said that." Gwen placed the basket she carried on the floor. "Here is some bread and cheese, the herbs you wanted, and some other stuff."

"What other stuff?" He rooted about and nodded his appreciation of the spoons and a tiny caldron Ardra had packed. He grunted his approval of a rolled parchment containing a crudely drawn plan of the fortress.

"I have marked the chambers in which the maidens are being held," Ardra said. "They are together in chambers near my father's, guarded by four men, in shifts of two on and two off, as at the grotto entrance. One only, the youngest, is allowed to wander, and she has become somewhat of a pet of the household." Ardra took a deep breath. "The oldest maiden is here." She touched a mark, shaped like a tear, with the tip of her finger. " 'Tis a chamber between those of my father and Narfrom."

"What should we do?" Gwen asked. She rolled up her sleeves and propped her elbows next to the map. Vad came to her side, and his shoulder brushed hers as he leaned over the map. A zing of heat pulsed where they touched. She shifted over to give him more room—and to give herself peace.

Vad absently tapped the map with the tip of his dagger

as he spoke. "We have several choices. I can go above and demand Narfrom meet me in combat, with the maidens awarded to the victor."

"Nay!" Ardra cried.

"Or I could rescue the maidens as quickly as possible and let Ruonail settle Narfrom as he sees fit once the women are no longer in danger. Did you think of anything everyone in the fortress might eat or drink?"

"The mourning wine," Gwen said. "I saw some men bring up these huge casks to the kitchen." She spread her arms wide. "They said they needed so much because everyone would be drinking to the dead men."

"Dead men?" Vad rolled up the drawing.

"Enec"—Adra's voice broke on his name—"and my two guards."

Vad nodded.

"I had merely to tell my father of their treachery, that they tried to harm me, and he wanted their heads. When I said they were dead, he accepted it gladly. I told him I purchased a few slaves at the settlement to help manage the boat on the return journey, and he accepted that, too. He was distraught that I could not obtain Nilrem's aid. He still cannot sleep."

"And the guards at the grotto entrance?" he asked.

"They never asked who accompanied me, nor did they get a good look at us in the storm. It is a testament to my father's grave illness that he was so unconcerned about the loss of his men. He was quickly satisfied—and this from a man who relentlessly fought his way to the height of power here in Selaw."

"His reputation is well known." Vad's expression was grim. "When a warrior loses his fighting spirit, his day is done."

"Nay. Do not say such a thing. He will recover. You will rescue the maidens; Narfrom will leave."

"What are the funeral plans?" Vad began to pace about the steaming pool.

Ardra continued, although her voice was still low and her head bowed. "The men's belongings will be burned in a few hours, the ashes scattered on the ice. As is tradition, a mourning vigil will be held in the chapel when the moons rise."

"And before the prayers," Vad said with satisfaction, "the mourning wine will be drunk. Excellent."

"Why would anyone mourn men who betrayed you?" Gwen asked.

"It is traditional to offer comfort to their families, whether what they did was right or wrong. No wailing, no outward grieving will be allowed, however. And . . . my father plans to use the ritual as a means of chastising those who might stand against him."

Gwen perched herself on a flat boulder. "What if the maidens drink the wine? It won't hurt them, will it?"

He shook his head. "Some it will put quietly to sleep. Others . . . let us say there will be constant attendance at the chamber pots while the people of the fortress empty their bellies and bowels."

Ardra made a face.

"Our time of opportunity will be very short. Guard changes are timed. If one of you can taint the wine, there will be little resistance from the guards—or anyone else. For those who do not sleep, the misery will be acute, but short-lived. It is the child that troubles me."

Gwen nodded. "I thought she might be a problem, too, when Ardra described her to me. She's everywhere and nowhere at once. I think I saw her running around with a few other children near the kitchen. Does she have long blond hair—all tangled? And a blue gown with silver embroidery?"

"Aye, that would be Liah." Ardra said. "What shall we do about her?"

"One of you must locate this Liah and bring her into these underground rooms. Make an excuse to separate her from her companions that will not raise a fuss."

He began to lay out the items Ardra had gathered. "I shall greatly enjoy testing my strength against Narfrom's."

"He is hardly a match for one such as you," Ardra said with just a touch too much admiration. Maybe Ardra had warned her off because she was, herself, enamored of Vad.

He sketched a quick bow in acknowledgment of her compliment. "I will also expect you to keep your father from interfering."

"I have no power over my father!" Ardra looked from Vad to Gwen and back. "Do not expect so much."

Gwen could not help feeling compassion for her. She remembered trying to persuade her own father that he should be supporting her and not her sister when R. Walter had decamped. It was like talking to a brick wall. To this day her father still believed it was Gwen who should bend.

"I trust you to do your best," Vad said. "As I will do mine."

"Once I get you to the upper levels, how will you persuade the maidens to go with you?"

Vad merely arched a dirty brow. Ardra looked from him to Gwen and lifted her hands in silent question.

"I think what Vad's not saying is, What maiden wouldn't go with him?"

"Ah," Ardra said with a smile. "Of course. And you are so obviously from Tolemac."

Ardra reached into the bodice of her gown and pulled out a small pouch of soft tanned leather. "I have also brought some herbs from the healer. Shall I dress your wound for you?"

Vad shook his head.

Gwen rooted about in the basket for something to do, but Vad plucked a leather pouch from her hands. "You must not touch what you do not understand. Some of these leaves are easily bruised."

He carefully spread out the contents of the basket. Ardra sat on a few furs and watched him work. She had packed a mortar and pestle, the small caldron, and a stone flask of oil that Vad muttered happily over for several moments.

Last, the basket revealed a half dozen or so pottery bottles with wooden stoppers. "These will do well for adding the potion to the casks of wine," Ardra explained. "At Narfrom's insistence, the wine is the very best. All will wish a taste."

Gwen put a hand on his wrist. "Before you start concocting your potion, let me clean your wound."

"After this task." He shook her off, and she joined Ardra on the furs, trying to ignore what was obvious here in the brighter light of the cavern: his knife's stone handle had no more hints of blue or green. It was a solid, dull gray against the gleam of the gold wrapping it. And yet, as he ground leaves, sniffed, added oil, heated his little caldron as if the slightest change in temperature was important, she had to admit he looked hale and hearty, whatever his blade handle might predict. His exhaustion had dropped away as he worked. "It's unfair that he's not only good-looking, but also handy," Gwen whispered to Ardra.

"Is he not perfect?" Ardra whispered back. "Look at his feet."

"Huh?" Vad's feet were rather dirty from traipsing about the cavern barefoot.

"Have you ever seen such symmetry? Such bones?"

Gwen gave Ardra a long look. "There's nothing special about his feet. You don't have a foot fetish, do you?"

"Foot fetish? What is that?"

"Let's just say, do you ever feel an urge to collect shoes, sniff them, and so on?"

"Certainly not! I am merely noting a thing of beauty, worthy of preservation in marble or wood." Ardra tossed her head, and the mass of her golden mane slid from her shoulder. It was held back from her brow by a circlet of silver. Her tawny eyes gleamed catlike in the fire's glow. Gwen felt disheveled, and woefully missed her hair dryer.

Then a thought occurred to Gwen as she inspected the alabaster smoothness of Ardra's complexion; maybe Ardra was more comfortable raving about Vad's feet than his face. "Frankly, I think his face is far more worthy of sculpture than his feet," Gwen suggested. "They're just big and dirty."

"They are not big," Vad said as he hunkered down and sniffed a spoonful of his potion.

"His ears are big, too," Gwen quipped. Ardra fell into a paroxysm of giggles, and for the first time Gwen saw the happy, youthful girl she might be if not weighed down by the gravity of her father's situation.

Vad glared at Gwen, and she gave him a toothy smile as she leaned near Ardra to keep her words private this time. "You know, his nose is not so perfect either."

With great seriousness, Ardra studied Vad. "I see nothing to criticize about his nose," Ardra whispered back.

"Take another look. The bridge is too high."

Ardra ran a finger down her nose as if tracing the perfection of Vad's. "Nay. 'Tis exactly what his face requires."

"Okay, what about his hands? Too big, just like his feet."

"No, you go too far. How noble he is, how strong."

"How can you accuse me of liking him when you're in love with him yourself?" Gwen said under her breath.

Ardra shook her head, her hair flaring out in a golden bell about her shoulders. "I cannot love a Tolemac warrior. It is against all my teaching. I might admire his form, his honor as a warrior, but only a Selaw man can command my heart."

Gwen realized that maybe Vad hadn't captured her heart because Ardra was already in love—or had been. "Enec? What about him?" Gwen touched Ardra's tightly clenched hands.

She dropped her eyes and bit her lip. "He was . . . unworthy of my attentions. A mere bowman, of good family, but . . . he is dead now."

Gently, Gwen took Ardra's hand. "I lost my lifemate, you know." Ardra nodded and looked up. Tears spilled down her cheeks. "You will find another to love one day."

Ardra shook her head and impatiently wiped her cheeks with the back of her other hand.

Gwen squeezed her fingers. "Yes. You will. And I'm not making light of your feelings, or what mine were. He will always bring an ache to your heart, but you will find room in there for another one day. There's a saying we have in Ocean City: 'Time heals all wounds.' And it's true." The only answer Gwen received was a return squeeze of the hand. "Let's see what cooking boy is up to. He looks neglected." Gwen rose and tugged Ardra to her feet.

When they knelt at Vad's side, he glared at them. "Are you quite finished criticizing me?"

"Criticizing? Were we criticizing, Ardra?" She nudged Ardra, who raised a small smile. Tracks of tears still marred her cheeks.

"No, Vad. We were admiring your many . . . skills," Ardra said with great tact.

He grunted. "When I have saved your father, I will ask for your oath of secrecy that no man of Tolemac will learn what I have been doing here."

Ardra took up one of several spoons Vad had laid out in a neat row and stirred his concoction. "I shall swear now. No man will know you have done women's work."

"I think you're wasting a payback," Gwen said.

"Can't you think of a better reward? Pot of gold? Cask of jewels?"

Vad's and Ardra's eyes were equally round and incredulous. "Ask for payment for such aid?" he said. " 'Tis more important that I maintain my dignity."

"There's nothing undignified about cooking. In Ocean City, men cook all the time. Some of my world's finest cooks are men. What's the big deal?"

"Amusing. Next you will say women can be warriors." Ardra smiled, her spoon poised in midair.

"You bet, if they want. Everyone's equal—or at least we try to make sure everyone has equal chances, male or female."

"So I heard once from your friend, Maggie," Vad said. "I thought she was just making up tales to entertain or entice Kered."

"No, it's true. We're far from perfect and have a long way to go, but we try."

"Of course you have a long way to go," Ardra agreed. "You must trek the ice fields. 'Tis a very long way."

Vad arched a brow and grinned at Gwen over Ardra's bent head.

Somehow being on the same wavelength with him warmed her insides. "I wouldn't be too worried about the cooking thing, though. You seem to be cooking up your first failure. Whatever that mess is, it smells like the inside of your boots," Gwen said, wrinkling her nose.

"And when were you smelling my boots? Are you sure you do not have a foot fetish?" Vad's deep laughter sent a bolt of pleasure through her.

She could not help a smile and a little smugness that Ardra didn't get the joke.

"Go, Ardra," Vad said, giving a final stir to his caldron. "This needs to cook for several hours."

Ardra extended the medicinal pouch and Vad took it, opening the drawstring top and sniffing. He grunted a thank-you. Gwen turned to follow Ardra from the cavern.

"Gwen. Remain here."

"Why do you want me to stay?" Gwen hopped up onto the flat boulder and sat by the drawing when Ardra was gone.

"It is tempting fate for you to be too long above. Instead you may tell me all Ardra left out." He leaned next to her. His scarred cheek looked fairly well healed, but only the finest of plastic surgeons would be able to restore him to his original perfection. How smooth his skin was despite the rough beard, the grime from their journey. A temptation to touch his cheek nearly overcame her.

"Why don't we fix up your arm while we talk?" Gwen hopped off her seat. She didn't really want to be in such close proximity to him. Hypnoflora flashback must be responsible for these nearly uncontrollable urges she had toward him.

He rolled up his long sleeve. Gwen stifled a gasp. The wound was puffy and looked painful. "It's a miracle you can still move it. Doesn't it hurt?"

"I am trained—"

"Yeah, yeah. To withstand pain, eighth-level stuff." She shook her head.

"Seventh." He grinned and touched the tip of her nose in an unexpected gesture of playfulness.

"Oh . . . seventh . . . sure," she said, losing her train of thought.

"If you are intent on playing the healer, take one of the bowls over there and mix a paste of the herbs and water for after I bathe," Vad directed her.

She sensed he could do it himself, but was deliberately sending her from his side. Maybe he felt the same urges as she? *Not likely. Don't read too much into his smile or touch,* she warned herself. He had recovered from their lovemaking quite quickly.

As she mixed the paste, she forced herself to do as Vad had asked—tell him what Ardra had left out. "Ardra got me back here very quickly this time. Why didn't she take the shorter route when she brought us here?"

He shrugged. "What are you saying?"

"What I'm saying is that when she urgently needed to talk to you, her path was pretty direct, but last night it took forever to find this cavern. Why the subterfuge with us?"

"Subter . . . ?" he repeated.

"Subterfuge. Deceit, ploy? Aren't we supposed to be on the same side?"

"Perhaps it is just the caution all Selaw are bred to when dealing with strangers. They have been dealt a hard life and must often fight off marauders who want the ice."

"And there's a definite tension in the fortress. The gossips think there's going to be some huge storm that will flood all of Selaw, washing everyone into the river to drown. They say they've never seen such a gathering of darkness."

"Do not be afraid." He rose and offered her his hand.

She stared at his hand, the strong fingers that had caressed her skin, skimmed her lips, raised flames of desire. She entwined her fingers with his.

"Get a grip, girl," she muttered.

"Why don't you also make use of the pool?"

Gwen's skin itched, and the temptation was almost overwhelming. "I suppose we'd better make sure you're really cleaned up or the maidens won't be tempted to run off with you."

"No temptation, no rescue?" He smiled.

She couldn't help smiling back. "That's right. No temptation, no rescue . . . Is there something more I can do to help with the rescue?" she asked impulsively.

"Why?"

She looked up at him. "What do you mean?"

"Why would you help us?"

"I want this all over and done. I guess I want to go home."

He placed a gentle hand on her shoulder. "And how do you think you will go home?"

"The same way you traveled to Ocean City—I'll cross the ice fields."

His fingers tightened; his words were hard. "If 'twas so easy, men would be doing it daily. 'Tis why the council sent me for the map in the dagger and accused Kered of being a traitor for taking it. No man has attempted to cross the fields and ever returned."

"Maybe they just really loved Ocean City," she said softly, shaken by his vehement assurance that no man had survived the journey. Her voice squeaked a bit when she went on. "Does that mean you won't try to get me home?"

"When we have rescued the maidens and released Ruonail from Narfrom's power, you will find Ruonail grateful enough to grant us a reward. I shall ask him for an escort for you—to Nilrem. Suitably protected and provisioned, you should be able to remain at Nilrem's until he returns. He will know how to assist you."

"And what will you be doing while I'm backtracking?"

"Fulfilling my quest. Returning the dagger and the map, and, I hope, regaining my sword." He clenched his fist, the knuckles white. "It is all I want."

"What if it doesn't work out? What's the worst the council can do to you?"

The expression that flitted quickly across his face just as quickly disappeared, and she knew he was not going to tell her. He shrugged. "They will deprive me of status." The words were simple, but Gwen imagined it entailed much more than she could possibly understand.

"I need something to wear," she said, changing the subject.

"Try these garments." He swept a hand out to the bundles he'd carried from the Selaw settlement. "They will not fit me, so you should make use of them."

"I suppose." She sorted through the miscellany of clothing and found a linen tunic so soft, she had to resist rubbing her face on it. There was no way she could put it on over dirty skin. Sounds behind her told her Vad was shucking his clothing. For a moment she gritted her teeth against the vision of his beautiful body—and the temptation to turn around and admire it. A splash and a stifled oath made her turn.

He was scrubbing at his hair with sand he scooped from the bottom in huge handfuls and dunking his head.

She pulled off all her clothes except her long, rough linen overshirt. It came to her knees.

"There's soap in Ardra's basket," she said. "So why the sand?"

"It will remove most of the grease. Soap is too precious to waste on such a task."

She sat at the edge of the pool, and tucked her chin on her knees and her shirt about her feet.

What a simple pleasure it was to watch him. The torches bathed him in a golden glow. The beautiful colors of the nearly transparent stones reflected light and lent a gemlike atmosphere to the chamber.

He stood up. The water barely reached his waist.

"Yikes," she muttered. Water ran in silver trails down his back and moved in a wide vee behind him as he walked toward the steps. Every move he made was fluid and strong. A sigh filled her chest, but she stifled it. He was unreal, from another world, a distrustful world, cold and cruel. And wasn't a person shaped by his world? Maybe he was cold and cruel inside.

No, she wouldn't believe that. Somehow there was no cruelty etched on his face. Whatever fine lines he had about his eyes and mouth looked as if they were put there by laughter and smiles.

A sharp, vivid image came to her: Vad, his eyes closed, his body moving over and within her. Then he had opened his eyes, looked down on her, and smiled. A bright rush of flaming sensation deluged her. It had nothing to do with the joining of their bodies and everything to do with the joining of their . . . *What? Souls? Minds? Hearts?* She couldn't explain it, just instantly knew she would never feel cold in his arms.

And she wanted to feel his arms around her again, unaffected by the seductive soap. She wanted to touch her mouth to the pulse at his throat and know again pure, unrelieved passion.

The thought of being lost in such a swamp of caring as she remembered from her visions made her rise abruptly to her feet.

Every muscle of his body was sculpted like marble, and perfectly set off by this dazzling cavern of turquoise and lavender. She tried, but failed to look away as he washed his upper body. Hers was on fire. Thank heaven, he had his back to her. He started to climb out of the pool.

"Don't you have any modesty?" she asked, fanning her shirt to cool herself and looking away as he stood on one of the steps and soaped down the rest of his body.

"You have seen all I have to offer. And . . . you need not look," he said with amusement.

"I bet you say that to all the girls," she muttered.

"No," he said. "Most women are happy to look at me."

"Sure. Who wouldn't be? Your genes should be registered as a deadly weapon." *She* was sure shot through with knee-wobbling lust.

"Could you put that in words I understand?" He stepped back into the water and stood there, hands on hips, the water lapping dangerously low on his belly. His honed chest, long arms, and corrugated stomach were a feast to the eyes. The three arm rings on his well-developed biceps told her how far from her he was in this world.

A quick dunk in the pool would cool her off. She slipped into the water, fighting down the shirt as it billowed up around her chest.

No. She was not going to be cooling off. The water was blood warm. Soothing underground springs moved the water about her legs in an imitation of the gentlest of whirlpool baths. It stimulated as well.

A splash behind her made her jerk around. The cavern was empty.

"Vad?" she whispered, glancing right and left. A rush of water by her legs made her leap toward the side of the pool.

He rose in a fountain of water, like a pagan water deity.

His laughter echoed about the small space. "Frightened? What did you think it was? A water dragon?"

"W-w-water dragon?"

"Aye. Of course, they have not been seen in many generations. 'Tis said they disappeared when man began to ply the sea in wooden ships."

He made his way through the water to where she stood. To avoid his intent blue gaze, she dug her toes into the side, boosted herself out, and stomped to where the soap lay on the step.

She washed her face and hands.

"I bathed you that day in the Selaw cottage," he said, coming up behind her. She froze, conscious of their closeness, the memories of that day, his nakedness, her wet shirt plastered to her hips and bottom. "I bathed your hurts with the hypnoflora soap. Are you still marked as you were then?" He didn't wait for a reply. His hands encircled her waist, turned her to face him, and drew her off the steps into the water.

"I'm fine," she managed.

No, I'm not. I'm lost.

His hands were gentle as he turned her chin, inspected her cheeks. "I am responsible for all your hurts."

"Shhhh," she said.

Every feature of his face was familiar to her now, memorized. His gaze was beguiling. Somehow she felt as if he could see inside her and feel every sensation she felt. Without hesitation, she touched her fingertips to his lips. A shudder of need ran through her.

"Kiss me," she said.

His hands flexed on her waist. Without hesitation, she went into his embrace. Strength and heat—from the water, from his body—suffused her.

"Vad . . ." She skimmed his lips with hers. She ran her hands up his arms, along his water-beaded shoulders, into his thick hair. In return, his hands gently stroked her back, up and down, up and down, as mesmerizing as the most potent hypnoflora. "Each time we touch, this heat, it . . . it runs through me. Can you feel it?" she asked.

"Aye," he said against her lips, drawing her lower one between his teeth and biting gently. "It runs through me like a river of flames." He kissed down her chin, her throat, her shoulder, to her breast.

"Please, Vad, make love to me," she said in a gasp.

"So sweet," he murmured against her heated flesh. He tongued her through the cloth, dragging his teeth back and forth, back and forth, with agonizing slowness.

Every bone in his body felt molten-metal hot. Weak. Able to be bent, molded . . .

Her fingers slipped into his hair and held him. "I want everything, all the heat, all the flames, all of it," she whispered, giving voice to what his body craved.

He met her gaze and held it. Answering flashes of desire followed her touch, like lightning flickering within his body.

Deprivation, he thought. *It is only the deprivation of three conjunctions of celibacy.*

She touched her lips to his chest. He felt the stroke of her tongue.

And knew he was lost.

Chapter Seventeen

"We cannot," he said, and gently disentangled himself from her arms. Clumsily, with his body intent on passion, not flight, he climbed from the pool. Wanting to deal honestly with her, he dried himself off and pulled on his tunic to conceal from her his continued arousal. "I cannot grant your request."

Finally dressed, he turned to her. Her eyes were huge and luminous, just visible over the stone lip of the pool.

Nilrem's throat, he swore silently. She was going to weep. He had always had trouble resisting a woman's tears. He went down on one knee by her. Her garment billowed about her hips in shimmering white. "One night, three conjunctions ago, I realized—or Kered helped me realize, for he was as much teacher to me as brother—that the women who so craved a night of my attentions cared not for what was in here." He thumped his chest with a fist. "If I wanted to share what was on my mind, my troubles, my dreams, there were no listeners. Save Kered. He suggested that I had merely to choose my next partner more carefully, someone worthy, a woman who was an equal, someone willing to see beyond my face. Kered's words kept me awake throughout a very long night of soul searching. Do you ever search your soul in the dark?"

A tear ran down her cheek, but she bobbed her head in agreement. *Good, she might understand then.* He clenched his fist to prevent himself from wiping her tears away. "That night I vowed my next partner would be a Tolemac woman worthy of an honorable lifemating. A virgin. One of a lineage of pride."

"Well," she said with a hitch in her voice, "I'm certainly not a virgin."

"Aye. Nor a woman of my place."

Should he continue? *Aye.* He must. He owed her that, at least. To begin seduction and then pull away even once was unworthy of him, even if that once was from the hypnoflora. He did not consider that an adequate excuse. She needed to hear it all. "I must ask your forgiveness for misleading you . . . arousing you to no purpose."

Her small shoulders rose and fell in a negligent shrug, but her eyes still looked wounded.

"I am an orphan, found with Kered on Nilrem's mountain when we were but children. Kered was adopted by the old high councilor, Leoh, and I was fostered with Kered, but only because we were found together. Nilrem stated that 'twas an ill omen to cast me off. And I was near death, unable to speak, eat, do the simplest of things. But Kered took on the task of encouraging me, forcing me to see my surroundings, eat. Nilrem said 'twas only that connection to Kered that helped me live.

"With Nilrem's encouragement and Leoh's kindness, I learned at Kered's side, was made a warrior to serve under him. It was been my whole life, that service."

She reached out and touched his fist. With great difficulty, he opened his fingers and allowed a moment's touch with hers—just the tips.

"I remember nothing of my childhood save the lessons at Nilrem's knee, by Kered's side."

"But Kered told you who you are. He said your name is Nicholas San—"

"Enough! Kered must be lying. He is seduced, has lost his honor." He shot to his feet in agitated fury.

"Then how do you explain how we got here? One moment in my shop, the next here? What of the family Kered said you had?"

"All dead? How convenient." The creeping doubts must be held at bay. Kered had lost his honor, lost his way. He, Vad, would not be mesmerized, turned from his goals as his friend had been.

"And the rest? You know a song from my place. Wanted pepperoni on your pizza. How do you explain that?"

"Magic." He knelt at her side again. She touched the back of his hand where it lay clenched on his knee.

"You told me warriors don't believe in magic." Her voice was low and insistent, seductive, each word sending a shiver of sensation to his belly.

He shrugged. "This is all I know—my life here." That uncanny heat still pulsed between them, tempted him to lock his hand on hers and bend his lips to her palm. To experience the beat of her heart against her breast.

Gently he put her hand away. "I am a warrior—here, in this place. That is all I am. But a warrior with no family has nothing beyond life in the barracks. And I want more. I want a living family—not a dead one. And what kind of life would my children lead with a man of no lineage to guide them? For their sake, I need illustrious ancestors. And for ancestors, I need to lifemate with a woman who is well connected. I might be able to serve as an honorable model, but my mate must provide the ancient pride, the breeding I do not have."

"Would a woman with such qualifications want a man who has no background?"

He rose and went to the map of the fortress, unrolled it, and studied Ardra's marks. "Just as the maidens will come to me, so, I expect, a woman of worth will as well."

"And that's it?" She climbed out of the pool. Her garment clung to her, tempted him with hints of high breasts and rounded hips. "You'll just beckon and this illustriously ancestored woman will meekly accept you? Aren't there going to be a few men in her life who will think an orphaned warrior less than perfect? Don't forget your face is scarred now."

He forced a smile of amusement he did not feel and turned his unblemished cheek to her. Her expression changed subtly, softening. When he turned full face, her rapt attention did not falter. "Until this accusation against Kered, there was nothing to be said against me. Only a councilor is above me in rank, and there are few councilors of mating age. Thus, my worth, scarred face or not, is great to a father who would barter his daughter's fate."

"I see." And he knew she did. "So much for widows from Ocean City," she said.

"Hold yourself separate from me," he warned. "If I had you, I would leave you." His voice sounded rough. It was his second warning, made as much for himself as for her. He had meant it the first time, and still he had embraced her, returned her kisses.

"I understand," she said, and wrapped a cloak around her shoulders. She began to shiver. "Don't let it concern you. I'm okay with it."

He knew she was lying. Her face had flushed into ugly red blotches.

"You have to understand that I'm no different from any other woman. I just wanted you for your body, too."

Although he knew she was lying to save her pride,

her words touched his composure. "Then 'tis best I have put you in your place—alongside the other shallow women of my acquaintance."

"The nonvirgin, shallow women of your acquaintance," she corrected softly.

"Aye," he said in a growl. The fortress plan wavered as he turned to examine it. Gwen would not get the better of him. "We must hope Ardra returns quickly." He needed someone between them, a buffer, a reminder of who and what he was.

"Your arm," she finally said after many moments of silence. "We didn't treat it."

Submitting to her gentle care was almost as heady as submitting to her kisses. She was matter-of-fact at her task, but still, she needed to touch him, smooth on the healing paste, wrap a heavy bandage about the wound.

Finally she completed the treatment and spoke. "Could you do me a favor?"

"What?"

"Go somewhere. I want to finish my bath and I can't with you around."

With a curt nod, he sheathed the jeweled dagger and took a torch to light his way. Within moments he found his steps leading him to a narrow opening he had found while Gwen had been above in the kitchen. Cold, fresh air bathed his face. He was out of sight and hearing of her ablutions—and temptation.

How long should he wait for her to regain her tart demeanor? Drawing the jeweled dagger, he twisted the hilt from the blade and slipped out the map that was the key to his honor. He uncurled the treasure map and turned it to the torchlight. What hope had anyone of surviving the perils guarding the treasures?

A thought had been swirling about in his head since the treasure map's discovery in Ocean City. Wouldn't the council expect him to open the dagger? look inside to ascertain the map was there before returning with it?

And if they knew about the treasure map wouldn't they expect him to then know he'd been used and resent it? Perhaps keep the map for himself? Or try to obtain the treasures himself and keep them?

And therein might lie the true test of his honor. Would he return with the map?

But if the council was testing him and he failed, never returned, kept the map for himself, would they not also be the greater losers? He put the map into the knife and looked on the icy world outside.

"Anything going on?" Her words were calm, distant. She was once more in control of herself. She'd garbed herself once again as a Selaw man, concealing her feminine form.

She peeked under his arm. But there was no concealing her heat. He could smell her: Ardra's soap, Selaw wool. No Ocean City seductive scents clung to her now.

What he wouldn't give to have that little scrap of fabric, what she called a dryer sheet, to remember the scent of her and her shimmery white and glittery silver gown. How it had captivated him.

Before his world had tipped upside down.

"Is this a window?" She prodded him in the side with an elbow.

He stepped away. "In a way. Come see. I noted there was a constant movement of air through here—cold air—so my curiosity led me to explore, thinking there might be another way from this chamber. Where do you think we are?" he asked.

"Beneath a mountain of evil?"

He laughed softly, the low sound sending a jolt of desire right to her middle. The "window" was a narrow slit two feet high. It started about three feet from the floor and revealed a small slice of the world outside. Indigo clouds, tinged with dark green, filled the sky. She leaned forward, her head and shoulders fitting comfortably through. With a deep, shuddering breath, she looked down. It was like being in a bird's nest on the side of a cliff.

She craned her neck and could just see the fortress overhead. In the distance were flat plains of white, tinged the color of the sky overhead.

A frisson of evil tickled her spine. This was not her world. "It's beautiful—in an ominous way," she said truthfully and sadly.

Vad was not from her world either.

"Aye." He bent down beside her, and she pulled back enough to allow him to share the view. "We are not deep in the bowels of the mountain, but in the outer skin."

"What's happening down there?" She craned forward and he clamped a hand on the back of her tunic. Would the sudden heat between them each time they touched ever go away? Sadly, the answer was yes—when she went away.

" 'Tis just the death procession."

Gwen watched the haunting beauty of the row of torches snaking along through the desolate white world beneath. A low sound, a mournful music of drums and some stringed instrument, reached her.

He tried and failed to ignore the wriggling of her bottom beneath his hand. "Ardra is late." He thumped his fist on the stone ledge. "The mourners will have returned, the funeral meats will be eaten, and the wine will have been drunk before she even comes back."

"We have something very similar in Ocean City, too. I remember when Bob died, everyone brought me food. I threw it all out. Couldn't eat for weeks. And the buffet after the funeral just turned my stomach—all that food, and everyone happily eating it. I felt like screaming, 'How can you eat when Bob's dead?' "

She slipped from her precarious perch and dusted off her sleeves.

Did she still mourn her Bob? In the tiny paintings in her home, one man had figured so often, he had to be her Bob. He did not look to be anything so special, but who better than himself to understand it was what was inside, and not outside, that mattered?

"Gwen, there is something I must tell you, should something happen to me. I know the key to the labyrinth."

"How'd you figure it out?" For the first time since their words at the pool, she met his gaze.

He scratched his brow. "Honor prevents me from taking credit."

"Really? Tell me."

"Take a close look at Ardra's pendant and the design around the amber stone: a maze of lines. It is unlike any engraving I have ever seen. It is also not like the traditional selaw patterns. When she left this time, she held it to the light."

Shadows were etched beneath Gwen's eyes. Her hair was sleek and wet on her head. He wanted to cup her face and touch his mouth to hers, make a better apology, erase the line between her brows.

As if he had conjured her, Ardra called to them from the cavern.

"I'm surprised to see her. Why isn't she in that procession?" Gwen asked, hurrying ahead of him.

Ardra moved quickly toward them. "Is the potion ready? We must hurry if we are to use the funeral wine!"

He nodded. "Everything is in readiness."

"How'd you get away?" Gwen poked through the large leather pack Ardra had put on the flat boulder and tried not to stare at the pendant dangling on a long silver chain between her breasts.

"I slipped away from my father by telling him I was ill, ill from the effects of those traitorous men's handling of me. It hurt to lie to him."

"The potion is ready, Ardra. I will pour it into these bottles. Put one in each cask of wine, no more, or you will cause more harm than good."

"Nay! You did not intend that I should do it? I cannot. I am afraid."

Gwen and Vad both looked at Ardra, who stood wringing her hands.

Gwen spoke first. "Afraid or not, there's a girl's virtue to think about, not to mention lives that are in danger. If you can't do it, I will. If Vad can trust me, that is."

What would he say? She held her breath.

"*You* would do it?" Vad asked, his head cocked to the side. "You would risk yourself for women you have never met over a matter not of your world?"

No mention of trust. The tightness in her chest loosened.

"Evil's evil. This Narfrom is a serious threat to those girls. This is no game."

No game. Had she really said that?

Chapter Eighteen

Vad was not content until they had made minutely detailed plans. He wanted every step gone over, each person's role defined, choreographed, memorized.

"And I bring the little girl here as soon as I've emptied the potion," Gwen said.

" 'Tis likely someone will see you, associate you with the illness, and set up a hue and cry, but it will not matter. We will be long gone by then."

"I had thought to go as I am now." He indicated his Tolemac garb. "The maidens will recognize the colors and know someone has come to their aid, but I think I can move about more boldly if I garb myself in Selaw gear."

"Your boots will give you away." Ardra pointed to the high black boots lying by the fire.

"I will go barefoot and be the quieter for it."

"Let me fix your hair before I go." Gwen placed the heavy satchel on the ground. At Vad's curious look, she added, "You want to be able to devastate them in one glance, don't you? Well, shave and let me braid it again; then you'll knock them dead."

He knelt and surrendered himself to her ministrations. "I am understanding you better each day. You do not really wish them dead." She smiled down at him and winked. "This understanding I am acquiring," he continued, "it frightens me more than facing a legion of unmated women."

"Shut up," she said softly, and gave her attention to his hair. It really didn't need to be braided. Clean and shiny, it was just fine falling down his back. And she regretted the offer the instant she touched him. It was better to appear untouched by his words, his rejection. It was better for her insides, her heart.

As the silk of his hair slipped through her fingers, she suffered from the proximity to him. She fumbled with the braids. The heat of his body reminded her of his embrace. The slow pulse at his throat drew her eyes. What had ever possessed her to think he would want *her?* she asked herself. Were his stories of vows just to soften the blow? To let her down gently? Make her think it was not just her ordinariness that made him refuse her?

She finished as quickly as she could in order to be away from him. The task of delivering the concoction was now upon her. Her stomach danced. With a last wistful look back at Vad, she followed Ardra. Nestled in her arms was the leather pack, now heavy with the pottery bottles filled with Vad's potion.

"I wish you would tell me how to get back to him," Gwen said.

"I cannot," Ardra said, her hand going immediately to her pendant and clutching it in a tight fist.

So Vad might be willing to trust her, but Ardra certainly was not. Perhaps her feeling of dread was misplaced. Vad looked healthy enough despite the color of his turquoise. She forced herself to put her concern aside. She had a job to do.

Ardra opened a door. Music from a stringed instrument could be heard in the distance. Gwen couldn't have found the kitchen again if her life depended on it. That thought frightened her silly.

The mournful sound of stringed instruments grew louder the farther along the final corridor they walked. Ardra whispered at her ear, "If something happens . . . wait by these steps." She indicated a spiral staircase like one found in an old castle, complete with worn treads and dangling webs. Gwen shuddered as they climbed up and up, expecting at any time to meet a warrior with a sword on the way down. "I will bring Vad here as soon as the first symptoms of the potion occur," Ardra continued.

"Okay." Gwen's heart beat faster when Ardra pressed a finger to her lips and then peeked through a tiny hole in a heavy woolen tapestry that covered an arch at the top of the steps. With a silent gesture, they slipped past it.

"Oh." Gwen almost gasped aloud. They were in a huge stone hall. Banners of amber and black hung from smoke-stained wooden beams. A hearth, as tall as a man, and wide enough to hold a Sequoia log, dominated one end. Here and there along the long side walls were arches like the tapestry-covered one they'd just come through. Some were entrances to alcoves with covered benches; others were draped with tapestries. A theme of ice and snow dominated the beautiful stitchery. From her courses in college she could tell that some were ancient, others fairly new, but all were the work of years of diligence.

But gorgeous as the lush tapestries were, the atmosphere was funereal. Despite the long tables draped with white linen, the gleaming silver goblets and plate at each place, the faces of the serving women and men were long.

"Remain near. I will ask my father when the wine will be served."

Gwen nodded and almost called Ardra back. She felt so alone, so near to danger. Whatever had possessed her to offer to dump the potion in the wine? Had she offered unselfishly or because she wanted to win Vad's approval?

And why was his approval so important? He wanted a Tolemac woman with a biblical number of "begats" behind her name. An Ocean City widow hadn't a chance.

A tug on her tunic made her look down. The gods are smiling on me, she thought as she looked into a grubby face surrounded by a tangle of golden hair. "Well, hello there," Gwen said to the youngest of the maidens.

"You have strange hair." The child's gaze took in the top of Gwen's head.

"Oh? At least mine is clean and neat. Would you like me to tidy yours?"

"Men do not tidy hair!" The childish peal of laughter rang through the silent rooms.

Whoops. She had forgotten her male attire. "The women appear to be very busy; 'tis why I offered," she said as an excuse.

"Silly man," the little girl said. Gwen glanced quickly around to see who might be watching them. Only a few serving women now moved about the tables, adjusting cutlery. They paid no heed to Gwen and the girl. Gwen needed to hide the bottles of potion. The little girl complicated the effort. She also prattled constantly.

"Where are we going?" she asked when Gwen hurried to a storeroom that Ardra's map had indicated held stored apples. Trying to maintain an attitude of purposefulness, she placed the basket on a shelf and rearranged a few others to conceal it. She polished an apple and offered it to the child.

"I have work to do now. Come along if you like, but do not talk so much. Have you no one to see you are garbed in a clean gown?"

"I am clean!" the child said, spitting half-chewed apple in all directions as she spoke. "You are impertinent. I shall have you whipped!"

Great. An imperious brat. "No, you will look at the front of your gown and see that I am quite correct. Come. When my work is done, I will help you wash up."

Without another word, Gwen hooked the little girl's hand and hurried her to the alcove through which Ardra had disappeared.

There was little excuse to linger in the great hall, but linger she must until Ardra returned. Gwen imagined being caught. Would Narfrom demand she be tossed over the fortress walls, a rope around her neck as punishment, just as he had the serving boy?

She heard strident male voices raised in argument. Before she could duck her head, two men tossed aside a tapestry and strode into the hall. They wore long robes cinched about the waist with belts embroidered with Celtic knotwork in gold and silver. One man's robes were the rich green of spring grass, his hair a loose silvery white mane about his shoulders. The other man's robe was as golden as his amber eyes. His singularly ugly face was framed by thinning blond hair held back in a wispy ponytail.

"Gwen Marlowe!" the ugly man said, his eyes wide upon her.

"Gary . . . Gary Morfran," Gwen said, her heart kicking into overdrive.

A vicious, angry expression crossed the man's face. "What the bloody hell are you doing here?" He took Gwen's arm, shoved the child away, and dragged Gwen though the alcove and up a set of steep steps. His grip was iron hard, his breath harsh and hot on her neck. "Say my name again and I'll slit your throat."

The older man followed them, sputtering questions in their wake. Gary whipped a door open and threw Gwen in. She fell to her knees.

Why, oh, why hadn't she recognized the name?

Narfrom.

Morfran. A knight of King Arthur's court, another survivor of Arthur's final battle. Why hadn't she made the connection between the names as quickly as she had with Vad's?

"It appears we have caught an interloper," Narfrom said to the older man.

Gwen sat back on her heels, dazed, her hands and knees smarting.

Gary Morfran of her world—Narfrom in this—stood before the older man who was clearly Ardra's father. Ruonail looked much like his daughter, though his hair was white. In the harsher light of this chamber, she could see his amber eyes were dull, and his skin paper thin and dry.

Narfrom, in contrast, looked in peak condition. He was not as tall as the Tolemac or Selaw men, but radiated an uncanny power that was almost tangible. He wore the heavy robes of a man of wealth, and Gwen had no doubt that under his sleeve she'd find arm rings—false ones, put there to deceive.

"This is a woman, you say?" Ruonail came close to her and inspected her from head to toe.

Wordlessly Narfrom grabbed Gwen by the collar with one hand and ripped open the front of her tunic with the other. He groped at the tight wrappings over her breasts and tore them loose. Gwen could only twist in his grasp. Screaming was not an option. The stranglehold on her collar guaranteed she had no air to breathe, let alone speak.

"Aye," Ruonail said softly. He raised a hand and

gripped Gwen's chin to inspect her face. "A woman. It is there for all to see, should they look."

Narfrom transferred his hold to her upper arms. The cold air of the chamber tightened her nipples. There was no greater feeling of vulnerability than being half-naked before two threatening men.

"Why are you masquerading as a man in my fortress?" Ruonail asked, his eyes sweeping her form.

She clamped her teeth on her lips. What could she possibly say?

Ruonail's fingers tightened. He tipped her face up. "Narfrom, can you persuade this woman to give an accounting of herself? This bodes ill for our plans."

"Nothing will happen to our plans," Narfrom said to Ruonail. "Come with me," Narfrom said by her ear, and jerked her half off her feet.

"Don't do this," she cried.

Ruonail whipped around, his rich green robes swirling about him. "She speaks as you were once wont to do. Is she one of your people? Is she party to your secrets?"

"Aye, she is of my people, but an outcast, a pleasure slave who gave little pleasure, I would imagine." He wrapped his arm about her neck, cutting off her air supply again and any protest she might lodge. "I will soon have her story out of her."

She opened her mouth to scream; only a croak came out. Narfrom did not give Ruonail any further chance to speak, nor Gwen for that matter. He dragged her from the chamber. A few steps along the corridor, he opened a door, struggling a moment with her as she tried desperately to break his hard grip. She kicked back on his shins and scraped her nails along his hands.

Narfrom swore and flung her to the floor. In but another moment, he snapped an iron manacle on her wrist.

"Sit up." He pulled her up by her torn tunic. The chamber was small and bare save for the bed—and two iron manacles attached by chains to the wall behind it.

One was already in use around her wrist; the other was wrapped around the wrist of a wide-eyed girl. Her bright blue eyes were close-set beneath unruly blond brows. Her long hair was so tightly braided it made Gwen wince anew just to look at her.

"Let me go." Gwen twisted in his grip. She fought him, but he was strong. One backhanded slap and she fell across the bed.

Narfrom stood up and straightened his long robes. "Get in the corner," he ordered the girl, pointing. She scrambled off the bed and crouched in the dimly lit corner at the limits of her chain. He leaned over Gwen's body and jammed a hand beneath her chin, stretching her neck, leaning his palm on her throat.

She clawed at his hand, but he merely grinned. When she fell still, he eased his hold. "Now tell me how you got here."

"Through the game booth."

He nodded. "Did you come alone?"

"Yes."

"How long have you known how to travel here?"

"I didn't know. It was an accident." She studied his face. "You're wearing contacts, aren't you? You've dyed your hair, too."

He grinned. "I'm the perfect Selaw seer, am I not?"

"Is that what your costume indicates? You're a seer? What are you predicting? The end of their world?"

His laughter rang through the room. "My, we are irritable, aren't we?" He spread a hand over her breast. She froze. "Now that shut you up, didn't it?" Slowly he slid his hand from her breast to her throat, wrapping his hand around it. "I could kill you and no one would care. Life is cheap here, and I find that concept quite exhilarating."

"You're sick."

His words frightened her less than the cold, reptilian expression on his face—one she remembered well. The last time she'd seen Gary Morfran, it had been at a virtual-reality seminar in London. He'd been wearing a Savile Row suit and accepting an award for the many advances he'd made to the business with his *Tolemac Wars* hardware.

He was the premier hardware engineer in the business. They'd spoken for over an hour at the dinner afterward, discussing the future of *Tolemac Wars*. Now she understood his curiosity when she'd said she knew the game's creator. Of course Gary Morfran would want to know all he could about the man who'd drawn this world.

Morfran was an unattractive man—not an ugliness of features, but of expression. He'd given her the shivers then, and he gave her the shivers now.

"When was the last time we met?" he asked. "Ah, yes. London. I thought you were . . . what is that word you Yanks use? Perky?"

"Perk you."

He threw back his head and roared with laughter, then just as suddenly sobered. "I want to know how you did it. Did the game creator show you how to get into the game?"

"Let me go and I'll tell you."

"Not a chance." He did ease his pressure on her throat a bit, and she sucked in a deep breath. "Now, I want every detail, and quickly. I've other places to be and other things to do."

"I can't really tell you anything. I was playing around in the game booth and I woke up here."

"Here?"

She knew instantly she'd made some error. "Well, not here. On some mountain somewhere." Was that vague enough? What if she was giving him some key to wreaking more havoc?

"Nilrem's mountain." He nodded. "Go on."

"That's it."

"That's not bloody all of it. How'd you get to the fortress?"

"Oh. I just walked, and then I found this settlement of Selaw. They were pretty suspicious of me, but then Ardra came along and said she needed to buy some slaves to get home, and they were perfectly happy to sell me . . ."

A sudden, bright flash of lightning illuminated the room in stark black and white; thunder cracked almost immediately. The scent of a smoky fire filled the air.

"What were you doing in this part of the fortress?"

"Looking for Ardra."

He seemed satisfied with the answer. "Does Ardra know you're a woman?"

What should she say? "I-I-I don't know. She looks at me funny sometimes, but hasn't accused me of cross-dressing yet."

He grinned. "Perhaps you will be entertaining after all."

"Will you let me up? Jeez. I could be on your side, you know."

"My side? Are there sides?" As if in answer, another roll of thunder sounded outside.

"Sure, your side and everyone else's." She smiled, waiting for his reaction, and her stomach clenched.

In a sweep of his amber robes, Gary released her. He pulled on her chain until she had to crawl to the foot of the bed.

"Did you invent the game gear just to travel to Tolemac?" she asked.

"Tolemac? I have never been so privileged as to make it to Tolemac. This"—he swept his hand out to encompass the stone walls with their narrow arrow slits—"is the closest I've come."

"Then did you invent the gear to travel here?" She pulled the tattered edges of her tunic together across her chest.

"No, that I cannot claim." He strode to the girl who still huddled silently in the corner. "But as I have stated in many of my seminars, there are advantages to using what providence places in your lap." The girl cowered away as he stroked the back of his fingers down her cheek.

Why did he speak so freely before the girl? A terrible, stomach-churning thought came to Gwen—perhaps he spoke so freely because he knew his words were destined to remain in this room forever. Maybe he intended to kill one or both of them. Or maybe, he planned on just cutting out their tongues.

Chapter Nineteen

Vad could not remain still. He wandered in and out of the stone corridors until he knew many of them by heart. Every now and then he had to lean against the wall as a wave of dizziness overcame him. Heat and cold alternately shook his body. He had thought the heat was just from his proximity to Gwen, but now he knew the truth of her words—he was ill.

The Selaw must have tipped their arrows with a slow poison. He laughed. If they had chosen a quick one, he would be dead. His laughter mocked him as it echoed along the damp stone walls surrounding him.

What a failure he was: a man without honor, about to go into battle against an unknown foe without his sword. He touched the hilt of his dagger. There was no need to look at the stone handle. He knew the color was dimming, graying, along with his strength.

He found the thundering falls in a grotto so huge, he could not see the sides or ceiling, only the river running through it and ending in a sudden drop into blackness. The bottomless pit.

The scant light of his torch gave little illumination to inspect the grotto as he stood among the dripstones, not translucent with color here, but glossy black rocks, crusted with ice where the water spray coated them. The chamber was cold. And yet there was a peace here amid the roar of the water and the sparkles of frost. He felt no evil, no sense of danger.

Quickly, conscious he was wasting time and his strength, he retraced his steps to the pool. He readied his bow, selecting the straightest of arrows, impatient for Ardra's return and news of the potion's effect. When no other preparations were necessary, he sat with his back to the rocky wall and leaned his head back. He closed his eyes.

Fever coursed through his body, and he prayed he would be strong enough to make it to Tolemac when the last maiden was released. Silently he repeated the names of the ancient gods, their consorts, their powers, the seasons, the days of each season, the names of the present councilors, the names of the past ones. Anything to keep the fever from possessing his mind.

A scent of summer flowers interrupted his recitation. He opened his eyes. Gwen stood before him. She knelt and touched her lips to his.

"I want you," she whispered. He touched her shoulder and it was bare. When had she removed her Selaw garb? Her smooth, cool hands soothed his brow, drew his head to rest on the soft cushion of her breast. His body was ready for her. The caress of her tongue on his throat swept his doubts away. She skimmed her fingers down his chest and plucked at the lacing over his manhood. He groaned.

"Vad?"

He was startled awake and shot to his feet. Ardra stood before him, a torch held high—not Gwen. The sense of loss was intense. His head ached. So did his loins. "Is the potion delivered?" he asked to cover his confusion.

The torchlight wavered as she shook her head and bit her lip.

"Why not?" he bit out.

"Gwen . . . she has been taken by Narfrom."

He turned away. All his awareness training vanished like mist over water. His heart plunged into his guts like the river over the falls. How could he have let her go alone to see to the wine? His throat ached as he spoke. "Has she been harmed?"

"Nay, but according to my father, Narfrom knew her name and said she was from his land. My father is furious with me that I should have purchased a slave who may have a treacherous heart."

"Who says her heart is treacherous?" Why did he feel so cold at her words? Narfrom was from Gwen's land? The implications were staggering.

Ardra placed a hand on his sleeve. "Is it possible she is not what we think she is?"

"And what do we think she is? Naught but a woman who has been brought to our lands against her will."

"But now she has Narfrom. If he is of her people—"

"What are you saying?"

"Would she not cling to her own kind if she found such a person? Would you not do the same in her place? And what did she do with your potion? When I went to tell her which were the funeral casks of wine, she was gone. That was when I discovered she was with Narfrom, but my father made no mention of finding the potion. Now your plans are all for naught, and the potion is gone."

Once Narfrom had gone, Gwen tried to coax some information from the Selaw maiden, or at least try to get her to come back to the bed. It took long moments to get even a murmur from her. "How long till he's back, do you think?" she finally asked.

"Do you speak his language?" the maiden whispered from her corner.

"Oh, sure. We're buds, don't you know." She smiled to reassure the girl. "I do not suppose you know of a way out of here?" she finished, making sure to imitate the Brit accent.

The girl came close, climbing gingerly onto the bed to crouch by Gwen's side. "We are doomed."

"Great. I am chained to a wall with a pessimist."

"I am Senga, daughter of Ranoc, a Tolemac councilor."

"Nice to meet you. Now, who has the keys to these chains?"

"Narfrom. He comes with a serving woman to release me each time I eat and need to relieve myself."

"You had to say that, didn't you?" Gwen muttered. All it took was the suggestion and she needed to go. She took a deep breath. "That won't do." She jerked on her chains. "Maybe we can pull these out of the wall."

Senga made no move when Gwen got on her knees and tugged at the chains, except to repeat her prophecy of doom.

Gwen frowned. "Now, why take that attitude? We'll escape."

"Nay. You are now a prisoner. There are now eight of us—the sacred number. It is all that was needed—one more maiden to complete the circle. Now we shall all die." Tears appeared in her soft blue eyes. They rolled silently down her thin cheeks.

Gwen wiped away her tears with her fingertips. "No, Senga, there are still only seven maidens in the fortress." She thought of the dream of Vad's body moving over hers. "I am definitely not a maiden. I have been well and truly bedded."

But Senga shook her head. "You do not understand.

There is more to maidenhood than whether you have lain with a man. I sense it in you, in the look in your eyes, the way you spoke to Narfrom. It is an innocence in here." She touched her chest, then her forehead. "It is a purity of mind as well."

"Well," Gwen said, thinking of all her meltdown imaginings about Vad, "rest easy. My mind's a sewer."

Outside, the sky flickered with long forks of light, and thunder rolled.

Gwen's jokes didn't even reassure herself. There was something more than the girl's insistence that made Gwen think, purity or not, they were all doomed.

There was no one to put Vad's potion in the wine.

A wave of dizziness made Vad lean on the bow he held in his hand. If Narfrom was from Gwen's land, had he not access to the mysterious weapons that put men to sleep and burned holes in rock? How frail his own weapons were against such a wonder.

He looked around at the magnificent walls of nature that had stood for thousands of conjunctions. Could Narfrom cut his way through them with but a single use of that mysterious weapon?

But, strange weapon or not, he had promised to rescue the maidens. "We will continue as planned and assume Gwen was taken before she could act. If we can get to her, she can tell us where the potion is." He dropped the bow and unbuckled his knife sheath. Then a thought came to him. "Ardra. Gwen's capture means there are now *eight* women prisoners. We cannot delay the rescue a moment longer." Slowly and deliberately, he pulled off his heavy woolen tunic, baring his chest.

"W-w-what are you doing?" Ardra stuttered, fluttering her hands and backing up, tripping over her hem and sending the remaining bow and arrows clattering to the floor in a cascading racket.

Vad buckled on his knife and slung the bow across

his back. Sweat glistened on his skin, the sweat of fever, though his mind was clear. He spread his arms and bowed. She gave a soft sigh, her eyes riveted to his bare chest. She licked her lips.

He gave her a grim smile. "What am I doing?" he repeated, unable to keep bitterness from his voice. "I am merely increasing the likelihood that the Tolemac maidens will come to me. One must use the gifts one has."

"We have to try to escape. Pull harder," Gwen said to Senga. Together they tried again to dislodge the iron pin holding their chains to the wall.

"If you are right and we are not doomed, then should we not just wait for a man to rescue us?" Senga asked.

"You know, there is not always going to be a man around when you need him. You have to learn to be resourceful on your own."

"There are always men around," Senga said, but she heaved on the chain. "Is not this Vad you told me about somewhere near, waiting for your signal?"

"Exactly. He is waiting for a signal. One that is never going to come if I do not get free. Now pull!" And he will never trust me again if I fail, she said silently to herself. Gwen hauled harder on the chains. "Damn it!" she swore, then quickly regretted the outburst as the door creaked open.

Two sentries entered, Ruonail behind them, a ring of keys in his hand.

"How many guards? And where?" Vad stabbed the fortress plans on the row of chambers where Narfrom was holding Gwen.

"You still persist in going after her?" she asked.

"Did you doubt I would?"

Ardra nodded. "You do not know what awaits you. Gwen may have told Narfrom you are coming."

"She has no reason to do so." He realized he must

choose. He must trust Gwen. To believe otherwise put his life and that of the maidens in jeopardy. "I do not think she will betray our plan."

"And if threatened with sale? Or losing her tongue?" Ardra persisted.

"I would imagine it is her tongue that will save her. She will talk her way out of danger."

"I do not know what else to say," Gwen continued. "I told Narfrom everything." Ruonail sat in a carved wooden chair, in his chamber, the fire roaring, the heat stifling, an impassive expression on his face.

Ruonail shifted in his seat. "There is a gathering of darkness outside. It began when you arrived."

Great. Blamed for the weather.

"I most respectfully disagree."

Ruonail sucked in his breath. "You, a mere woman, a slave, disagree? With me?" He shot to his feet. A tremor ran through his thin body.

Gwen hastened to placate him. "I mean no disrespect. I spent many hours with your daughter, and she told me of the strange changes in weather, this darkness that has fallen over the fortress. It began before I arrived."

Gwen saw on his face an acknowledgement of her words. "What else did my daughter confide in you, a slave?"

"Her love for you," Gwen said softly.

Silence, save for the crackling of the fire in the hearth and the crack of thunder outside, filled the chamber.

Narfrom strode in just as Gwen thought Ruonail was about to speak. "All is going well. The feast is about to begin." Then his steps slowed. "Why is she here?"

"I wanted to know more of her, of her land—and yours."

"We have no time. You must put in an appearance, as we discussed, warn the rest of them what befalls a person who dares turn against one of your family."

"Aye. I must offer a warning." Ruonail's shoulders seemed bowed with an invisible burden as he left the chamber.

When he reached the door, Narfrom stopped him. "Ruonail, we have no time to ascertain this slave's true loyalty. I want to put her to the test."

Ruonail nodded. "It would swiftly end the matter."

When Ruonail was gone, Narfrom pulled a woolen gown from a coffer and tossed it toward her. "So you charmed your way out of your bracelet?" Narfrom propped himself against a table and crossed his legs at the ankles. The casual stance did not fool Gwen. He still looked like a viper about to strike.

She ignored the dress. "I didn't have to use my charm. Ruonail sent for me." Gwen wished she were beautiful. Maybe then she could charm someone into believing Narfrom was evil. "May I ask you what you want in this world?"

"Everything."

"But you have quite a bit of everything in our world, don't you?"

He gave a bitter laugh. "Ah, our world. Too many competitors for the power and wealth. Here I will rule. And when it bores me to do so, I shall simply take a little tax-free wealth home with me."

"I thought the Selaw were just recovering from starvation."

"But their future is so rosy." He leaned so close she could feel his breath on her cheek, and gave a quick bark of laughter. "One of the dead men, Enec, he worked for me. He was a . . . spy of sorts. Did you know the Tolemac councilors have been camping for weeks at our borders to negotiate a lifemating for their head councilor?"

The way he so easily said *our* borders told her he had come to think of Selaw as his.

"Enec's angelic face allowed him to insinuate himself

quite easily in many beds—Tolemac slave beds. The male slaves were happy to help him access the maidens and the females—they talk."

"So what? What can they tell you? How many ice cubes fit in a wagon?" Ardra would be heartbroken to know of Enec's part in the kidnapping of the maidens.

Narfrom laughed. "You are cheeky. No, this time the slaves told him some very interesting tales of a famous warrior who is seeking a fortune."

A cold, sick feeling spread through Gwen. Had Enec guessed who Vad was from the first moment they'd met?

Vad studied Ardra's plan of the fortress. The corridor of chambers in which Gwen and the maidens were being held ran east and west. Each end of the corridor had a set of spiral steps linking it to the great hall.

"You will need to enter from the western end and distract the guards while I enter from the east," he said. "Do not react to anything I do except as an innocent onlooker. You do not want it to appear that you are aiding me."

Ardra led him to a door that opened into a dark alcove. To his right was a set of winding steps. Before him was what he at first thought was a wall, but then realized was a heavy tapestry.

She indicated a small hole through which a glimmer of light shone. Dust tickled his nostrils as he looked out on the great hall, filled with rows of Selaw mourners. It lacked the opulence of a Tolemac hall. The women were well dressed, but their garments did not have the same richness of embroidery as those of Tolemac free women. There was little conversation, but the hall was still noisy with the sounds of cutlery and servants bustling about.

He tried to steady his erratic breathing. His heart beat felt rapid and fluttery in his chest. How much simpler to act if the crowd was moaning and groaning over a hundred chamber pots. He wiped sweat from his brow.

Where was Gwen?

"I don't get it," Gwen said softly. Her stomach did a little dance at Narfrom's smug smile.

"Don't you see? I have seven councilors in my power. They will do whatever I want to save their daughters. Surely a daughter is worth changing a few votes, a treaty possibly. Or even donating this fortune the warrior seeks to my retirement fund. I could rule here very soon."

"What of Ruonail? Isn't he ruling?"

Narfrom waved off her words with a negligent hand. "An old man. When I mate with Ardra, all will accept me as his heir."

His eyes glittered with amusement. "Old men die."

A shiver ran down Gwen's spine. So Ardra had it all wrong. He might want to ravish Senga, but his personal designs were on a different maiden. She changed the subject before he realized how much of his plans he'd revealed to her. "Which came first? The game or this world?"

"This world exists quite independently of the game, my dear. Don't you understand any of it?" He shoved off the table and began to pace. "I was fifteen when I saw a man disappear. He was dotty, a bumbling cretin who worked for my father's engineering firm. But he had hobbies. Marvelous hobbies to a young man of curiosity—"

"You," Gwen interrupted. She was definitely going to die. He was pouring out his every thought much too indiscreetly.

He nodded. "It took me days to believe in his disappearance, but finally, when he did not rematerialize, I understood I'd witnessed a miracle." He pounded his fist into his palm. "It took me thirty years to repeat what he'd done. The bastard had encoded his notes. I made several rather disastrous mistakes first—lost a child. Another boy who witnessed the little tragedy started drawing this world a few years later. Luckily that's all he did as he grew up—draw it. When the time was right, I talked him into making it into an incredible virtual-reality experience." He snorted back a giggle. "Little did he know he was drawing a real place."

Abruptly he strode to Gwen's side and knelt by her. His touch on her cheek was icy cold. "What were you wearing when you disappeared?"

"Wearing? My nightgown."

"Any jewelry?"

She shook her head. She'd taken off her earrings and her wedding ring. Then she remembered the ring on Vad's hand as he held hers. She could not let Narfrom know about Vad. "No, I'm wrong. I had a ring, but I lost it."

"Celtic?"

She nodded.

"I was right. If one can wait for the extra electrical energy produced by a storm, and if one wears certain designs, the power of those ancient interlacing patterns channels that energy and you go into the game. I must stop thinking of it as a game. It's a world all on its own." He stood and stroked the beautiful embroidery at his waist. "See these designs? They entwine endlessly, linking, channeling the energy."

"Sounds strange to me. Are you saying that a man, whom you saw disappear, invented some machine to bring him here using Celtic designs?"

Narfrom shrugged. "I do not know what he was trying to accomplish, but he knew the ancient legends, had scores of books and photographs of caldrons and weaponry that had been found in rivers, once offerings to the ancient gods. He studied the designs, coincidentally or deliberately, we will never know. And he must have come here. It would account for the legends of the lands beyond the ice fields. These people have not the level of technology to cross that vast wasteland themselves and return to tell about it."

"What if one of my customers is wearing Celtic designs and plays the game during a bad electrical storm; will she or he be sent into the game?"

"Not without a certain type of conjunction. I used to think only a lunar conjunction would do, but I have found that if the power of a storm is great enough, you can still travel on a lesser stellar conjunction. I can now make the journey at will. It takes but two things: power and design, both Celtic and heavenly."

Power and Design. It had been the title of Gary Morfran's talk in London. "What about the weapon rumors? Doesn't the description of that coveted weapon match the game gun? Isn't the Tolemac council trying to find a way across the ice fields to find it?"

"Oh, yes, you are well informed. Tolemac and Selaw both wish for such a weapon. A totally useless endeavor." He reached inside his robes. "Why would anyone need a game gun when there is this?"

Every cell in Gwen's body went cold. Narfrom strolled casually to her and raked the barrel of a gun, one that looked alarmingly similar to R. Walter's, across her cheek.

Chapter Twenty

Vad searched the many faces for a glimpse of Gwen as he stood behind the tapestry, his insides knotted with concern. No, he was lying to himself. This was far stronger than concern. Deny it he might, but there was a tie between him and Gwen, a connection. The thought of her in danger sent a rush of blood through his veins, a call to defend that shook him with its intensity.

Somehow he knew in that moment that if the connection was severed, he would suffer for it, perhaps forever. She was more than just a woman who knew the world of his night dreams.

A sudden silence made him put his eye to the hole again. At the far end of the room, a man rose from his place before the warming fire of the hearth. The glow lit his hair in a silver blaze. The man must be Ruonail, Ardra's father.

"We are gathered to mourn the loss of three of our men," Ruonail said, his voice thundering down the hall. "The men betrayed my daughter's trust and endangered her life. It is fitting and proper that they lost theirs in the process. Stand and raise your cups."

The company rose, metal goblets held high in their hands. Untainted wine was in them, Vad supposed. *What an opportunity lost.*

Ruonail spoke when all were silent and every eye turned to him. "I drink to their souls. May they never find rest."

A gasp ran through the hall. Voices rose in an angry murmur. Some drank; some did not.

"Silence," he roared across the room. "You will drink! I command it. Drink to their unrest. To their eternal walk on the ice, never to find peace, their punishment for harming one of my family. Drink, or you shall join them."

Ruonail threw back his wine in a single gulp. After a moment's silence, others also drank their wine. Like a ripple across a pond, the arms rose around the room, one after another, and the Selaw people drank.

"Nilrem's throat," Vad swore. Ruonail might be ill, but he still commanded his people with an iron will.

"Go now. Cross the hall," he said to Ardra.

She lifted the edge of the tapestry and slipped away. He watched Ardra walk quickly across the vast chamber. Whispers followed her. Ruonail half stood; then when Ardra did not look in his direction, he sat back in his place.

Vad moved quietly from the tapestry and up the steps. According to Ardra's map, the room with the five maidens together was three rounds up and a few doors from the room housing Narfrom's favorite. And where was Gwen?

The stairs circled to the left to give the advantage to the right-handed warrior coming down. Vad moved his blade to his left hand. He kept his bare shoulder to the stone wall as he silently ascended.

Three rounds up, he stopped and imagined the two

guards, each with drawn swords, standing at each end of the corridor, facing the steps.

He heard Ardra. "How fare the maidens?" she asked.

The murmur of a man's voice answered her, though the words were indistinguishable.

"I wish to move this coffer to my chamber," Ardra said quite loudly. "Would you two men help me? A few steps only?" How persuasive was her soft, feminine request. Vad heard the sound of a man's footsteps moving away from his end of the corridor.

Glancing cautiously around the wall, he saw the guard place his sword on the wooden floor and smile and nod at her. His fellow guard did the same. He would have had their arm rings for such a blatant lack of discipline.

Silently he stepped up into the corridor. The men bent to lift a banner-draped coffer.

He rushed forward, kicked the back of the closest guard's knee, and slammed his knife hilt into the temple of the other. Turning back to the first guard, he kicked him in the groin.

He whirled to where Ardra stood, her eyes wide with alarm. "Make not one sound," he cautioned her for the conscious guard's benefit, his blade held beneath her chin. She nodded and collapsed in a credible faint.

He bound each man with his own belt and gagged the unconscious guard with a strip he tore off the man's tunic. The other guard was too intent on his injured groin to make much noise. Vad grabbed him by the collar and dragged him to the door of the room that held five of the maidens.

Next, he pulled the unconscious man to the door as well. Last, he returned to the coffer. Over it lay a faded Tolemac banner, one taken in a border skirmish, he supposed. He swept the banner off the chest, tied it loosely about his waist, then checked the coffer for weapons. It was empty.

Vad knelt over the still-gasping guard, drawing

Gwen's little fruit knife. " 'Tis said this knife is for cutting away sections of flesh. I think 'tis more suited to cutting out an eye. What say you?"

The guard gagged and choked, his eyes wide. He croaked for mercy. With the tip of the curved knife, Vad traced the line of the guard's eye socket. "How many guards are inside this chamber and the next?"

The man began to beg pathetically for mercy. There was only an old woman to see to the maidens' needs; just one guard watched the other one, Narfrom's favorite, the man stammered out between whimpers. Of Gwen, he seemed to know nothing. Vad rose, then dragged the man by his tunic to the other guard.

Female whispers came to him. Silently he eased the door open. Five young women, ranging in age from about fourteen conjunctions to nearly twenty, were nestled like spoons on a bed. Their bare feet were tied. Their eyes opened wide, as did their mouths, at the sight of him.

He touched his lips with a finger and gestured to the gray-haired woman who dozed at the hearth. They nodded, first one, then another down the row. Swiftly he untied their feet.

Their gazes followed him as he circled the edge of the room, moving behind the woman. He undid the banner from his waist and twisted it into a rope.

Quickly he dropped the makeshift gag over the woman's head and across her mouth. She jerked awake and bucked against the cloth. He tightened it and knotted it in one motion.

Then he showed himself. The woman froze. She stared up at him. He knelt at her eye level and touched her shoulder gently. "I mean you no harm," he whispered. "But you will be most uncomfortable for a bit." As he spoke, he tied her arms and legs to the chair. Next he returned for the two guards and tossed them on the bed. Soon they, too, were trussed like spring lambs.

When he turned around, the maidens, dressed alike in long white bed robes, were standing in a row by the door. Their heads moved as one, following his progress around the chamber as he gathered their shoes.

"Come with me." He had no need to say more. They linked fingers and followed him wordlessly. Just before he opened the door, he turned back to them. "Obey me." They bobbed their heads and smiled. He felt as if he were being considered as a meal. "No matter what happens, you are to remain silent. Utterly silent." He eased the door open and peered out, then jerked back into the room as he felt a warm hand on his back. "Do not touch me!" he said in a hiss.

The maidens put their hands behind themselves and nodded vigorously. He sighed.

"When it is silent below, we shall go down into the labyrinth." Fear lit their eyes. They darted glances at each other. "Do not be afraid."

A whisper of sound alerted him to one maiden's movement. He grabbed her hand in midcaress. "You do not obey very well, do you? There is rope enough to bind your hands should I find it necessary."

The young girl had not even the decency to hang her head or drop her eyes. She smiled up at him with a look of adoration he had seen too often to be flattered by. Perhaps he would not wait for the mourners to leave the hall. It might be safer down there than up here with the women. Surely, in his weakened state, they could overpower him . . .

"I keep my gun hidden, even from Ruonail," Narfrom said. "I like this society in its primitive state. They're no match for me just as they are." Narfrom sighed deeply. "It is such a burden to be the most superior being in an entire world."

His words chilled her to the bone. "So Ruonail isn't interested in crossing the ice fields for weapons?"

"All of Selaw wishes to get across the ice fields and gain the marvelous weapons of legend." He laughed. "They just don't understand there is no 'beyond' the ice fields. But I have convinced Ruonail that bartering ice for weapons is senseless. He has become convinced he wants gold and jewels. After all, when you have enough gold and jewels, you can buy all the food you want—and all the weapons. And who has the gold and jewels? Tolemac."

Narfrom smiled. "My dear, there is what amounts to a mountain of gold outside, just waiting to be turned into the real thing. Ruonail just needed someone to show him how to use the ice to the best advantage. He was stupid to agree to the peace treaty. Ruonail trades the ice for food! Moronic! But now, with hostages, I am this close"—he held his fingers two inches apart—"to trading a worthless quantity of frozen water for a fortune."

"Or a map."

"Map?" Narfrom grabbed her arm and hauled her close. "Who said anything about a map?"

"You did." She hadn't even realized she'd said the word out loud.

"I said fortune. Not map. What do you know about a map?"

"Slaves talk," she said.

"Oh, yes, they do. Somehow I think you know more than you let on."

Gwen shook her head. "I just heard about a map, nothing more."

Narfrom gripped her by the throat. "We shall see. They have a wonderful test of loyalty here in Selaw. Should you pass the test, you will need to keep my secrets, work for me, not against me, or I will see you offered to the slaves that mine the ice. They haven't had a woman in months. They work shifts of eight men on and eight men off. Can you handle eight men, Gwen?"

She tried to remain calm.

"Put the dress on." Narfrom pointed to the gown she'd done her best to ignore.

"Here?"

Sweat broke out in small beads across his brow. "I want to see the goods. Maybe you'd be wasted on ice miners. Now change." He raised the gun.

She knew its power, understood the threat. Turning her back, she pulled off her torn Selaw clothing. The gown was silky smooth, long, flowing. Its high neck was embroidered about with the familiar Celtic knotwork in turquoise and amber. Narfrom's hands settled on her shoulders. "You are lovely," he said, his breath scented with wine. Then he pulled back. "Did you hear something?" He walked toward the door, gun in hand.

Was Vad outside rescuing the maidens? She had to distract Narfrom. "I can't do up this dress. Can you help me?"

He veered back with a grin. "How nicely you ask. I would be happy to help you."

As he came to her, Gwen strained her ears for some sound beyond the heavy wooden door, but heard nothing. There were thin ribbons down the back, which Narfrom tied tightly, pulling the gown snugly against her chest and abdomen. When he finished, he slid his hands about her waist, then up the silky cloth to cup her breasts. He stroked the barrel of the gun over her nipples. "In our world, you're a bit out of shape. Here, you're perfect."

Gwen remembered the rumors about this man, the London tabloid headlines that had linked him with the beating of his girlfriend—a beating that had left the woman comatose. After that, he'd disappeared for months—in jail, she'd thought. Now she wondered if he'd come here to escape prosecution.

She stepped decisively away from his embrace. "Don't touch me. I can't see any reason why we should be enemies—I have no loyalty to anyone here—but if you so much as touch me again, you're dog meat."

His eyes glittered. "Lucky for you, you're not my type. I much prefer the subservient ways of Ardra. She knows her proper place. You've been indoctrinated for far too long in the equality of women. Such a waste." He waved his gun toward the door. "Now come, I've a charming little room where you will be quite comfortable until Ruonail is free to attend the testing."

Vad led the maidens to the bottom of the winding steps to where Ardra stood waiting behind the tapestry, gripping her pendant. Together they led them down into the first levels of the labyrinth. His heart pounded at the amount of noise the maidens made. He stopped Ardra at the first door. "What of the child?"

"She is in the kitchen, sorting beans."

"Is she safe there while I return above? There is one more maiden to save, and I must find Gwen." Ardra nodded, and he took the steps up two at a time and hastened back along the still-deserted corridor. It was his best hope that Gwen was inside with Narfrom's favorite.

He eased the door open. A naked man was climbing onto the bed—and a woman. Seeing Vad, he leapt off and grabbed his sword from the floor.

Vad snatched the jeweled dagger from his belt and threw it. It was not a throwing knife, but it found its mark.

The man fell to his knees, the gaudy hilt protruding from the center of his chest.

With a cough, he fell forward. Vad caught him, drew the knife, and let the man collapse. He wiped the knife on the bedcovers, sheathed it, and leaned close to the woman. "You must be silent if I am to take you away from here."

The young woman nodded, her eyes wide, a fist pressed to her mouth.

Gently he pulled the woman's skirts down. "Was that Narfrom?" he asked her with a gesture to the dead man.

"Nay. A guard."

"Where is Gwen?"

"Ruonail has her."

He took in the manacle, the other empty shackle, and swore silently. Bowing his head, he gathered all his concentration, applied every awareness lesson he had ever learned. He opened his eyes, wrapped the woman's chain about his hand, grasped the pin, and pulled.

Nothing.

Sweat broke out all over his body. He closed his eyes and gathered his strength and will and pulled. Slowly, so slowly he almost did not believe it, the pin shifted. His hand and arm shook with the effort. The pin gave way.

He scooped the woman into his arms.

She linked her arms about his neck and began to weep. Within moments she was with the other maidens. He pulled Ardra aside. "She may have been forced by a guard, and most certainly witnessed his death, so go gently with her. She says your father took Gwen, but she is not in the hall with him. Where can she be?"

"Narfrom must have taken her to one of the prison pits. It is all I can think of."

"And where are these pits?" Gwen in a pit? The image was not to be borne.

"Beneath the fortress, by the river entrance, but above the water."

"Take the maidens below to one of the caves. They need to be hidden away. And do not forget the child!"

Ardra did as he bade. How long she was gone, he did not know. His impatience ate away at his composure. He saw in his mind the guard between the maiden's thighs, and imagined a similar fate for Gwen. His mouth was dry.

Then he imagined heavy iron manacles around

Gwen's wrists, saw her in an earthen prison with nothing but a grate overhead for air and light. Either fate was intolerable.

When Ardra returned, she quietly led him to a set of storerooms. "The child is gone—wandered off again. She will be punished for disobedience this time. We must go on without her and hunt for her on our return." Ardra pulled on his arm. "No one will notice a little noise as the mourners make their way to the chapel for the final funeral prayers, but I bid you, go quietly."

She opened an iron door and led him toward a simple, oft-used corridor. This was not a hidden part of the fortress. This was a common prison entrance.

Ardra lifted a hand, and he hung back while she proceeded. She turned a corner, and he heard her voice take on an imperious tone. "Who is in these pits?"

"Why do you ask?" came a man's response.

Ardra gasped. "Narfrom. Father? What are you doing here?"

Vad took a step closer to the corner to better hear the men.

"My child, you must be gone. We are going to test this slave. Go," commanded a voice Vad assumed was Ruonail's.

"Nay. You cannot." There was a scuffle and the sound of a grate being lifted.

"Go. Now," Ruonail repeated. "Get to your chambers."

Ardra came around the corner in a rush. She ran into Vad's arms. He slapped a hand over her mouth so she would not give him away. He lifted her into his arms and silently carried her out of earshot. "What is going on?" he whispered.

"They are testing her." Ardra touched her amber pendant with a trembling hand.

"You must stop it." He placed her on her feet and implored her with every fiber of his being.

"Me?" Her eyes widened.

"You know the test," he said in a hiss. "Burning. Coals in her hand or an iron on her breast." He had not the strength to argue. He did something he had never done before to a woman. He went down on one knee and bent his head. "I beg this favor. You can stop the test. I ask it of you."

Chapter Twenty-one

For a few moments Vad knelt in silence; then he felt Ardra's hand on his head. Her words were barely audible. "How can I refuse you?" Then her voice strengthened. "You have brought the maidens to safety. I will try to stop the test, although I have never had the power to command my father. Now please rise. You shame me."

The effort to rise to his feet was almost too much. His head felt swollen; his ears rang.

His imagination painted the scene: Gwen, her hand extended, or worse, her breast bared for the hot iron. If the wound festered, she would be taken out on the ice fields and abandoned. In Tolemac they had no ice fields. They would have set her out at the rise of tide and let the sea take her.

Ardra turned and walked resolutely away. He followed to the corner and nocked an arrow. Every sound, every scent, every touch of air on his body was heightened by his desire to know the outcome. Should Ardra fail to have the test stopped, he would step out and kill whichever man performed the test, most likely Narfrom. He was slipping, failing. He had not asked the most important question—how many other guards were at the pits, men who were not speaking? He would just have to keep shooting until he ran out of arrows—or was stopped.

Gwen stood before Ruonail and Narfrom, her chin high. She would not allow them to see how disconcerted she was. She blinked away the torch smoke that drifted toward her.

"This slave knows about the treasure map. How, I ask? We must determine the extent of her knowledge." Narfrom spoke rapidly, his voice hypnotic, and cataloged all the reasons she should be tested. Her eye color, her outcast status, her lack of arm rings, and last, the one that startled her most, the fact that if she truly had been sold by the Selaw to Ardra, why was there no *X* on her breast to mark the transaction?

Ruonail paced, a frown on his face.

An indefinable flow of heat eddied about her sheer gown. It reminded her of the heat that flowed from Vad to her each time he touched her. Was he near?

What would the test be? Some question she had to answer? She ran over all the little clues she remembered from the game. Which chiefdom wanted what. Who was allied with whom. She prayed they'd ask her something simple, like how many councilors made up the Tolemac council or how many moons were overhead.

Ardra, her back straight, came around the corner. Ruonail froze. "What are you doing here, daughter? I told you to be gone."

Narfrom frowned and gripped Gwen by the upper arm. "Shall I have the guards recalled?" His fingertips bit into her tender flesh. She stifled a moan. "Shall I have Ardra taken away?" Narfrom asked.

"Father, I beg you, do not send me away until you have heard me." She made a deep bow.

Her father turned from Narfrom, his hands thrust out in a gesture almost of supplication. "You should not be here, my child."

"Aye. It is my place. Is this not my slave?"

"Go to your chamber. This business is not for you to see."

"I have seen a testing before, Father. Do you not remember? When mother was alive?"

"Ardra! How can you bring that up now?"

She knelt at her father's feet, her silk gown a molten gold pool about her body. Its fineness was a sharp contrast to the stone floors and the ugly pits only a few feet away. Gwen suddenly understood that whatever the test was, it would be no simple quiz of facts. Tears ran down Ardra's face.

But she did not bow her head as she spoke; she kept her eyes on her father's face. "I have asked little of you. Give this slave into my care, Father. Please, I beg of you."

Narfrom stepped forward, but Ruonail raised a staying hand. "You have been a good and obedient daughter. Will you answer a question before I make a decision?"

Ardra nodded.

"Why is this slave unmarked?"

Gwen felt a flush of heat stain her cheeks.

"I would not allow it. What purpose does it serve to scar a woman so men might know how many beds she has lain in? I hate the custom. It sickens me. We do not mark the male slaves so we women can count their lovers."

"And yet you have never spoken up before. Why now?"

Ardra folded her hands about her pendant. "We have just mourned three men who died in treacherous acts. Perhaps if I had been thinking for myself, saying what

I thought all along, the men would not have thought me such a useless sheep before whom they could do as they pleased. I have no authority here, and yet I am your heir. It is time I took my place at your side and made a few decisions."

Ruonail smiled. "I have waited long to see some spark of courage in you. Rise. I will spare your slave."

"How dare you!" Narfrom dragged Gwen backward to the pit. "You old fool. You forget what we have planned," Narfrom said. "You forget what our goal is. This slave—" he gestured at Gwen—"may yet ruin those plans. We must test her."

"I have made my judgment. You must abide by it, as should any man."

"You will regret this decision."

"I regret all we have planned between us." Ruonail thrust his daughter aside as he approached the pits. "It is time to release the maidens and make some recompense to appease their fathers' ire. We will bring only war upon us, such a war as has not been seen in generations. Tolemac will not need to trade for the ice; they will simply annihilate us and take it! I was a fool to believe in vague rumors of treasures and maps!"

"You coward," Narfrom said in a low voice only Ruonail and the two women could hear.

"How dare you!" Ruonail swung around.

Narfrom shoved Gwen into Ardra. They went down in a flurry of skirts. Gwen screamed.

"Hold." Vad stepped into the chamber. He aimed at Narfrom's chest, but it was to Ruonail he directed his words. "Take the women to safety. I will deal with this one."

Gwen was on her feet before Ruonail could reach them. As Ardra went into her father's arms, Narfrom smiled. It was reptilian, frightening, but no less frightening than the dull metal object he drew from his robes.

"I knew this would come in handy one day. Drop the bow or I kill one of the women."

Vad ignored him. "Ruonail, if you wish to salvage any of your reputation, take the women away."

Narfrom shifted his aim to Gwen. "Make the man see reason, Gwen. When I came across Liah in the kitchen, she found my gun a more fascinating object than the bowl of beans she was counting. If your champion is not interested in saving your life, what about hers? Explain what a gun is, Gwen, and how it works."

The gun was aimed at her chest. Gwen's heart thudded dully. "Vad—"

Narfrom gasped. Ruonail swung to where Vad stood. "You are Vad?"

"Well, well," Narfrom said, smiling. "It seems we can avoid violence. How pleased I am to meet the famous Vad."

"What is it you hear of me?" Vad asked.

Gwen edged around behind Ruonail toward Vad. Somehow being near him seemed terribly important. She felt a thickness in the air, a gathering of something awful. It shimmered around them. She could taste something bitter and ugly on her tongue.

A rumble of thunder shook the stone edifice.

"Enec, one of the dearly departed," Narfrom said, "garnered some pillow talk that you were after a very valuable map."

"Pillow talk?" Ardra whispered. She glanced at her father.

Narfrom spared her a brief sneer. "Talk after lovemaking, my dear. Loose talk. He was excellent at gathering those little gems that make a man's planning so much more effective."

Another crack of thunder sounded, almost in the chamber with them. Even Narfrom glanced overhead. "Where is the child?" Vad asked, tracking Narfrom as he moved around the chamber.

"Liah? I will give her to you in exchange for the map." Narfrom halted by one pit and tapped it with his toe. Everyone looked down. "Oh, Liah is not in here. That little minx would have been howling up a storm if she were here. But you will never find her, never know her fate if you do not hand over the map."

Vad tipped his head. "It is a fair exchange. Bring out the child and I will give you the map."

A sickness rose in Gwen's belly. His words were casual, but she knew the map was everything to him. Did Narfrom know that the map was in the dagger, right there for all to see, the handle in plain view? He had only to shoot Vad and he would have it.

Her knees nearly buckled. She glanced about for some weapon to help defend Vad.

"Ruonail. Liah is in that little room where you like to meet your concubine. Bring the child here, and we will have riches far greater than any you can get with the ice."

"Father, do not aid him. Return the child. Do not take the map. We do not need the Tolemac treasures."

There was a pair of chains lying in a neat coil on a table by the chamber entrance. Gwen estimated how long it would take to get to them.

"Stand still," Narfrom barked at her. "I can shoot him in the knee, or the heart, before you can even lift those chains from the table."

She froze. All eyes save Vad's swung toward her.

"We are about to realize our dreams, Ruonail." Narfrom took Ardra's hand and pulled her close to his body. He encircled her waist and spread his hand over her middle. "We will have everything with no bloodshed, no sacrifice of maidens, no pain and suffering, if you just get the child. Go now."

With but a moment's hesitation, as if he now understood that Narfrom could harm more than just the Tolemac maidens, Ruonail swept out of the chamber.

No pain, no suffering. Not true. Vad would suffer. But his face was a study in serenity. No one but she would know how he must wish to bargain anything but the contents of the dagger.

Ruonail was gone only a few minutes. Ardra tried to run to him, but Narfrom shoved her back. Ruonail kept the child between himself and Vad as he walked her to where Narfrom stood.

Narfrom held out his hand, the gun once more visible, aimed at the child's small blond head. She was avidly taking in her surroundings, unaware she was in danger.

"What use is the map to you? You can't go on a treasure hunt yourself," Gwen said. She took a step toward Narfrom, but he raised the gun.

"The map alone will be worth a fortune—millions—to certain collectors back home." Narfrom turned to Vad. "Are you ready?"

But Vad directed his words to Gwen. "Be easy. It is just a piece of paper, not worth a life. Come take the map to him and bring me the child. His weapon may be deadly, but I am counted an excellent shot with mine as well. I would gladly wager my shot against his."

Gwen's legs felt rubbery as she withdrew the dagger from its sheath. She felt the full weight of the gun's power trained on her back. The evil in the chamber was thick, like smoke. Only here by Vad could she breathe normally. Heat emanated from his body. She quickly twisted off the handle, withdrew the map, and thrust the dagger back into its place.

How small was the paper; how big were the consequences for her warrior. Her warrior. Although his eyes were on Narfrom, he smiled. "Hand it over, Gwen."

She offered the child one hand and gave away Vad's future with the other.

A tremor shook the building. Ozone filled the air.

Gwen looked at Narfrom, who smiled and gestured

her toward Vad with his gun barrel. "Do you remember what I said, Gwen? Power and design."

Narfrom touched his embroidered belt. From one moment to the next, he disappeared.

Gwen threw herself into Vad's arms.

"Thank the gods he did not harm you," he murmured against her hair.

His body was flame hot. All the desires and fears of the last few hours ran through her. She locked her arms about his waist and hiccuped to keep back her tears. He touched her shoulder. "We must see to the others."

She stood back and looked up into his eyes. "You're burning up with fever."

"Nay, it is just you, woman. You are the one who is warm."

"Wait! I don't think we've seen the last of him." She looked at Ruonail and Ardra, who were standing and staring at the spot where Narfrom had disappeared, as if frozen into ice like the glacier outside. "How do we explain him?"

Vad shrugged. "I do not want to. I just want to be gone from here. Let them puzzle out his magic."

He held out his hand to the child. She took it, and, still glancing over her shoulder to the spot where Narfrom had stood, she followed him,. Ardra led her father after them. Ruonail stumbled along like a broken man.

Gwen wrapped one arm about Vad's waist. "I have to tell you what I learned from Narfrom. It might make a difference someday," she said softly, so the child would not be privy to the tale. "Narfrom is from my world. He's obviously figured out a way to come and go from there at will, but that's not what's important. His name in my world is Gary Morfran. I feel so incredibly stupid not to have thought of it. My only excuse is tiredness, finding myself here, not really believing. . . . Never mind all that."

Vad watched her face pale to the color of her gown.

"Steady yourself. You are just frightened. Save your tale until we have settled this little maiden."

How she hated to wait. They saw Ruonail up the steep steps to his chamber. He barely acknowledged his daughter as she told him she was taking Liah away. Gwen watched Ardra leave her father and take the child by the hand.

No one challenged them as they went down to the lower levels. A murmur of prayers floated on the air; voices could be heard singing. No sentries challenged them. All was silent, as if the guards had deserted the fortress along with Narfrom.

Every step in the oppressive, dark corridors told her Narfrom might be gone, but only temporarily. Would the amount a collector might pay for an ancient map be enough to satisfy him?

Gwen detoured to the storage area to retrieve the basket with the bottles of potion. She threw a couple of apples on top for Vad to eat.

Right before they lifted the tapestry to cross the great hall, Gwen tried to make Vad listen to her once again.

"Remember how I told you where your name came from? Nicholas Sandav. Remember who Sandav was?"

Vad made an impatient gesture.

"Make him listen, Ardra. In my world Sandav was a famous warrior who survived one of our legendary ruler's last battles—"

Vad nodded when Ardra raised a brow. "There is a legend in Gwen's place that tells of a warrior whom no man would engage, lest they harm a messenger of the gods. She thinks I am somehow the embodiment of that warrior."

"No. I think you are one of his descendants. But listen!" She touched his bandaged arm. "You have to listen or this wound on your arm might be the least of your worries. Another warrior survived along with Sandav.

His name was Morfran. And he didn't survive because he was a great fighter, or gorgeous like you. No. He lived because he was so ugly, so dark, no one would fight him in case he was—"

"A messenger of evil," Vad finished for her.

Gwen could only nod. Her fear was cold and deep. "This man from my place, his name is Gary Morfran. He must be a descendant of this ugly warrior. And he is evil in my world. He was accused of beating a woman nearly to death. And remember, in this world he had a boy hanged!"

"But Narfrom is gone," Ardra cried. "We need no longer fear him."

"Don't you feel it? Narfrom may be gone, but that evil feeling is still here. Maybe he came back in another spot or something. He could be waiting around the corner."

Vad still could not believe what his eyes had told him. But he had seen a weapon such as Narfrom's once, seen its power, known his bow and arrows were useless if the man had decided to fire on any one of them.

"Narfrom is evil, as is Morfran," Gwen continued. "In legend, Morfran's mother was the goddess of darkness. Her totem spirit was the sow—"

Ardra reeled away, a hand to the wall, the other to her stomach. "Nay. Nay." Liah cowered away from her emotion.

"What is it?" Gwen ran to Ardra's side. Vad moved more slowly, but it was into his arms that Ardra turned. She buried her face against his bare chest.

A stab of jealousy twisted in Gwen's middle. She took Liah's hand and held it tightly. They did not need to lose her again.

Ardra raised a tearstained face to Vad. She spoke only for him. "My mother died because she accused my father of having congress with one of her trusted slaves. My father denied it, but my mother, thinking to force my father's confession, demanded that the woman be tested. My father agreed. He did the testing himself. I remember my mother's cold anger, the woman's tears. The slave died of her festering wound, cursing my mother. Within a few months, my mother sickened and died. I know 'twas the curse."

"Wound? Festering? Died? What are you talking about?" Gwen asked.

Vad held his bow out to Gwen, who took it automatically and then wished she'd refused. It merely freed him to fold Ardra into a tighter embrace. "A testing, Gwen, involves forcing the slave to hold a burning coal, or the placing of a heated iron to her breast. If the wound festers, she is evil. 'Tis believed by the ignorant that the evil inside will seep out at the wound site."

The bow shook in her hand. "Oh, my God," she whispered. "You saved my life, Ardra."

"It was nothing. Vad asked it, and I could not refuse him."

Gwen looked at him. He shrugged and looked away. Had he really cared about her fate, or had he simply felt a sense of responsibility toward her?

Ardra continued, "My mother's slave wandered in her fever, as is so often true in such deaths, and I took my turn to nurse her. She called on the goddess of darkness, begged us to sacrifice a sow for her. I had never heard such things before, but they frightened me. I remember her every word."

Gwen and Vad exchanged looks over her head. "Then we are all connected somehow," Gwen said. "Oh, why didn't I remember this stuff when I first heard his name?"

"I agree. Narfrom is evil," Ardra said softly. "And if he can command the powers of darkness, as the woman did in killing my mother, we are all lost. Vad must find Narfrom and destroy him, or this will never end."

"I do not believe in such nonsense." Vad put Ardra

gently aside. "Only an evil man would take innocent maidens hostage, then threaten their lives—that evil I will believe—the desire for power. The desire that twists a man. But this other evil? The goddess of darkness being mother to some ancient warrior named Morfran? It is all just legend."

"Please listen, Vad." Gwen blocked his way. "Narfrom appeared and disappeared. That wasn't some legend! I think there's going to be a battle. The light against the dark. Sandav against Morfran. Good versus evil. I thought it before. And Narfrom may be gone for the moment, but I think the battle is still to come."

"Whatever omens you read in our names, or in your memories of ancient legends, Narfrom has what he wanted. And if the map is not enough, even now he may be on his way to gain the treasures. What need has he to bother with me?" He turned and walked away.

Chapter Twenty-two

Ardra held Gwen back from following Vad. "Enec was part of this treachery? He conspired with Narfrom?" Her voice quavered.

Gwen tried to soften the blow. "I think he was seduced by the treasures."

"Then it is best he is dead." She wiped her eyes. "We must take the little maiden to the others."

"Hide the maidens somewhere. I don't believe this is over," Gwen said, and before Ardra could protest, she ran after Vad. She reached his side as he crossed the silent hall. She felt exposed, sure some guard would jump out and challenge them. He was a tall, blond, half-naked target. "Where is everyone?" she asked when she reached his side.

"It is tradition for a priest to offer prayers after the funeral wine," Vad said softly.

"Ardra's going to take the child to the others. I asked her to hide them."

He nodded his approval, but did not slow his steps.

"We will depart at the sunrising tomorrow. I may have only a dagger, but I am still going to take it to the council."

There was nothing she could say.

"If you are so afraid, go with Ardra and hide with the maidens." He leaned on his bow and impatiently thrust his braids behind one ear.

"No." She felt a cold breeze swirl about her ankles. "I won't leave you. What if Narfrom returns? I could help you."

He smiled and shook his head. "That thought will make me sleep at ease this night."

"No smart answers," she said, and hooked the heavy basket over her arm.

Vad marveled at her. She had been so close to harm, and here she was offering to defend *him.* Just as he knew his fever stemmed from a tainted arrow tip, so he knew men often assured the results of a test by dipping the iron rod in poison. He would wager Narfrom would have called for a brand, not a hot coal, if Ruonail had allowed the test. If all Gwen said about Narfrom was true, he could not have afforded to have someone who knew his background talking to Ruonail or Ardra.

He was responsible for Gwen. That responsibility was not the burden he expected. "Come. You are in need of a bath."

They entered the lower labyrinth. Ardra caught up with them, said she would hide the maidens at Gwen's request, and led them to the corridor from which they could find the steaming pool. "I must return above and speak to my father," she said. "He must provide guards tomorrow to protect the maidens on their journey home. What will you do until the sunrising?"

"Sleep," Vad said.

Gwen shook her head. "I don't think I'll ever sleep

easy again. But it's freezing down here. I'm going to change my clothes."

Vad watched her walk away, the basket still clutched in her hand. The hem of her gown was dirty; her hair was sticking up in the back.

She was beautiful.

Ardra interrupted his musings. "I will lodge the maidens in a cavern I know by the grotto entrance, at least until the tides change. It is dry, and it will take little time to move them into a boat from there. But the tides will not change until the sun is overhead." She lifted her necklace from around her neck. "I want you to have this as a token of my thanks for saving the maidens. It is the key to the labyrinth. You will always be welcome here."

He held it in his hand and rubbed his thumb over the well-polished center stone of amber. "I am honored."

She bowed. "I will go above and see my father. Now that the maidens are released, he must also offer some recompense to their fathers to . . . encourage their silence. I will return when it is accomplished."

Vad watched her go. He thought of his journey to Tolemac. It was imperative he arrive before vintage month. Or perhaps it mattered not where he went. What good was an empty dagger? What good was his life from this day forward?

And yet he could think of nothing to do save complete his journey.

He dropped the bow and arrows to the ground and raked his fingers through his hair. Every muscle in his body ached. For long moments, he contemplated his next move. He plucked the one remaining torch from its bracket and headed for the warm pool. Perhaps a long soak in the water would ease the throbbing in his arm.

Then he admitted to himself he just wanted to find Gwen.

A thin, high scream echoed down the corridor from the direction of the thundering falls.

He ran into the tunnels, then stopped. He consulted the pendant, lifted his torch to be sure of the way, then carefully walked forward. His torch cast demonic shadows on the wall. According to the pendant, the falls were almost straight ahead. He stood still and listened. He heard nothing and ran blindly.

His instincts led him well. A lone torch lit the mammoth cavern of the falls. He skidded to a halt by the thundering waters, his heart in his throat. He cast his torch to the ground to free his hands. It hissed and extinguished itself in the slick moisture on the grotto floor.

Gwen stood with her back to the falls, her heels inches from the abyss. Mist dampened her gown so it clung to her body and surrounded her in a sparkling array, like transparent gems in the light of the one torch smoking on the wall. A tall man held the tip of his sword to the center of her chest.

Enec.

"Don't come any closer, Vad," she called. "He'll kill you."

"I told you he would come if you screamed." Enec grinned. He stood half-turned so he could keep an eye on both Gwen and Vad. "Shall I make her scream again?" he asked Vad.

Vad shook his head. "Why are you not dead?" he asked softly. Enec shifted the sword, and Gwen groaned. He froze.

"You left me to die. But a lovely Selaw woman found me and nursed me." Enec swung his gaze between Vad and Gwen. "Surely *you* can understand the power of a kind woman's succor? I finally made my way here and found that the maidens were no longer prisoners."

"And are soon to be in the bosom of their loving families." Vad noted the gauntness of Enec's features. His eyes were almost burning flames in his face. A tremor ran through the hand that held the sword.

"It is really you I want, Vad," Enec said. "You ruined

my plans. Imagine my dismay when I discovered the fortress mourning my passing. And imagine my surprise when two well-trussed guards described their captor. An angel come to rescue the maidens! What lunacy. But then, here you are. An angel I could not kill—last time. Now I think I can."

Enec laughed and shifted the point of his sword over Gwen's breast. "Ruonail will regret this piece of business. The maidens will tattle to their fathers, and Tolemac will send an avenging army, I suppose."

As if he had forgotten Vad, Enec skimmed the flat of the sword up and down Gwen's stomach. Vad took a step. Enec jerked in his direction. "Do not move, or I will kill her in your place."

Vad froze, his eyes on the sword and the quick rise and fall of Gwen's breast. "What do you gain from her death?" he asked.

"Revenge. It is a petty emotion, but I had hoped to claim Ardra. Whatever objections Ruonail might have had to our mating, Ardra would have overcome them—if I had had my reward for taking the maidens."

"What could possibly have swayed Ardra to mate with a man such as you?" Vad asked.

"The Vial of Seduction, of course," Enec answered softly. "Now my plans are dashed to pieces."

"You will never escape this labyrinth."

"No?" He reached into his dirty tunic and brought out a pendant just like Ardra's. "Ruonail gave it to me long ago so I might come and go."

"What of the guards?" Vad asked. "Did they not wonder at your return from the dead?"

"They never saw me, not this night, nor any other time I have come and gone on my errands. I much prefer a good climb to a boat ride, and there are several 'windows' to choose from."

Vad remembered how he and Gwen had watched the funeral procession. Why had he not thought of it as an access point? Because he had been stupid with fever and distracted by Gwen.

Gwen stood so close to oblivion. She had been brought here by his carelessness. He studied Enec and the position of his sword—and Gwen.

"Do not move, my Ocean City warrior woman," Vad warned her. He could tell, as if she were whispering her plans in his ear, that she intended to take action. "Allow me to deal with him."

"Ah, yes, Vad, come deal with me," Enec taunted. "But you will fail. This time I will ignore your face. I will see only your Tolemac heart and cut it out."

Gwen's body tensed at Enec's words. Her eyes were wide.

Vad tried to communicate with her. *Do not move,* he silently ordered her.

She gave an imperceptible shake of her head and shifted one foot.

Then he saw it in her hand—an apple. Even from where he stood he could see the whiteness of her knuckles and the smooth redness of the apple's skin.

Do not do it, he silently begged. Behind her the river flowed, the falls sent up their spray, the abyss yawned.

She lifted her hand. Enec turned to her. The apple hit his temple. Instead of falling back, he lunged forward, into her. Her arms windmilled slowly, impossibly slowly. Vad leaped for her, felt her hand, gripped it. She clung to him, her fingers icy, wet, slipping.

"Vad," she choked, and went over the edge. He held on. His injured arm trembled with the effort to support her weight and maintain his grip.

He sensed movement behind him. With a shout of pain, he hauled her up, grabbed her gown by the back, and heaved her onto the slippery edge.

Enec slashed at his belly with the sword. It swung in vicious arcs. The man had no competence, but was a deadly threat nonetheless. They slowly circled around the cavern, moving in and out of the torchlight, a sword length apart.

With a glance over his shoulder to see where they were, to see if Gwen was safe, Vad edged sideways, away from her, hands extended. He wished desperately for his sword.

Vad timed the sword's swing. Slash. One, two, three. Slash. One, two, three.

Vad kicked out, connecting with Enec's knee.

The sword flew from his hand, over the falls. For a moment Enec stood poised on the edge, his arms outstretched. Then dropped backward.

Enec made no sound as he plunged into the abyss.

On the wall, the lone torch sputtered and died.

"Vad," Gwen whispered in the darkness. "Where are you? Find me. I don't know where you are . . . where the edge is."

"Do not move," he said. "I will come for you." He felt as if someone had pulled a black cloth across his face. The mist touched his skin like fingers. *Close your eyes and see,* he said to himself. *Imagine where she is.* He put out his hand and took cautious steps toward her voice.

She went into his arms eagerly. He pulled her body against him.

He edged away from the abyss, sliding his feet, feeling the ground until his back came up against a wall. He leaned on it, Gwen in his arms, and took a deep, shuddering breath.

She was still and silent except for the hitch of her breath. He cupped her face and bent his head.

He found her mouth, the hot moistness of her lips and tongue. Not seeing, he could only feel. Every inch of his skin was on fire. She spread her hands on his shoulders. Flames flared under her touch. He groaned deep in his throat, gave voice to all the pent-up need he felt for her.

As he had dreamed, her fingers plucked at the laces over his manhood. He swept his hands down her back, cupped her buttocks in his palms.

Her fingers were gentle on him.

He wanted nothing of gentleness.

For long moments there was only his selfish need, her warm hands, her mouth on his throat, and a flaming burning in his belly to have it done.

She said his name. It sent a shiver of awareness through him—awareness of where they were, who she was, and what they were doing. This was no dream from which he could wake. There was no hypnoflora to confuse his senses.

He wrapped his arms about her and lifted her high against him. The warmth of her breasts cushioned his head as he leaned in to her. She tasted sweet, her nipples hard as he dragged his teeth over them. With a whispered question and her assent, he laid her down. She slid his breeches off his hips as he lifted her gown.

"You are silk," he said at her ear, sending a shiver of sensation down her neck as he knelt, poised to sheathe himself as she so desperately wanted. "A silken tie. And you have bound me to you."

"Vad," she said his name aloud. He moved inch by slow inch into her, filling her. She thought her heart would burst. No air entered her lungs; her heart no longer beat. There was nothing save him, that exquisite point where they met.

She lifted her arms and embraced him, hung on, for a storm broke over him.

It raged in silence, buffeting her with waves of sensation, heat, flames of want. She twisted, gasped, cried out as his release triggered hers. The cry echoed around them, prolonging the moment like the ripples of aftershocks that ran through his body and hers in the wake of climax.

He shuddered in her arms. Heated breath stroked her neck. Wet skin moved against wet skin. Hard muscle pressed on soft tissue. Thundering heart met thundering heart.

She slept, fearing nothing in his arms, her legs entangled with his. Long hours later, something woke her. It was so dark she couldn't see her fingers inches from her eyes. The mist of the falls blanketed them, but she felt no cold. She touched his shoulder with her lips. How hot he was, how salty his taste.

And she wanted to devour him. He shifted on her, and she sensed that he was looking at her. What did he see in his mind's eye? His hand began a slow movement on her hip, a featherlight caress, mirrored by his mouth as it traced the veins and arteries along her neck, her shoulder, along the inside of her arm. It was almost as if he could feel the heat of her inflamed blood and wanted to trace it to its source.

They linked fingers in the dark. She guided his hand with hers, over her breast, to her stomach, and lower. Her hips arched to his caress, to the knowing way he touched.

How simple it all was in the dark, with no one to see or judge what they did. And she knew it was just this one time, this once in the anonymous blackness where she could be what he needed and he could forget what he wanted.

He sought her mouth and she kissed him hard, then gently, explored the textures of him, bit him gently on the lips, the chin, the throat. She laved the smooth planes of his chest, his hard stomach. His hands moved restlessly in her hair. With slow, languid touches of her mouth she made love to him, memorized him from knee to shoulder, his taste, his scent. She memorized it all for later, when he was once again a warrior and she but a slave—when she was gone.

This time, when he entered her, she held herself motionless. When he tried to move, she clutched him tightly and whispered to him to lie still. She felt a frantic need to hold on to the moment, to freeze it. For when he found his release this time, she knew it would be the end.

He lay in her arms, every muscle of his body held rigid at her request. His lips feathered her with soft kisses on her eyelids, her brows, her mouth. But one traitorous part of her couldn't hold still, and with a moan, she arched her hips to him.

They came together, riding the same need, frantic for the same end. He said her name once. Then she lost herself in his passion, deaf to the words he murmured at her ear, enveloped only in his touch, his fierce embrace. She felt his teeth on her shoulder and cried out as a flicker of pain met an outpouring of ecstasy.

Chapter Twenty-three

Gwen became aware of a faint glimmer of light raising sparkles across the frost-rimed rocks. She rubbed her eyes. Yes, it was light. She broke from Vad's warm embrace, shaking his shoulder. "Someone's coming," she whispered by his ear.

He rose slowly, like a bear awakening after a long winter's nap. How magnificent he looked in the dim light—and how unreal. No man should be that handsome, that perfect. He gathered his scattered clothing, and she remembered that he did not revere his perfection. Indeed, he thought it a burden.

Self-consciously, she pulled on her gown, then turned away as Vad dressed. When no one burst in on them, she tiptoed to the grotto entrance and peeked out.

"Vad, look," she called. He joined her. Sequentially along the path, torches burned. They flamed low in their brackets, telling her how long they'd been asleep.

"Ardra," Vad said, looking down at her. "She must be marking our path back for us."

Gwen gathered her rush basket and the flagons of potion. She felt her face flush with the knowledge that if Ardra had lit a path for them back to the cavern, she had probably seen them, heard them. Gwen wanted to bury her face in her hands in embarrassment, thinking of the abandoned way they'd made love, sure of the knowledge they were not only unseen, but also unheard.

Had Ardra come after them?

And how long had they slept in each other's arms? No, Gwen thought, I won't think about his arms, sleeping, any of it. She avoided eye contact with him, afraid to see regret in his gaze.

"Should we tell Ardra about Enec?" he asked softly.

She shook her head. "No, she thinks he died on the river. She's already mourned him. Why reopen the wound or add to her pain?"

"Come." Vad held out his hand, and she accepted it. Every step away from the grotto was a step away from intimacy, and a step toward an inevitable separation. At the steaming pool, she hastily washed herself and pulled a linen tunic over her head, aware of his intent scrutiny. His gaze touched her like fingers skimming her skin.

But he would not allow her to avoid him. He knelt before her and took the laces from her hands before she could cross-garter her legs and don her male persona.

I won't think about his hands either, she thought as his strong fingers wrapped up her legs.

"Gwen, look at me." She lifted her eyes to his blue ones, dark here in the light of but one last torch, his irises so huge his eyes appeared to be black. "We must talk."

She shot to her feet. "Gee, in Ocean City that's never a good way to start a conversation." She grabbed a cloak and swung it about her shoulders.

"I do not know how to say this. You are making it more difficult."

She lifted the extra bow and cradled it in her arms,

across her chest, before looking up at him. She took a huge breath and smiled her best smile, imbued it with all the happiness she did not feel. "I know what you're going to say, Vad, and you don't need to. Please don't worry about me either." A lump burned in her throat, but she swallowed it. "We were celebrating life after coming so close to death." She went on quickly before he could say anything that would rip her heart right out of her chest. "That's all. But it was a beautiful celebration."

He gripped her upper arm. "Is that all it was? Celebrating life?"

"Sure. What more *can* it be?" She didn't wait for him to answer. "I'll carry these, too," she said, and fumbled the extra arrows into a pile like giant pickup sticks.

His brow furrowed. "And what of my dreams?"

"Dreams?"

"Aye," he said, coming to her and taking the arrows. He carefully packed them into a quiver. "I had dreams there as we lay sleeping. I have had them before, only this time they had such detail, such clarity, I cannot explain it. You wanted me to examine my dreams. Well, I am ready."

So he was concerned about the dreams he'd had, not about trashing his vows or breaking her heart.

He went down on his haunches and used the tip of the jeweled dagger to make a drawing in the black dust of the cavern floor. "I dreamt of this."

Irresistibly, she was drawn to his side. Perhaps it was the black dust that rendered his crude lines so clear. *London taxi*, she thought immediately. With agitated strokes, he drew another, object. *An airplane.* When he looked up at her, his eyes wide and questioning, she forgot her own heartbreak. He must be remembering. He must be who Kered said—Nicholas Sandav, a missing child from her place and time, descendant of another man of wondrous beauty.

"Nilrem's Seat of Wishes?" he asked softly, his blade hovering over the taxi.

She shook her head. "No. It's called a car. Like the one you saw in Ocean City." Did she have the energy to explain internal-combustion engines?

With a sweep of his hand, he erased the plane. "And this is not some fantastic bird that haunts my nights?"

"No." She said it softly, for his agitation was evident in every line of his body.

"Vad. Gwen. If we wish to arrive under cover of darkness, we must hurry."

Ardra stood before them, dressed in elegant white wool with gold embroidery. The hood of her cloak framed her face and drew attention to her lovely features.

"We're ready. Lead the way," Gwen said cheerfully, faking a smile and hefting the quiver of arrows over her shoulder.

When she looked at Vad, he had once again donned his warrior mien. Any hint of his earlier passion or the confusion of the last few moments was buried far beneath his surface demeanor. Any fears he had about returning to Tolemac without the treasure map were buried even deeper.

"We have no time to waste if we wish to return the maidens under cover of darkness." And so saying, Ardra swept away from the cavern. Gwen had little choice but to follow; Vad's footsteps were a constant reminder of his presence behind her.

They had been longer in the grotto than Gwen had suspected. Light burst on them. It dazzled their eyes, poured a bronze gleam over the fortress cliffs. She shaded her eyes for a few moments, until her eyes readjusted to life in the outside world.

The huge red orb of the sun was almost overhead. At the grotto entrance, Ardra's people were readying a boat.

This boat was large and magnificent. It had a tall mast and seats for six or more oarsmen.

At the sight of Vad, the maidens screamed and surrounded him as if a pop star had arrived. They bubbled over with thanks for rescuing them.

"I did not do it alone. You must offer your gratitude to both Gwen and Ardra." When the maidens made no move, he said in a disapproving voice, "Give them thanks. Now." He gently shook off the youngest maidens, who clung like barnacles to his legs, and urged them in the direction of the women.

The maidens offered a flurry of thanks to Gwen and Ardra, then returned immediately to Vad's side.

Gwen watched him. He lifted Liah into his arms. The child tugged at his straggling braids, and he said something that made them all laugh and Liah do it again.

Get to work, she chastised herself. She climbed into the boat and helped Ardra place several painted boxes in the bow.

"He is very patient with their foolishness," Ardra said. Gwen couldn't speak. She feared what her voice might betray, so she merely nodded.

"You are different."

Gwen's head jerked up. "Different? What do you mean?"

"It is difficult to put a name to the difference." Ardra shrugged. "But there is something . . . it is in your eyes. He took you last night, did he not? That is it. You are filled with sadness because he has no place for you in his life."

"You know, Ardra, he did not *take* me. That's not what lovemaking is—taking. I *gave* myself to him, and there's a big difference. Remember that when you fall in love. You're supposed to give, not take."

Fall in love. When had it happened? When had she passed from admiration of his face and form to something else?

She knew the exact moment: when he had come after her.

But she made a decision. "Vad suggested that your father might be grateful for ridding the fortress of Narfrom's evil influence. Would that gratitude extend to an escort for me, back to Nilrem's mountain?"

Ardra looked from Gwen to Vad. "If you are sure you wish to leave him, my father will most certainly grant you an escort. You have but to ask."

Gwen followed the direction of her gaze. A ray of red sun burst from behind a cloud and filled the grotto with an uncanny light, painting the walls copper. Vad looked bronzed, like a sculpture—beautiful and unreal. "I'm sure," she said softly. "When Vad leaves with the maidens, I'll go to Nilrem's mountain."

Unfortunately, Narfrom had spent plenty of time telling her how to get *into* the game, but had not told her anything about getting out. She would have to trust that it all worked smoothly in reverse. She would spend the journey to Nilrem's mountain praying for rain—and praying that Narfrom never returned. Perhaps the fair sky was a harbinger of better times for them all. She prayed that Narfrom was truly gone from this world. Although she knew it was shameful, she wasted a few moments hoping he'd get hit by a bus in hers.

Tears pricked at her eyes, and she bent to inspect the furled sails to conceal her face from Ardra's too-knowing scrutiny.

They worked together in silence, Ardra fussing with embroidered pillows and soft woolen blankets, Gwen surreptitiously checking the sheets, lines, and sails.

The sound of marching men filled the watery fortress entrance. Gwen turned and looked up the steps. Ruonail stood there, wrapped in his rich green robes, flanked by his guards.

The maidens hid behind Vad. Liah wrapped her arms tightly about his neck and buried her face in his hair.

"Do not be afraid," Ardra said firmly, and Gwen relaxed. It felt odd not to be fearful. She'd just spent the last few days in a state of high-level anxiety.

Vad gave only a slight nod of his head to acknowledge the older man. Ardra bowed deeply, and Gwen followed suit. Why annoy Ruonail when she intended to ask him for a favor?

"Esteemed warrior," Ruonail said from his place at the top of the steps. "Please assure the maidens I mean them no harm."

"Harm has already been done," Vad responded.

Ruonail nodded. It was then Gwen noticed the tremor in his frame. When he descended the steps to the edge of the pier, he leaned on one of his men.

"No compensation can make amends for the damage done here in this last month." Ruonail accepted a heavy walking stick from one guard. It was topped by a golden knob set with amber. It was not decorative, but necessary without the guard's arm.

"Then you have come to bid us good journey?" Vad set Liah on the stone pier and, with a hand on her head, guided her behind him.

"Aye. But before you go, would you accept a reward for helping me . . . see the error of my ways?"

"I need no reward except this." He swept a hand in the direction of the boat.

"What I have to offer you is infinitely more valuable than a simple boat."

"Father." Ardra put out her hand and, with a guard's assistance, climbed back onto the pier. She wrung her hands. "Father. I beg of you, not at this time."

Her father gently stroked the back of his hand down her cheek. "I did it all for you. I wanted you to have everything that was denied your mother for being born Selaw and not Tolemac."

"Please. I have never been discontent with my lot," Ardra said. "I require nothing."

"Silence, child." The words were gently spoken, but a very specific order.

Ardra subsided, but her hands continued their agitated motion.

Ruonail drew himself up to his full height. "I have been beguiled by a man's stories of power. But now I am recovered. Ardra informed me you have taken time from your own urgent concerns to save these young women. She is filled with admiration for your sacrifice. Thus I wish to offer you the greatest possession I have—my daughter. I offer her to you as a lifemate."

The world spun a moment, and Gwen needed to grasp the smooth wooden mast for support. *Lifemate?*

Gwen looked from Ruonail to Ardra, then to Vad, whose impassive features gave no hint of his thoughts.

No one looked stunned. Did that mean she was the only one who had not seen the possibility? Gwen's stomach churned. She sat down heavily on one of the supply boxes, a vicious headache behind one eye.

Ruonail lifted his stick to the red sun. "We Selaw share the same light, earth, and sea as Tolemac, and yet we have fought for generations. I have jeopardized the first fragile peace, perhaps irreparably, should the Tolemac councilors fail to accept my compensatory gifts." He indicated the seven boxes in the bow of the boat. "To truly know peace, we must join together. As we speak, Tolemac is negotiating a lifemating between a Selaw princess and your high councilor, Samoht. If one of his warriors were to take the same step, it would start our chiefdoms on the road to a deeper, firmer peace."

What horse hockey, Gwen thought. He'd just kidnapped seven maidens, chained them to walls, and he spoke of peace. She had to bite her tongue to keep silent.

"You have not demonstrated any wish for peace. Senga will bear the scars of her manacle for all her days," Vad said with a small loss of his usual control.

"What damage has been done to these others, I can only conjecture."

That's it, Gwen cheered inside. *Reject the old hypocrite.*

"One must start a journey of redemption at the site of one's sins." Ruonail made his halting way to where Vad stood. "Selfishly, I know that should Tolemac learn of my . . . foolishness, 'tis likely I will be beheaded—"

"No, Father, please."

Ruonail lifted his stick, and his daughter fell silent. "Do not fear the truth, daughter. I face possible beheading—banishment, at the very least." He turned again to Vad. "If you take my daughter as your lifemate, no man would dare harm her when she is alone here at the fortress, prey to unscrupulous men. We both know that the sun-rising after I am gone, hordes of men who seek to possess all I have will descend. Ardra will need a strong man such as you."

Vad smiled. It twisted his scar with wry amusement. "I see Ardra did not tell you of my own predicament."

"Aye. She did, and Narfrom had other thoughts on your lack of sword. I need no display of weapons. A man either demonstrates honor or he does not. It is not necessary that you give your answer now. I will hold Ardra bound to you by my promise until you have accomplished your quest. Perhaps the knowledge that you will have my blessing to rule my fortress will compensate you for what Narfrom took from you. Return when you have dealt with the council, and we will sever or seal a pact of mating at your wish."

"And should you be gone ere I return from the Tolemac capital?"

"Then I beg that you will look kindly on my precious daughter and offer yourself as her protector and lifemate."

With a sweep of his robes, Ruonail returned to his

place at the top of the steps. There, framed by a stone arch and his men, Ruonail raised a hand.

"A woman alone is prey in this world. A woman between the coveted ice and the men of power is not only prey, but also a prize. Think of the power you will have as her mate. Think of how you will be able to influence the use of the ice."

Gwen's body went numb. It was as if the intense heat from Vad's body was only a distant memory. Wind scoured her cheeks and cut straight through her short cloak.

"I send Ardra with you to the Tolemac councilors. They are not so very far," Ruonail continued. "The council is camped at the border. The negotiations for Samoht must be very close to being signed. If you take Ardra to them, she will help plead your case as you attempt the restoration of your sword. Take what help she may offer you, be it only the comfort of her companionship." With those words, Ruonail left them.

"Vad, my father makes great sense when he says I should accompany you." Ardra slipped her hands into her cloak. She paced along the pier before him. "As a woman, I can escort the maidens without suspicion, see their fathers, intercede—"

"I do not need intercession." Vad began to herd the maidens into the boat. Despite his words, he made no objection as Ardra climbed aboard.

Gwen put out her hands to each girl and helped her to a seat. Several guards, the designated sailors, jumped in behind them.

Vad put Liah in last, hoisting her high overhead before settling her on a cushion. The gesture was playful, but Gwen doubted he was in a playful mood. The maidens each clamored for his attention, for a place at his side.

Gwen took advantage of the noise to challenge Ardra.

"You knew what your father was going to propose, didn't you?"

"I suspected." Gwen hated the pity in Ardra's eyes.

"Since when? Before we rescued the maidens? Or even before that? At Nilrem's cave? Did you know what reward your father had set for freeing him from Narfrom's influence?"

"Nay. You go too far. I sought only Nilrem's wisdom, or a means of breaking a spell. How could I know Vad would be there?"

It was almost impossible for Gwen to reply. Despite the obvious truth of Ardra's words, Gwen felt betrayed.

"Last night, my father and I spoke for long hours of my challenge to him over the testing. It was then he hinted at his plan." Ardra glanced at Vad, who was swamped in maidenly hugs. "You were not about last evening. I could not tell you what I suspected."

Not about last evening. Of course not. She had been making love by the waterfall. While overhead, Ruonail was planning Vad's marriage—to someone else.

"But you don't object to the match, do you? After all, Enec is dead, isn't he?"

"That was unworthy of you." Ardra swung around. She took her place in the bow, the perfect consort for the perfect man.

Unworthy. Yes, old Gwen was unworthy of a man like Vad. He was husband material for a politically connected wife—like Ardra.

Gwen looked at him, surrounded by his seven new friends. Liah had curled up in his lap and lay fast asleep, her face tucked into the crook of his arm. The others were no longer in their designated spots on the boxes of bribes. They were clustered around his boots and leaning on his arms, also sound asleep.

He'd do well with children, she thought. *Lots of them, following him about like the Pied Piper.*

I was right to avoid entanglements, she thought. *They*

lead to heartache. She took in a long, shuddering breath, but it did nothing to ease the sharp pain that lodged in her chest.

With a low command from Ardra, one of the Selaw escorts picked up an oar and began to shove the boat away from the pier. Gwen knew it was now or never. She jumped from the boat.

Chapter Twenty-four

"By the sword!" Vad burst from the gaggle of females and snatched the back of Gwen's tunic. He held her dangling over the water, half-inclined to drop her in. "Have you lost your senses?"

"Put me down," she said with all the heat he loved.

Gone was her sad demeanor, her almost skittish, colt-like behavior. Fire snapped in her eyes. He swung her back into the boat and dropped her onto the blanket-covered deck. He stood over her, his hands on his hips, and offered her his most menacing glare. "You are foolish, woman."

She struggled to her knees and jerked her tunic back in place. The men were staring at her bare stomach, exposed by his rough handling.

"So what? And don't call me woman. I have a name, damn it. How dare you . . . I have every right to leave if I want." Her little chin jutted forward; then her face altered, shifted, her eyes widening, her mouth dropping open. "Your sword."

"It is a knife . . ." he began, but then saw what she

did. Although not close to its once-vibrant color, the knife handle was clearly more blue-green than gray. He felt an easing, a loosening within him.

"You're better," Gwen said with a smile so sweet, he wanted to somehow capture it forever.

She was swamped by maidens who climbed over her to surround him. The boat rocked dangerously, and Ardra snapped a terse command, which was instantly obeyed, to everyone's amazement. The maidens took a seat, one to a box, knees primly together, hands folded, but eyes still avidly on his knife—or his groin. He could not tell which.

"Aye," he said. " 'Tis a wonder." He touched his brow.

Ardra nodded and gave him a smile, but somehow it did not light up his insides as Gwen's had.

"You must have done something, eaten something healing," Ardra said.

He had eaten nothing save an apple Gwen had fed him in the darkness. He had done naught to restore his health, unless one could believe that the power of her embrace was healing.

Red swept over Gwen's cheeks.

She was thinking as he was. The seven maidens, the escort, and Ardra were all staring in fascination at her face. He must divert their attention.

"You have not explained yourself. Why were you leaving the boat?" The instant he opened his mouth, the maidens, at least, snapped their attention in his direction.

"Ardra promised me her father would see I was returned to Nilrem's mountain." She mirrored his stance, hands on her hips.

"I will see you to Nilrem's mountain." The maidens' heads swiveled back and forth. He did not relish the public expression of her anger.

"When? After your quest is over? After your sword-restoring ceremony? Or maybe after your lifemating ceremony?"

"You are impertinent," Ardra said with a gasp. But when he raised his hand, she held her tongue.

"The 'when' will wait. It is only the 'why' you need know. You are my duty. My responsibility. I take my responsibilities seriously. I brought you to this place, and I will return you."

"Marvelous." Gwen sat cross-legged on the blankets, arms folded over her chest, her face turned away.

Ardra resumed her place and renewed her orders to push off.

"Do not think to try such behavior again, do you understand?" he said. "It is important we have use of your ability to sail this vessel, should these men prove more oarsmen than sailmen."

"It's sailor, not sailmen," she corrected.

Let her think he needed only her sailing ability. If it kept her off guard, so be it. He needed time to think of what she meant to him and how to communicate with her so Ardra could not hear his words.

When he settled back in his place, an icy wind in his face, the maidens once again clustered about him. Their scents and little muttered sounds interfered with his thinking.

Gwen sat with her back to him, her chin on her fist, staring straight ahead.

Would he ever lie again in the dark and not feel the silk of her cheek pressed to the back of his hand, or the warmth of her tongue down his belly, or the scalding heat of her tears as emotion overpowered her?

With a glance, he looked at his chest, where his tunic gaped open. No, he could not see red welts from the burn of her emotion, but inside it still flamed.

The heat of her passion had taken the place of the heat of his fever. In other circumstances, he would lifemate with her, for the idea of any man, even her perfect Bob, touching her with intimacy, lapping her nectar, sheathing himself in her silk, made him want to draw his sword and . . .

His sword.

A warrior without his sword was unworthy of any woman. When he regained his sword, his fortunes would turn. Of course, he had no idea how he would exchange a worthless dagger for a warrior's sword. Perhaps Gwen would think of some plan.

He must concentrate on the upcoming confrontation with the council, when he would present the empty dagger. The time drew near. He put his hand to his waist. The jeweled dagger was not in its sheath.

Searching among the folds of Liah's cloak, he found her little hand wrapped around her purloined treasure. He eased it from her palm, cleaned the sticky handle, and sheathed it.

Ruonail knew his gifts would not placate any father, and that the councilors could not hide their daughters' kidnapping for long. To save their heads, the councilors would heap the blame on the Selaw, fuel another war, turn all attention away from themselves.

The sound of the dipping oars and creaking wood was hypnotic, his fatigue deep, but his anxiety about the upcoming meeting kept him wide-awake.

The terrain gradually grew less rocky and greener. The wind no longer harrowed the cheeks, and sweat began to run down the faces of the oarsmen. When Ardra ordered the men to put ashore, he gave Gwen no opportunity to sneak away.

Instead he snagged her arm and marched her into the bushes.

"I could use a little privacy," she said coldly.

"I will give you a few moments, but you must give me your word you will return to this spot. We must speak privately."

Her stormy look boded ill for her return. "Swear it," he repeated.

"Okay. Okay. I'll be back." She disappeared into the greenery, her garments helping her to blend with the foliage. It was a Selaw trait, this garbing oneself like one's surroundings. Ardra's cloak would make her nearly invisible on the ice, and he supposed one of the boxes contained green gowns and cloaks.

True to her word, Gwen returned to the small clearing where he stood. "What's wrong with your hair?" he asked as sun pierced the glade in a sudden and final farewell to day.

"My hair?" She smoothed the short strands from her forehead.

"Aye." He moved closer, and despite an inner warning that he should not touch her, he stroked back the silky tresses. "It is turning dark near your scalp. Are you ill?" He touched her cheeks and forehead, which were mercifully cool.

"Oh, dear." She frowned, and he had to resist a need to smooth the furrow between her brows with his thumb. He dropped his hands and stepped away from temptation. "I suppose my roots need a touch-up."

"Roots?"

"Yes. This is really hard to explain. By roots I mean where my hair grows from my head. The color needs . . . to be painted on again."

"Painted on? You have gone too long without proper sustenance. I shall tell Ardra to delay the journey until I may prepare a meal. Fish, I think. I know some root vegetables that will amply supply not only flavor, but have healing—"

"Vad. Stop. I'm not hungry." She gave a long sigh and dropped to the ground. "Sit. This is going to disillusion you."

"Disillusion me? How could your hair offer me disillusionment?" But he sat beside her.

"I'm not really blond." She stroked her fingers through the soft cushion of dead pine needles and exposed the rich soil beneath. "My hair's really this color, maybe a little lighter. I was a blonde when I was a baby, but the color changed over the years, which is not uncommon in *my* world."

"Why would you not be content with what you are?"

She looked up, and a smile, one of sadness, crept over her face. "Blondes have more fun?"

He gently sifted his fingers through her hair, examining the dark roots. "You are discontent with your life? Your circumstances? You thought that if you were blond, your life would be more pleasing?"

"Well, put like that it sounds pretty pathetic." She leaped to her feet—away from his touch? "It's not discontentment. It's fashion. Everyone does it, even happy people. Just think about women's clothing. Do they ever change the design here? Make the sleeves wider? Or narrower?"

"Constantly."

"Then you can understand this. Women in my place change their hair color as often as they change the designs of their clothing."

He shrugged. "Despite your words, I think you are discontented with your life there."

Her little chin stabbed the air again. "I'm sure there are a few Selaw who wish their eyes were blue, and maybe someone, somewhere, might even want brown ones like mine." Then she lowered her gaze and jabbed the toe of her soft boot into the dirt. "I'm sure you didn't drag me out here to analyze my life. What do you want?"

The muscles of his legs and back protested as he stood up. He stretched and wished he had had the time to soak in the steaming pool. "I wanted to explain why I could not let you stay at the fortress."

"Is that all? You were quite clear: you needed a sailor.

And how dare you prevent me from going to Nilrem's mountain? Who do you think you are?" Tears glistened in her eyes.

He gathered her stiff form into his embrace. She smelled so sweet, felt so warm. "I could not allow you to remain at the fortress. Ruonail would not have been there."

"What are you talking about?" The tears slid down her cheeks. He skimmed one away with his thumb. "Had you remained behind, you would have found no Ruonail to help you, for he would have been long gone, onto the ice to face his end in his own way, or perhaps to an ally in another chiefdom who would give him shelter.

"Ruonail's meaning was veiled to protect Ardra, but clear to me. He intends to leave immediately. He does not plan to be at the fortress when a Tolemac legion comes to deal his fate."

"Poor Ardra," she said softly, and leaned into his body.

"Aye. Even now I imagine he is gone. A man capable of kidnapping, and more, will not spare his able warriors to escort a slave to Nilrem's mountain. You are safe only with me."

She nodded against his chest, her nose rubbing on the cloth and sending darts of desire into his loins. Carefully he set her away from him.

"When these matters are decided, I want you to lifemate with me."

Her mouth fell open; she staggered. Lest she fall, he put out his hand, which she grabbed and clutched. "I don't understand."

"And why do you not understand? Did I not tell you the the next woman I lay with would be my intended lifemate? Did you think I just tossed my vows over the abyss with Enec and took you for a night's pleasure?"

"I don't know what I thought." She pulled away and tucked her fingers under her arms. She paced the small clearing, agitated, glancing everywhere but at him.

"I saw you standing there at the edge of the abyss and knew I could not bear to see you die. I knew in that instant that we were tied together. I said as much as I joined myself to you."

"I thought they were just . . . words spoken in passion."

"You insult me."

She shook her head. "I don't mean to insult you. But you can't lifemate with me, not here."

"I will find a way."

"I'm not a virgin. And what of Ardra? Ruonail offered you everything he had. A beautiful daughter to be your lifemate. Political power to influence peace. A treat of a fortress with its own hot tub. Warriors to protect it all."

"That is why we must talk. I felt something like this might occur. I cannot insult Ruonail by rejecting his offer, and yet I cannot join myself to Ardra—or any other woman—when you are everything to me."

"I-I-I am?" Tears ran unchecked down her cheeks.

"Aye." He embraced her, and this time her body was pliant, molding willingly to his. A shudder of need for her ran through him.

"But I'm not a virgin."

"As to that, neither am I." He kissed her brow, her lips, lingering there, tasting her sweetness. "I do not understand it. Perhaps it is magic, but you are part of me now. That only makes my predicament worse. You must face it, Gwen, my life is uncertain. The council may strip me of my arm rings."

She whispered against his lips, sending a hum of sensation to his heart. "So what? We'll leave then, go to Nilrem's mountain together and go to Ocean City—"

A man's voice called for all to board the boat. Time was slipping away.

He set her aside. "If the council still wishes to consider me a traitor, they will not simply strip me of my arm rings and set me free to pursue my own path. At the worst, I am a dead man; at the least, they will sell me into slavery. And even if they allow me to keep my status, I cannot just put aside Ruonail's offer and say, No, I want this woman here, this slave, instead of a lifemating with an important Selaw heiress."

"I thought the mixing of Selaw and Tolemac was a bad thing."

"If the mix is between slaves or the lesser free folk. But who will not honor the offspring of rank, duly joined in a ceremony sanctioned by both chiefdoms? As you said, rank has its privileges."

Another shout drew his attention. "We must go. Think of some way to turn this empty dagger to our advantage. Think of what I have said; think of some plan that will allow us to be together and yet not injure Ardra. For she is blameless in all of this. She will be a woman alone when she returns to the fortress. And as Ruonail stated, a woman alone is prey."

He snatched her into his arms, then kissed her with all the heat and desire coiled inside him. "Know this well, Gwen—you are mine, and I intend to claim you."

Chapter Twenty-five

Twilight of the next day fell before they rounded the river bend that took them from Selaw territory to Tolemac. Undulating hills smoothed out to a wide valley, through which the river wound like a ribbon of blood under the setting Tolemac sun. Soon the night would belong to the moons, and surely, Gwen thought, the moons belonged to Tolemac, echoed by the color of the people's eyes, the gems in their belts and on the handles of their daggers.

Nestled in the valley, as far as the eye could see, stretched a city of tents, dotted about with the flicker of large fires. The tents were high-peaked pavilions with fluttering banners. It all reminded her of what a medieval tournament might have looked like. She imagined from the division of the tents on either side of the river that some were Tolemac and others Selaw.

In the midst of the light-colored tents on the Tolemac side, a cluster of a dozen or so were stark black against the hills.

"Who has all the black tents?" Gwen asked as she helped the maidens disembark from the boat in a natural cove that screened them from view of the valley.

"If they fly the standard of a single rose then Samoht has brought his personal guard—the Red Rose Warriors. They are known far and wide for their prowess as fighters." Vad stood on the bank and helped unload the boxes. When the boat was secured from both Selaw and Tolemac view, each person attended to washing up. Vad shaved with the razor-sharp edge of the jeweled dagger, and, along with the seven maidens, Gwen found it hard not to sit and stare as he worked.

Ardra changed into a green cloak edged with gold and purple. Senga braided Ardra's hair, then wound it about her head like a crown.

"Shall I send one of my men to Senga's father to inquire how he wishes to effect the return of his daughter? Surely one Selaw servant will not excite any curiosity. A lifemating negotiation will not be hostile. I imagine many Selaw are dining in Tolemac tents, as well as the reverse," Ardra said.

Vad nodded. "I am loath to send another man to do my tasks. But it makes sense."

"I could accompany him and see if I can contrive a private talk with the councilor."

Ardra kissed each maiden, and then, with but a moment of hesitation, kissed Gwen's cheek. She went to Vad. Before him, she bowed deeply, then, without a word, she melted into the night with her escort.

While the maidens spread blankets on the ground, night fell. Vad knelt by the water and gathered plants in the bright orb's glow.

It silvered his hair, cast a gleam on his clean-shaven face. Gwen sighed aloud. He looked up, smiled, and beckoned her near. She crouched by his side. In his hand he held a few flat leaves. He tore one and held it to her nose. It was peppery. "These will add a touch of flavor to the fish he catches." Vad nodded toward one of Ardra's men, who was setting out a small net. "If nothing else, we will dine well."

"Vad, what if this doesn't go well? Have you thought of that?"

He gave a negligent shrug, but she knew he cared deeply. "Isn't there something else you could be besides a warrior?"

He looked into the distance. "Nothing."

"I don't believe that," she said. "I didn't start out to run a shop. I was going to be a famous fabric designer, but circumstances changed that. I met Bob, he died, and I just couldn't sell his business. Now I love it. I love the games, talking to the people, playing the roles. Come on. Use your imagination; dream a little."

Ardra's man brought Vad a long, silver fish. He cleaned it and then wrapped it in the peppery leaves. Tucking the fish into the banked coals, he sat back and stared into the fire. "I would like a kitchen with three fires going at all times, a kettle constantly on the boil, and three men or women who love food to do my bidding." He grinned. "Most especially to clean the fish." Then he lost his smile. "But a man does not cook unless on the move with his company, or in a place where a woman is not available."

She imagined him in her grandmother's kitchen, a chef's apron about his waist, a wooden spoon in one hand. She laughed aloud at the image, because in her mind's eye, when he turned around, he wore only the apron and nothing else.

"What amuses you?"

"Nothing." She swallowed her delight.

Later, when the savory fish was but a memory, Gwen licked her fingers and sighed. Ardra burst from the shadows, her man running at her side.

"Disaster," she cried, and fell into Vad's arms. "All is discovered." She clutched his sleeves and gulped air.

With great calmness, Vad held her shoulders and shook her. "Steady. Start at the beginning. Tell us calmly."

Ardra nodded, and then broke into tears.

"I will tell you," Ardra's man said. He was a nondescript man of the same tall, blond stamp as the rest of the Selaw men. "As Mistress Ardra and I approached the tents, we heard a terrible commotion. Many folk were streaming toward a tent larger than the others."

"The council meeting tent," Ardra managed to say, then fell to sobbing.

"I asked a man tending a horse what was the matter and he said one of the councilors had been caught with another's lifemate."

"And?" Vad stifled an urge to choke the information from the man.

"And the wronged woman started screaming and tearing her hair, bemoaning her missing daughter and her mate's perf . . . perf—"

"Perfidy." He could imagine the rest. "And everyone became privy to her lamentations, thus alerting all to her daughter's plight, and so on to the other councilors."

The man bobbed his head in agreement with Vad's words.

"Ardra, bathe your face; we must go to the meeting tent immediately with the maidens. It is cruel to hold them from their families even a moment longer."

"But we haven't thought of a plan yet to explain the missing map!" Gwen cried. She peeled Ardra off Vad's chest and wiped her tearstained face with a wet cloth.

"I will take my chances." Vad stepped into a pool of moonlight, and Ardra gasped when she saw he was garbed in his Tolemac colors, once again a warrior from his tunic to his high black boots. "I want each maiden to stand with another. Youngest first, oldest last. Ardra, hold Liah's hand and keep a close watch on her. Gwen, walk a few paces behind us and keep your eyes downcast. It will serve to make you appear a proper servant."

The maidens lined up like ducklings behind their mother, and Gwen had to run to catch up when Vad immediately led them up the riverbank.

Her stomach danced as they approached the Tolemac camp. They excited great curiosity as they passed along the rows of tents, but the men who sat about the campfires merely rose and watched them, murmuring among themselves. No one challenged them, perhaps because of Vad's uniform, perhaps because they had children with them.

One tent, twice as large as the others, stood a bit apart. Torches ringed it. Men stood at attention, long spears in their hands at every tent stake. Angry voices could be heard. It sounded like dozens of men were talking at once. The apprehension in Gwen's stomach turned to stark fear.

Vad lifted his hand for them to wait and said only one word to the sentry at the tent flap: his name.

The sentry disappeared a moment, and the brief glimpse Gwen had of the inside was of splashes of color and many men about a large round table.

Silence fell inside the tent. When the sentry returned, he threw back the flap and gestured them in.

Vad pointed right as he entered, and the maidens, led by Ardra, took places against the canvas wall. Gwen's heart thudded hard in her chest.

The tent was awash with the scents of men: leather, oiled metal, sweat, and horses. There were no women present, and no one stood and cried with joy at the sight of his missing child. Utter silence had fallen.

Gwen counted twenty-four councilors at the table. The high eight sat in ornate chairs, with silver goblets and plates before them. Three men sat on more humble stools between each councilor. Banners of many colors, the Tolemac form of heraldry, lined the wall.

It was magnificent and frightening. Not one man smiled.

Vad knelt before one man, who stood at his approach. The man touched Vad's head and broke the tense silence. "Rise."

Gwen noticed he was not called "esteemed warrior" here, as he had been in the fortress.

Vad walked the table and accepted a similar touch on the head as he knelt at each chair. When he returned to the original man, he placed the jeweled dagger on the table. A murmur ran the length the table.

"Most esteemed High Councilor, I have brought you the dagger," Vad said. "I have also returned the maidens."

So this was Samoht. He was younger than she'd expected. He was also lean and handsome, his hair more brown than blond. His bright blue eyes raked the women. "This is most unexpected."

Vad nodded, and Gwen guessed the less said the better.

Samoht returned his attention to the dagger. He examined it, and finally twisted off the handle.

He upended it. An audible moan rose from the councilors. Samoht shook it, peered into it. "Is this some jest?"

All eyes turned to Vad.

"There is no jest," Vad said. "I gave the map to Ruonail's partner in this treacherous kidnapping. The man's name is Narfrom. I exchanged the map for Liah. I do not regret it."

No one spoke. Several heads turned toward Liah, then back to the high councilor. Finally Samoht cleared his throat. "What of Kered? Why is he not with you? Did you find him?"

Vad nodded. "I did. He had no intention of using the dagger, and knew nothing of its contents. It is a slave who holds him there, in a place called Ocean City, far across the ice fields. It is not a desire for treasure, or worse, a desire to plan treachery against Tolemac. He and his woman await the birth of their first child."

"How can we know this to be the truth?" asked one of the councilors. He was obese, overflowing his stool, his stomach straining his rich red robes.

Vad turned to him. "Because I say it is. And I do not wish to be questioned by a man who cannot even rise to welcome home his daughter."

A gasp ran the perimeter of the tent. Senga burst into tears. An expression of pain crossed the fat man's face, then his countenance smoothed to a doughy impassivity. His voice was low and trembled as he spoke. "I am at the tenth level of awareness. Do you think it worthy of me to show such emotion?"

"Aye. It would bespeak your concern for her."

"You tread without fear," Samoht said to Vad.

Vad swung in his direction. "What have I to fear? That I will be accused of treacherous acts? Or that I will be asked to a trek across the ice fields, a journey to almost certain death? Or should I fear the consequences of returning here to men who said they wanted one thing, but really wanted another?"

Several councilors put their heads together and whispered urgently.

The fat man rose. His stool fell over. "Let us be done with pretense. Our daughters"—he stabbed a finger at six men at various points about the table, each one a lesser councilor—"were taken, their lives threatened unless we tried to change the ice treaty. We have not tried, have we?"

"That is so." Samoht nodded. "Continue."

The other men rose. First one, then the other gave a piece of the story. Their beloved daughters had been taken, but they were determined that no matter what—even the painful deaths of their loved ones and the inconsolable misery of their lifemates—they would stand firm and do nothing to change the ice treaties.

Two other maidens began to weep. Gwen wanted to hug them, but she was disguised as a male servant and knew she couldn't do it.

Liah hid her face in Ardra's skirts.

Samoht sat heavily in his chair. He rubbed a hand over his face. "Sit." The seven men sank into their seats. "This is a diabolical mess. When may we expect more of Ruonail's demands?"

"Ruonail will be troubling you no longer," Vad said. "He has banished himself." Ardra made a small sound in her throat, and Gwen forgot her role and squeezed her hand. Vad continued, "I have brought his daughter, Ardra, to offer her father's sincere apologies." He beckoned her near.

Ardra went, her head held high, but Gwen saw the small trembling of her hands. She dropped to her knees before Samoht. The maidens crowded about her. "My house has always been honorable. I offer no excuse for my father, save madness."

Why didn't she mention Narfrom?

"Perhaps, if no harm has been done to the treaties, the councilors could step down, and the issue could be put in the past," said a councilor who was in a favored chair near Samoht. His long hair was gray and thick, his robes the white, black, and gold of Vad's uniform. He had a military air.

A frown knit Samoht's brow, and Gwen felt a shiver of fear again. "You are generous with your advice this night, Tol." Samoht seemed a hard man, and Gwen pitied the Selaw princess whom he would wed.

"The young often need advice." Tol smiled. "If Ruonail has banished himself, we are saved a visit to that cruel clime to take him. You know we would have lost many men trying to breach such a fortress. Let us be practical. The beloved daughters are returned." Tol pointed a finger to a councilor in ivory and blue. "Ranoc shall make what amends he can to his lifemate." His finger then shifted to a man who wore black and purple robes. "Srob's mate shall be scourged, as is proper in a faithless woman. All will then be as it was. New men will join the council; peace will continue." Tol yawned and scratched his own ample belly.

Scourge the woman, do nothing to the husband? Gwen had to bite her tongue.

"And what of our warrior here?" Samoht pointed the empty dagger at Vad.

"Ah. He has performed most admirably. As these fathers will attest." Tol smiled about the table. Seven heads nodded agreement. "He must be endowed with more than just a beautiful face to cross the ice fields and return. Surely, to keep his arm rings, he can be persuaded to show us how he did it. If not, I imagine he will spend his days as a pleasure slave to a woman whose mate is no longer capable of servicing her."

Laughter broke out around the table.

How could Vad stand there so calmly? Gwen's hands were locked in painful fists at her sides. She wanted to choke someone.

"Speaking of servicing," Samoht interjected, "are any of the maidens soiled?" Every head turned in their direction.

The young girls crowded close to one another, Senga at the center.

Vad answered. "Senga was attacked by her guard, but she fought him valiantly and is still intact. She should be rewarded for her bravery, equal to that of her esteemed older brother, who I know commands his own company."

"Hmmm," Samoht said. "And the others? Untouched, are they?"

"By men? Aye. But they need the comfort of their mothers."

"Take them away," Samoht said to several of the sentries standing by the tent flap. Ardra rose and shepherded the young maidens ahead of her. "Nay," Samoht barked. Everyone turned. "I wish Mistress Ardra to remain."

Gwen made a decision to stand unobtrusively by Ardra's side, her eyes downcast. Perhaps she'd just be considered an invisible servant.

"What have you to say for yourself, Mistress Ardra of the Fortress?"

She dropped back to her knees. Torchlight cast her hair in a golden crown. "I humbly ask to return home." Her voice trembled. "If it is as Vad states, and my father is . . . gone, the people will need me. They are as loyal to me as to my father. I ask if I might offer my allegiance to you, the Tolemac council, that you will trust me to maintain the treaty."

"Nonsense. A man must be appointed," Tol said. "Then we can get back to these mating plans for you."

Samoht nodded. "Aye." He pinched his lower lip and contemplated the pleated ceiling of the tent. His gaze returned to Vad. "You failed to bring Kered home," he said.

Vad nodded, but his gaze was steady.

"He brought the dagger," Tol said.

"Empty!" Samoht roared. He slammed a fist on the table. "What use is an empty dagger?"

Tol ignored the outburst. "Forgetting the dagger for a moment, I never understood what use Kered could be to us, Samoht. The man was besotted with his slave, a lamentable folly to be sure, but hardly worth our notice. If he wished to make a fool of himself, so be it." Several heads nodded in agreement, and Gwen felt a loosening of tension in the tent.

Then Samoht turned his eyes on those who were nodding. Several froze. "You consider Kered's desertion of his duties mere folly?"

"Kered was as brave a warrior as ever wore the Tolemac colors," Tol said softly. "He did all we asked and more. I begrudge him nothing, especially as he so willingly gave Vad the dagger. He did give the dagger willingly, did he not? He is not lying dead somewhere, a knife between his shoulder blades?"

Everyone turned to Vad.

Vad nodded. "He is well. Indeed, as I said, Kered was as ignorant of what the dagger contained as I was. He gave it with his blessing."

"And so we come again to the empty dagger and the map that is now in the hands of Ruonail's partner, this Narfrom."

Gwen held her breath. She felt as if a judge were about to issue a sentence. Vad looked unconcerned, calm. What did he feel inside?

Tol continued. "I have loved and lost children. I believe I, too, would have exchanged a piece of paper for a child." The tension loosened in Gwen's chest. "It seems Kered was never out to harm Tolemac. Only you, Samoht, seemed intent on his return and punishment. Perhaps you allowed your personal enmity to cloud your judgment?"

"*This* man's loyalty is still in question!" Samoht said, rising from his place, his long robes swirling about his legs. "*You* may be sure there is nothing to Kered's departure, but *I* choose to believe otherwise. For all I know, Kered is here, the map in his hands, seeking the treasure as we speak."

"You go too far," Vad said. Gwen saw his hand go to the hilt of his knife. "I have stood here and heard myself and my friend maligned. If you wish some proof of my loyalty, I can think of no other. You bade me return with the dagger and I have. I cannot return the map. It is in the hands of a man who will surely use it for ill. But at the time, I felt I had no choice. You cast aspersions on my good name."

"Your good name?" Samoht said with a sneer. "Who

is your family? How many generations back can you trace your roots?"

"Enough." Tol slapped the table with his palm. "Let us put him to another test." At the word *test,* Gwen felt sweat break out on her skin. "Have him draw what he remembers of the map, and then use it. Have him obtain the treasures for us. If this other villain, Narfrom, has it, it is in Vad's interest to get there first."

Gwen felt sick to her stomach. No, she thought, don't ask him to get the treasures.

"As for Ardra," Tol said, "until we decide what is best for the fortress, she should remain here. Perhaps as a reward for bringing us the treasures, we could mate her to Vad."

Samoht crossed his arms over his chest. "And should Vad decide to keep the treasures for himself?"

"Everyone knows only a brave and honorable warrior can use them. That makes such treachery pointless."

A murmur of satisfaction swept the table.

Resuming his place at the table, Samoht held up his hands for silence. "This is my decision. Should anyone wish to oppose me, he must do so now. The seven councilors must step down for keeping silent about the abductions. They will take their families back to their chiefdoms, and make penance of two arm rings to the Tolemac council." One man moaned and dropped his head. "Their daughters of mating age will be given lifemates immediately. Should their maidenheads prove to have been breached, they will be sold as slaves. Mistress Ardra will remain in our custody until Vad obtains the treasures. He has five sunrisings."

"Five," Ardra whispered. "Impossible."

"You have something to say, Mistress Ardra of the Fortress?" Samoht impaled her with a glare. Gwen felt its ice, as if he'd sent a winter wind whipping through the tent.

"No, Esteemed Councilor."

"Excellent." Samoht held out the jeweled dagger. It was passed from one councilor's hand to another until it reached Vad. He took it.

"And if we send this warrior to gain the treasures, what weapons do we grant him?" the man called Ranoc asked hesitantly, almost apologetically.

"Weapons?" Samoht repeated.

"Aye. We do wish him to succeed, do we not?" Ranoc said.

"Tol, you have more experience in such matters. What weapons should we grant this man?" Samoht asked.

The older man pursed his lips and stared at the ceiling. "We have taken his sword," he said finally, "so it is not possible to give him another. Let him request one weapon to aid him in his hunt—save, of course, a sword."

Samoht threw his arms out in a deceptive gesture of generosity. No kindness or concern lit his austere features. "Name your weapon."

Vad answered with little hesitation. "I have the use of a sturdy bow, but could use a supply of arrows."

Samoht nodded his head and raised his hand. The guard at the tent flap disappeared and returned in a few moments to drop three arrows in a clatter at Vad's feet.

Three! Three would never be enough. Gwen bit her tongue to keep silent.

Vad did not blink or glance down. Any anxiety he felt at being sent on a treasure hunt with few weapons was well concealed behind his seventh-level awareness training.

"And . . ." Vad continued.

"And?" Samoht dropped his hand. "One weapon is all we will grant you."

"It is not another weapon I request, but two horses."

Samoht nodded his head and crossed his arms over his chest. "Vad shall deliver the treasures in five sunrisings. Is there any dissent?"

No one spoke. Gwen looked at Tol, who had seemed more reasonable than the others. But Tol was picking his nails with his own dagger point.

Vad bowed to the council and turned on his heel. When Ardra tried to follow him from the tent, Samoht called her back with a sharp command.

Gwen's mouth dried. She glanced about. No one was watching her. A Tolemac guard picked up the three arrows and followed Vad. With her head down, she ducked out of the tent. No voice called her back; no heavy hand fell on her shoulder. She almost ran to stay close on Vad's heels and avoid notice.

Once he was a few yards from the council tent, Vad turned and took the arrows from the guard, barked an order for him to remain where he was, and stomped away.

Vad muttered all the way through the city of tents. He stopped once, kicked a pot from the three-legged iron stand on which it sat by a fire, grabbed it by its long handle, and thrust it into Gwen's arms.

Gwen shook at the idea of a treasure hunt with only Vad's long knife and a handful of arrows. They stopped in an area on the outskirts of the tents, where a rope cordoned off a section filled with horses and guarded by a dozen men. Surely they would question her presence? Hanging back near a tent, she glanced about. Every eye was on Vad as he examined horses and selected two, and no one seemed to pay any attention to her, so she picked up a leather pack lying on the ground. A quick peek told her it wasn't a feed bag.

At the riverside, Vad tethered the horses to a low branch and ordered Ardra's men after their mistress. When they were gone, he kicked dirt on the coals of the fire, tore the coverings from the seven bribery boxes, stared at the contents, and swore. "Even in appeasement, the man was treacherous."

Dirt and stones spilled from the boxes as he threw them into the river. "Mount up," he ordered her.

"We can't go now," Gwen said. "You can hardly see your hand in front of your face, it's so overcast. There's no moonlight." Every muscle in his body was tense with anger. "Get a good night's sleep, and we'll start when the sun rises."

"By the sword," he swore, and disappeared into the shadows.

Gwen ran to the edge of their small camp, then stopped. He was angry and disappointed, and probably felt betrayed on all sides. Maybe he needed to let off some steam. After all, he had expected to get his sword back, not go on an impossible treasure hunt.

But that left her alone with a fire that was almost out. She did what she could to coax it to life, but succeeded only in extinguishing it completely. Finally she admitted defeat and wrapped herself in a blanket.

What if Vad didn't come back? What if she was abandoned here? A rustle in the undergrowth reminded her that she was in an alien place. What creatures were stirring? What became of women slaves who had no one to look after them?

He wouldn't abandon her, would he? Exhaustion tempted her to lie down by the cold fire, but fear kept her sitting upright, peering into the trees where Vad had disappeared.

"Come back, Vad," she whispered.

Chapter Twenty-six

Vad woke her by brushing a finger over her cheek. She struggled up on one elbow, but could not see his face to gauge his temper.

"Come." He offered his hand and pulled her to her feet. They walked along the river for about half a mile, then stopped at a grassy bank. The air was almost warm. Or was it his presence that warmed her inside?

The clouds had parted, and the Tolemac moons were high overhead in a purple velvet and diamond-studded sky.

"Gwen?" She smiled up at him. He lifted her fingers to his mouth. "Forgive my temper." He turned her hand and touched her palm with his lips.

"You're not angry anymore?"

"I have had much time to think. Perhaps this is for the best. I will obtain the treasures and demand the ultimate reward."

"Ultimate reward?" She could barely talk. His tongue traced a figure eight on her palm.

"Aye," he whispered against her skin. "I shall ask that they grant you at least one arm ring, that we might lifemate."

"Arm ring?" She said the word, then gasped. He licked up her wrist, over her pounding pulse. In moments he had her tunic over her head. A breeze kissed her bare breasts as his mouth kissed her throat.

Her breeches slid easily down her hips and legs, snarled on her crossgarters, but yielded to his knife.

He slashed the thongs and threw the thin strips of leather to the dew-studded grass. She shivered, then grew hot. He peeled off his tunic and dropped it. A liquid rush tore through her as he stripped his own breeches and boots off.

Naked, aroused, he stood before her.

"The last time we made love," she said softly, "was in total darkness. This time I want to see your face. I want to watch every muscle move." She skimmed her fingers down the valley of his chest. His muscles leaped beneath her fingertips. "I want to see the expressions on your face." Then a thought came to her, and she bit her lip and withdrew her hand. "Your expressions will change, won't they? You won't hide what you feel from me with your awareness training?"

"Sweet Gwen, I will hide nothing of my thoughts." He took her hands and placed them on the honed muscles of his chest.

"Thank you," she said, and plucked at his nipples until they were tight points. He bit his lip and groaned. She learned every valley and ridge of his chest just as she had in the grotto, only this time she kept her eyes on his face, a face now beautiful to her not because of nature's kind arrangement of bones and flesh, but because it truly was a window to how good he was, how kind inside.

His eyes were black in the night, his hair a silver blaze about his shoulders. The snap of a twig made her jerk her hands from his stomach and turn.

"It is only a night creature, a very small one," he said, and wrapped his arms about her waist. The feel of his hard body, his arousal nestled against her buttocks, made her groan in turn. He spread his hands over her stomach and then slid them up to cup her breasts, much as Narfrom had. The memory made her shiver, and she clutched Vad's hands tightly to her. "Narfrom touched me like this."

His body went taut behind her. "I will kill him the next time I see him."

"It was to intimidate me; he felt nothing for me, but I want to forget." He gently caressed her, soothing her nipples and inflaming them at the same time.

"I want my child to drink from your breast. I regret this implant you have."

So do I, she said to herself. She turned in his arms to see his face. "Make love to me, Vad," she said, and locked her arms about his neck.

He placed her on the ground and granted her wish. She was so aware, every sense heightened by her intense need for him, that she imagined she felt every ridge of his fingerprints as he traced her hip, her inner thigh. She could not get enough of him. She stroked his back, his buttocks, cupped him in her palm, and finally bent her head over him.

"Gwen." He gasped and arched off the velvet grass. She straddled his thighs and used both hands to measure him and bring him pleasure. He groaned and bucked his hips. When she could tell he was at the limit of his endurance, she sat back, massaged the long muscles of his thighs, and whispered soothing words until he relaxed and fell still.

Then she began again, rubbing her hands in long strokes over his body. Every nuance of his pleasure streaked across his face. He arched his head back and moaned, and finally snatched her into his arms and flipped her over.

But he did not do as she expected and enter her; no, he did everything she had, only much slower. He ran his tongue and hands from her shoulder to her toes, touching and laving her with infinite patience.

"Now, please," she said, and he slid up her body.

"Look at me," he whispered against her mouth. She opened her eyes and stared into his. "I love you, Gwen from Ocean City," he said, and slid into her.

She wrapped her legs about his hips and hung on for the ride she knew was coming. "I love you, too." His eyes closed; a groan tore from his throat. She felt every inch of his hard, deep thrusts, each hot spurt as he came. An answering hammer of blood and flare of heat coursed through her as she came with him.

"Wake up," he said at her ear.

She groaned.

"We have a moment or two before the sun rises and we must go."

"Uh," she said as his hand moved to her inner thigh. "Go?" She should know what he was talking about, but her brain was fried.

"Aye."

She remembered now. He caressed her with a light touch, and her body rose instantly to a fever pitch. She reached for him; he was more than ready. "My noble warrior," she teased as she encircled him.

He peeled her fingers away. "No. Not yet. I have waited three long conjunctions to lie with the woman I desire, so I wish it to be nothing but the best of pleasure for you. Let me prepare you." He leaned over her and kissed her nose.

She cupped his face and stared into his beautiful blue eyes. "No, don't prepare me. You prepared me three times last night, and if you do it again I'll have a coronary."

"A coronary is bad?" He took her hands and stretched them out to the sides.

She found her wrists pinned to the grass. The long length of his body over hers, his gentle imprisonment of her hands, made her heart thunder in her chest. He nudged her thighs apart with his knee, and she felt the flame-hot heat of him.

With a soft moan, she answered him. "A coronary is very bad. It means my heart will stop beating, from too much . . . joy. So no more preparation. Please." She gasped when he bent his head and his long hair skimmed her breast. "Please. No preparation." The words barely made it past her lips as his teeth closed over her nipple.

"Just this?" he asked a moment later as he sheathed himself.

"Yes," she cried out at the heat of him, the hard feel of him inside her. She tightened her legs about his hips.

In the near-dawn, with the sky brightening each moment, she could see the love in his gaze. "Free me," she said, and he did.

Vad went down on one knee by the fire. He made a quick sketch of the map. Gwen watched as he placed an eight-branched tree in the center, then surrounded it with other symbols.

"Choose a peril," he said with a gesture at the drawing. Behind him, pale pink tinted the dawn sky. "Should I fight the sow, the hounds, or the dragons?" he asked.

"Gee, none of the above," she muttered. "The map reminds me of an island."

"Not an island, an area—the Forbidden Place. It is believed that the perils surround the tree to protect the treasures buried there from those who would seek them for the wrong purpose."

"What's a right purpose?" She rested her chin on her knees, watching his shoulders ripple through another shrug, and sighed. They were great shoulders.

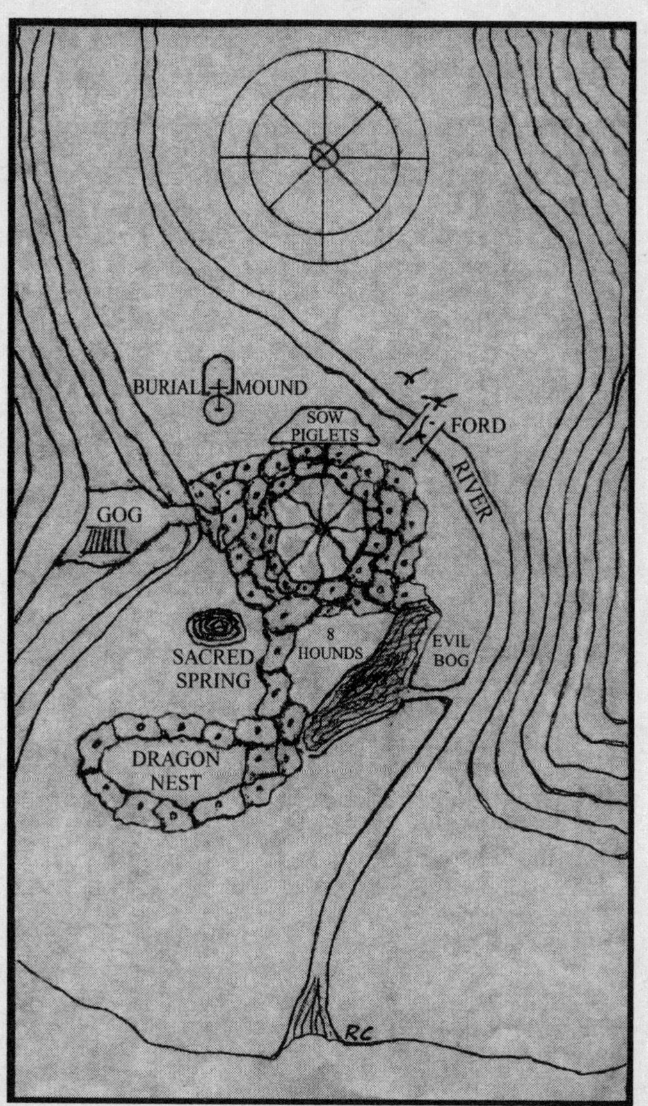
BURIAL MOUND
SOW
PIGLETS
FORD
RIVER
GOG
8
HOUNDS
EVIL
BOG
SACRED
SPRING
DRAGON
NEST
RC

"Nilrem chose the tree and the Forbidden Place as a challenge to man's honor. No one has succeeded in finding the treasures—or the wisdom it is said will be gained in the bargain. Perhaps the treasures do not really exist."

"You didn't mention this honor bit to Narfrom. He's going to be a bit put out if he finds the treasures and they don't work. Do you know how to find this eight-branched tree without the map?"

"I believe so. Certain items I remember on the map are known places. Gog—"

"What's gog?"

"Gog was a sleeping giant of legend. If you look for him now, you will see but a steep mountain to be climbed. The Raven's Ford, the sacred spring, the evil bog, these are all known places. The former two were sacred places of worship in the ancient times, and the latter is still believed by many to harbor evil spirits."

"By all means, try to avoid the evil spirits."

He smiled. "The ignorant cling to their beliefs despite what the priests might tell them." He tapped the river ford. "The Ford of Ravens. 'Tis said that if one sees a woman there, instead of ravens, she will show you your death in the reflection of the water."

"Marvelous," Gwen said. "Avoid that place, too."

"Would the pack of eight hounds be preferable?"

"Can't you come up with any other numbers? Why not nine? Or five? I'm sick of eight," she said tartly. She tried to remain calm. How could he speak so casually about this latest quest?

"You must be fatigued," Vad said, then yawned and scratched his belly.

Gwen felt her face flush red. "You're not?"

"I slept. But I imagine the folk who guard the tents slept little from all the yelling. A compliment to my prowess, I believe it was, all your yelling."

"I did not yell, or maybe just a little. Oh, stop. Please." She hid her face in her hands.

* * *

Vad loved looking at her. He now knew every hair on her head, the shape of her ears, the taste of the soft skin behind them. To distract himself from the thought of soft skin, he bit into one of their remaining apples.

"Weren't there piglets on the map? They sound non-threatening," she said.

"Their sow is the size of three horses, each piglet the size of one. Her milk is a burning acid, and the piglets suckle and spit the liquid at intruders. If the piglets are male, they have razor-sharp tusks."

"What an image."

Gwen stared up at him, and he found himself mesmerized by the depths of her dark eyes. He forced himself to think of perils instead of seeking the peace of her embrace. Never had he known such contentment. For the first time he understood Kered's need for Maggie, understood how Kered had given up all for the woman he loved. Under other circumstances, would Kered have given Maggie up to protect her?

Vad hoped Gwen would understand what he must do.

"Other than deadly milk, is there anything else special about the sow?"

"She has bristles about her snout that cause an itch so terrible, you will die of it, your skin hanging in bloody tatters from your scratching."

"That's more information than I need," Gwen muttered. "What about the hounds?"

Vad shrugged. "The hounds have fangs that drip poison. A gash from their teeth will fester immediately. They are said to run more quickly than the fastest horse and swim faster than a snake."

"Then it will be the nest of dragons," Gwen said, her voice trembling.

He cast the apple core into the shrubbery. "Dragons spew venomous spittle. It eats through the skin. Some people are not susceptible to it; others die writhing in pain as the sores eat away their flesh."

"I have a confession to make." Her words were soft sounds, scattering the images from his mind.

He went down on one knee by her and tucked several strands of her hair behind her ear. "What? You desire me again?"

"Men. They think only of making love."

But her smile belied the sharpness of her tone, and it was not making love he was thinking of. No, he was thinking of her smallness and vulnerability.

"I borrowed some stuff on our way here." She handed him a worn leather pack. "I hope you won't be too angry with me."

He looked inside and grinned. "Do you know what we have here?"

Gwen watched him pull out a bundle of soft cloth. "What is it? A weapon we can use?"

"Better than that—bread." He unwrapped a loaf of bread, tore off a piece, and handed it to her.

They ate. More time wasted.

"What will you do with the cooking stand?" she asked when he was packing his horse for the journey.

Silently he held the iron handle and brought it down in a harsh swipe. "A favorite weapon of women, it is said."

"Used on the heads of their cheating lifemates, I presume." She shivered, the bread in her hand forgotten. "You'll have to choose your own peril. I can't help you. They all sound so frightening. Before coming here, the worst peril I'd ever faced was Mrs. Hill."

He grunted. She encircled his waist and laid her head against his chest. "What's your best weapon, Vad?"

"The sword," he said.

"Oh . . . I'm so sorry." She squeezed him hard.

"I have my own confession to make." He steeled himself for what he must do. "There is not much choice between the perils; each is a formidable challenge. But the choice is already made for me."

"Why?"

"I have been given only five sunrisings. This is the first. I have no choice but to go straight to the tree—through the bog, past the hounds." Each moment he spent here by the fire with her was just more delay.

"We can do it," she said softly.

A brisk wind rose. He looked at the sky. It was just about light enough to begin his journey. It was clear, almost cloudless. He could not imagine a blue sky. Then the earth seemed to tip and spin. In his mind's eye he saw the strange thing Gwen called a plane in the sky, a blue sky, with a trail of pure white behind it.

He shook the image off.

"I. Not we. I will not be taking you with me. When I am gone, seek Ardra in the camp. She will be permitted her own servants and will thus be able to protect you."

"What?" Her body had gone stiff in his arms. She stared up at him with a look so vulnerable, he felt skewered in his vitals.

"I am not staying with Ardra!" She jerked from his arms and stood there, her mouth open. Then she threw her bread at him. "How dare you! How dare you make love to me all night, then abandon me in the morning?"

He brushed the bread from his chest and struggled to maintain his composure. "You cannot come with me. Do you really think the council expects success? My death is far more likely."

"Damn the council then. Let's take the horses and go to Nilrem's mountain. We can go home to my place and live happily ever after." Tears ran down her cheeks.

"Happily ever after." He said the words slowly. "You expect too much." He carried the purloined pack to his horse. "I am thinking only of your safety."

Gwen watched him prepare the horse. Only one horse.

"I don't need you to look after me—or anyone else!

And what about returning with the treasures and asking for an arm ring for me?" Her skin felt hot, her hands cold. There was a burning pain in her throat. "Was that a lie?"

"No," he said, and reached for her, but she evaded his touch—his seductive touch. "I did not lie to you. If I am successful, I will do as I said. And you will be there, in the camp, safe and protected to attend the ring ceremony."

How military he looked, how implacable, how stubborn, in his Tolemac warrior uniform, creased from being carelessly discarded during lovemaking.

She wanted to shriek. "You knew you were leaving me behind last night, didn't you? You knew it even as you made love to me. That's why it was so intense, wasn't it?" Every muscle in her body ached from the night of passion. Her heart ached, too.

"Aye. I knew it last night. I knew I could not allow harm to come to you."

"I knew it, too." She pressed her fingers to her mouth. "I knew it. You told me so in the cavern. You said if you had me, you'd leave me."

"I am not leaving you. I am protecting you."

She sank to her knees and hugged her arms about her ribs. The pain in her chest was enormous. Ardra had known it, too. A man as beautiful as Vad would never stay with one woman, she'd said.

"Rise. I must go. You must go." He put out his hand, but she ignored it.

"Go. Just go then. But I'm not going to stay in some camp with Ardra! And if you come back, *she'll* be the one undergoing a ceremony with you—a lifemating ceremony. Damn you."

She ran from him, reached the bushes, and in a burst of speed flew blindly toward the cover of trees.

The low branches snatched at her hair. She ran until the pain in her side caused her to fall to her knees in a swath of grass, trampled green grass, trampled from their lovemaking. She knelt there and wept. He was never coming back. He'd die, or abandon her for another, worthier woman. *Ardra.*

Chapter Twenty-seven

Gwen pounded the trampled grass with her fists. Vad had known he was leaving, known it each time he'd kissed her, touched her. If *she'd* known . . . she would never have made love to him again. How much easier it was to take rejection without the scents and aches of lovemaking still lingering on your body.

A crackle in the undergrowth made her leap to her feet. Would Vad come after her? Gwen strained her ears for the jingle of harness or the sound of footsteps, then peered into the dense tree cover. When she heard nothing, she wiped her tears and tried to compose herself. The effort was too great. She sank to the spot where he'd made love to her and silently wept.

Of course he didn't want her. She wasn't from his world. She was a liability. She brought him no illustrious ancestors, in fact, had only a family she neglected badly.

She thought of her mother, her father, her sister, even R. Walter. They'd never know what had become of her.

And what would become of her if she stayed here? Would she serve Ardra? *Never.*

It hurt all the more because she liked Ardra. Ardra was sweet and gentle. Ardra had saved her life. What courage it had taken to stand up to her father. What man wouldn't want her?

Gwen faced the reality of going home. Somehow. Now. Not later, when Ardra was enjoying the Selaw equivalent of a honeymoon with Vad, but right now. The mental picture of Vad lying on a bed, a real bed, with someone else, was too much to bear. She pressed her fists to her temples to block out the image.

"I have to get away," she said aloud.

Then she realized that if she left, she'd never know if Vad survived his treasure hunt. The thought of him alone in an evil bog, surrounded by . . . bog things made her skin crawl. No matter what her own fate must be, she had to know what became of him.

She worried about Narfrom. The sky was a clear, bright lavender overhead. Maybe he was at Sotheby's auctioning the treasure map, claiming it was for *Merlin's* treasures. He might also be out there somewhere seeking the treasures himself. She still believed the ultimate confrontation with him had been postponed, not prevented.

Another flood of tears overwhelmed her. Why hadn't she resisted Vad? Her pain was of her own making.

Then another thought intruded. Why had Vad needed two horses? Had he originally intended to take her with him? Maybe he'd been disappointed in her lovemaking, and had had second thoughts. She cringed and dropped her head onto her knees.

Why would a man so spectacular be interested in her? Because there was no one else available? She wiped her tears on her sleeve again.

The whicker of a horse made her swing around. There sat Vad atop a sturdy horse, the reins to the other in his hand. "What do you want?" She scrambled to her feet and jammed her hands on her hips.

"I want to know why you further delay me by running away."

"Delay you? Just go. Leave me alone. I'm not completely stupid. I can find my way to your precious Ardra."

He threw a leg over the front of the saddle and slid to the ground. "My precious Ardra?"

Gwen wiped her nose with the back of her hand, conscious of how she must look, her cheeks grimy with tears, her hair a mess from rolling on the ground half the night.

Slowly he walked nearer until he towered over her. "You think because I inhabit this form, I have not the integrity to remain true to one woman—you."

"You were leaving me behind."

For a moment words escaped him. "For your safety," he finally managed. How easily he had found her. He, too, would have come to this place to lick his wounds, the place where they had joined themselves so ardently. They were more alike than he cared to admit.

"Your tears," he said, "are not about waiting in the camp for me to return. They are not tears of fear that I may be devoured by some menace on my way to the treasures, are they?" Her silence was answer enough for him. "Do you think I declared myself and meant none of it?" he nearly shouted.

Her gaze slid from his. "Vad, I—"

He threw up a hand to silence her. The evasion of her eyes said so much. "You think a man who is beset by the attentions of women is easily drawn in by them. That is what you think, is it not? You think I am incapable of constancy! You think a woman perhaps more beautiful than you, or more . . . By the sword. I am sick of it. I was leaving you behind because I could not bear to see you hurt."

"Vad. You have to understand. Every man I've ever loved has left me. I—"

"Every man? Your Bob? You blame him for dying? Then well you should blame me, too, when I am rotting in the evil bog. Believe that I am doing so to make your life miserable."

He boosted her into the saddle, trying not to think about how small and delicate her bones felt in his hands. He could not remain here one moment longer.

"You make me sound petty. I'm not petty." She gripped the reins in a tight fist.

Better her anger than her tears. "You are petty. You are doubting. You have no trust. And yet I must take you on this treasure hunt. I have lost far too much time to return you to my 'precious Ardra.' Now, instead of concentrating on the perils, on finding the treasures, I must spend every moment worrying about your safety." He handed her the jeweled dagger. "You will need a weapon."

"I'm sorry." Tears ran freely down her cheeks.

Sorrow would not sway him. "Your apology means nothing." A small hiccup joined her tears. The little sound ate at his composure. More followed. By the time he settled himself in the saddle, he had not the heart to continue chastising her. "Perhaps you were just not thinking clearly," he finished.

"I promise I won't be a burden. I can help you. I just know it."

Her simple words scattered what remained of his ire. What worthier woman could he ask for than one willing to battle perils at his side? Perhaps one more predictable. "You will follow my orders. You will do only what I tell you, when I tell you. Is that understood? And when we return, we will deal with your inability to trust me, to believe in my love for you."

They rode in silence for about an hour, by Gwen's reckoning, along a path that edged the river. She hated staring at his broad back. It seemed stiff with displeasure—because of her. Several ravens sat in the top of a tree and tracked their progress. They reminded her of the fortress, and that reminded her that Vad might soon be Ardra's husband.

"Vad. What if the council insists you lifemate with Ardra? How can you say no?"

He did not even look over his shoulder. "Whatever I decide to do about Ardra will have nothing to do with my love for you."

"Oh?" What the heck did that mean? "You'll lifemate with Ardra, and keep me on the side? Is that what you're saying? Well, no way."

He hauled on his reins, holding his mount in place until she caught up to him. A muscle twitched in his jaw. Even his hair looked angry. "By 'keep you on the side,' " he snapped, "do you mean as a concubine?"

"Yes."

"How could you think so little of me?"

The fact that her doubts had the power to hurt him amazed her. She'd never been on the giving end of pain. It made her feel very small and very contrite.

"Can I start over?" She felt the tears gathering again, but fought them this time. They were a weakness he probably deplored. Women about to cross an evil bog should not give any outward sign of frailty. "I just think when you get back—and you will get back, I know it—the council will offer you Ardra, and you'll have to take her."

"Ardra is not some package to hand around. The council may offer her to me, or may not. How I will answer I do not know. Perhaps I will say aye to a mating with her. Perhaps not."

She let her horse drop back behind his. On second thought, maybe weeping was a good thing.

* * *

They allowed the horses to pick their way daintily through the outskirts of the bog. Vad took her reins and led her horse as the ground began to grow more uncertain underfoot. The trees thinned and took on a ravaged look. He spoke over his shoulder. "Before we are deep in the bog, I have but one request of you."

"What is it?" Her horse stumbled a bit in the softening ground.

"I know the value of a family. When we complete this journey, should you return to your place, make peace with your parent, your sister. They must grieve for your loss."

Return to her place. Could she ever leave him? Yes . . . if the council gave him to Ardra. She had too much respect for the woman to horn in on her happiness.

Maybe the wandering wiseman, Nilrem, could help her go home. But wait, she had watched Narfrom disappear. He had done it right there in the fortress, not on some mountain under the direction of a wiseman.

Power and design, Narfrom had said.

So theoretically, *she* could leave at any time. No, she couldn't. She couldn't envision life without Vad. It was not possible to spend the rest of her days looking at him glowering down on her from a poster, playing his game, turning him off and wishing for what could not be.

She hadn't wanted another man in her life, hadn't wanted to face another heartbreak. This time it hurt as much as she remembered—times ten. How could she have fallen in love with a man who was too handsome for words and too kind for his own good?

But no matter how painful her love for him, no matter how alien and frightening his world, she now knew the only way she'd leave him was if he sent her away.

Gwen strove to be nonchalant. "Maybe one day I'll make peace with my parents. You'd really like my mother. And she'd love . . . your eels. This experience certainly makes holding a grudge against my sister seem—"

"Petty. Is Rwalter a good match for your sister?"

"Perfect," she said, and for the first time she meant it. "They have everything in common. My sister was my best friend until . . . she met R. Walter. I miss her friendship."

Vad nodded and held up a hand. He listened a moment, then signaled her forward. "I understand. It must be similar to what I feel at the loss of Kered's leadership." He talked of the accusations leveled against himself and Kered.

Gwen could hear the continued pain in his voice at how his reputation had not been enough to stand against Samoht's accusations. "This Samoht must have a real grudge against you," she said.

Vad shrugged. "Samoht's grudge is more with Kered, but as his lieutenant, I must stand in his place."

"You took it with admirable grace," she said. "I wanted to leap over that round table and smack his arrogant face."

Vad turned in his saddle and grinned. "You are a fierce little warrior woman."

Black water, with an oily scum, seemed to surround them. She wrinkled her nose. "Boy, this place stinks."

Remnants of ancient trees rose like black spikes from the water. The dry or firm places were growing smaller. Afraid of becoming lost, or being unable to find her way back, Gwen used the jeweled dagger to cut slashes on the bare tree trunks whenever she could manage it without falling out of the saddle.

The sky grew overcast; the sun retreated. "We'll get out of here before it gets dark, won't we?"

Vad shook his head. The idea of this place in the dark was more than intimidating. At least in the fortress the ground was solid underfoot.

Vad pulled up his horse. She watched him scrape a

fungus growth from a tree trunk. "Dinner," he said, and placed it in the worn leather pack. He slowly grew more talkative, losing some of his stiffness with her.

The murky ground near her burped a bubble of gas. She grabbed her nose and wheeled her horse back.

"Here." He offered her a strip of cloth that had been wrapped about the bread. She held the cloth to her nose.

"You asked me before what my best weapon was, and I answered my sword. Then I started to think, perhaps it is not a sword that will triumph here. Perhaps I could—"

"Feed the hounds something noxious, like the stuff for the mourning wine? Did you bring my basket?"

"No."

"Oh, too bad. It had that potion you cooked up for the maiden rescue. And apples."

He dug about in his saddle pack and held something up. "Would you like one now?"

She accepted the apple and tucked it into her tunic. "Does this mean the potion's somewhere in your pack, too?" He nodded. "Then maybe it's not such a bad thing that we couldn't use it at the fortress."

"Aye. This time I will invite eight to dinner—hounds, that is."

Gwen smiled behind her cloth. His next few words took away all her humor.

"From this point, we must beware of outcasts and water creatures."

"Outcasts? Water creatures? Sure. No trouble. I'll just keep my eyes peeled."

"I know you are not going to peel your eyes, but especially you must look for Wartmen. They often venture into the bog, perhaps to hunt the ravens. A raven pie is very satisfying."

It took most of the day to go only a few leagues. The horses wouldn't go faster than a walk, and Vad stopped repeatedly to scrape fungi into his pack. Gwen began to pride herself on spotting the ugly growths before he did. As they went deeper into the bog, new growth appeared, long, cobwebby strands that crossed the paths and clung to their hair and horses, draping itself from branch to branch.

She continued making her marks.

Vad raised his hand. As she drew to his side, every muscle of her back and legs aching from the tense ride, she saw what he did: three men. They were swathed in fur cloaks like the one Vad had left in Ocean City. Dirty beards covered the lower halves of their faces. One stepped ahead of the others. There were no weapons in view beyond the usual knives.

With a stiff nod, Vad dismounted and handed her his reins. Slowly, his hands out at his sides, he advanced. The first man met Vad, and the two hunkered down and spoke. Gwen wished she could hear their words. A second man, with some sort of crusty growth on his cheeks—warts, she realized—gave her a wide grin. Could he tell she was a woman? Gwen thought not. Her cloak would conceal most of her form, and the hood hid her face and hair. Nonetheless, the man was certainly happy about something.

Vad came back to her side. "They are hungry. I have invited them to share a meal with us. In exchange they will guide us from here to the hounds."

"Is it necessary to have a guide?" As the men drew near, she realized they all had the growths on their faces and hands.

"If we wish to move forward when night falls, aye."

"But they look scary," she whispered. "One of them keeps grinning at me."

Vad nodded. "They outnumber us, probably covet the horses, but we have little choice. I did not want to alarm you, but without the stars or sun to guide us, we could just as easily be going in circles."

Gwen glanced at the heavens and realized it had been

over an hour since they'd seen anything of the sun. The sky was a flat, greenish gray blanket overhead, hiding the lavender heavens.

She gathered what she could of dead branches while Vad unsaddled the horses. The three men stood on the periphery of the activity and murmured among themselves. Plotting?

After constructing a small fire on one of the few dry spots in the bog, Vad speared several of the fungi with sticks and held them out. While the men and Gwen held the sticks over the coals, Vad divided the apples and bread and explained to the silent men that when they left the bog, the remaining food would be theirs.

Gwen desperately wanted to visit the bushes, but was afraid to leave Vad alone, or to go off on her own. She watched the Wartmen devour the fungi. Taking a tentative bite, she almost groaned with pleasure. It tasted like steak, tender, succulent steak. Her stomach growled with pleasure.

The Wartmen's strong odor almost ruined her appetite. It was less uncleanness than it was a feral scent. One man stood. He opened his cloak, separated his clothing, and relieved himself into the undergrowth. Gwen felt heat rush into her face.

"Gather some dry wood," Vad ordered her, pointing to a deadfall. She watched him conceal a small grin when she scrambled quickly behind the snarled screen of twigs and moldy branches, grateful for his attention to her privacy. The ground beneath her feet was soft and spongy. There was little that was dry. Even a few moments away from Vad made her nervous they might attack him.

Several hours later, full night had fallen, and they were still unscathed. The three men carried torches and led the way. The bog was filled with black shadows, but not silence. Gases burped as they passed, birds cawed, small things slithered from their path to hide in the undergrowth. The horses labored.

Gwen cursed their guides' stamina. But to give them credit, they were quick to point out hazards. Finally Gwen noticed a freshening in the air. Vad ordered a halt. He slung one of their packs to the ground and clucked at his horse to go around the men. Gwen stuck close to Vad's side as they left the three Wartmen.

"The attack will come now, I sense it. They like to gnaw on the bones of the dead."

"Gnaw?"

He eased from his saddle, blade drawn, and tossed her his reins. "Ride ahead and wait for me."

She opened her mouth, then remembered not to be a burden and kicked her horse to a trot. The ground was firmer, but the soft, dark night concealed small hazards. She pulled up and listened. A man shouted. Another answered.

Her heart's hard beat concealed all intelligible sounds from her. It was all she could hear—that and the rush of her blood. The horses danced in agitation, almost jerking the reins from her hand. "Stay," she said softly to them. "Stand." Hers responded, but the one Vad had ridden was rearing and pulling, almost dislocating her shoulder.

Vad burst from the night, a white specter, hair blowing, cloak flying like wings behind him. He leaped into his saddle, shot her a quick nod, and urged his mount to a canter. Gwen followed on his heels. Weaving between barely seen trees, they rode hard. When Vad finally pulled up, he shifted around to look at her. "They did attack as I expected. However, it lasted only a few moments. Their dinner was well laced with a few drops of my potion. They have their breeches about their ankles right around now."

His teeth gleamed white in the shadows. "Oh, dear," she whispered, then burst into a laugh. "You didn't!"

He held out his hand. "They fought valiantly for all of three or four thrusts of their blades before 'bowing' to their pain and suffering." Impulsively he pulled her close by the hand and kissed her mouth. "Come. We must find a dry spot to await the dawn—not far off, by my estimation. I do not relish being lost so close upon the edges of the bog."

They dismounted near a faint gleam of gray interspersed with the black stumps of trees. It was not boggy ground. It was a spring, bubbling softly from the earth. "Do not drink it," Vad said. "Some springs are poison in a bog, and we have no way to tell the difference." He stamped about with his boots and declared the ground firm. "Sit."

Gwen sat beside him. "I was afraid they were killing you," she whispered. He answered by turning her head and bringing her mouth to his.

"I cannot remain angry with you," he said against her lips. Gently he explored her cheeks with his fingertips, opened her cloak, and in a moment she felt the warmth of his hand on her breast. "Your skin is so silky, just one of the ties that bind me," he said as his fingertips stroked her. "No matter what fate has planned for us, remember you are mine. You are mine."

He felt every beat of her heart against his palm, reveled in the changing textures of her body as he ran his fingertips over the smooth skin of her breast, returning again and again to the hard, small crest. Each skim of the tip delivered up a moan from her throat. He swallowed each soft sound with his mouth. His body was rigid with want. It was all he could do to keep his groans silent.

When her hand ran along the inside of his thigh, he failed and gave voice, muffled, against her lips. He held her head with one hand, caressed her with the other, and entreated more of her touches. Her palm on him was ecstasy—hot, gentle ecstasy. With but a few light grazes of her fingers, she reminded him that no other woman had this power to make him forget dangers in the dark or dishonor in the day.

"I wish we could make love here, take what time we need," he said, pulling her hand away. "But I fear our friends will not be indefinitely discommoded, and the sun is making itself known."

He covered her mouth with his for a final kiss. The taste of her was sweetness itself. Her fingers entwined with his, and she brought his hand to her mouth. Each small kiss she placed on his hand pierced his insides with desire.

The lightening of the sky told him there was no point in delaying. With a groan, he rose and pulled her to her feet.

After a long kiss he helped her mount up, and they began the final leg of their journey. The sleepless night of following the Wartmen had taken its toll. Her horse scrambled over a fallen log and rocked her in the saddle. For a dangerous moment she hung half-on and half-off the saddle. Vad grasped her by the collar and heaved her back into place. She had to be more careful if she didn't want to cost him more time. "I doubt Narfrom could get through that bog alone."

"We have left him a rather plain trail to follow, should he be behind us."

Gwen whipped around in her saddle. "Behind us?" She saw nothing except acres of forbidding trees, their twisted, leafless arms like hands reaching for the sky, and the hollow impressions of their horses' hooves. Swinging back to face him, she said, "It would be a tough walk."

"Perhaps Narfrom has no need to walk. Perhaps he will use his magic."

Just as she opened her mouth to reply, an eerie howl filled the air. The hair on her nape stood up. The horses shied. Another howl joined the first. Yips followed. "Only eight hounds? It sounds like dozens."

Vad frowned. "The legends put the number at eight. I know not what the reality may be."

He dismounted and calmed Gwen's horse, then led the two mounts to the shelter of a large tree much like an oak. Gwen climbed down and rubbed her bottom. In a moment Vad's hands supplanted hers, massaging away the aches. How easy it would be to lean back into his gentle embrace. "Enough of that, Vad, or the treasure will never be dug up."

Together they walked their horses to the summit of a low hill. A glower of angry clouds filled the sky. A brisk wind lifted Vad's hair and whipped it about his shoulders.

"Oh, my God," she whispered. On the broad, flat plain before them at least a dozen hounds roamed, pacing to and fro like impatient cats caged at a zoo. And they had only three arrows.

Chapter Twenty-eight

"Why did I ever braid your hair?" Gwen muttered as her fingers were rubbed almost raw from the task Vad had set her. He had cut long strips of bark from a tree and shown her the stringy inner lining. Now she was braiding the stringy lengths into long pieces of twine. No sooner had she made a reasonable length of the stuff than Vad took it, made a snare, and disappeared into the undergrowth to set it.

Finally, after most of the morning was gone and her fingers were nearly bleeding, she was done, and so was he. A row of small creatures lay before her. But despite the growling of her stomach, she had no appetite for the raw meat Vad chopped and mixed with the potion.

He carefully rinsed the stomachs of the creatures in the spring and then stuffed them with the mixture. Her nose wrinkled as Gwen tied up the small sacs. "Well, Vad. I've lost any appetite I've ever had for meat."

He patted with a certain pride the little row of sacs lying at his feet.

"I sure hope this works. At least as well as on the Wartmen," she said with a smile. He looked very disheveled, his white tunic grimy from setting snares in the undergrowth. She plucked a few errant leaves and twigs from his hair, then traced the livid scar on his cheek. "This is healed, now."

He touched his knife handle. "And this restored to good color. Your touch is healing."

When Vad put the meat sacs in his pack, she held it at arm's length.

"I am hoping it puts them soundly to sleep, or keeps them too busy to care who passes them," Vad said. "Come."

Vad climbed a low hill, and she had to run to catch up with his long strides.

"Do we have enough of the meat?" she asked.

"It will have to be enough," he said quietly. "Hope this wind stays in our favor, too." He went down on his haunches and idly plucked blades of grass. "I do not want to be attacked by them all at once, so we shall have to lure them one by one away from the pack."

Gwen sat next to him and felt she needed to whisper. There was something eerie about the way the hounds paced. "It almost looks as if they're guarding something, doesn't it?" Their hair was pure white, their bodies sleek. They were larger than any dogs Gwen had ever seen, like a cross between a Great Dane and a mastiff. "If we could get to that tree, maybe we could climb it and toss the meat down from there."

Vad sighed. "It would be humiliating for a warrior to sit in a tree."

"No one will see you." Gwen patted his arm.

He sighed again, louder. "I wish we had more arrows." Before Gwen could comment, he had returned to the horses. After a quick examination of the packs, he told her to sheathe her weapons, and strap on anything else worth taking. She chose the heavy cooking stand.

Vad slung the pack and the nearly empty quiver of arrows over his shoulder. Loaded with weapons, they crept down the hill. They reached the tree with little trouble. The hard wind carried sound and smells away. But they could do little to conceal the noise they made climbing a tree only a few yards from the hounds.

One hound swung its head in their direction and lifted its lip in a low growl.

"Up!" Vad ordered, almost catapulting her into the air as he planted a hand on her bottom. She landed hard against a low branch and imagined the tear of fangs along her legs as she dangled over the head of a hound who rushed the trunk.

Vad shoved her into the boughs and then followed. She scraped her knuckles and chin climbing quickly to an upper branch. When she looked down, she saw they were surrounded. "What's the plan now?" she asked. Her branch shook with her trembling. Below, the tree was ringed by the hounds, who stood on their hind legs and growled.

"*Their* plan is to wait us out. When we are sleeping and fall, they will pick our bones clean. I knew this tree was not for warriors."

With more anger than skill, Gwen watched Vad hack away some of the foliage to give him a better view of the hounds. He pitched one small sac of meat toward the hounds to gauge their reaction. In a ferocious mass, they fell on it, tore it to pieces, and snapped it up. Gwen felt the bile rise in her throat.

"Too many eating it that way. It will never work." He handed her a squishy ball of meat.

"What if we throw it farther away? Maybe we can scatter them."

"Well done, Gwen." He kissed her hard. "Toss a sac as far away as possible."

The ground looked very far away, the snapping jaws far too close. She climbed a bit higher and edged out on a limb. It bowed a bit, and she quickly retreated to a steadier perch. The sac of meat was sticky. She wiped her hands on her tunic and then pretended she was throwing a softball from home plate to the outfield, letting the sac of meat fly.

One hound reached the meat first, and snapped it up in one gulp.

"Another?" She put out her hand.

Vad shook his head. "We wait to see what effect it has."

They leaned against the trunk. The hounds circled, jumping up against the trunk, snapping and snarling. She kept her eye on the one who'd taken the meat. Was it her imagination, or was the hound moving slower? No, she was right. The hound circled, whined, paced away, back and forth, then fell on its side.

"Excellent." Vad handed her another sac of meat while he prepared to lob one himself.

They worked as a team, pitching and throwing the meat sacs at various distances. "We should save some for the return journey," she said.

"If we have them to save," Vad said. Two sacs went astray. One broke in the air, showering the hounds with the meat.

Finally the hounds lay in blissful sleep. Only two sacs of meat remained—not enough to get them back safely. Neither of them mentioned the fact.

"What a team," she said as he assisted her to the ground.

"Quickly." He broke into a run. She followed, the heavy cooking stand thudding against her back. Then he skidded to a halt. There before him, his huge head swinging back and forth, stood a hound as tall as a pony. "Stand back," he cried.

She froze in her tracks. The hound watched them, licked its chops, and raised its head. It howled, a wild, baying sound echoing across the distant hills.

"Back up," Vad said softly. His hand moved slowly to his shoulder and the quiver. With infinite patience, he pulled an arrow, then with lightning speed nocked it, drew, and let fly.

The hound leaped as the arrow found its mark. With a shriek of unearthly pain, the hound landed on Vad. They went down together, rolling.

Gwen screamed and ran in circles. The dog raked Vad with its fangs. Blood splattered across the ground.

She reached for her little dagger, then shoved it back home. Hefting the cooking stand from her shoulder, she edged around them. The hound savaged Vad's arms. She swung and connected in a sickening crunch of bone. The hound reared back and turned on her. With a low snarl, its fangs bared, it crouched, ready to pounce. Vad drew his knife. As the hound jumped at her, he thrust the blade home. It dropped instantly, its muzzle but inches from her toes.

Gwen ran into his arms. "Oh, God," she whispered. His face was streaked with blood, his sleeves long ribbons of red. She tore off her cloak, ripped out the lining, and wadded it against the gashes on his arms.

Vad suffered her ministrations for only a few moments, then broke away, wiped his knife on the grass, and sheathed it. He began to sway. She put her arm under his and supported his weight.

"It's just a few cuts," she said, wiping away the blood. "I don't even think you need stitches. How lucky. Wow. That was scary."

Vad looked down at his arms. The hound's bite was poison. He had told her so, but she must have forgotten. He didn't have the heart to tell her that even now, he could feel an itch moving through his veins. The wounds would fester. Quickly.

"Come on. Maybe there's water up there by those trees and we can wash off your cuts."

He followed her. She strode determinedly up the hill. Under other circumstances, her killing blow would have saved his life.

At the top of the hill she contemplated the grove of trees. "Well, no water here. Let me look those cuts over." She took his arm. "Not so bad." She ripped up more of her cloak and made makeshift bandages. "It's not pretty, but I think the bleeding's stopped."

"Gwen. We must talk."

She jerked away. "I told you, that's no way to start a conversation. Now start counting branches. I thought there'd be just one tree here, but there's at least seven or eight."

"Gwen." He hooked her arm. "We have to talk about what you are going to do. Now. While I am capable of helping you."

Tears welled in her eyes. "No," she whispered. "You'll be fine. I know it."

He pulled her close. "We will look for the treasures. Perhaps you can use the Seat of Wishes to return home."

"This is my home," she said. "Here, in your arms."

How could he answer that? "Perhaps you are right. I feel fine." But for how long?

They walked hand in hand from tree to tree. Then Gwen pointed off to a distant hill. He saw what she saw: a lone tree, its eight twisted limbs lifted to the sky.

The tree was larger than he had expected, the distance to it greater than he had guessed. Walking took concentration. He grew light-headed. How like his fevers in the grotto felt this poison in his system. And maybe it was the same poison, used by the Selaw, milked from hound fangs.

He took a surreptitious glance at his knife handle. He tucked the handle inside his cloak so Gwen would not see it.

"Eight branches. Perfect." She knelt at the base and began to dig with her dagger. He set her aside and drew a digging tool from his pack. It took all his resources to concentrate on the task and not the poison coursing through his system. She remained kneeling at his side, her eyes on his face.

"Nothing." He sat back on his heels and wiped the sweat from his brow.

"There has to be something." She jumped into the hole and dug furiously.

While she scattered earth in all directions, he stretched out and watched clouds race across the sky. A philosopher once said a man's life passed before his eyes right before he died. A swirl of images, or visions, raced through his mind as the clouds raced across the sky.

A woman—he now knew without doubt she was his mother—offered him a smile. A man climbed into one of Gwen's "planes." The child, Kered, held his hand. Together they jumped up and down, laughing.

They were memories—from his life in Gwen's place.

He lost his doubts and knew his visions of the dark place, the enveloping mist, and the hand reaching for his were real. A curious peace fell over him.

Gwen blew hair out of her eyes and climbed out of the hole, which was filled only with tangled roots. "What should we do next?" She turned around. "Oh, no." Vad lay face to the sky, eyes closed. "Vad. Vad." She embraced him, kissed him, her tears bathing his face. "Open your eyes, Vad," she begged.

His lashes fluttered.

"Come on. Please. Don't leave me." His eyes opened, then rolled closed again. "Damn you, don't leave me." She slapped his cheek. Slowly he shook his head and sat up. Then he fell back again.

"I am not quitting."

He had said it before—when they'd first met. "That's right. You've crossed the ice fields. Now open your eyes." Nothing. His skin was hot and slick with sweat. The hound's poison was working through his system. She had denied the legend, dug in the hole instead of watching over him.

His blade handle was once again a dull gray. She shook him again. "I love you. I love you. You can't leave me."

He didn't respond. She shook him harder. "Come on. Use your awareness training. You fought the fever in the grotto; you can fight it now!" His body shuddered. He opened his eyes. Such beautiful eyes. "Wake up! You can't leave me here alone."

The apple? Or lovemaking? Which did it? Which cured him? She hacked an apple into small pieces.

As she had in the dark night, she touched the juicy slivers of fruit to his lips, but he did not take it. Instead he pushed her hand away and struggled into a sitting position.

"It was not the apple that made me well," he said. His hand was hot in hers. "Help me to rise."

When he was upright, he swayed a bit. "You made love to me."

"Yes. Do you think . . . I mean . . . can you?" She held him about the waist and helped him to a cairn of rocks near the tree. Every nerve of her body was tense with joy that he was upright and moving.

"As Nilrem is fond of saying, the spirit is willing, but the flesh is"—he looked at his lap—"weak."

She laid her head on his chest and encircled his waist. "We have the same expression in Ocean City. Please fight the poison. You're so hot. Don't let the fever win."

He set her aside. The world spun before his eyes; she grew large, then small; his breath seared his lungs. "I have failed you. Failed to find the treasures."

"No. No. There has to be some secret to this treasure stuff." She knelt on the ground at his feet and drew the map in the dirt with the jeweled dagger. "Isn't this about what the map looked like?"

But concentration eluded him. Her words slipped and slid through his mind. "It looks . . . incomplete." He licked his lips.

Thunder murmured in the distance.

"What was that?" she asked.

"A storm, but it is far off."

She directed her attention to her drawing. "I know what's wrong; it's missing the compass." She slashed two crossed lines into the dirt.

"What is a compass?" He stared at her drawing. Something tugged at his memory, but evaded his grasp.

"You know." She touched the lines. "The thing that shows north and south, east and west."

He shook his head. His mouth was as dry as the Scorched Plain. "There was no direction marker on the map."

"Then what does this symbol represent?" Her dagger traced the radial lines she had drawn.

"Lunar and solar feast days."

"Feast days?" she said. "What do feast days have to do with . . . Oh, my." She bit her lip and scratched her nose.

How beautiful she was, how innocent and sweet. He could not leave her alone here to die. The hounds would wake soon. She had nothing with which to fight them. He closed his eyes and gathered his strength. Opening them, he saw her staring up at him, her dark eyes bright with wonder.

"Don't you get it, Vad? The feast days must be important to finding the treasures." She embraced him. "Think, my love. Is there a feast day coming? Is there?"

My love. A quick burst of life, or simple desire, ran in his veins. He looked down at her drawing, then up at the heavens. Clouds filled the sky. "Where were the moons on the last clear night?" How far apart were they?

Where in their journey across the sky? "One day more," he managed to say. "Just one day more."

She hugged him hard. "You have to hang on. You have to."

How sweet was her embrace, how warm the cushion of her breasts against his chest. "I . . . think . . . my flesh is willing now."

Her tears wet his cheek. "Not a chance," she whispered at his ear. "Now come rest."

He let her lead him to a grassy spot. She wrapped her cloak about him, held him close, whispered promises of success when the sun rose. He did not answer. He had no false hope to offer. He would not live to see the sun rise.

During the night, Gwen filled in her hole and replaced the sod. If Narfrom came, she did not want to make it easy for him to find the treasures. Vad lay insensible beside her. She stroked his cheek, which was red-hot, dripping with sweat. There was no water to bathe his face, clean his wounds, or wet his dry lips. Her tears were the only moisture she had to offer. As they ran down her face, she wiped them away and touched his lips with them. Each time, he opened his eyes and smiled. She would see his blue eyes in her dreams.

Forever.

A cold night wind rose, whining about the bare arms of the treasure tree. What men did for honor and for fortune. How meaningless it all was in the end.

A short exploration showed her that the hounds had recovered and were roaming the plain. She did not dare look in any other direction.

She didn't believe in dragons; a nest of them would send her over the edge.

If Vad died, how would she get past the perils? And more, how would she get home?

Did she even want to live if he died?

She opened his cloak and tunic, then pressed her ear to his chest. His heart beat, but rapidly and faintly. Unable to resist, she kissed his smooth skin. His hand settled on her head—the first sign of life in hours. Anxiously she rose on her knees and tried to rouse him. He muttered "pepperoni," then fell still again.

She thought about the legends she loved and how she was living a legend at that moment with a man who would forever haunt her waking hours—and her sleeping ones. He lay so still, his unblemished cheek facing her, beautiful and silent—a sleeping beauty. She leaned forward and kissed his cheek. His flesh burned against her lips; sweat soaked his hair. "I can't allow you to just . . . drift away," she said. "I can't."

She climbed astride his body. His knife lay in its sheath, and she pulled it from the leather with shaking hands.

The handle was ebony black.

"No. *No. No!*" She gripped the icy handle in her palms and placed it on his chest. She entwined her fingers with his. The blade lay like a cross on his bare chest, pressed to his heart.

His ring gleamed gold in the moonlight. The orbs overhead seemed to call him, but Gwen was determined he would stay with her. She knelt with her legs on either side of his hips and clasped his hands about the hilt, squeezing as hard as she could.

"Come back to me, Vad. Come back. I need you."

The orbs chased each other across the sky. Failure nudged at the edge of her composure. Each beat of his heart seemed fainter. Her tears ran between their fingers, but she let them fall unchecked to drip between the spaces and run over the icy black stone.

Her head grew dizzy, hot, filled with his feverish heat. The blade handle heated, his hands grew almost too hot to touch, but she hung on. Energy zinged through her veins, swam through her system.

It centered on his hands, and hers, and the blade.

Power and design. The power was hers—and his: the simple power of their love, and not wanting to give it up. The designs twisted and wrapped endlessly through his ring, along the crossguard of his blade, through their entwined fingers. She felt the power following the design, surging, moving, spinning through her consciousness, drawing her life force, linking them together, nourishing him.

How long she knelt over him, she did not know. Her legs went numb; her hands flamed. She forced her mind to ignore the heat, the feeling of melting flesh, and hung on. She whispered nonsense to him, whatever thoughts came to mind, calling him back, begging him to fight off the poison and live.

Chapter Twenty-nine

Gwen took a deep breath and opened her eyes. Dark streaks of red, like blood, colored the indigo sky. Dawn broke. The edge of Vad's tunic tickled her nose where it lay on his chest. Her fingers were frozen in place around his knife.

His beautiful, gold-wrapped, turquoise blade handle.

"Thank you," she whispered to whoever listened.

"Get off me." Vad's hips and chest heaved beneath her. "You are heavier than a Gulap. Get off me."

She rolled away and lay on her back, laughing.

"What amuses you so?" He staggered to his feet and pulled his tunic straight.

"Absolutely nothing. A few hours ago you were dying, I was praying over you, your knife handle was black as coal. Now you're wonderfully . . . cranky."

He touched her cheek, his voice husky. "My blade was black?"

"As Narfrom's heart." She covered his hand with hers. "I thought you were dead." Tears welled in her eyes again. "I will not cry!" She burst into tears.

He gathered her into his arms and squeezed her. Her heart beat against his hand; her breath feathered his chest. "How?"

"I just . . . just held your hands all night."

"I thank you," he whispered against her brow, feathering kisses there. "You saved my life."

Gwen struggled from his embrace. "Look!"

He turned and stared. The eight twisted branches of the tree were in bloom. White petals like flakes of snow drifted from huge blossoms nestled in dark, glossy leaves.

"A gentle scent," he said, plucking a bloom and holding it to his nose. "But not as seductive as your scent, the scent of the white squares."

Gwen limped to his side. Her knees were wrecked from kneeling all night. She giggled. "You really like those dryer sheets, don't you?"

"Only when they are coupled with your scent."

"I'll never be able to look at a dryer sheet quite the same."

He lifted her high and kissed her hard. Then he went down on one knee and offered her the bloom. "Thank you for my life."

She felt a true flush of happiness. "I just did what felt natural."

He rose and tucked the bloom behind her ear and kissed her forehead. "I will look after you always."

Always. That sounded like forever. Now, in the bright Tolemac dawn of purple skies, she felt some of her doubts returning. She smiled and forced the feelings deep inside. "Come on. Let's dig. We have only three days to find these treasures and get . . . back."

Vad frowned. Why was she reluctant to accept his thanks? Why did she avoid his gaze? What was in the sky to make her little brow wrinkle?

He set her aside to do the digging himself. As he thrust the tool into the dirt, he heard the thunk of metal on metal. "By the sword," he swore. "Carefully now," he directed as she knelt at his side and began to dig around with the jeweled dagger. In moments they had a small cooking caldron on the grass. Nothing else remained in the hole.

"Look." She tipped the dirt out of the caldron, and with it spilled several objects.

"The treasures." They examined the unprepossessing objects. He unwrapped a dirty cloth and revealed a golden game board. A handful of tarnished silver men rolled out onto the ground.

Gwen picked them up. "Is this the game that predicts—"

"A battle's victor? Aye. If it were an ordinary game, each player would move his men outward from the center to claim territory. The player with the most territory wins. Simple."

"But *this* board plays by itself, right?" she asked.

He nodded. "Aye. I am sure this is what the council most craves." Carefully he placed each piece back into the caldron. "Let us not tempt fate. I have found, to my dishonor, that a wager on a game is hard for me to resist."

"Then don't go to Atlantic City," she said.

"Not even for a war conference?" He lifted her chin.

She smiled, but pulled away. "Nope. Not even for a war conference. Let's look at the rest of this stuff." She bent over the rest of the objects: a simple whetstone, a thick brown bottle, a knife with a short, curved blade, and a ring, which she held up to him. "This is certainly too small for your fingers, or most men's, for that matter. One of the treasures is missing, isn't it? Shouldn't there be eight?"

"Aye. No Seat of Wishes."

"Will the council be satisfied with just these?"

He rose and dusted off his hands and knees. For a moment he stared at his torn sleeves, the dried blood roping his arms. "They had better be."

"The treasures don't look like much."

"It is their powers, not their appearance, for which they are valued." He shook the cloth and draped it about her shoulders.

"Ohhh. I'm warm." She drew the edges of the cloak together and nuzzled her nose into the folds. "This reminds me of how my gloves felt in winter when I'd put them on the radiator to warm. It's . . . toasty."

He pulled it off her and draped it over his own shoulders. "The Cloak of Warmth," he said. "Gwen. I can smell wet wool from. . . . mittens?"

"Yes. Mittens."

With reluctance he took off the cloak and stared at his hands, the momentary vision gone; but the feel of the material was still on his skin, the scent in his head.

"What's this for?" she asked, the whetstone in her hand.

"Watch." He took the whetstone and restored the edge to the curved blade, then showed her the simple technique so she could sharpen the jeweled dagger.

"If these objects only work for a brave, true—" she began.

"Honorable."

"Honorable warrior . . . that means the treasures must consider me to be—"

"Honorable. Brave and true." He lifted her finger and slipped the tarnished silver ring on it. "The treasures recognize what is within."

The ring was heavy, thick with tarnish, the interlocking engraving just visible. "What does the ring do?" she asked.

"It is called the Ring of Invisibility."

She inspected her arm, her hand, her legs. "I'm still here."

"I do not understand it." But he understood the surge of want that ran through him as she twisted and turned, each move emphasizing her form in the snug breeches.

"Should I keep it on?" She held out her hand.

If she moved it to her middle finger, it would look like a mating ring.

"Keep it. It is lovely on your hand. Perhaps I can clean it for you later."

"Are you hungry? We could test the caldron."

"I am hungry." He drew her against his body and whispered in her perfect ear, "But not for food."

Dark clouds obscured the Tolemac sun. Gwen hugged him tightly.

"I think you shall not be testing *my* caldron."

"Narfrom!" Gwen gasped.

Vad felt no surprise, only anger as Narfrom strode up the hill. In his hands he held a weapon, larger and somehow more dangerous-looking than the one he had used in the fortress. Gwen quivered in his arms.

"How did you get here?" she asked.

His weapon aimed at them, Narfrom trotted up the hill. He wore his amber robes, his gold and silver belt. "Dragons are no match for an AK-47." The only word Vad could think of to describe his posture was *preening.* "Now put the treasures into that little pot and hand them over."

Gwen did as he commanded, her eyes on the gun.

Vad stood as still as a statue, but felt compelled to tell Narfrom the truth. "They will not work for you. You have no honor."

"Is that so, pretty boy? I have a very interested collector who will pay big bucks for the treasures, working or not. Let me give them a little look-see before I go. I'd hate to think you'd cheat me now." Narfrom motioned Gwen to Vad's side and pawed through the caldron. Gwen closed her fist over the ring.

"This is it?" He rose, stiff with anger, and tucked the

curved blade in his belt. He cast the cloak aside and walked across it. "Where's the rest of them?"

In concert with his anger, the wind rose and the sky darkened.

Vad shrugged and sat on the cairn of the rocks, his boots crossed at the ankles. "Perhaps someone has been here first."

"Bloody unlikely. Did you see those dragons? Did you?"

"Ah, no," Gwen said, inching closer to Vad. "We came by way of the hounds."

Narfrom raised his gun. "Where are the rest of the treasures? The Vial of Seduction? Where is it?"

"The brown bottle is the vial, I assume," Vad said.

Narfrom shook the bottle, pulled the wooden cork, sniffed, recorked it, and tossed it on the ground. "Just dirt. Bloody dirt. Where is it? You're tricking me."

The ring was cold and hard in her palm. "Is that all you're interested in? Seduction?" She wanted to punch him in the face.

Vad restrained her with a hand on her arm. "Perhaps the vial was made of delicate glass. It may have been broken, the powder scattered conjunctions ago."

"Ardra would be mine if I had even a pinch of that spice!" Narfrom paced, the weapon loose in his hands.

"When will you give up?" Gwen asked.

Vad kicked Narfrom in the knee, snatched the weapon, and sent it sailing away. With a shriek of anger, Narfrom ran after it.

In two strides Vad reached him. The little man was stronger than he looked; his own warrior's strength had been sapped by illness. They circled, grappled, managed only to land a few glancing blows, before Narfrom ripped from his grip.

Narfrom drew the sacrificial knife.

Vad drew his long blade, the smooth turquoise handle a comfort in his hand.

Gwen held her place at the cairn of rocks, the trampled cloak clutched in her hands. The wind rose. It howled around them. The sky darkened to a purple so deep it was almost black.

They circled and stalked each other.

"When you're dead, I'll have Gwen and then Ardra. I'll chain them side by side, and they can take lessons from one another." Narfrom howled with laughter.

A rumble of thunder followed.

Narfrom's words meant nothing. But the curved blade in his hand meant everything. It was sacrificial. What honor was there in sacrifice? For whom would it strike a killing blow?

A crack of lightning tore the sky. "Come for me now." Narfrom beckoned. "I'll give you a scar on the other cheek—right before I slit your throat."

"Let us not play games," Vad said, and walked straight to the man. Their blades engaged with a ring of metal on metal. The battle was joined: good against evil.

Gwen murmured a prayer as the men fought. The sky overhead flashed with lightning. Streaks of rose and violet and indigo darted through the heavens. The wind rose, shrieking all around them.

Vad gave Narfrom no room to maneuver, fighting close, his wounds opening and splattering blood on Narfrom's robes. But the robes were Narfrom's undoing. He stumbled back and tripped.

Vad stepped on Narfrom's wrist. "Drop your blade." Narfrom's hand fell open; the knife dropped to the ground.

Gwen watched in horror as Vad bent to retrieve it. Narfrom held another weapon in his left hand, a smaller but no less deadly version of the gun Vad had kicked away. It was aimed at her chest.

"Back up, pretty boy, or I put a hole in your girlfriend." Narfrom plucked the treasure knife from Vad's fingers.

She watched Vad. He stood as if unconcerned, but his eyes were on the gun. He's going to go for it, she thought.

"Narfrom," she cried to distract him from Vad. "You can't get away with this. This isn't your world." She gestured to the hillsides, the long vista to the bog. A scattering of snow followed the arc of her arm. "Vad," she whispered. She swung her arm again, the ring icy in her palm. The scattering of snow became a sweep of wind and ice. It blanketed the eight-branched tree, the treasures. Vad. Narfrom.

"Stop it!" Narfrom cried. "Stop it or I'll shoot. I can't see. I can't see!"

But she ignored him, for he was no longer visible. The world wasn't visible.

Vad burst into the circle of calm surrounding her, wrapped his arms around her waist, scooped her high against his chest. She lifted her arms overhead and he turned, spinning her around, laughing at the joy on her face. He whirled her about as if he were alone with her on a polished ballroom floor. The winds rose; the snow flew. Where they spun, the earth remained clear, a central vortex in a blizzard of ice.

Vad lifted his face to hers. Her lips were as warm as her body against his, as warm as the love he felt for her. "My ice woman," he said. "I dreamt you; you called me to you."

She wrapped her arms about his neck and kissed him.

"Call me anytime," he said, "and I will come to you. For you are mine."

They stopped spinning, dizzy, staggering. The wind died. It fell silent with a soft sigh. The sleet hissed to the ground. A twig snapped in the brittle cold she had created.

"Oh, Vad. It's beautiful." She felt a lump form in her throat. She'd done this, made this happen. Or the ring had.

The hillside on which they stood was blanketed in snow. Icicles hung from the eight-branched tree. The red Tolemac sun laid a candy-apple red glaze over everything.

"Narfrom?" she asked softly, afraid to disturb the silence.

They looked about, but Narfrom was nowhere to be seen. Vad shook out the cloth from the caldron and placed it over her shoulders. It enveloped her in a marvelous warmth.

They searched the hillside and found him inches from his gun, covered with snow. Vad flipped him over. Narfrom's boot was caught in the hem of his robe; the curved blade was embedded in his chest, his hand still on the hilt. The earth beneath him was dark with blood.

"Sacrificed to his ambition," Vad said. "Another treasure worked for us, protected us." He leaned over and searched Narfrom's robes for the treasure map, found it, and with triumph gave it to Gwen. "This will prove we were not lying."

"Oh, no. I feel . . . terrible." She hugged her stomach, then leaned over and threw up. She raised a hand before he could say a word. "Don't say it, I'm not feminine."

"I was going to say you are too compassionate. He needed to be punished for the hanging of the serving boy, if nothing else." Vad took the AK-47 and the smaller gun, and buried them along with their master in the hillside, far away from the eight-branched tree and any future treasure seekers.

"What now?" she asked as he scattered the last of the earth over the grave. They stood on the hillside and watched the snow melt in the Tolemac sun. "How are we going to pass the hounds?"

"We do not need to pass them."

"Then how do we get home? Ah, you're thinking about the dragons Narfrom killed, aren't you?"

"Nay. I am thinking of the dreams I had when you were healing me." He took her hand and led her back along the hillside to the tree. "I remembered who I was, my mother, how I came to be here."

"Mittens?" She squeezed his fingers.

"Aye. I remembered mittens, too." He scratched his scar. "And something called Wheatabix."

"That's not a word in my vocabulary."

"Perhaps one day . . ." He let the sentence die away.

One day might never come. Gwen's stomach churned as he turned from her and looked out over the landscape. What was he thinking? Wishing? Regretting? "How are we going to get past the hounds?" she asked to prod him back to the here and now.

"The Seat of Wishes."

"But it's missing."

"I think not." His strong hands wrapped around her waist, and he lifted her atop the cairn of rocks. "Can you not sit here and look over the countryside? Think on your fate? Contemplate your future?"

"Make a wish?" she asked.

"Aye." He scooped up the caldron and sat at her side. "It cannot hurt to try."

She snuggled her hip against his and wrapped her arms around his waist. She linked her fingers around the handle of his knife and made sure her new ring was lying against the engraving.

"What should we say?" he asked, a frown on his face.

"I don't know. Why not . . . 'Take us to the Tolemac council'?"

Vad swore and pushed Gwen aside. He lay half-on and half-off a small padded stool that was digging painfully into his manhood inside the Tolemac council tent. Luckily, it was a deserted Tolemac council tent. Gwen moaned. He regretted pushing her away, and made amends by helping her to her feet.

"Wow. That was incredible." She rubbed her elbow. "One moment there, the next here."

Vad studied her face as she swayed in place. "Your face looks green."

She dumped the treasures out of the caldron just in time to throw up in it.

"I guess I don't travel so well." She smiled wanly and peered into the caldron. "I hope this doesn't affect its magic."

"Are you often sick?" he asked, stroking her hair from her damp forehead. He spoke softly, mindful of sentries who might be patrolling outside. The council tent was deserted, dim, but lit enough from the residual glow of the sun for him to see she was going to faint.

He pulled her to Samoht's seat and pushed her into it.

"I'm never sick," she said over the caldron. "Well, just that once when we arrived on Nilrem's mountain."

"You are with child." He crossed his arms on his chest and grinned.

Gwen flopped back in the chair and put a hand to her stomach. "I can't be. Remember? I have an implant."

"I know what I know. I have bathed you in my seed. You are with child."

She groaned. "Can't you express it in a different way?"

"I have loved you at the appropriate time of your cycle. Is that more to your liking?" He grinned even wider.

"No, it's not. And I'm not." She would *not* be pregnant. It wasn't possible. She could not be pregnant here. Not here where children of slaves were . . . slaves. "What's our next step?" she said hurriedly. "Other than cleaning this caldron?"

"We will garb you for the presentation. I will no longer hide who you are, or why I must be joined to you." He took the caldron with a sour look and held it at arm's length. Gwen gathered the rest of the treasures and followed him as he lifted the tent flap and stepped boldly into the camp.

With all the authority of a true Tolemac warrior, Vad demanded to be shown to Ardra's tent. Three sentries accompanied them. Ardra dwelled in one of the black tents marked with the distinctive banner with a single red rose.

Vad handed the caldron to a servant crouched by the tent flap and ordered him to clean it out. Ardra rose from the nest of pillows on which she sat.

"Vad!" She ran into his arms. Gwen did not look away. They looked great in each other's arms, but now she understood who really belonged there. How Vad would accomplish it, she didn't know.

"Mistress Ardra," he said very formally, setting her aside. "Can you secure garments for Gwen? A gown, something very . . . feminine. I do not wish to have anyone mistake her for a male when we go before the council."

"You will wait for the morrow, will you not? You must rest."

"I will not be given such a choice," Vad said. "Even as we speak, I imagine the sentries are informing Samoht I have returned."

Two men threw back the tent flap. When they would have led Vad to the council tent, he asked and was granted time to bathe and attire himself appropriately. He had merely to show his bloodstained sleeves and his wishes were granted.

A flurry of orders were given, servants dispatched for clothing, hot water, food, healing herbs.

When Vad was gone, Gwen quietly requested a few supplies of her own. Ardra raised a brow, but gave the orders anyway.

Finally Gwen found herself alone with all she needed.

She bathed and nibbled on soft bread and honey. Next she put on the gown a servant had brought.

It was perfect: white, long, flowing, delicate, and silky. But best was the matching sash.

With a tiny brush in her hand, she deftly made a series of dots on the length of cloth that comprised the belt. She then examined the small pots of dye she'd requested. Her hand trembled when she began but, after a few moments, grew steady. Slowly, in the colors of berries and barks, a pattern grew on the belt. An interlocking pattern. Knotwork. The echo of Vad's knife, his ring, and the ring on her hand—a ring she must surrender to the council.

Vad borrowed a clean tunic, one lacking the gold embroidery of leadership. But he did not care. He no longer intended to lead anyone anywhere.

When dressed, he donned an empty sword scabbard and strapped on his knife. Then he smiled at the shiny, clean caldron. In moments the rest of the treasures were inside, and he was threading his way through the city of tents to the council's. He noticed that everywhere he went, two sentries followed a few paces behind. The council's lack of trust no longer bothered him. There was only one person's trust he cared about.

He met Ardra returning to her tent. "Ardra, I must speak to you before I address the council." He drew her aside, out of earshot of the sentries. "I know that when I present the treasures, I will be given a reward. I seek only the return of my sword, the restoration of my honor, but I know Tolemac politics. The councilors will try to bind the fortress to them and benefit from its location at the ice fields. They will ask me to lifemate with you."

"I would obey," she said quietly, with a low bow.

Chapter Thirty

Vad acknowledged her bow with one of his own. "I, too, Mistress Ardra, would lifemate with you if I had not already given away my heart. I can offer you only my sword, my strength, my able help to defend your fortress. My heart belongs to Gwen. Where she is, there I wish to be—no matter where that place is.

"But if I must go to the fortress, it will be as your protector only. And Gwen goes with me. I will ask that the council grant her an arm ring, that we may lifemate, but if they refuse, I will still honor her as if we had vows between us. I ask but one favor of you, mistress—bring Gwen to the council tent under your protection. Should something happen to me, aid her in whatever she asks to see herself back to her home."

Ardra sank into a low curtsy, her skirts pooling in gold around her. "So be it."

His two sentries approached. They formed more of a guard than an escort. At the council tent, he took a deep breath and entered. Seven seats were conspicuously empty. Vad made the customary obeisance and then stood at an empty seat. "I have brought seven of the treasures, most esteemed councilors, and the map."

The councilors handed around the map, glancing at the perils and then back at Vad. Their expressions confirmed his guess that they had not really expected his return. Quickly he explained Narfrom's use of the map to go after the treasures, and his subsequent death by misadventure.

"And why only seven treasures?" Samoht asked, picking idly at a thread on his flowing black robes embroidered at the breast with a single red rose. "Surely our charge was to bring all eight treasures, was it not? Tol?"

Tol scratched his beard and yawned. "I do not recall." He looked about the table at the other councilors. "Did we actually state eight treasures or did we just say treasures?"

The lesser councilor on his left whispered in his ear. "It seems we asked only for treasures."

"Esteemed councilors," Vad interjected. "If I may explain the missing treasure? The Seat of Wishes is a cairn of stone set by the eight-branched tree. It is not possible to transport it. Nor would it work, I imagine, without the perspective one has when sitting upon it. It is situated just so to allow contemplation—"

"Enough of the Seat of Wishes. Let us examine the treasures we have. Where is the Vial of Seduction?" Samoht paced behind his seat—A poor sign, one that indicated that he was angry. Vad wondered if Samoht had been called from the bed of one of his pleasure slaves, or if the lifemating negotiations were not going smoothly. Was that why he wanted the vial? To aid him in securing the Selaw daughter?

Vad handed the brown bottle over to Samoht. "The Vial of Seduction." A hiss of disappointment ran around the tent as the councilors examined the heavy brown bottle and sniffed the dirt.

"Show us the rest of the treasures," Samoht demanded, slamming home the stopper on the bottle and casting it aside on the table much like a piece of refuse.

As Vad put the caldron on the table, the tent flap lifted and Ardra entered with Gwen a few paces behind.

No one paid the women any heed. The councilors were completely absorbed by the objects he placed before them. He donned the cloak and then offered it to the councilors to feel the heat radiating from it. A few councilors asked to try it, but with red faces, they found it offered them no warmth. None of the others wanted to try it. Next he set up the game board. When he placed the last tarnished piece in place, everyone gasped. A game began to play.

Tol swept the pieces off the board. They rang together in melodic harmony as they rolled on the table. "Are we sure we wish to see our fate written here? I suggest we think well on this before using it."

Samoht touched the curved sacrificial blade with a long fingertip. "I wonder how many generations ago this was used to sacrifice to the ancient gods? Still quite sharp, isn't it?"

"I have sharpened it for you." Vad set the whetstone in place.

"None of these are remarkable." Samoht picked up the whetstone and drew his own dagger. After several passes of the stone on his blade, he frowned. "Is this some kind of jest? This is useless." No one contradicted him. He dropped the stone to the table. "Where is the Ring of Invisibility?"

Vad strode to Gwen. "Demonstrate the ring for the councilors."

She walked with great poise to where Samoht stood at his chair, a glower on his face. She swept her arm out. Wind and snow blew on the table, the councilors, the guards. They all threw up their arms to protect their faces.

"It cloaks you in storm, hides you in ice," Vad explained. "Hence you are not visible."

Tol smiled when Gwen lowered her arm. "And who are you?"

"My name is Gwen." She dipped into a curtsy, not sure what to do.

Vad held out his hand, as she had expected. She slipped off the ring and placed it on his palm. Without it, the only designs she wore were the ones about her waist. Grief filled her. They would order her taken away, or give her over to Vad. Which would it be? Her suspense could not last much longer. She trusted Vad to *want* to follow his heart, but knew that the reality of the situation might dictate he could not.

Vad passed the ring to Samoht, who swung his arm about and then cast the small silver ring onto the table with a grunt of displeasure. He picked up the caldron. "What is the purpose of this?"

"No honorable man will go hungry with this caldron. It is said in legend that the caldron will cook any food instantly," Vad replied.

Samoht snapped his fingers. A guard stepped forward. "Bring a haunch of pork and water sufficient to boil it."

As they waited, Vad felt his first prickle of doubt. It was the only treasure he had not used. Each of the others, including the ring, had performed as the legends suggested.

Within moments, the water and pork were delivered, the caldron filled. Nothing happened. The councilors left their seats and peered into it. "Surely," one remarked, "a fire is necessary?"

"No fire is necessary." Vad held his breath.

The councilors each took turns removing and dropping the pork into the caldron. Finally Samoht, in a low, tense voice, ordered Vad to try his hand. Heart pounding, he stepped to the table. The pork lay on a platter. He lifted it with his long knife and dropped it into the water. Instantly the water seethed with bubbles, steam rose, and the pork cooked, the rich scent of meat filling the air.

"Well, well. The legends say only an honorable warrior may use the treasures," Tol said. "What does that make us?"

"This is errant nonsense!" Samoht said. He tried in vain to sharpen his blade again. Each pass of the whetstone only further dulled his blade. He threw it into the caldron. The water stilled. "Are you telling me none of us is honorable?"

Tol began to laugh. "The man sent after the treasures seems to be the only one who can use them, and I will wager he is also the one man who does not want them! Until we make some amends for our own behavior, I think these treasures belong in the vaults."

"Just what do you want, Vad?" Samoht said with a snarl. He crossed his arms, his anger clear. "Your command back? Your name struck from the rolls of infamy? Your sword?"

"All of those things. And none." Vad met his eyes. "When I crossed the ice fields, I did so in hopes of regaining my honor. I sought honor from dishonorable men." He had not known until he met Gwen that honor came from within. The legends had said the warrior who obtained the treasure would gain great wisdom. And so he had. "Honor is here." He touched his chest. "It was always with me, a part of me. No man, not you, esteemed High Councilor, nor any of these other councilors could take it from me, nor give it back."

Tol stood up. "Where is Vad's sword?"

A guard placed a long silver sword on the round table. Gwen could see the long gleaming blade, its engraved crosspiece, its turquoise handle wrapped with gold. It was the twin to Vad's knife.

"You would give this man his sword after the slur he has cast on us?" Samoht sat in his chair, an insult to the standing older man and Vad.

"Nay, I do not wish you to give it to me," Vad said quietly. He strode forward and lifted the sword from the table himself and sheathed it. "I will take my sword from no man's hand."

Several councilors nodded their approval. Tol came around the table and clapped Vad on the shoulder. "Which of us spoke up and told Vad it was these objects we wanted, most especially the game board, when we sent him across the ice fields? Which of us was willing to challenge the others and reveal the lie that would only cast dishonor on us? Which of us has been able to use the caldron? Or the other treasures? Only one man. And for that matter, even this little slave has more honor than we." Tol pointed to Gwen. She trembled as Samoht impaled her with a glare. "Even she can command at least one of them." Tol shook his head. "Vad seems to be the only man among us with honor."

A heavy silence fell in the tent.

"And now, esteemed High Councilor," Tol said to Samoht at the head of the table, "we come to the issue of Ardra and the Fortress of Ravens."

Gwen thought she would be sick. She swallowed and crossed her fingers. Vad nodded his head briefly to acknowledge the issue.

Samoht stared at the treasures. "It seems we need to provide *honorable* protection for Mistress Ardra. It has been proposed you take her to mate as an adjunct to my own joining with the Selaw chieftain's daughter."

"With due respect, I decline. I have given my heart to another." He put out his hand. Gwen slipped hers into his, comfortable for the first time since entering the tent. His strength filled her. The heat of his ring warmed her fingers.

"With all due respect, you cannot lifemate with a slave," Tol said gently.

"With all due respect, you will lifemate where I direct you!" Samoht shouted.

"With all due respect, she is as honorable as the most able warrior. Each treasure works for *her*. I ask nothing else, save this: that you grant her an arm ring to make the match one you can approve. But arm ring or not, she is mine," Vad finished.

A cacophony of noise burst forth.

Tol waved the councilors to silence. "This does not help Mistress Ardra, nor serve us at the fortress. Can you not keep this little woman for pleasure . . ." The expression on Vad's face was thunderous and halted Tol. "Never mind that idea. Well, we have a pretty dilemma. The fortress is so very valuable to us."

Vad nodded. "I offer my protection as a warrior, a commander of the fortress guards. I decline only the offer of Mistress Ardra as a lifemate."

Samoht snorted. "You will mate where bidden."

"I have come to think quite highly of Mistress Ardra," Tol said, picking at his nails again. "Perhaps, as my lifemate has been dead these last seven conjunctions, Ardra might consent to a lifemating with me instead of Vad. That would mate her where we want and free this young warrior to make a fool of himself. My household guard is more than sufficient to defend the fortress."

Gwen tried to force her face to remain neutral as the men argued. Her cheeks were hot.

Tol looked back and forth between Vad and Gwen. "I cannot, however, countenance an arm ring for this slave. It would set a dangerous precedent. Imagine! Next men will want to free their concubines to mate with them. Preposterous!"

Gwen's heart sank. Vad's fingers squeezed hers.

"Come forward Mistress Ardra. You shall make the choice," Samoht directed with a tight smile.

"That is hardly fair," piped up one councilor. "I know he is scarred now, but still, what woman would not choose this warrior?"

Every head nodded. Samoht's smile widened. "Indeed," he said, and Gwen knew that had been his intention. And perhaps it was all the punishment Samoht could contrive for Vad for proving the council's dishonesty.

Ardra would choose Vad. His scarred face would not matter to her. She would choose, and Vad would obey. Vad would obey because of the very honor he'd demonstrated. And she, Gwen, would still be a slave in this world. Without thought, her fingers traced the design on her belt. She could not live in this world without Vad. She could not live as a slave or have a child in slavery, either.

A guard pulled her away from Vad and closer to the tent entrance. The scent of the guard's leather garments made her stomach dance.

Ardra, her gaze searching those assembled, found first Vad and then Gwen. She walked very slowly forward. Gwen smiled. Whatever Ardra decided, Gwen would not blame her. Samoht and the council were playing their own game, and she and Vad and Ardra were each just a game piece on the board of their politics.

Samoht stood. "Mistress Ardra. You have heard all of the discussion about the fortress and its fate. The council has decided you must lifemate. The fortress will fall without proper guidance. I offer you two men, both more than worthy of your hand, both well able to hold the fortress. I give you Vad or Tol. You must choose one for a mate. Which is it to be?"

One of the councilors licked his lips and hid a smile behind his hand. Samoht also had a cynical smirk on his face.

Ardra sank into a curtsy before the men. "Most esteemed councilor, I thank you for the courtesy of a choice. The answer is simple. I choose Tol."

"What?" Samoht sat down hard. "You choose a man older than your misbegotten father to lifemate with when this man . . . this warrior could be your choice?"

"Aye." She walked around the table to stand at Tol's side. Her voice quavered a bit, but her gaze was steady and so was her hand as she offered it to Tol. "I have had many talks with Tol. He understands the needs of the fortress and my people. I trust him to see to their care."

Vad bowed as he turned to go, but Tol called him back.

"Take this as compensation for the loss of the fortress." Tol handed him the small silver ring. Vad closed his fist about it and nodded. He strode to the tent entrance and took Gwen by the hand. He pulled her out into the Tolemac sun.

"Come, we need privacy for what we will do."

Gwen hurried behind him, past the tents, to the river, into a grove of trees, and still he walked with long strides, almost pulling her along with an urgency that frightened her.

Finally he stopped. They stood at the edge of a small clearing. Soft green grass spread like a carpet at their feet.

He placed his hands at her waist. "I watched your hands. They touched this design over and over as the councilors discussed our fate. You painted it, did you not? Painted it so you could go home?"

She nodded. "I was afraid of what you would be forced to do. What your honor might force you to do."

His bright blue eyes were grave. "We have both had our moments of distrust. But I tell you now you may always trust in me. I am free now. I can fight the council for an arm ring for you, or . . ."

"Or?" she whispered.

"Or we can go where no one has arm rings and begin our own illustrious line."

"Are you sure?" she asked, going into his embrace, laying her head on his chest.

"Aye. I am sure."

"Not everyone is honorable where I live, either."

"Then we will be two more to balance the scale. I wish to see where I was born, where my parents are buried. I want my child to live without slavery. I want to see you heal the rift in your family."

She leaned back. "I think we'd be just in time for Thanksgiving—that's a festival sort of thing where everyone . . . gives thanks for all the gifts they have."

"I have one gift I must thank your father and mother for—you."

Tears ran down her cheeks. A huge lump filled her throat. "You're just the man to cook the dinner, I think."

He brushed his lips across her forehead. "I would be honored. Do they like eels?"

Gwen laughed through her tears and kissed him hard.

Then he slipped the silver ring on her finger. "Wear this ring, be my ice woman, call me to you, and I will come." He set her aside.

Gwen felt her heart pounding in her chest. Vad stood at the edge of the clearing, his hand on his sword hilt—the sword that meant so much to him.

The sky was clear. Not one cloud marred its lavender perfection. She stood on tiptoe and lifted her arms to the heavens. The ring on her finger grew cold. She turned, twisted her arms, sent a swirl of snow, a whirl of wind through the clearing. Snow covered the grass, filled the sky, obscured the sun. Obscured Vad.

Would she ever see him again?

She spun in the world of white, each turn of her body filling the air with more flakes, more cold. Each lift of her arms intensified the storm, whipped her dress in sharp snaps against her legs. All around her the world, every tree, each blade of grass, glistened, sparkled with snow, ice, and frost. Only her small space was green and warm.

Her ears filled with the howl of the wind; her body shook with the power of the storm.

Vad stepped out of the glittering snow. His blond hair flew about his shoulders. He was her warrior.

Beautiful. Sensuous. Alluring.

She put out her hand and beckoned him to her. He came forward and stepped into her circle of warmth, his hands on her waist, on the unending design she'd painted on the belt.

"Take us home," he said.

VIRTUAL DESIRE
by Ann Lawrence

Enter to win a beautiful Celtic-inspired sword pendant!

You fell in love with the passionate tale of Vad and Gwen. Now you can own a replica sword pendant just like the one Vad sought to regain his honor! Just correctly answer one simple question based on the love story in *Virtual Desire* by Ann Lawrence and you'll be automatically entered into our special Grand Prize Drawing for a sterling silver Celtic-inspired sword pendant.

- Pendant is approximately 3.25 inches long with a turquoise handle wrapped in 14 karat gold inlaid wires. Both the pendant and 24-inch chain are solid sterling silver. Original sword pendant designed and created by bladesmith/ goldsmith Jot Singh Khalsa of Millis, MA. Celtic engraving and sculpting executed by Ron Skaggs of Howe, IN.

For further information about this Celtic sword pendant or the 35 other sword/knife pendant patterns available, please contact LifeKnives directly:

LifeKnives
368 Village Street
Millis, MA 02054 USA
E-Mail: LifeKnives@AOL.com
Phone: 800-442-8162
Fax: 508-376-8081

LifeKnives

Knife Jewelry to Cut through Life's Challenges and Achieve Excellence

Please see opposite page for official contest rules and entry form.

This contest is co-sponsored by Dorchester Publishing Co., Inc. and Ann Lawrence. For news and exciting contest information, please visit their websites at www.dorchesterpub.com and www.annlawrence.com.

OFFICIAL ENTRY FORM

Win a beautiful sterling silver Celtic-inspired sword pendant! Just correctly answer the following question based on Vad and Gwen's story from *Virtual Desire* by Ann Lawrence. Be sure to give your complete and correct address and phone number so that we may notify you if you are a winner. (Please type or print legibly.)

Which of the following landmarks is never mentioned in *Virtual Desire*:

a.) The River Ford
b.) The Burial Mound
c.) The Dragon Nest
d.) The Evil Bog

(Please type or print legibly.)

NAME ______________________________

ADDRESS ______________________________

____

PHONE ______________________________

E-MAIL ADDRESS ______________________________

MAILING ADDRESS FOR ENTRIES:
Dorchester Publishing Co., Inc.
Department AL
276 Fifth Avenue, Suite 1008
New York, NY 10001

OFFICIAL CONTEST RULES: No purchase necessary. Must be at least 18 years old to enter. Only one entry per envelope. Use of a photocopy of an original entry form is acceptable. To obtain free entry forms, visit the website of Dorchester Publishing Co., Inc. www.dorchesterpub.com. Entries must be postmarked by January 15, 2001. The contest is open to all residents of the U.S. and Canada, excluding employees and families of Dorchester Publishing Co., Inc. and the Hearst Distribution Group. A random drawing for all contestants who correctly answer the above question will be held at the offices of Dorchester Publishing Co., Inc. on or before February 1, 2001. Odds of winning are dependent on the number of correctly answered entries received. Any illegible, mutilated, altered, or incorrectly filled-out entry forms will be disqualified. Not responsible for lost, late, misdirected, damaged, incomplete, altered, illegible, or postage-due mail. Entries become the property of the sponsor and will not be returned. The Grand Prize will be mailed to the winner on or before February 15, 2001. If the prize is returned to Dorchester Publishing Co., Inc. as undeliverable, the prize will then be awarded to an alternate winner in a random drawing. The Grand Prize is a sterling silver Celtic-inspired sword pendant. All additional expenses, such as applicable taxes, are not included and are the responsibility of the winner. Prize is guaranteed to be awarded. Void where prohibited by law.

This contest is co-sponsored by Dorchester Publishing Co., Inc. and Ann Lawrence. For news and exciting contest information, please visit their websites at www.dorchesterpub.com and www.annlawrence.com.